Evangeline:

Paradise Stolen

Volume III of the Series
Evangeline: The True Story of the Cajuns

M.M. Le Blanc

BIZENTINE
PRESS

EVANGELINE: PARADISE STOLEN
Volume III
by M. M. Le Blanc

©2019 BizEntine Press
Cover Design: ©2019 BizEntine Press
All rights reserved.
ISBN: 978-1947471-05-4

Cover portrait "Evangeline" in locket, painted by Jules Dupré, ca 1840's,
Courtesy Warren A. Perrin and Acadian Museum of Erath
Photograph courtesy Lucius Fontenot, 2005

Cover photograph "Evangeline" engraving by James Faed, 1863
Courtesy Museé acadien de l'Université de Moncton

This is a work of historical fiction about the author's ancestral heritage and genealogy, based on and inspired by historical events, incidents, figures and places and the author's oral and written family histories. Characters, names, places and events are used factually, with dramatic license and/or are the product of the author's imagination. Any resemblance otherwise is purely coincidental and unintentional.

Manufactured in the United States of America by

BizEntine
PRESS

Evangeline:

Paradise Stolen

Volume III

Helene Lebrun
7215 NW 214th St
Alachua, FL 32615

BOOKS by M. M. Le BLANC

FICTION

EVANGELINE: PARADISE STOLEN, Vols. I & II, True 1st Ed.

EVANGELINE: PARADISE STOLEN, Vols. I & II, Ltd. 2nd Ed.

EVANGELINE: PARADISE STOLEN, Vol. III, True 1st Ed.

EVANGELINE: PARADISE STOLEN, Vol. I, eBook

EVANGELINE: PARADISE STOLEN, Vol. II, eBook

NON-FICTION

Vol. 1, CHEAP PROTECTION: Copyright Handbook for Films

Vol. 2, CHEAP PROTECTION: Copyright Handbook for Screenplays

Vol. 3, CHEAP PROTECTION: Copyright Handbook for Teleplays

Vol. 4, CHEAP PROTECTION: Copyright Handbooks for TV Projects

Vol. 5, CHEAP PROTECTION: Copyright Handbook for Music

FINANCING INDEPENDENT FILMS: 50 Ways to Get the Golden Goose, Not a Goose Egg

THE ACADIAN MIRACLE, 50th Anniversary Edition

THE ACADIAN MIRACLE, 53rd Anniversary Edition with Index

THE TRUE STORY OF THE ACADIANS, 90th Anniversary Edition

THE TRUE STORY OF THE ACADIANS, 93rd Anniversary Edition with Index

COLLECTIVE WORKS

ACADIE THEN AND NOW, Author, "Acadians in Belle Île en Mer"

L'ACADIE HIER ET AUJOURD'HUI, Editor, "Les Acadiens de Belle Île en Mer"

For the descendants of the Exiled Acadians
and everyone who loves history.

Commemorating the 264th anniversary
of the Unlawful British Deportation from Nova Scotia
of the French Acadians, Ancestors of the Cajuns.

Merci, St. Gabriel.

Author's Note

While this is a work of historical fiction, the author conducted years of scholarly and genealogical research of actual historical documents, archival records and diaries, leading to the inclusion of numerous authentic historic details in this novel, including, but not limited to, text from correspondence and character dialogue.

Additional information and research about the period of the Acadian Exile, as well as the political and social conditions leading up, and resulting from, the Exile may be found in two non-fiction books written by the same author:

- *The True Story of the Acadians, 93rd Anniversary Edition with Index* (BizEntine Press, 2019), and,

- *The Acadian Miracle 53rd Anniversary Edition with Index* (BizEntine Press, 2019), with a full Bibliography of over one hundred historical sources from the 1700's, 1800's and 1900's in English and French.

HISTORICAL SUMMARY
Grand Pré, Nova Scotia
1524-1755

"Et in Arcadia Ego."

- Virgil

Acadia was discovered in 1524 by Giovanni da Verrazzano. He chose the name "Arcadia" in honor of its beautiful trees reminiscent of those in the idyllic land of Sannazaro's poem of the same name. By 1603, Acadia was settled by French fishermen and in subsequent years, by trappers and waves of French colonists.

Acadia changed hands in 1713 pursuant to the Treaty of Utrecht between France and Great Britain which ended the War of the Spanish Succession. By virtue of this Treaty, England gained control of the Acadian territory from France and renamed it Nova Scotia. The Treaty obligated England to treat the French Acadians as neutrals, allowing them to practice their Catholic religion freely and exempting them from bearing arms against France and their allies the Mi'Kmaq Indians. In return, the Acadians signed an oath of allegiance to King George.

For decades, the Acadians had honored their oath to remain neutral and refrain from bearing arms for their mother country against England. In return, they had expected the English to honor the Treaty and allow them to practice their religion freely. But it should have come as no surprise to the Acadians that the English would not keep their promise, as they had not kept any promises they had made.

For decades after the Treaty was in effect, the English military in Nova Scotia had demanded that the French Acadians sign an unconditional oath of allegiance to England, including disavowing their own religion and agreeing to fight for England against France in any war. The Acadians refused to agree to such modified oath, but continued to honor their oath of neutrality.

In July 1755, British King George II issued an Edict which had been discussed for generations over the past century as the "Acadian problem."

The King ordered Nova Scotia Lieutenant-Governor Charles Lawrence to exile all the French neutrals whose families had lived in the French territory of Acadia since 1603.

Lawrence appointed Lieutenant-Colonel John Winslow to conduct the secret operation in Grand Pré, though other British officers implemented the same scheme in other towns populated with the French Acadians.

But even worse than the Acadians being exiled and losing everything they owned was the division of families and boarding onto separate ships. British soldiers tore wives from husbands, children from parents, and betrothed couples from each other. The order was given because of English paranoia that the "large heathen Catholic families" would regroup in exile and return to Nova Scotia to fight the British and recover their lands.

Winslow deceived the Acadian men and boys over age nine into presenting themselves in the St. Charles Church in Grand Pré on September 5, 1755, for a reading of the King's Edict. The Edict forfeited their property to the British Crown and ordered the Acadians out of the land where their families had lived for generations. When the males entered the Church for the reading, they were locked inside for weeks until ships arrived to deport them, while their wives, children and elderly relatives remained ignorant of the situation and pined for their return.

Despite the Acadians' unwavering adherence to the Treaty for forty-two years, the King's Exile order directly violated the terms of the Treaty during peacetime. Although the Acadians had done nothing to justify their deportation, George II nevertheless banished them forever.

The Acadian Exile began in the fall of 1755 and continued in waves for years as English militia hunted and, in many cases, killed Acadian runaways on the spot. The Exile sparked yet another war with France the following year. That conflict would come to be known as the Seven Years' War in Europe, and the French and Indian War in the Colonies, which ended in 1763 with the Treaty of Paris.

The Exile of the French Catholic Acadians by England's King George II was an act of genocide, disbursing the Acadians throughout the British Colonies, France, England and the Caribbean as leaves scattered to the winds.

*

The saga of Evangeline continues from *EVANGELINE: PARADISE STOLEN*, Volumes I and II, Part IV, Chapter 42.

Part V

In Love and War
1755 - 1756

"We are now upon a great and noble Scheme of sending the neutral French out of this Province, who have always been secret Enemies, and have encouraged our Savages to cut our throats. If we effect their Expulsion, it will be one of the greatest Things that ever the English did in America; for by all Accounts, that part of the Country they possess, is as good Land as anywhere in the World: In case therefor we could get some good English Farmers in their Room this Province would abound with all Kinds of Provisions."

- *Pennsylvania Gazette, September 4, 1755*

CHAPTER 43
Burning

Grand Pré, Nova Scotia

The shrieks of a soaring eagle reverberated from the cliffs above Grand Pré, Nova Scotia to the beaches of Minas Basin below. Other birds screeched in response, and the cacophony pierced the fog settling on a group of British ships in the harbor.

But the English troops onshore and on ships in the bay ignored the birds' cries. The men would have been surprised to learn that the calls were not made by birds at all, but by members of the Mi'Kmaq First Tribe, dedicated allies of the Acadians. But today, the soldiers were pre-occupied with their mission. They were to deport all the French Acadian men and boys over age nine from their homeland forever.

Prince Kitok Mius, the sole son of Mi'Kmaq First Nation Chief Mahtok, surveyed the devastating scene from a tree high above the beach. It was only October, but the snow flurries had begun early, signaling the onset of an especially harsh winter. British soldiers had marched Acadian men and boys to the beach from the makeshift prison in St. Charles Church. Under the watchful eyes of Lieutenant-Colonel John Winslow and his trusted Captains Turnbull and Adams, troops had loaded the prisoners at bayonet-point into rowboats. Kitok could only imagine the grief and powerlessness the Acadian men felt as they waited futilely for their families to join them.

Kitok looked in vain for Winslow, the leader of the British troops in Grand Pré. He had arrived at the British fort not two months earlier to implement King George's brutal order to exile the Acadians. Shortly after his arrival, Winslow had imprisoned the French Catholic parish priest Père Rivière and sent him to be sold into servitude in Bostontown.

Subsequently, the Lieutenant-Colonel had conveniently moved into the priest's lodgings at the rectory to keep an eye on the men who had been imprisoned in the Church and to maintain the women's false hopes that they, too, would be boarded on the same ships as their men.

Yet today, after months of planning, Winslow had found the deportation activities too disagreeable to his temperament. He had left the operation in the hands of his cruel officer Captain Turnbull and had returned to town. Turnbull had relished loading the Acadian men and boys onto rowboats to be boarded onto the deportation ships.

Winslow's deportation plan was cruel and brutal. He planned to exile the Acadians in animal cargo vessels whose holds had been rebuilt to accommodate three times the number of people as animals. This was required because the Acadian population was much larger than originally calculated by the British. Winslow had approved the inhumane plan to build three windowless cells about four feet tall within each hold into which the human cargo would be loaded. Additionally, the food stores had been woefully underestimated, so rations were scarce. Stores of food and water bought for the initial September deportation date were contaminated due to delays in the arrivals of the ships. Yet Winslow did nothing, knowing death and disease on the ships would be rampant and any surviving Acadians would be too weak to retaliate.

Soon, Kitok's long-time Acadian allies against the British would be sent hither and yon. Kitok had overheard Captain Turnbull boast about sending his enemy, Gabriel Mius d'Entremont, leader of the Acadian resistance, to the most notorious prison in England -- London's Westminster Gatehouse. Kitok feared he would never again see Gabriel, his closest friend and a distant relation. The Mi'Kmaq prince knew nothing of English prisons, but he had witnessed the cruelty of the English military leaders in Grand Pré. He felt a great foreboding for Gabriel and a shiver overcame him.

Before the Acadians had been imprisoned in the church, Kitok had devised a rescue plan with Gabriel who circulated the strategy to members of his underground Acadian militia. By the time the men were loaded onto the ships, they were all aware that if they could get off the transports, the Mi'Kmaqs would remove them from the water to safety.

Kitok had directed Mi'Kmaq braves to hide in trees and in the woods near the cliff watching for men jumping off the boats. He had strategically deposited bundles of dry clothes, blankets and food in the woods. And he had horses at the ready to help the Acadians make their getaway. They had planned to take the runaways into the mountains beyond Grand Pré or to New France by the overland trail. Both treks were dangerous but would discourage English soldiers from following the fugitives.

Kitok had also sent two braves from the trees to the British garrison at Grand Pré to seize all the documents they could find, hoping to learn details of the ships' destinations. Kitok's plan was to join them. They would burn the fort and all of its contents so the English would not know that the Mi'Kmaqs had learned the evil details of the Exile. By learning where the ships were bound, Kitok would be able to track their whereabouts and send aid or help them escape and return home. But those documents were not in the fort. Winslow had apparently kept them hidden elsewhere.

The English Captains, Turnbull and Adams, had been ordered to give the Acadian women false assurances that they would embark once the men had boarded. They carried out their plan well. Troops were already loading the men onto the ships before the women learned of the ruse and marched to the beach themselves. Turnbull ordered the troops to protect the side of the beach farthest away from the cliff where Kitok and his braves were watching.

Pouring forth from the woods came women, children, old folks in carts, people stumbling with canes, women carrying newborns and pregnant women in the rear. They shouted and cried as they hurried through the rocks and sand toward their men in the rowboats and on the ships. Panic and chaos ensued as the women rushed toward the water's edge seeking their husbands, sons, brothers and fathers.

The soldiers diligently pulled women back onto the shore, but so many eluded them that Turnbull enacted a cruel plan. He organized a long line of British soldiers armed with bayonets and muskets to block access to the water at the edge of the beach. He ordered, "Use your bayonets and muskets if necessary. Prevent the women from leaving the beach. Shoot any who enter the water trying to join their men."

Hours later, the last of the Acadian men had been loaded into the rowboats while the women stood helplessly on the beach. Separated family members watched in agony as their fathers, husbands, sons, brothers and grandfathers were boarded onto transports that would take them away forever to unknown destinations. Wives, daughters, sisters, parents and young children cried out in distress at the thought of never seeing them again.

Kitok watched British soldiers led by Captain Turnbull tear French fathers away from sons and load them onto separate boats at bayonet point. His heart ached as he saw young boys cling to their fathers or men try to swim to join their sons, only to be shot without warning.

Kitok winced as he saw a woman break through the troops and wade into the water. She dropped into the freezing sea, hit by a young soldier's musket ball. A young boy let go of his mother's hand and scampered into his father's arms in a rowboat being filled with other prisoners. When the father refused to release his son, a soldier grabbed the screaming boy from his crying father. Refusing the entreaties of his mother, the soldier thrust a bayonet into the little boy's body and tossed him into the water, his blood pooling near the father's boat. The father kept his hand in the water touching his son's blood for as long as he could until the rowboat was shoved out into the bay towards a ship.

Several women who preferred death to living without their men disobeyed Turnbull's order and broke through the line of soldiers. Within minutes, each felt the cold metal of the bayonets pierce her body before dying at the water's edge. Their bodies were abandoned on the bloody beach.

Turnbull threatened the Acadians remaining onshore saying, "Anyone who attempts to retrieve and bury these traitors shall be hung on the nearest tree until dead." The last thing the Captain wanted was a "heathen" ceremony which could create chaos and injure the troops.

The most prominent French Acadian to be exiled was Royal Consul Lord René Le Blanc de Verdure, the royal French Consul and Notaire of King Louis XV. He was Evangeline's father and became her sole parent when her mother Lady Eugenie de Beaufort had died giving birth to her.

Le Blanc had been rowed to an old hull along with the aging Acadian men. His royal status was ignored by Winslow, and subsequently, by Turnbull. From his vantage point, Kitok could see that the small boat did not appear in the least to be seaworthy. The last glimpse Kitok had of René was of him being marched down into the hold of the vessel by armed troops.

Kitok turned to the other end of the bay and watched sadly as his good friends Gabriel Mius d'Entremont and Marc de la Tour Landry were forced to climb aboard the last empty ship in the harbor.

Kitok focused on this ship and emitted his soaring eagle cry to the other Mi'Kmaq braves hidden in the trees near the beach and on the cliffs above. The powerful bird call meant, "Be watchful. Prepare to move soon." Kitok's code alerted his braves to be ready to rescue Gabriel and the other Acadians on that ship.

But before the Indians could take action, a group of twenty-four Acadian men led by Francis Hébert made a daring escape from one of the ships by shimmying down a rope on the side of the ship hidden from view of the beach. They swam to shore and escaped into the trees on the side of the beach not guarded by soldiers.

When they arrived, Mi'Kmaq braves were ready with dry clothes, blankets and food for the trek to safety beyond Grand Pré.

Turnbull learned about the escapees and he ordered two soldiers, "Bring Consul Le Blanc to me." When René arrived, Turnbull ordered, "Talk to the families of the men who escaped. Warn them that I shall kill all of them unless the men return and re-board their transports."

Consul Le Blanc did as he was told, and convincingly. He knew Turnbull would not stop at killing the families, but if he were to learn of

Kitok's plan, he would hunt the Mi'Kmaqs as well, though the English had left them alone as a general rule.

The men who escaped from the ships had changed back into their wet clothes and hidden the dry ones so as to not reveal Kitok's plan. Turnbull waited near the trees with several troops to set an example for any future escapees. As soon as the returning men walked out of the woods, British soldiers shot and killed the first two arrivals, a father and son.

Francis Hébert, the organizer of the escape, was a Grand Pré boat builder and sailor with years of maritime experience. Turnbull's men beat Francis badly, then dragged his family to his house and workshop to watch troops torch them. The flames of the burning buildings shot so high in the air they could be seen from the beach. There, Acadians bowed and prayed that Turnbull did not burn the family alive as retribution. Francis' eldest daughter Marie died trying to save her mother. And Francis' wife nearly died of grief watching a bloody and beaten Francis being rowed back to the ship from which he had tried to escape to return to his family.

The other returning fugitives feared they might meet the same fate. To protect their families, they bravely marched to the beach and presented themselves to Turnbull. The Captain ordered the disobedient men whipped until their backs bled. Then they were rowed to the last boat in the harbor, the one bound for the London prison. They would join the other Acadian men believed by Winslow and Turnbull to be the resistance, including Evangeline Le Blanc de Verdure's fiancé, Gabriel Mius d'Entremont, and Jeanne Lambert's fiancé, Marc de la Tour Landry. They were dumped onto the deck and chained together, then pushed down into the hold.

The cruelty of the British officers and troops did not deter Kitok from his plan. He and his braves remained ready in the forest to assist escapees, but no others appeared. Turnbull had sent messengers on every ship to issue a threat to kill the family of any escaped prisoner. None of the Acadians made any further attempts to escape. They preferred acquiescing to their unknown fate rather than subjecting their families to Turnbull's cruelty.

At that point Kitok realized the futility of his plan to help his friend Gabriel escape. Having no living relatives in Grand Pré, Gabriel had no reason to fear Turnbull's vengeance. His mother Diane had died before the trip to Acadia and his father Henri was killed in a surprise British attack while on a peace mission to Halifax that summer. Still, Gabriel would refuse because of his honor, his love for his fiancée Evangeline and his respect for her father, René, the French Consul.

Most of the large cargo boats had set sail, now appearing as ghostly ships in the fog. Kitok could not fathom the unspeakable horrors that awaited the Acadian women without their husbands and older sons to protect them. He and his tribe would determine a plan to protect the remaining Acadians and to prevent more tragedy.

As their men sailed out of the harbor, the women on the beach sang Catholic hymns of hope and prayer. Their voices carried across the water as they sang with deep emotion through their tears. Soon, their beloved men on the ships joined in the songs. Their voices meshed in harmony as loved ones strained to see each other one final time before disappearing from view.

Kitok returned his gaze to the water below and the ship Gabriel had boarded. He thought he saw a woman's head bobbing in the waves close to the boat. He looked again, more closely this time, but saw no one. He was about to signal his braves to head back to their camp when he saw the woman lift her head above the water for a moment before it disappeared again. Kitok guessed the female swimmer was Evangeline heading towards Gabriel's ship. Fortunately, she was out of the line of sight by the British troops on the far side of the beach. At least for the time being.

Then Kitok noticed a British officer being lifted up onto the deck of the same ship. It was none other than the cruel Captain Turnbull. Clearly, it was Turnbull's intent to punish Gabriel and his militia on their way to their final destination.

Kitok peered down at the troops who were trying to organize the Acadians on the opposite side of the beach. They were paying no attention to the last ship which would set sail at any moment.

Taking no chances that Turnbull could see Evangeline, Kitok signaled his braves. He shrieked his eagle cry again. One by one, he heard the cries of the Mi'Kmaq braves loyal to him. The call of the crow from Sitting Fox, of the blackbird from Running Bear and of other birds from braves strategically positioned along the edge of the forest, near the beach, and behind rocks and in trees on the bluffs above the harbor.

When Sitting Fox and Running Bear got the sign from Kitok, they quickly climbed down the trees on the bluff and set their pre-arranged plan in motion. The other braves did the same. Meanwhile, Kitok turned his attention back to the ship. He saw Evangeline raise her arms out of the water to Gabriel. He and declared his love for her from the deck above.

Boom! Kitok felt his heart stop when Turnbull shot his musket into the water below. As if in slow motion, Evangeline disappeared under the water and he heard Gabriel's painful cry as piercing as an eagle shriek.

"Evangeline!"

In the thickening fog, Kitok watched Turnbull drag Gabriel down into the hold. In the water, he saw not Evangeline's head but a red pool ripple on the surface of the water. As the fog enveloped the ship, Kitok knew he had to take action.

He shrieked a formidable eagle cry and dove straight down from the cliff into the water near the spot where he had last seen Evangeline. Running Bear and Sitting Fox followed, their dives from the cliffs through the fog taking them into the icy bay below.

Kitok could only pray that they could find Evangeline. Perhaps she had swum underwater and found refuge in the rocks of the cliff. Kitok's powerful strokes under the water brought him nearer and nearer the boat. But as the ship sailed away, he saw no sign of Evangeline.

Raising his head, Kitok gasped for air through the bobbing waves. The other braves swam to the surface, shaking their heads as they filled their lungs. Then the three of them dove under the freezing water again.

Kitok prayed as he had been taught by his parents Chief Mahtok and Princess Snowbird, and by the Grand Pré priest Pere Rivière at the Masses he had performed in their Mi'Kmaq Village.

"Please God, please keep Evangeline alive and show me where to find her," Kitok whispered.

He rose to the surface and filled his lungs while scouring the beach from one end to the other. Evangeline was nowhere to be seen. He realized she could not have swum fast enough to rejoin the women. And soldiers had blocked the road so she could not have taken that route. Was she still alive, or had she died at Turnbull's hand?

Kitok could not fail at his mission. He had promised to protect her if anything happened to Gabriel. She must still be in the treacherous water. But if so, where? And why couldn't he see her?

The other two braves surfaced again empty-handed. They submerged themselves again. Evangeline's body was not visible anywhere in the murky waters. Still, Kitok had faith that God would protect her. She was the most loving, generous person he knew, Acadian or Mi'Kmaq, who had always put others before herself. She had even risked her life to help Gabriel and Kitok with their resistance movement against the English soldiers.

Kitok knew Evangeline was a devout spiritual young woman and that God would not have taken the life of such an innately good person. And he believed he could save her, if he could find her.

Just then he saw a limp body in the dark, swirling water just ahead of him. He compelled himself to swim faster, faster until he grasped Evangeline's hand. Sitting Fox and Running Bear swam over to him. Together they propelled a motionless Evangeline to the surface of the waves.

Evangeline's eyes were closed, her face contorted and pale, her lips already turning blue. Her precious locket that Gabriel had given her had escaped her neck and floated in the water. Unseen by anyone, the waves carried the chain and locket to the sandy beach where it lay untouched until it would be found by the unlikeliest of persons.

With powerful strokes, the Mi'Kmaqs swam and carried Evangeline to shore, hidden from the soldiers on shore by the thick fog.

In the heavy gray mist, the last ship sailing away carried Gabriel and his fellow Acadian rebels to Westminster Gatehouse Prison. The ghostly vessel had set its course for England. Away from home. Away from Evangeline.

CHAPTER 44

Snows

Grand Pré

On the beach, Acadian women watched in agony as the ships carrying their male family members sailed into the fog. Knowing their loved ones were leaving, perhaps forever, the women wailed incessantly and beat their breasts. Little did they realize, nor did their men sailing away from them, how permanently their lives would be changed by the voyage.

Adding to their misery, the names of the transports that took their men away belied their true purpose. *Swan, Swallow* and *Elizabeth* sounded soft, benign, even friendly. Yet too many of those who survived the horrific trek would pray for death to release them. They would weep with happiness that deceased family members and friends did not have to endure their hell on earth. But that was in the future. At present, all they could do was pray.

Christine de Castille fell to her knees. She was the French housekeeper who had become a nursemaid and substitute mother to Evangeline when René's wife Eugenie had died giving birth to her. Christine prayed for the health and safety of not only her love René but of all the Acadians exiled that day.

"Lord, please keep them safe. Reinforce their hope and resolve to meet us again one day. And, especially, do not let the old hull sink. René knew it had been sabotaged. Please protect him and all the Acadians on board and bring them safely back to us. Bring my René back to me. Amen."

The infirm who had been carried to the beach in carts desperately wished for death. Old women like Yvonne Poché hobbled along the beach thinking of nothing but their husbands who had been loaded onto the old hull. She comforted herself knowing that her Alain and the other Acadian men were with Lord Le Blanc, who would protect them as best he could.

Jeanne's mother, Lorraine Lambert, had difficulty with her walking cane that stuck in the sand with each step. She could do nothing but hope that her husband, Jean, would safely reach his unknown destination and that she would join him there before long.

The other women joined hands and began saying the Lord's Prayer aloud. "Our Father, Who art in heaven...."

Farther down the beach, Jeanne knelt and bowed her head, praying quietly to herself. "Dear God, I pray that you hold my fiancé Marc, my father Jean, and all the other Acadian men in Your hands. Prevent any harm from befalling them. Give them the strength to follow Your will. And please let Evangeline be safe. We know not where she is but pray that she is alive and safe. And, please show Marc the way to find me. Amen."

Snow flurries whipped past the pitiful scene of the crying women and girls on the sand as soldiers tried to round them into manageable lines. The Acadians ignored the troops and wandered up and down the beach at the water line. They sought a last glimpse of the ships through the dense fog.

Béatrice Gaudet held the hand of her mother Anne who either did not understand or chose to ignore the gravity of the situation in which they found themselves. An orphaned eight-year old boy named Francis Melanson had been living with Béatrice and Anne. Evangeline had found him alone and crying after his mother had been killed by soldiers months earlier. Francis followed the women walking on the beach. He watched Anne kick up shells and giggle without understanding the situation at all.

Béatrice peered into the fog but there was no sign of the ship on which her nine-year-old brother Pine had been forcibly boarded. She adored her brother, one reason why she had readily accepted to care for Francis.

Anne stopped every now and again to pick up a shell or piece of broken wood on the beach, oohing and aahing over each one as if it were of immense value. She pocketed her treasures in the apron she wore over her dress. Once the items were safe, she wrapped her cloak tightly about her and looked around furtively to make sure no one had seen her but Francis. She trusted him to keep her secrets safe.

But she needn't have worried. No one else was watching her, not even the troops. They were busy rounding up the women rushing around as they fretted over loved ones and friends they might never see again.

Each Acadian on the beach felt the piercing loss of family and experienced untold anxiety over their fate to be shipped to parts unknown. The soldiers had not confirmed their scheme, but the Acadians were not naïve. They knew they were to meet with the same destiny as their beloved men and boys. They, too, would be shipped out. It was not a question of if, but rather, of when. But the looming question in their minds was where. Where would they be sent?

Many hoped against hope that they would arrive at the same destinations as their loved ones. But Christine knew better. Gabriel and Kitok had revealed to René, Evangeline and herself the cruel British plan to separate the familes and ship them to different ports.

Unknown to René, before the men were exiled, Christine had devised a plan to learn more about the British scheme. She flirted shamelessly with Winslow, hoping to gain access to his personal quarters. When he invited her to dinner and attempted to gain carnal knowledge of her, she spiked his win with an herbal sleeping potion. He fell fast asleep and she rifled through his documents. None had the exact timing of the exile but did specify the plan to separate and ship family members to different destinations.

But before René could develop a strategy, the Acadians were imprisoned in the church, then exiled. The espionage Christine conducted was all for naught. Winslow and his troops applied the brutal plan perfectly.

Troops deposited the last of the Acadian men in the ships and rowed their small boats back to shore. The commanding officer, Lieutenant-Colonel John Winslow looked up every now and again, but preferred to sit still on his horse and read his Bible. With Captain Turnbull re-assigned to the ship of Acadian "rebels" and their leaders Gabriel and Marc, Captain Adams was now the ranking British officer under Winslow. Adams kept looking at Winslow for direction, but he refused to look up. Adams took that to mean he was definitively in charge and acted that way.

As guilty as he felt when he read his Bible, Winslow still believed he would best obey King George's Edict to divide and ship the families on separate ships if he duped the women into believing entire families would all leave together. He intentionally lied to them about the fate of their men, assuring them they would be notified when the men were released from the church and ordered to board the ships.

But when the time came to exile the Acadians, Winslow issued orders to his troops. "Herd the men out of the church at dawn and lead them quietly to the rowboats on the beach." Winslow told the officers, "If any of the men break their silence, do not hesitate to use your weapons. Bayonets ready!"

The troops had instantly pulled out their sharp instruments and affixed them to the edge of their guns. The Acadian men winced and the young boys cowed at the thought of being punished by such a painful instrument. With the threat of the bayonets looming over the Acadians, the British troops had quietly marched the men from the church through town, into the trees and down the hill to the waiting rowboats and ships. Winslow's orders were carried out to the letter without so much as a whimper from the Acadians.

The Acadian women never imagined that Winslow would lie to them, especially after they had kindly quartered and fed so many troops. Those soldiers had eaten at their tables, slept in their homes and been treated with respect. It slowly sank in that Winslow never intended for their families to be together. At that point, the women realized they had been tricked and began to cause chaos.

From their formations at the waterline or at the trees, the troops watched the Acadians closely. Lieutenant-Colonel Winslow had promised a hanging to any soldier that allowed an Acadian to steal a rowboat and head for any of the ships. That would have upset Winslow's perfect plan of dividing up the heathen families.

From his vantage point at the opposite end of the beach from Kitok, Winslow clutched the Bible tucked within his waistcoat. He vehemently muttered to himself, "The heathens shall not be allowed to reunite in the same destinations and strengthen their ranks with more children. That can never happen. They would surely march north from their drop-off points and fight to take back their ancestral lands. They may be heathens but they are still too powerful a force against the troops here. These lands now belong to the King and they shall make the Massachusetts Bay Colony the most powerful of all the Thirteen. No, that shall not happen if I have to string up every last one of them."

Winslow harrumphed and nudged his horse forward. He was thankful he had left some armed guards at the fort, but he saw the chaos on the beach and shouted to Captain Adams, "Dispatch the troops from the fort to the shore save one guard." Adams was happy to get an order and implemented it immediately.

Winslow stroked his Bible and murmured to himself, "Let my officers handle the women when they learn that I misled them. The Acadians are all papists and are the cause of their woes. They had the chance to convert to our King's one true church but refused. This is their own doing. They deserve what they get and what they get shall not be gentle."

Winslow's lies to the Acadian women had generated swift and strong mistrust of all the English. From that point forward, the Acadians refused to believe any assurances the officers or troops gave them. For some, their disobedience resulted in death. For others, grief of lost loved ones.

Christine moved throughout the Acadians, trying to calm their distress and relieve their suffering by saying a prayer. But it became clear that many preferred death by drowning to living without their loved ones. She noticed a little girl running towards the water, crying out. "Mama. Mama." Her mother was floating in the water, stained red with Acadian blood.

However sad, the woman's body was not the lone one. There were dozens of corpses floating like small icebergs on the water heading into the fog.

Christine raced to grab the child before she reached the icy waves. "Child, come to me. Do not go in the water."

But the little girl ignored Christine's warning. Just at that moment, a soldier called out, "Halt!" Without waiting, he shot the child. She dropped into the water near her mother, her blood pouring out and staining the waves redder.

Christine stared at the soldier in anger and disbelief. "How could you kill a child? She did you no harm. Such a senseless death. Why?"

The soldier shrugged. "Heathens got to learn to obey orders. All of youse is the enemy, no matter the age. Now get back with them others."

Christine ignored him and ran toward the water, screaming as she went. "Children are not the enemy. She was innocent and shall have a Christian burial."

She picked up the child's body, intent on burying her. But before Christine knew what had happened, she felt a brutal force. She never saw the soldier's musket when the butt of the gun landed squarely against her cheek. The sickening cracking sound told her everything she needed to know. Stopped violently in her tracks, she fell to the beach, dropping the child's body and clutching her mangled face.

The soldier stood over her. "If that ain't enough, just try it again. How many times we got to tell youse heathens. Stay aways from the water. Go back to them others."

Christine begrudgingly sat up and when the soldier walked away, she made the Sign of the Cross and planted a kiss on the child's forehead. "Go with God, child. And pray for all of us." She reached under her cloak for the bag of herbs she had tied to her skirt. Pulling out some odd-shaped leaves she spit on them, rubbed them together then placed them like a poultice on her cheek. Instantly she sighed as she felt relief. She tore off a long cloth swatch from her underskirt and tied it from head to chin to soak the blood and keep the wound taut.

Farther up the beach, Béatrice held her mother's hand. Anne chatted to no one in particular. "Monplew jaxny flup." When Béatrice said nothing in response, Anne started to yell. "Deslem hinguit!"

Béatrice leaned down and patted her mother's head until Anne calmed down once more. She continued gurgling in a near-whisper. "Jaxny flup. Surkno relp murr." She picked up the snowy sand and tried to eat it until Béatrice brushed it out of her hand. Anne then folded her arms and refused to hold Béatrice's hand.

Frustrated, Béatrice told Anne, "Come with me, mother. We must find Christine and our other friends." Anne understood and traipsed behind Béatrice.

Seeing a shiny object in the sand, Anne bent down and picked it up. It was Evangeline's locket and golden chain. Anne held it up to Béatrice, who was walking ahead of her and did not see what her mother had found. Anne hid the golden prize in her pocket with her shells and other hidden treasures and again wrapped her cloak tightly around her. She scampered to catch up with Béatrice. Béatrice kissed her mother's cheek and held her hand tightly as they passed a group of soldiers warming their hands over a fire. Francis skipped along behind them.

The troops were exhausted from the physical labor of dragging women and children from the sea intent on following the ships carrying their men away. Captain Adams issued orders loudly to the soldiers, "Attention! Get the prisoners in line. Prepare to march back to town."

As Adams galloped from one end of the beach to another, he surveyed the chaos with disgust. At the waterline, many Acadians were still trying to swim toward the ships now enveloped by the fog. Christine and Jeanne did their best to hold children back, but many eluded their grasp. The little ones quickly drowned trying to reach their grieving mothers who welcomed death, despite the orphans they made of their children.

Anne Gaudet and Francis sat in the middle of the beach, playing in the snowy sand. Gurgling her nonsensical language to the young boy who clapped and smiled, Anne was completely unaware of the dangerous soldiers surrounding her.

Captain Adams yelled at the troops by the water. "Fix your bayonets and aim them at the prisoners until you can herd them into some kind of order. Don't let me see any more chaos when I return."

Without staying to supervise, Adams kicked his horse and rode up to the woods. He gathered troops to form a line and prevent the Acadians from returning from the beach to their homes in town.

At the water's edge, soldiers fumbled and stumbled as they attempted to corral the Acadians into a line. Their efforts remained unsuccessful, largely because many of the Acadians ignored them and waded to their death in the icy water.

Snow fell in earnest now. A cart holding an old couple, presumably grandparents or even great grand-parents, appeared too exhausted from the march or from grief to move. Soon, the aged Acadians were covered in the white powder and became as stiff as marble statues.

Lieutenant Wicker tried to prod the women into marching by raising his musket, but they would not budge. He looked around but there were no commanding officers who could make a decision to shoot or leave them as they were.

"Get up, yer lazy heathens. Get out that wagon and move. That means now!" Wicker prodded the couple in the cart with his rifle butt. No response. He pushed the old man sitting on the edge of the wagon. The man fell out of the cart onto the beach, his body frozen solid.

Wicker tried the old woman. "Stand up, I say. Off that wagon!" When he received no response, Wicker made up his mind to make her sorry for her disobedience. He muttered to himself. "Every dead heathen makes this place better." He pointed his musket and aimed.

Just as he was about to shoot, Captain Adams rode up to Wicker and issued an order. "Leave them and join the other troops. They need help at the treeline." Adams said in a tone harsher than usual. He pointed to the soldiers near the woods blocking the Acadians on the beach from returning to town.

"Do not allow anyone off this beach until I give the order. Hear me?"

Wicker nodded. "Yes sir, Captain." He lowered his musket and ran to the edge of the woods, joining the line of soldiers. Like them, Wicker raised his bayonet and pointed it at the moving mass of women and children. He ignored their wails, the loudest of which was a young woman crying out as she rocked her baby.

Wicker turned his gun and beat the woman to the ground with the rifle butt. She lay on the beach, her blood staining the white snow. As the baby fell from the young mother's arms, Christine rushed up and grabbed it, but she was too late. The infant had already frozen to death.

Christine stood and raised her arm to protect against Wicker, who had raised his whip. Just as he was about to strike her, Béatrice rushed up and knocked Christine to the ground. Summoning her courage and a smile, Béatrice told Wicker, "She won't bother you, sir. She is very ill. See?"

Christine obliged by doubling over and coughing as hard as she could. She avoided Wicker's eyes but carefully watched his weapon and his whip. Wicker snorted and motioned with the whip. "Back in line. And don't let me see any more trouble from the likes of youse."

"No, sir. No more trouble. I promise." Béatrice nodded her gratitude then grabbed Christine and hurried up to the treeline. They joined the other Acadians waiting to return to their homes.

Christine looked around furtively. When she saw Wicker joking with another soldier, Christine whispered her thanks to Béatrice. "What would I have done without you? Thank you, dear Béatrice."

Béatrice hushed her. "We should escape into the woods. Hopefully, the Mi'Kmaqs would rescue us and take us to safety in their mountain caves. I heard they are impossible to find otherwise."

Christine nodded. "Yes, René said we could rely on our friends. When we get back to town, let us stay in our houses until midnight, then slip into the forest. No need to search for the Mi'Kmaqs. They will see us. But we must bring food and many blankets, as the snows are coming so early this year."

Béatrice grimaced. "Let us hope the soldiers have not robbed our homes of all the winter food."

Christine said solemnly. "I took precautions and hid some beneath the floorboards along with several guns and a pouch of coins that René gave me. I do not know if any of it is enough."

"It shall have to be," Béatrice replied.

Christine's spirits lifted and her face brightened. "I feel better knowing we have a plan once we get back to town. You and I can spread the word amongst the other women as we did when we saw our men marching to the ships."

Béatrice nodded. "If we move in small groups, hopefully the soldiers will not realize what we are doing until we are gone."

The two women clasped hands and gave each other a quick hug. Suddenly Béatrice panicked. "Where is my mother? And Francis?" She spun around and called out to the crowd. "Mother, where are you? Francis?"

Béatrice wrung her hands in consternation. "Oh, where are they?"

Christine pointed to Anne and Francis sitting nearby in a pile of sand topped with snowflakes. "Don't worry, Béatrice. Let her stay in her own world a little longer. Francis is with her."

Béatrice watched Anne tossing handfuls of sand all around to her heart's content as she gabbed to Francis continuously. He did not understand anything but pretended to, which was good enough for Anne. Béatrice shook her head and disagreed with Christine. "You don't understand. She's unpredictable. She could just walk up to a soldier and try to be playful, but the troops are so short-tempered, they would shoot first and not give it a second thought."

Christine grabbed Béatrice's hands to reassure you. "Don't even think about that. She will be fine. Francis will watch over her."

Béatrice pulled away and began running towards her mother. Suddenly, Captain Adams rode up out of nowhere and blocked Béatrice's path. "Just where do you think you are going? Back to the treeline." Adams put his hand on his whip.

Béatrice stopped and quickly waved to her mother, then focused her attention on Adams' whip. Anne saw Béatrice and waved back in dim recognition. "Blerkey nuse durfit?"

Béatrice fell to her knees and pleaded, "Captain. Please let me get my mother. She is just over there. She is dim-witted and confused."

Adams refused to relent. He pointed to the treeline and cracked his whip threateningly in the air. "She shall not be confused about this."

Out of Adams' sight, Christine grabbed Anne and half-carried, half-stumbled with her toward the trees and away from the Captain. Francis ran behind Christine, fearful of the soldiers. Christine covered Anne's mouth. "Hush, Anne. We must be quiet now."

Anne clumsily put her finger to her lip and smiled. Christine thought she understood and mimicked Anne's gesture. "Yes, Anne. This is a game. We are going to see who can be the quietest. Quiet as a mouse."

With that, she helped Anne to stand. "Up we go, Anne. Let's run to our friends near the trees. Quiet now. No talking. Let's play the game together." Anne nodded as she hobbled along, still pressing her finger to her lips. Francis lagged behind, staring at the soldiers, then rushed up.

Watching them, Béatrice slowly rose and wiped tears from her eyes. She was relieved that her mother was safe in Christine's care.

Adams turned his horse around slowly. He did not see anyone in the direction where Béatrice had pointed. "Where is the old woman?"

"My mistake, Captain. I see my mother in the line with the others. I shall join her now. Thank you, sir."

Béatrice trudged toward the woods on the sand wet with melting snow. Béatrice chose to join a group of Acadian women she knew rather than her mother and Christine. She did not want the officer to know which woman was her mother. He might inflict retribution.

She made a good decision because Adams sat on his horse watching her. Finally, Adams cracked his whip and dug his heels into the side of his steed. "Go, boy. Let us check on our troops on the other end of the beach. I am ready for this assignment to end. I long for civilized company again, not a group of uncooperative heathens."

Anne started to panic. She pointed out to Christine the soldiers and their guns and bayonets. Béatrice ran up, grabbed her other arm and whispered, "Quiet, mother. Everything is alright. We must be very quiet now. You, too, Francis. Not a word, alright?" The young boy nodded, too afraid to speak. Anne patted Béatrice's face, nodding and touching her finger to her mouth. "Kliken. Anne klicken."

Béatrice nodded. "Yes, mother. Klicken. Quiet. Be very quiet."

They waded through the still-falling snow to join the other Acadian women. Everyone on the beach shivered in the cold, but their minds were not on the temperatures. Rather, they felt a greater horror of loss and grief amidst the contrasting beauty of the snowfall. Still, that did not deter their mission to gather close to remaining family and friends and build fires for the little warmth they could bring.

A few brave souls darted into the woods unseen, returning with fallen branches for firewood. Under cover of night, Christine searched for herbs and plants with healing properties. She had a feeling she would need them sooner than expected.

But other Acadians who tried to escape were not so lucky. Soldiers followed them into the trees. Cries of pain were heard. Soon a gruesome trail of red snow and bodies littered the path into the woods.

When the soldiers traipsed out of the woods, they wiped their bloody bayonets in the snow. The dead Acadians were grieved by their loved ones, who blessed them as fortunate to escape the upcoming tribulation.

CHAPTER 45
Fort

Grand Pré

Further down the beach from the beautiful trees where the Acadian women were being herded back into town, Kitok and Sitting Fox carried Evangeline from the water. During their rescue, the chain to Evangeline's locket had broken and the jewelry had floated in the sea. But the waves that lapped onto the shore had gently carried the locket onto the sandy beach, where Anne Gaudet had found it.

Around the bend hidden from view of the beach and the bay was a small inlet with a cave carved into the cliff rocks. Running Bear had arrived before Kitok and Sitting Fox at the cave. Inside, he had cooked a thick soup in a pot over the roaring fire he had built.

The two Mi'Kmaqs carried Evangeline along the beach to the cavern. They were fortunate that snow fell into the opening to the cave which obscured it from the soldiers' view.

Kitok and Sitting Fox laid Evangeline on thick bear skins and covered her with woven blankets. Running Bear stoked the fire to generate more heat. She was nearly incoherent but Kitok understood her when she said, "Gabriel? Where is Gabriel?"

Kitok put his hands on her shoulder and whispered, "You are safe, Evangeline. I promised him I would keep you safe. I must tend your wound before anything else."

Kitok dressed the wound, cleaned it and put a paste on it. Evangeline nodded as the pain subsided. Then she moaned as she remembered what happened. "The ship. Turnbull sent him to the ship. I swam to see Gabriel. Turnbull shot me." She looked at her arm and saw a cloth had been tied and that the bleeding had stopped. Kitok nodded. "Red river paste," he said, reminding her of the Mi'Kmaq medicine woman White Bird who had taught Christine and Evangeline how to make a poultice from plants that stopped a wound from bleeding and healed it quicker.

Evangeline tried to get up but shivered and crawled back under the covers. She gratefully drank the soup from the bowl that Running Bear handed her and drifted off to a fitful sleep.

Confident that Evangeline needed time to recuperate but would heal, Kitok murmured instructions to the two braves. "Sitting Fox, you and I go to the fort. Running Bear, stay and protect Evangeline. Kill any English soldier who nears. Do not hesitate."

The braves nodded and agreed in unison. "Yes, Prince Kitok."

Kitok wrapped a bear fur around his shoulders and headed out into the snowy weather. Sitting Fox grabbed his own fur cape, staying a stone's throw behind Kitok. The two Mi'Kmaqs moved quickly around the bend of the cove and skirted the edge of the cliffs. Hidden by the heavy snowfall, they made it across the far end of the beach.

Kitok continued to the treeline without being detected by the soldiers on the beach. He whistled his eagle call to Sitting Fox, signaling to wait until it was safe to move.

Sitting Fox was about to run into the woods when he saw a group of Acadian women moving toward the rocks near him. They were seeking shelter from the snow which was falling heavier. He ducked behind a rock, but in the snow flurries, the women did not see him.

The Acadians were merely a few yards away from him when two British soldiers headed for them, running hard. Sitting Fox then saw Captain Adams trotting his horse toward the women.

Adams called out to the Acadians. "You there. Time to return to town. Go with my troops and you shall be safe."

The Acadians were completely distrustful now of the English. But when the soldiers brandished their bayonets, the Acadians had no choice but to follow them. The troops rounded them up and led them to the other side of the beach where groups of Acadian women, children and old people were lining up at the treeline. The soldiers took their job seriously, and none of the Acadians wanted to test their resolve. The bayonets were bloody but still sharp enough to do their job.

Adams stayed near the rock, and looked out at the bay. The departing ships seemed like figments of his imagination through the fog. But he had seen them, loaded them and sent them on their way.

"Soon we will be rid of all the treacherous papists," he said aloud. "Then I can move back to civilization. How I miss Bostontown."

Sitting Fox crouched lower behind the rock when he saw Adams jump off his horse. The Mi'Kmaq pulled his knife from his sheath, never taking his eyes off Adams.

But as it turns out, Sitting Fox had nothing to worry about. Adams merely wished to relieve himself, his spray bouncing off the wall into the snow-topped sand. When he was done and his breeches were adjusted back to normal, Adams breathed a sigh of contentment. "Only a little while longer in this horrid place." He mounted his steed again and trotted back down the beach to supervise his inferior officers and the troops.

Once Adams had left, Sitting Fox quickly dashed into the woods. Adams turned and thought he saw a shadowy figure in the snow running through the woods. He stopped his horse. Sitting Fox and Kitok did not move a muscle.

Adams trotted his horse closer to the treeline. At the edge of the woods, he saw nothing. He nosed his horse slowly into the trees. The Mi'Kmaqs were well-hidden by foliage and their fur cloaks. Adams peered through the misty trees as if he saw something.

Hiding under the fur behind a grove of trees, Sitting Fox watched as Adams peered through the trees near his spot. Adams suddenly realized what he was watching. He chided himself, "A bear? Didn't know they descended this close to the water, but no time to take a chance." With that, whether or not he was satisfied with his research, Adams reared his horse and galloped back to the troops at the other end of the beach.

Kitok had moved ahead in the woods the minute Adams galloped off. Sitting Fox peered through the trees waiting for Adams to disappear, then wasted no time in making up the distance between himself and Kitok.

Before long, both of them were deep within the trees' thick protection, unseen by anyone on the beach. Together they traipsed uphill and soon arrived at the road leading to the English fort near Grand Pré.

Once Kitok was within eyesight of the fort, he shimmied up a tree. He had seen rows of soldiers and hoped his intuition was right. His vantage point offered a clear view of the entire fort.

Kitok saw only one sentry manning the entry gates. The plump young man carried no rifle and sat on the ground, eating his lunch. The lookout perch was empty. No candles burned inside the offices of the fort, indicating that all the officers were elsewhere, most likely at the shore.

He was not surprised at the empty fort. He chuckled to himself. "Winslow does not know the first rule of war. Do not expose your weakness. He should have posted more armed guards at the headquarters, even if simply for show." He chuckled to himself. "And the second rule. Never forget your enemies have friends. He was so predictable in sending nearly all his troops to march our Acadian allies to the ships. And that will be his downfall."

Kitok suddenly let out a loud eagle screech to the other Mi'Kmaqs, signaling, "No armed troops at the fort."

Below the tree, Sitting Fox responded with his crow call that acknowledged, "Ready when you are."

Kitok was content. His plan was ready to be implemented at the fort. Actually, it was just a group of two-room houses surrounded by a wooden palisade and simple barracks. Abandoned for years, the military post had been refurbished at different periods since the Treaty of Utrecht which had transferred France's Acadia to England.

The latest renovation had been made a few months earlier when Winslow was assigned to the fort by William Shirley, Commander-in-Chief of the British Forces in North America. Shirley had transferred many more troops than the fort could house, forcing Winslow to quarter many troops in Acadian homes. The cost was minimal, to be sure, but the Acadians provided both room and board until a tent city could be built for the troops in the town square and new barracks were built for the officers. Yet, even after the improvements, the garrison was still nothing more than a small post and several houses surrounded by fences and a sentry tower.

At the conclusion of the negotiations with the French Consul René Le Blanc for the quartering agreement, Winslow had remarked to his Captain Turnbull, "How easy it is to dupe the French. They are completely trusting of us. They even consider us their neighbors. What fools they are."

Winslow had tried to hide his resentment when Shirley had uprooted him from his spacious red brick home in Marshfield, near Bostontown. Winslow had been enjoying what he considered the perfect life. His sumptuously round-bellied, well-endowed wife Mary who constantly barked orders to Cook to make whatever dishes he desired, especially his favorite onion pies. Servants who cleaned his rooms to perfection and dropped their tasks to restock his favorite tobacco. Most importantly of all, silence and solitude when he wished it so, though he did not understand how his wife could keep his young sons so quiet.

Winslow harrumphed. "What kind of life do I have now, with no one at my beck and call worth half a twit? I had better be given a reprieve to return to my comfortable home. No more assignments in such a prison as this forsaken backwoods hole."

He returned his focus to the day's events, and observed the carnage in the woods and the desperation on the Acadians' faces. He knew they had no trust in him now, but he cast off the thought and mused, "How utterly fascinating that the few words of the King's Edict would change their entire world. To many, this Exile is a death sentence or perhaps a prayed-for relief.

I pray that I am not forced to supervise the women's exile, but the guilt piles on higher each day. I hope to be soon relieved of this miserable duty. But most of all, I pray to return home for the warmth of Mrs. Winslow in my bed at night and for the hot onion pies that Cook makes with such care."

Winslow kicked his horse and galloped up the hill. Passing the quiet but depressing fort, Winslow was eager to return to his quarters in the house of the exiled priest Père Rivière, next to St. Charles Church in town.

He hoped his remaining time in Grand Pré would be short and that Commander Shirley would agree to send a replacement. He would soon learn his prayer would be answered. Another officer would be assigned to the fort in his stead, but for Shirley's reasons, not those of Winslow.

*

In Bostontown, Commander Shirley had decided to replace Winslow after he began to doubt Winslow's loyalty in doing his duty. Shirley's spies within the English Council had warned him of Winslow's tendency to feel strong guilt.

The Commander feared Winslow might be too weak-willed and would release the Acadian women rather than completing the second part of the King's Edict and plan to exile all of the heathens. If that happened, Shirley would fail in his plan to sell the fertile Acadian land to English planters and annex Nova Scotia to the Massachusetts Bay Colony that he governed. And he was not a man who failed, nor allowed any officer under his command to do so, either.

Shirley sat in his office, downing a glass of wine as he lectured a young aide, "Of all the emotions a commanding officer can have, guilt is the most dangerous. Never let your heart do the thinking for your head. The feeling of guilt is the one that eats loyalty from the inside until there is none left."

The aide quickly saluted and stammered, "Yes, sir, Commander. I mean, no sir, Commander. I have no feelings, no guilt, no other feelings at all. Except my gratitude to you for this position. And my loyalty, of course."

Shirley waved him off as he poured himself a glass of wine. "Dismissed."

The aide saluted again and practically ran out of the building. Shirley's temper tantrums were well-known throughout the army headquarters, and it was best not to be seen or heard when the Commander was in a foul mood. The young man quickly disappeared from the office and the building, but Shirley never noticed.

The rich lands developed by the Acadians had turned into the breadbasket of the Colonies, envied by others who were not as successful in their own farming pursuits. Then, too, the French supplied nearly all of the salted cod and colorfully-dyed fabrics which delighted the women in all thirteen of the Colonies.

The plan would make Shirley the most powerful Governor of all the Colonies, which was even more important than his role as the English army Commander-in-Chief. He realized the more territory he had, the more taxes he could collect, which in large part he could maneuver into his pockets.

He could not afford to have this plan fail. His financial backers had loaned him substantial sums on his guarantee that the Massachusetts Bay Colony would become the richest and most valuable of them all.

But no matter what Winslow did, Shirley knew he could not allow anything to compromise the second phase of the Exile. He spoke aloud as if his aide were still there, "I must congratulate myself for planning ahead. I have removed a disloyal officer from my ranks just as a surgeon cuts out a gangrene. Winslow shall be replaced with a stone-cold officer in his stead. There shall be no risk of failure and no hint of emotion in the ranks who must follow their orders to the letter. The second phase must conclude successfully and profitably. My new man shall make certain of it."

Shirley dipped a quill into the ink pot on his desk. With a flourish, he scratched his name on the orders recalling Winslow to the Massachusetts Bay Colony and replacing him with a new commanding officer, Captain Phineas Osgood.

After sending his orders, Shirley leaned back in his huge leather chair and plopped his boots on his large wooden desk, sighing contentedly, "Ahh, the next part of the Exile shall go according to plan. And if those little heathens think they can escape into the woods, then my phase three with my hunting parties shall certainly take them by surprise. Especially when they learn they shall not be granted any mercy. They shall get their due even if they escape the first Exile and do not board the transports. No, runaways shall be hunted like the animals they are, for years if necessary, then strung up or stuck with the cold steel of the bayonet before they shall be allowed to escape the King's Edict of banishment. One way or another, I shall rid the province of those heathens."

Shirley nodded, pleased with himself in the knowledge that he had his King's trust. In his reverie, he cackled in the empty room, "I shall have more gold than I can count once this deed has been finished. And my backers shall reap a tidy profit as well."

*

In the tree above the English fort, Kitok signaled to Sitting Fox to circle around the main building while the fat and happy guard took a nap. Sitting Fox scaled the wall and dropped inside the fence. Then he unlocked one of the gates and tossed Kitok some rope.

Kitok grabbed the sleeping guard and gagged and tied him before he could fight. Kitok tossed the guard over his shoulder, but the man wriggled off and landed with a heavy thump on the ground.

Kitok sat on the ground, watching the guard with amusement as the young man struggled unsuccessfully to free himself of his ties and yell through the gag. When the guard gave up his fight, Kitok stood and dragged him into the woods, where he tied him to a tree hidden from the road.

Kitok joined Sitting Fox in the fort. They spread out and each struck his flint to a torch, which quickly lit the wood wherever it landed. They hastily ran throughout the fort, igniting wooden palisades, outbuildings and fences. Soon the entire fort caught fire. Dark smoke and flames lit the skies above Grand Pré.

The two Mi'Kmaqs escaped the burning garrison moments before the gates crashed to the ground in a pile of burning timbers. The Mi'Kmaqs dashed back into the woods heading towards the cave and Evangeline.

Back on the beach, Lieutenant Wicker was the first to see the flames spurting from the fort. He raced to meet up with Captain Adams.

"Captain? The fort! It's burning, sir!"

Adams looked in the direction Wicker pointed and issued orders without hesitation. "Send half the troops back to the fort. Have them start a bucket brigade to put out the fire."

"Yes, Captain."

"I shall lead the remaining troops and herd the Acadians back to town." Adams fired shots in the air to emphasize the urgency of the situation. He rode swiftly up and down the beach, shouting orders to the troops. "Line up the Acadians and move them up the hill and back to their homes."

Wicker spread the word to the soldiers on the beach. At the treeline, Wicker directed the troops with a loud shout. "Surround the prisoners and march them forward." He added, "If anyone hesitates or gets out of line, use the butt of your musket until the order is followed."

Soldiers fired shots into the air to frighten the Acadians, which motivated many Acadians into helping family and neighbors climb faster. Some soldiers grabbed people stuck in the snow and beat them until they half-dragged themselves up the hill.

When one cart became stuck in a steep snow bank, two young soldiers tossed the aged Acadians passengers onto the ground. "Get up yer lazy heathens," said one of the soldiers. But the Acadians refused to budge, either because they could not or they preferred to die where they were, of grief, fright or cold.

The other soldier shrugged, "Let 'em be. We got to join the others." The two soldiers hurried to march with the line of troops herding the Acadians in a snaked line up the hill through the trees. Some Acadians moved slowly, and several collapsed. The two old Acadians thrown from their cart were too exhausted to move forward. They lay in front of Francis, who tried to help them up. In doing so, he fell. The three bodies blocked the line from moving forward.

Adams noticed the line had stopped and ordered a soldier to determine the cause of the delay, shouting, "Knock those bodies a few times. Check if they are sleeping."

Walking a bit ahead, Béatrice realized Francis had left Anne's side and turned to see if she could find him. She cried out when the soldier took the butt of his musket and hit Francis and the two old people on their heads. The boy died instantly, but the elderly Acadians clung to life, moaning softly.

Béatrice put her head on Christine's shoulder, wiping her tears. "Their cruelty knows no bounds."

Christine shushed her, reminding her, "He is with his mother in heaven now, and you must think of your own. Do not call attention to yourself."

Béatrice nodded, realizing she was right. She turned back, grasped Anne's hand and moved alongside Christine and the others up the hill.

Below her, the soldier jeered at the old couple, "If ye is alive, get going." But neither of them moved. "They is not moving, Cap'n."

Then Adams issued a general order. "From here forward, use your bayonet to check each body lying on the ground. If they don't march, they die. No exceptions."

The soldier dutifully thrust his weapon into the two old people who breathed their last lying next to each other. Other soldiers pushed their bayonets into the bodies of Acadians on the ground. Blood spilled into the snowy ground but no one cried out.

After assuring they were dead, the troops marched over the corpses and pushed the living forward.

As the Acadians marched forward, most were oblivious to the soldiers' threats and jabs. They plodded ahead, mourning the loss of their loved ones and praying silently, many without the energy to speak. They held onto each other for moral and physical support as they trudged up the hillside toward the smoke and flames of the burning fort.

Soldiers had doused most of the fire, but the fort itself was engulfed in smoke. Only the back buildings in the barricade were still burning. The troops had formed a human bucket brigade, still handing off pails and buckets of water to put out the flames.

The British soldiers tried to make order out of chaos as they led the Acadians down the road leading to the fort. Many fiercely brandished their bayonets to keep the Acadians in line as they passed the burning garrison.

From the treetops, Kitok and Sitting Fox watched the Acadians hike forward in a state of despair as if they were the walking dead. Soon the women and children disappeared from the Mi'Kmaqs' view on the road leading to Grand Pré.

The Mi'Kmaqs saw only the cruelest beauty before them that evening -- the deserted beach strewn with belongings, the fog which had enveloped the Acadians, and the magnificent trees crowned by red flames and smoke spewing from the fort.

Captain Adams sat on his horse and stared at the smoke still wisping from the blackened timbers strewn near the road. He roared when he saw the half-burned British flag lying in the dirt.

"The flag! Pick up our glorious flag."

Weary Acadians ignored the Captain's frantic shouts and continued to trudge toward their homes.

Adams pointed to a soldier and ordered, "You, there. Deliver the flag to Lieutenant-Colonel Winslow at once!"

The soldier obediently picked up the smoldering banner and trotted into town. Following him, the parade of grief-stricken, half-frozen Acadians moved slowly forward, guarded by the English troops.

Soon thereafter, the area surrounding the fort was quiet. The nearby woods were empty of people. The troops and French Acadians were locked in their homes. The main street of Grand Pré was empty. Candles flickered in windows, and smoke curled upwards from the fireplaces in Acadian residences. Troops had been moved from the tent city into the church to await their next orders.

*

Kitok and Sitting Fox ran from the fort through the trees and down the hill to the deserted beach and into the waterfront cave. Kitok's sole interest was to restore Evangeline to health and help her find Gabriel. He planned to escort Evangeline to the Mi'Kmaqs' winter home in the mountains. There, he could protect her from English troops and keep her away from the transports.

He was also certain that his family would welcome the daughter of their great French ally Lord Le Blanc as one of their own. But first, she must heal and build her strength.

Inside the cave, Running Bear guarded Evangeline. He waited for her to wake so he could prepare another meal. He had melted snow for her to drink. At long last, Evangeline opened her eyes. She gulped the bowl of water down to the last drop.

When Kitok and Sitting Fox arrived at the cave, they found Running Bear guarding the entry, still concealed by fog and falling snow. None of the English soldiers on the beach had thought to look their way. But if they had, they would have seen only gray rocks through the mist.

Entering the cave, a blazing fire welcomed them and warmed the entire space. Light danced on the stone wall where Evangeline sat. Wrapped in a fur blanket, she had finally stopped shivering.

Kitok sat next to Evangeline, making sure she was comfortable. Running Bear handed her a bowl of thick liquid. "Eat. Make better."

Evangeline accepted the bowl gratefully. "I find myself very hungry." She sipped the soup gratefully. "I cannot find words to express my gratitude to all of you."

Kitok nodded. "I am glad we found you. I could not lose you or fail my friend."

Evangeline smiled ruefully. "Hoping to be with Gabriel again is the only way I can move forward. I refuse to give up." She paused, then continued, "You must think me foolish for jumping in the water. The odd thing is I didn't feel the cold as long as I kept moving toward Gabriel. But when I saw that sadistic Captain Turnbull…." Her eyes filled with tears and she shook her head, unable to continue.

Kitok put his hand on her shoulder. "No need to speak. Just eat."

CHAPTER 46
Escape

Nova Scotia

The women who had been herded back to their homes in Grand Pré had virtually no chance to escape. Troops were quartered with them at all times. They felt great anguish at their fate to be exiled.

Yet some families had avoided their fate by leaving Grand Pré before Winslow read the King's Edict, like those who followed the Broussard Brothers through the woods to the French island of Île Royale north of Nova Scotia. Other Acadians headed for the woods, living off the land and heading for safety in the French province of Quebec. And some made the arduous trek into the mountains and met the Mi'Kmaqs, their long-time ally.

These bold Acadians defied Winslow's order and abandoned possessions and homes, planning never to return. Many, but not all, avoided capture by the British troops that began to patrol the woods after the first Exile. Those who left on their own relied solely on themselves. Adèle and Claude Arnaud and their daughter Pauline were three who escaped in this manner.

Like most of the other Acadians, Claude had trusted the British for the seventeen years that he and Adèle had lived in Grand Pré. But he had gradually joined Gabriel in realizing they were covertly fighting against the French despite the peace treaty with England. A surprise British attack on the Acadians was thwarted by Gabriel, who convinced the men to hide many of their weapons in anticipation of a raid, which happened not long after.

But it was the last letter Claude received from his half-brother Laurent just before the Edict was to be read that convinced Claude to leave. Laurent was the illegitimate son of Duke de Rochefort who had acknowledged his paternity and had bequeathed Laurent a fortune and a château in Provence. Laurent had written Claude every year inviting him to move in and serve as his valet. Claude had lost a wager years earlier promising to do so if Laurent had ever married a titled Lady, which he did -- Lady Véronique of Navarre. Laurent's last letter, marked "URGENT," had warned Claude of an impending war with England and begged him to sail to France via Quebec City on a Captain Boucher's ship, for which Laurent had prepaid for Claude's entire family. All the Arnauds had to do was travel to New France undetected by the British soldiers hunting Acadians fleeing from the Exile.

Claude knew this was the right solution at the opportune time. He reminded Adèle, "You have spoken wistfully of not being in Le Havre when your mother died. You could visit her grave and spend time with your sister Claire and her husband Michel Broussard in Le Havre."

Previously Adèle had objected to moving, but this time she knew he was right. "The English have never been our friends but we lived in harmony with them until their deceptive actions. What will they do next?"

Claude was adamant. "When I appear for the Edict reading, I want to know you and Pauline are safe with the Mi'Kmaqs." Adèle and Pauline took refuge with their allies while Claude went to the church. When Winslow locked them in the church, Claude did not fear for his family's safety.

*

Claude had been locked in the church with the other Acadian men and boys for over a month, since September 5, 1755. But he had escaped into the woods outside Grand Pré due to the ingenious plan of Consul Le Blanc to dig a tunnel from the church cellar into the woods. René had only allowed the single men to leave since Winslow had threatened to hang the family members of any Acadian man who escaped. But Claude convinced René to let him leave since his family was already out of harm's way with the Mi'Kmaqs and they had a plan to depart immediately for Quebec City.

Adèle and Pauline were hidden in the tent of White Bird, the tribal medicine woman, who traveled with Chief Mahtok and his wife Singing Bird. Along with Kitok and the braves, they were the last group to leave. They were packing their remaining possessions before heading for their winter caves in the mountains. When they learned the Acadians had been imprisoned in the church, they did not know how Claude would escape but prayed for his safe return and promised Adèle they would wait as long as need be.

Claude planned to travel overland, hiding in the woods and forests until they could reach the first French fort out of English territory. There, he would send word to one of Adèle's ribbon and cloth vendors who had supplied her couture dressmaking business. Merchants who traveled from Quebec City were allowed past Nova Scotia checkpoints by English soldiers who often bought pretty ribbons for their women back home. Claude believed he and his family could hide in the vendors' wagons amongst bolts of fabric and boxes of notions to elude capture at the British checkpoints.

After Claude was imprisoned, Adèle and Pauline waited for him in a pre-arranged clearing in the woods. The night he escaped through the tunnel he joined them in the woods. They had a joyful reunion and returned to the Mi'Kmaq village where Chief Mahtok gave them provisions of food and animal traps, as well as some of the weapons Gabriel had hidden with the Mi'Kmaqs when the British had seized the weapons from Acadian homes.

At dawn, the Arnauds said their goodbyes to the Mi'Kmaqs and set out on their trek in the harshest of conditions. With the snowfall, they made little progress due to snowdrifts in some parts of the woods and icy patches in others. Nonetheless, they were determined to reach first destination, the French Fort Gaspareaux, within a week. There, Claude hoped to stay under military protection while he searched for a way to contact the vendors.

It took them twice as long to reach the fort, but when they approached it all was quiet. Claude thought it odd, so he hid his family in the woods, watching and waiting for any sign of activity. At dawn, soldiers raised the English flag and told the Arnauds all they needed to know. The English had captured this French fort. They had to find another way.

As they walked deeper into the woods out of view of the fort, they came across a family of Acadians who had stopped in a clearing to rest. One of the men, Jean Foret, warned him, "Our French troops surrendered to the English months ago but were forced to remain silent to prevent a warning to other French garrisons. The British officer promised to keep them prisoners but instead hanged three officers, claiming they tried to escape. We saw the entire incident. Our soldiers were killed as a warning."

Claude could hardly believe it. "How did you escape?"

"My farm was half a day's journey away. After the surrender, British soldiers rode throughout the province. They ordered us to present ourselves at the fort within a fortnight but refused to explain why. It did not sound right to me so we abandoned our house and hid in the woods, hoping to make our way to Île Royale, a French island north of Nova Scotia."

Claude wanted to pepper the man with questions but asked just one. "Did you know the British planned to exile the Acadians"

Foret grimaced. "One of my brothers had an intuition to leave rather than listen to the King's Edict. He took his family into the forest, and they stopped here to warn me before they continued on their way to Île Royale. I think some of the Acadians who escaped went to live with the Mi'Kmaqs until spring. Some of the others made their way to New France."

Claude commented, "We are heading there ourselves to board a ship bound for France. Have you any advice?"

Jean warned, "Trust no one. British troops continue to search the woods and the shores with the help of some Acadians who offer fugitives a place for the night. The turncoats then report their countrymen and receive a bounty from the English and a reprieve from exile. I fear when all the Acadians are removed, those traitors will be shipped out or killed as well."

Claude agreed, "I shall never again trust the British. Thank you, sir. I shall be mindful of your cautionary words."

Foret pulled some dried meat and a bottle of wine from his sack. "For your journey. Food is hard to get without running into soldiers."

Claude gratefully accepted and offered Foret a coin. "Please take this. It is not much, but perhaps you will be able to buy something with it."

Foret pocketed the money and said, "It will be very useful when we join my brother and his family. I bid you good luck."

Claude responded, "Godspeed and thank you." He led Adèle and Pauline deeper into the woods. He had to find a way to contact Adèle's vendors since they could not travel overland to Quebec City on foot without starving, freezing or being captured. They traipsed in the woods, digging holes in the ground and covering themselves with leaves and branches to keep warm at night. When their food ran out, Claude trapped squirrels and rabbits and Adèle found edible plants and water. She was thankful Christine had taught her such skills on their walks in the forest near Grand Pré.

After several weeks of furtively traveling while foraging for food and water, the Arnaud family arrived at another fort, this one flying the French flag Though shivering from enduring freezing nights and snow-filled days, they were not disheartened. They tried to enter, but the garrison was locked.

An armed guard on the ramparts above asked, "Who goes there?"

Claude replied, "French Acadians loyal to King Louis seeking refuge. Claude Arnaud, a former King's Horseman, with my wife and daughter."

"Where are you going? Why are you stopping here?"

A weary Adèle snapped, "We are escaping the British exile and need assistance to travel to Quebec City where a ship awaits us."

A young soldier opened the gate. "Me job is to take youse to the Cap'n."

Claude asked, "And the name of your Captain?"

The soldier grinned, "Oh. Course. He's famous around these parts. Cap'n Peltier. Him and a handful of soldiers fought off the English that took down the Acadian towns of Beauséjour and Chignecto over the summer days."

Claude nodded, "We learned of it in Grand Pré, but were in no position to take sides. We had taken an oath to be neutral in any conflict between our French King and England."

They arrived at a small house at one end of the fort. The soldier knocked loudly on the wooden door. From inside came a gruff voice, "Enter."

The soldier opened the door. With a half-bow, he urged the Arnauds to enter. "Cap'n will see youse now."

Claude escorted the two women in, as much to support them in their exhausted state as to provide a gentlemanly service. The Captain stood and said in a kind voice, "Captain Peltier at your service."

Claude explained their situation. "We are fleeing our homes in Grand Pré. The British plan to deport every Acadian and disburse them throughout the Colonies."

Peltier furrowed his brow. "We assisted a small band of Acadians recently with provisions. They had decided to travel overland to Quebec City but were captured not far from here. The route is very dangerous and armed British soldiers roam freely."

"But this is French territory, is it not?"

The Captain nodded solemnly. "It is indeed. However, who can stop an armed militia intent on taking prisoners? If we sent our troops out into the snow looking for every British soldier, I fear we would lose most of them to skirmishes or the biting cold. We simply cannot afford to leave the fort."

Claude's shoulders dropped in despair. "I see. Could we at least rest here and regain our strength before we move on? We are hoping to send a message to one of my wife's vendors who runs the trail between Quebec City and here selling fabrics and women's goods. We hoped to hide in his wagon on his return visit to New France."

Peltier nodded and queried, "If you are fortunate enough to reach Quebec, where will you go? What will you do?"

Claude smiled. "My brother has arranged passage on a ship to France if we can only reach the harbor."

The Captain clapped Claude on the back and said in a warm voice, "I believe I can spare a soldier to help you on your trek." He glanced over at Adèle and Pauline, who stared at the table laden with piping hot dishes of food and bottles of wine. It seemed like days since they had eaten anything other than roots or berries. Captain Peltier followed Adèle's gaze and politely asked, "Madame, I was about to sit at table. Would you and your family care to join me?"

Before she could say a word, Adèle Arnaud swooned and dropped to the floor in a crumbled ball. When she came to, a midwife who was married to a soldier in the fort was sitting next to her. "You are with child, Madame," she said, to the delight of Adèle, Pauline and Claude, despite his concern for her health during the dangerous journey.

Adèle clasped Claude's hand, "We shall all be fine. Do not worry." But Claude knew that until they boarded Captain Boucher's ship and it arrived safely in Le Havre, he would feel apprehension for his growing family.

Captain Peltier sent a scouting party to nearby towns that left messages for Adèle's vendors to contact the fort. The Arnauds remained in the fort and weeks went by without a word from any vendor until one day Adèle's main fabric supplier, Curtram Abbey, drove his wagon up to the fort. He was overjoyed to see Adèle and meet her family.

He quickly agreed to Claude's plan to hide them in his wagon on his way back to Quebec City but suggested building a false bottom in the covered wagon. He and Claude constructed it, adding a large wooden box where the Arnauds could just fit by laying side by side on their backs. It would not be comfortable but it would be safer than hiding in the wagon.

Captain Peltier agreed to send an armed soldier dressed in driver's clothes who would be prepared to subdue any British soldier who attempted to search the wagon beyond the cursory glance at a few of the boxes and cartons. The state of the road was risky at best for a pregnant woman, but Adèle calmly assured the men that all would go well.

As the spring thaws began, the wagon was finally ready and they set out on the trail for New France. They ran into the first English checkpoint on the border between the French and English provinces. Inside the hidden compartment, the Arnauds had held their collective breaths at hearing the English soldiers bark orders to Abbey and his second "driver," "Present yer papers. What yer got in the wagon? Open them boxes and cartons."

When Claude heard the sound of bayonets thrust in cartons of supplies and stacks of fabric, he silently blessed Curtram for his idea. Several soldiers jumped inside the wagon and stomped the floor, kicking dust through the cracks into Claude's face which nearly caused him to sneeze. Adèle realized what was happening and she squeezed his hand to stop him.

Pauline's shoulders began to shake, and tears began to stream down her face. She had reached her breaking point after weeks of nearly starving during the day, freezing at night and narrowly avoiding attacks by a wild boar and a skulk of foxes. The soldiers walking above them made her fear she could not go on. She whispered, "What if they find us?" Claude held her right hand whispered, "Say a silent prayer. We shall be fine. God shall protect us. Pray now." She blinked her eyes to stop the tears and prayed.

Suddenly, the Arnauds felt the wagon move as soldiers jumped off the floor onto the ground. They heard Curtram talking to the soldiers, "May I offer each of you a ribbon for your fair lady? Take your pick."

After a minute, they heard an English soldier shout, "Youse can pass." The checkpoint barrier grated their ears as it was opened for the wagon. The soldier added, "Me girl will be pleased with the silken flurry."

The wagon lumbered along the road away from the soldiers. When the soldiers were out of sight, Curtram called out to Claude, "Only one more checkpoint. A soldier I know, lessen the English got bold and set up more traps. It is New France but they figure rightly the French troops ain't going to monitor the road."

The Arnauds worried when they heard a soldier call, "Halt!" but Abbey passed easily through the checkpoint after he gave the soldier a bolt of cloth for his wife.

From then on, the Arnaud women felt relieved, but Claude's anxiety did not dissipate until they arrived in the harbor. There, Claude, Adèle and Pauline piled out of the wagon, profusely thanked Curtram Abbey and the soldier, and rushed to the wharf in search of Captain Boucher and his ship.

*

In the dark cave in the dead of night, Kitok woke Evangeline. "If you can travel, we should go now."

Evangeline nodded, "Do what we must lest the English find us."

Kitok and his two braves, Running Bear and Sitting Fox, surrounded her and led her past the fort. They traipsed quietly past the sleeping sentries and darted undetected into the woods beyond the fort and Grand Pré. Kitok knew every inch of the land in the area, having served as a translator and tracker for the English military years earlier. As Evangeline rested, he and the braves collected berries and plants and set traps, cooking the small animals in an earthen pit to prevent alerting the English with a fire's smoke.

By dawn, the small party had passed all of the Acadian farms. As the morning light poured across the fields, they found themselves in the last outlying property nearest the mountains, the most treacherous part of their journey because the flat fields were exposed. They stopped to find food and water for the final journey that would take them up into the mountains.

Kitok halted the group and gazed at the farmhouse, then at the barn. Neither humans nor animals stirred, which was unusual. A typical morning would see the farmer's wife drawing water, the children gathering eggs and the farmer setting his plough harness. But Kitok did not even see anyone relieving himself outside the house at the start of the day. He slipped quietly into the barn to check for soldiers and entered with Sitting Fox cautiously behind. They scoured every nook and cranny, all the horse stalls, and the lofts where male children would sleep since the main house was too small.

The dearth of activity confirmed to Kitok that the farm had been abandoned by the family, either on their own terms or forcibly by British troops relocating outlying Acadians to town. Kitok was satisfied they could hide in the barn as troops typically checked a house first and their noise would alert the Mi'Kmaqs and give them time to escape. He led Evangeline into the barn and arranged a pile of blankets as a bed. Watching Running Bear twirl twigs to produce smoke for a fire, she quickly fell asleep.

Kitok checked the main house and discovered it had been ransacked but he managed to find a sack of dried corncobs inside an overturned cupboard. In the cellar, Sitting Fox found it empty except for a near-empty barrel of flour, a jug of rum and an urn half-filled with oil. He managed to scoop enough flour into a bag for flatbread and carried the jug and urn with him.

They stepped into the morning light and gazed at the bare fields. They felt confident they could find food left behind, but an English search party on horseback could also see and capture them.

Aiding escaping Acadians was a death sentence for the Mi'Kmaqs. Evangeline's punishment would be brutal rape by English soldiers yearning for the wifely duties of their spouses. The taking of female prisoners by force was encouraged by officers to instill obedience in captured women. English officers would ignore Evangeline's status as the French Consul's daughter, claiming they were protecting her from a hanging.

Kitok turned to Running Bear and Sitting Fox. "We must risk being seen in the fields to find food for our journey. Search for anything left from the harvest. Take care to stay hidden. Send your signal if you see soldiers."

The braves crept in and out of rows of plants, but they had been thoroughly picked or impounded for British troops. An hour later, they returned with a handful of potatoes and several tomatoes pecked by birds.

Evangeline woke to the aroma of Kitok's roasted rabbit. Sitting Fox had found an iron pot in the house and proudly cooked flatbread studded with corn. The little party dove into their bread, potatoes and rabbit in tomato sauce. Passing the rum, the braves smiled. Evangeline timidly took a sip from the jug, then took a long swig before passing it to Kitok.

When the meal was over, Kitok stood. "I shall get water from the well. We shall need it once we start climbing. But first, we hide you from soldiers." The three Mi'Kmaqs dug out a hole in the middle of a large haystack, creating a small lean-to inside the space. Evangeline climbed in, grabbed Kitok's hands and said tearfully, "I shudder thinking I could have died but for you. I would have never seen Gabriel again."

Kitok replied quietly. "Gabriel is my brother. I would do anything for him. I cannot do more for him, but I shall take care of you." They closed the opening and said, "We shall return soon. Stay here and do not move." He looked back at the haystack and saw it would take a keen eye to spot her.

He sprinted toward the water well, where a young British soldier stirred on the ground. Kitok hesitated. The soldier stood quickly and yelled, "Halt!" Kitok kept moving slowly. "You there. I ordered you to halt."

Kitok had three choices. Stop and be captured. Run and risk being shot. Or rush back to shelter and expose the others. But he took none of them. Instead, he walked slowly toward the soldier. The young man was caught off-guard and had trouble getting to his feet. Kitok handily disarmed the soldier and hit him over the head with his rifle butt. Kitok hurt no one unless they threatened his family. And Evangeline and the braves were his family.

CHAPTER 47
Shirley

Bostontown

For a hundred years, France and England had been in a constant state of contention, though not always actively engaged in battle, by the time the English Council met in Halifax in 1755. The reprehensible plan to exile the Acadians had been discussed by the English Council off and on for that entire century.

But this time, the plan was accepted. William Shirley, Commander-in-Chief of the Militia in the Colonies, made the proposal which the Council approved and sent to King George. The King finally decided to issue his deportation Edict and seal the fate of the Acadians.

His Edict ordered that every Acadian man, woman and child would be exiled without further delay and without mercy in the cruelest manner possible. Families were to be separated and put onto separate ships bound for different destinations. The King could not afford to take the risk that the large French Catholic families could reunite and return to overpower the few British troops and take back their land.

At long last, Shirley had the authorization of the King, echoed by Governor Lawrence, to do whatever he thought necessary to carry out the plan. Shirley took matters into his own hands, consulting with Vice-Admirals Edward Boscawen and Savage Mostyn at the meeting of the English Council in Halifax on matters relating to the transports. "How many people will be put on the ships?" Boscawen asked. He was the practical one and wanted to determine the number and size of ships and the foodstuffs required to sustain the prisoners and crewmen on board during the voyages.

Shirley had tapped Lieutenant-Colonel John Winslow for the job of supervising the Exile, a decision he would come to regret. Winslow had attended the English Council meeting where the details of the exile were to be decided. A man who had his nose perennially stuck in his Bible, Winslow looked up and gave them a number of Acadians to be exiled, "This is merely an estimate, mind you, because those heathens breed without thinking. My best guess is about two thousand souls from Grand Pré. Half as much from Annapolis Royal and the other nearby villages."

No one in the meeting gave the estimate another thought. No census was taken, no family count was made. Winslow's guess was accepted as fact. But he rarely took time off from his prayers and Bible reading in his quarters; therefore, he had no idea how many Acadians lived in Grand Pré, or any other Acadian settlement for that matter.

Winslow's lack of information would soon become a huge problem. The population was many times the number projected, meaning the British would need many more times the number of ships allotted to exile the Acadians. When they realized the error, the solution they devised was shocking in its cruelty.

Boscawen nodded with contentment. "We need only increase the usual number of persons per ton to reduce our shipping costs considerably."

Admiral Mostyn chimed in, "Instead of two passengers to a ton, we should be able to board three or four, maybe more. That will, without a doubt, leave more in the budget for our Council, to use as we see fit."

Of course the Council members had agreed. They were in agreement with anything that put more money in their pockets. Armed with the necessary answers, Commander Shirley took the assignment back to Bostontown.

There, he contracted with his personal friends, Charles Apthorp and Thomas Hancock, to provide all of the transports to exile the Acadians from Nova Scotia. Proprietors of the Boston Mercantile Company, Apthorp and Hancock had the excellent reputation of being able to procure, build or lease any size ship anytime, for the right fee. Shirley was confident they could fill his demand for ships.

Shirley knew his friends could help him in his determination to rid the territory of the blasted Acadians once and for all. Like many other loyal British military officers, Shirley was exasperated by discussions of an Acadian exile that were foiled for decades by oral and written treaties between France and England.

Shirley's post was not only powerful, but it was also very profitable for him. His friends' prices were never the lowest ones, but they always included the biggest bribes back to Shirley, who was also the Governor of the Massachusetts Bay Colony. In paying the tributes, Apthorp and Hancock were assured that their boatbuilding site would hum with orders.

Shirley argued to himself that the British treasury had no idea of the cost or value of things in the Colonies. He could always justify the high prices to the military account manager. He simply bemoaned the lack of skilled labor which cost more for experts, and the difficulty of obtaining materials which cost more for supplies, and the weather changes in the Colony which cost more for shipping, and so on. Shirley wanted to assure himself a money pot upon his retirement from the military. Corruption was, indeed, a way of life in the Colonies.

*

As Shirley approached the shipyard, he reflected on how he had amassed the power he had today. Riding his fame with the troops and his favor with the King, Shirley was not about to lose the prestige and control his position gave. And he knew he would be able to profit greatly from it.

But to increase his personal wealth, he knew he had to surround himself with friends who could also make money on the military contracts he could send. That was where his friends, Apthorp and Hancock, came in. He had made an appointment to check on the status -- and cost -- of the additional ships needed to exile the remaining Acadians caused by Winslow's erroneous population estimate

Shirley trotted his horse into the yard to take stock of his friends' business. The large fading sign on top of the large brick building read, "Boston Mercantile Company of Apthorp & Hancock." Starting their business of leasing boats from a small wooden shack, they had built a successful empire. The building abutted their manmade marina, where anchored cargo boats bobbed in the waves of the choppy water.

The proprietors of the business were worried about Shirley's visit. They feared they might lose their commission because they still did not have enough ships.

Apthorp spoke first. "We cannot deliver all the ships by the deadline."

Hancock agreed, "We must devise an excuse that Commander Shirley can readily accept. Without his military contracts, our business cannot survive."

Apthorp asked, "What do you have in mind? I surely cannot conjure up a half-cocked reason. The man is very smart."

Hancock paused a moment before speaking. "Were I in his shoes, I would act no differently. He holds our fate in his hands. That truly is power."

Apthorp clasped his partner's shoulder. "We had best be prepared to answer his questions before he asks."

Hancock added, "And hope he shall not try to renegotiate the price any lower."

Shirley appeared in the open expanse of the yard. He observed workmen with hammers and construction tools enter and exit ships under construction like insects scurrying in and out of an ant pile. Shirley watched his two friends arguing at the other end of the yard. He had no idea that their quarrel focused on who was to blame for the unfinished ship works.

Apthorp was the more aggressive. "You were responsible for the materials, but you failed to order them in time. We are short the finished lumber we need."

Hancock replied icily, "You did not provide the funds to me in time. Thus, I was forced to pay more per board and ended up with fewer pieces But, we have more than enough nails for the proper amount of lumber, thanks to my ability to negotiate with the ironworks owner."

Apthorp was about to attack again when he noticed Shirley trotting toward them. The two men stopped their bickering and greeted Shirley with a smile.

"How do you do, Governor Shirley?" said Apthorp.

"Good day to you, Commander Shirley," Hancock said.

Shirley retorted, "It is not a good day if the rumors I hear are correct. Is it true that my ships are still not ready? The ships that must be sent to Minas Bay? The ships that Governor Lawrence ordered? The ships for which I made a substantial payment in advance, based on our many years of working together?"

Apthorp pleaded. "Commander, let us discuss this in more pleasant surroundings in our office. It will be warmer and more comfortable."

Shirley nodded quickly. "So long as I get the answers I need."

Hancock said agreeably, "Of course, sir, of course."

Shirley dismounted and handed the reins to a young boy shivering in the cold, whose sole job it was to tie horses at the railings. Hancock rushed to open the office door and bowed to Shirley, who stomped in and sat at Hancock's desk. Without waiting for them to take their seats, Shirley lit into them.

"You were given the exclusive contract to provide all the ships to exile those heathens. I was very generous with you, agreeing on a per-head lease price. And you agreed to meet my conditions, the most important of which was to provide a sufficient number of boats by the deadline. You failed this task miserably. We are in August, and you are just now saying it is impossible to send passenger ships to Minas Bay before spring. We need them in October. Read your contract."

Apthorp said, "Commander, sir, be reasonable. We have had so many weather delays."

Hancock quickly agreed. "Yes, weather delays. And the, how shall I say it, the tributes we had to pay to the other government types."

Apthorp jumped in quickly, "In addition to yourself, of course, sir, but the local officials demanded quite the sum. Our costs have doubled, I am sorry to say. We must raise the price to deliver the ships on time."

The two boatbuilders cringed for what they knew was to come next. Shirley exploded. "Absolutely unacceptable! You are already getting paid thrice what you should."

Apthorp gently interrupted, "Ah, but a large part of that is being returned to you for your -- generosity."

Shirley waved him off angrily. "Nonetheless, you should be able to convert the ships at the original price. And you say you bribed local officials? Which ones? Give me their names."

Apthorp looked like he was about to explode. Hancock had to take control. "Commander Shirley, let me explain."

Shirley fumed. He was still furious that Winslow had grossly under-estimated the Acadian population on which the order for ships was based, but he waved at Hancock to continue.

"We are constructing some works in the holds of twenty vessels but can increase that number to twenty-four with the materials we have and the price of the contract. Take a schooner, for example. Most are built to hold one hundred tons of cargo. Generally, no more than two persons per ton would voyage if on a passenger ship of that size. This limits the ship to two hundred souls traveling somewhat in comfort. Yet, you required us to provide space on each ship for three to four times as many persons."

Apthorp timidly added, "With our adjustments, you can squeeze in a greater number, many times over what such a ship would normally carry."

Shirley nodded. "Harrumph. As it should be."

The two shipbuilders looked at each other, unsure of what to do, so they waited respectfully for Shirley to continue. He did not disappoint. He pulled out a cigar, which Apthorp quickly lit with a match he struck on the bottom of his boot. Shirley crossed his massive legs with his muddy boots on the desk where Hancock usually sat. Hancock cringed but said nothing.

Shirley barked, "Well? How shall you honor this contract and send the ships to the commanding officer in Grand Pré?"

Hancock said calmly, "The specific requirements you asked for in the passenger ships could not be met, as the materials were unavailable in the Colonies to match the interior wood finishes. We were constrained here and are still awaiting the special order from London. They have said nothing can be shipped during the winter so that means those ships shall not be finished until late summer next year."

Apthorp interrupted, "The cost of conversion is nearly the equivalent to building four little boats within each large ship."

Shirley was infuriated. "Impossible! You get all of my military contracts. You shall cover the excess costs, plus make your usual payments to all of the officers."

Apthorp ignored Shirley's outburst. "We anticipated the issue and came up with the idea to use animal cargo boats to keep the costs reasonable. It is a bit more than the original cost, to be expected, since the number of passengers increased many times over."

Shirley scoffed. "How will you fit so many men in the holds of a cargo boat? The space is limited, especially with the bulkheads, troughs for food and water for the animals and such."

Apthorp replied, "Hear us out. This is the only solution we could devise in a timely manner."

Shirley kicked his boots on the desk and motioned to continue.

Apthorp explained, "The most reasonable and efficient solution is to redesign the interior of the cargo ships. First, we remove the floor timbers and bulkheads in the holds. That opens more space for use." He rolled out his construction plans. Apthorp pointed out the various parts of the drawings, explaining the dimensions.

"In a ship originally designed for one hundred fifty tons of cargo, the hold is usually twenty-four feet wide by forty-eight feet long, but we have removed the unnecessary elements and extended the hold by nearly twelve feet. Removing the timbers raised the ceiling height to fifteen feet. In the expanded space, we divide the hold into three levels of about four feet high."

Shirley nodded. He was not disturbed by the fact that triple the passengers would be crowded into small, windowless locked boxes without fresh air. He did not give a second thought to the fact that the Acadians would be forced to travel in rough winter seas, endure freezing cold weather without proper clothing, be fed substandard food, and face disease and unsanitary conditions for as long as three months. He did not think about the fact that the adults would not be able to stand erect in their little box, since the height was only four feet. Nor did Shirley worry that there would be too many men and boys stuffed into each converted hold to all lie down at the same time. He felt no guilt about any of it. He, as the other members of the English Council and their King George, believed the Acadians deserved what they got.

Shirley nodded in understanding. "So we can exile at least six hundred in one ship instead of two hundred? That is appealing."

Hancock nodded. He was glad Shirley liked the plan. "Not only fewer ships, but less victuals."

Shirley quizzically looked at him. "Save money on the foodstuffs? Why is that?"

Hancock said offhandedly, "When they are crowded in those conditions, many will quickly become ill. They will either die quickly or will be too sick to eat. That reduces the food needed for the others."

"What conditions exactly are you thinking?" Shirley was intrigued.

Apthorp drew in a breath, then explained their reasoning. "Since you will want to push as many prisoners into the holds as you can, they will have no room for bags or personal items. Not even extra clothing like a cloak or shawl. Naturally, a voyage in the Atlantic in the middle of winter will be cold, but they will be huddled together and will get warmth in that way. The cargo ships are not for passengers, so there are no fire boxes. The wood planks are old and drafty. It is altogether natural that some passengers will die of the cold, in addition to the illnesses."

Hancock added to the horrific plan. "And, since they will be tightly confined to their holds, without any facilities for waste, et cetera, it is quite possible that they might catch the dreaded pox."

Apthorp nodded, "Yes, outbreaks of the pox have been known to happen on long journeys without sanitary conditions and at least an occasional whiff of fresh air on deck."

Shirley nodded with satisfaction. "I do believe you gentlemen understand your mission now. It is critical to fit as many persons as possible in your vessels. No matter they are for cargo only. Build them out with haste and get them to Minas Bay by the mid of October if you wish to get paid. I have run out of patience with you. And to top it off, you have caused a great headache that not even my wife's remedies can cure. What say you to that?" Shirley tossed his cigar to the floor. Hancock quickly stomped it out and wrung his hands, signaling Apthorp to speak for both of them.

"We assure you, Commander, you shall have your ships on time. Perhaps even early, if the tides work in our favor. But in any case, you shall have what you need."

Apthorp assisted Shirley with his overcoat. Shirley put on his military hat, which he tipped to the two shipbuilders. "Do not embarrass me. There are too many others who would love to be in your position." He handed Apthorp a note. "Even with the increased passenger estimate, we reduced the food stores needed for the transports. Here is the list."

Apthorp perused the paper. "We shall have no problem filling it, Commander."

"You shall receive no more business in the future if you fail. You do understand, do you not?" Shirley opened the door and strode out, not waiting for an answer.

The two men nodded as Shirley exited. Hancock rushed to close the door and leaned back against it, breathing a sigh of relief. Hancock said, "That was a close call. We might not have saved our contract if not for your brilliant idea to reconstruct those old cargo ships."

Hancock asked, "But if we have to provide more food? Can we still make a profit?"

Apthorp read the note Shirley had given him. "We ration five pounds of flour, one pound of pork or beef and a handful of rice and beans for each person per week. Methinks we shall make a pretty penny."

As Shirley rode off, he smiled. "Even at the higher price, I still have a pretty penny left over from the sum Governor Lawrence shall pay me."

He laughed aloud at the additional funds that would soon be his. He was anxious to dispose of the women on as few ships as possible, thus keeping more for himself. That would happen soon, but not soon enough for him.

CHAPTER 48
Town

Grand Pré

Two soldiers entered each Acadian home, partly to be fed and to sleep and partly to keep an eye on everyone who lived therein. Captain Adams had warned them to be vigilant and to listen for whispered schemes to escape or, worse, to plan an uprising against the troops.

Christine broke away from the other plodding women and rushed into the partially-open door of the Consulate, fearing what she would find. Two soldiers, Wesley and Rollin, attempted to enter behind her, but Christine summoned her courage and strength and held them back.

"The French Consulate is French territory. No English allowed," she managed to say as she pushed the door closed and bolted it from the inside. She then lifted and pushed a heavy hewn log between two iron holders on the door frame. René had insisted on this additional form of security to lock the building from the inside and block entry from the street. She silently thanked him for his foresight, feeling safe inside the building, at least for the night.

The stunned soldiers looked at each other, then tried to push the door open but it did not budge. Wesley yelled out, "Open the door, hussy." He turned to his fellow soldier, "Help me, Rollin."

Rollin banged his rifle butt against the lock, trying to break it. But the heavy iron latch did not budge. He turned to his buddy and shrugged, "Give it no mind. We can get a place in any house we want."

Wesley agreed and they took to the street. They spied an old Acadian couple disappear into an alley, moving as fast as their rickety legs could carry them. Rollin ran after them and before they could close the door to their cottage, Rollin's tree-trunk leg blocked it. The Acadians threw up their hands and huddled together in the corner. Rollin waved Wesley in ahead of him. Then the door shut.

In the French Consulate, Christine rushed to the back door and pushed the hewn log into place bolting that door and making the Consulate a locked fortress. Other soldiers soon arrived and tried kicking and pushing the back door open to no avail.

Christine brushed her hands and smiled with grim satisfaction. She spoke her thoughts aloud. "The Consul would be proud." Exhausted, she sank into the nearby chair and burst into tears. "René, my love, where are they sending you?" She shook her head, trying to regain her composure. She had to take hold of her emotions and rely on her faith. She had to believe René would survive and find her.

But doubt quickly crept back in. Christine shook her head violently, not allowing herself to hope. She fell into despair realizing she did not know where René's ship was going and that she would most likely not be sent to the same place.

She lit a candle and walked slowly through René's office, trying to convince herself to think only positive thoughts. She knew he would want her to be strong. After all, he had promised to meet her in the port of New Orleans in the French territory of Louisiana. But she could not fathom how to meet him when she did not even know where she was going to be sent.

She wanted more than anything to meet René but she was still reeling from the fact the he was gone, and that she might never see him again. Christine knew she and the remaining Acadians would be exiled soon, and her fear of being shipped to an unknown destination was almost too much to comprehend.

At the same time, she realized she would have to put her own desires to the side. The other women in Grand Pré would be relying on her. They would be looking to her for strength and leadership, as they had for years before the Exile. She felt torn. She had been a housekeeper fulfilling the needs of René and Evangeline for so long that she felt she had lost her independence. She was only one woman. How could she save her friends and neighbors on her own?

Realizing she was too hungry to think any more, she decided to cook a good meal. She knew that always made her feel better. She pushed the kitchen chairs out of the way, then moved the table off the floorboards.

Using a wooden spoon, she dug into the grooves between the boards, raising up a small board lodged between two larger ones. Reaching in, she pulled out a woven bag stuffed with food -- winter vegetables, baked bread and dried meat. She peered into the space. The other food bags were still there. They would serve her and other Acadians well when they escaped into the woods.

She flew down the stairs into the Consul's office and looked in his wine cabinet. Empty. She looked around and spied a bottle that had fallen behind the cabinet. She pulled it out and pushed herself to climb back up the stairs.

Opening the wine and laying out the feast on the table, she felt encouraged. A dismal thought entered her head. What if Kitok and the Mi'Kmaqs do not find Evangeline? She shook it out of her mind and took a bite of the meat and a sip of the wine savoring it in the calmness of the Consulate.

Just then she heard soldiers yelling along the street. She checked the door again. It was firmly locked and buttressed by a log. No unwanted visitors would get into the building tonight.

After she had eaten, she took the candle and walked slowly down the hall to René's room. In the candlelight, she looked around at the neat, simple room just as he had left it when he went to the church for the reading of the Edict. Her eyes welled with tears as she sat on his bed and smoothed his pillow. She lay her head on it and wept. She felt like he had been gone an eternity, yet it had only been a day. She fell asleep worrying about how she would find him in New Orleans.

When she woke, it was dark save the sputtering candle. She picked up the wool scarf René had tossed haphazardly onto the bed. She slowly raised it to her face and rubbed it against her cheek, taking in the aroma of his scent. She decidedly wrapped it around her neck and slid out of bed, then slowly walked out of his room down the hall carrying the melting taper.

Entering her bedroom, Christine lit a fresh candle at her bedside, then walked to the window. She parted the heavy cloth curtains and peered outside. Snowflakes silently dotted the main street which was empty. Christine shivered and pulled the curtains back in place. She gazed around the room and opened the armoire, filled to the brim with clothes, hats, shoes and bags. She stared at her beautiful dresses. Her favorite shawls. Her colorful collection of silk hair ribbons.

Shaking her head, Christine pulled out a small travel bag and reminded herself she had no room for luxuries now that winter was already upon them. She packed things she would need for the trip. A thick blanket. Warm sweaters. Woolen dresses. Her favorite shawl. A warm cape. She allowed herself to close her eyes and imagine René's arms around her, just for a moment.

When she opened her eyes, she sighed and packed her winter clothes in the bag. She set her sturdiest boots and thickest stockings next to the bed. Then Christine walked out of her room and up the stairs to the top floor. On the landing, she pushed open the door to Evangeline's room.

She saw her exquisite wedding dress and veil laid out on the bed, left there when Evangeline heard the call that the men were being marched out of town. Christine touched it gingerly. On an impulse, she picked it up and carried it back to her room, folding it into her nearly-stuffed bag. She wanted Evangeline to have the wedding of her dreams to the man she adored in the dress she loved, just as Christine hoped to become René's wife.

She knelt next to her bed and bowed her head, "Dear Lord, have mercy on the souls of all of the Acadians. Those who have been taken on ships and those of us who are yet to go. Please show us the way to find each other again. All these things in Jesus' name I pray. Amen."

She rose and curled up on the bed, holding René's scarf to her face as she dozed off into a fitful sleep.

*

In their home, Béatrice Gaudet and her mother Anne were alone. The soldiers either forgot about them or were unaware that they were in the house. She helped Anne out of her wet clothes into a warm gown, then wrapped her in a blanket and sat her on a rug by the hearth. Béatrice added more logs to the burning fire and set a pot of soup to boil. She had only a handful of carrots and some beans but she knew she could make it tasty.

Béatrice warmed her cold hands over the fire and sighed. She watched Anne play, oblivious to their predicament. Anne gurgled happily, tracing her finger through some spilled flour on the floor. "Drestoplatte."

Béatrice patted her hand. "You are fortunate, Mother. I am so thankful you don't understand what is happening to us."

Anne cooed contentedly looking up at her daughter. Béatrice nodded repeatedly, more to convince herself than Anne, who she knew did not understand. "Somehow, we shall survive this ordeal. Our faith will see us through. I know it. I just know it."

Béatrice slipped into the only bedroom in the house and pulled out the warmest clothes she could find for herself and her mother. She tucked them into a large sack and brought it into the main room. Anne had fallen asleep on the rug by the fire. She was so still and looked so peaceful that Béatrice woke her to make sure she was still breathing.

Anne pointed to the soup and babbled more nonsensical talk. "Glatgon somi pirnak." Béatrice patted her mother's hand and served her a heaping bowl. The two women dug into the soup with gusto. Béatrice momentarily brushed away her pain and distress as she watched her mother happily enjoying the meal.

*

When the Acadians were installed into their homes, Winslow called the troops into the church. They trudged through the snow-filled dirt in pairs from their assigned homes and sat in pews awaiting their commander. No one knew what he was to tell them. As dusk settled on Grand Pré, the soldiers chatted among themselves. Captain Adams entered and pointed to Wesley.

"Light the candles. The commander is arriving soon." Wesley quickly performed the task. Once that was done, Adams walked up to the altar and hit his rifle butt on the wooden floor for attention. The soldiers were instantly silent.

Winslow entered, walking proudly upright, carrying his Bible for all to see. He stood at the front and addressed his troops. "I congratulate each of you for the fine job you did today. Some deaths were necessary, I understand. Those who disobeyed orders had to be punished. To those of you whose bayonets were bloodied, consider that a badge of honor. You did your duty to your King and to your God."

He surveyed his men who were listening with all ears. "Our mission is nearly accomplished, but we must continue to carry on until we are rid of every last heathen."

At this, the soldiers murmured loudly in agreement. "Hear, hear."

Winslow cleared his throat and the troops quieted themselves. "You are on the precipice of a history-making event. You are about to rid the King's land of these French Acadians forever. Englishmen have tried and failed for a century, so be proud of what you are doing. Each of you is a hero today for your effort."

Winslow paused so that his words could take effect. And take effect they did. Soldiers jumped up and clapped, or stomped the floor or cheered loudly. Winslow looked at Adams and they nodded knowingly to each other. They had no doubt of the loyalty of their troops, who would see the mission to its very end. Winslow raised his hands for silence. Instantly, the troops silenced themselves and awaited more directives from their commander. He did not disappoint and explained the plan to expel the remaining Acadians from the entire territory.

"When the ships return to exile those Acadians who remain here, you are to say nothing to the families under whose roof you are living. I shall post a meeting notice on the church door requiring the presence of everyone, young and old. After they are seated in the church, you shall march them back to the sea and onto the rowboats for ships to their final destinations."

Captain Adams looked out at the soldiers and as if he could read their minds, he asked, "Lieutenant-Colonel, may I ask a question, sir?

Winslow nodded, "Certainly, Captain."

Adams continued. "Are we to know the destinations of the prisoners?"

Winslow peered over his Bible and said in an icy tone, "They shall be sent far away from here. Some as far as France. Others will be left on the shores of our King George's colonies." He turned back to face the troops, "The key is not telling the heathens where they are going. Lack of knowing will cause such consternation that they will be more docile. They will be more manageable because they will worry about something they cannot change as they follow our orders. Where they end up is not their business, nor ours. They shall find out soon enough. As for our end of this bargain, it is unimportant where they are going. We only care that they shall soon be gone."

Captain Adams nodded.

Winslow snipped, "If there are no more questions?"

Captain Adams bowed in consternation. He realized too late he should not have asked the question. But he felt remorse for the dead Acadians. And if no one else felt for them, he did. They had been good neutral subjects, always ready to feed a soldier, always respectful when meeting troops on the street. Why were they blamed for their nationality? English and French had lived together in Grand Pré for nearly half a century. Why now? Why must they leave their homes now? Adams was conflicted in his thoughts even though he was devoted to his King and his military service. He did not know what he would do if he were in the same position as his commander.

Winslow continued, "The main reason for your being quartered with the Acadians is to remain attentive to their activities. Remember who they talk to. Follow the head of the house as she goes about her daily chores. I sense that the women are more dangerous than their men ever were, despite the young resistance fighters we sent to Westminster Gatehouse. They may be up to something. Tell me, who is staying with the women in the French Consulate? We must keep a close watch on that one."

No soldier raised a hand. Winslow glared at Adams.

"The ones living there are the Consul's daughter and, as I understand it, his fiancée. Why are there no soldiers in that building? They are the most dangerous of all. They are educated and well-respected by everyone. They may have already hatched a secret plan and we have no news of it. How are we to quell a rebellion when we have no spy in the ranks?"

Winslow pulled his whip from his side and cracked it loudly. The soldiers, as brave as they were, flinched. Wesley looked at Rollin. Rollin shook his head, but Wesley decided to take a risk. He raised his hand. Winslow pointed him out with the whip. "You, there, soldier. Name?"

Wesley jumped up and saluted. "Wesley Jackstone, sir."

"Well, out with it. Do you have any information about this situation?" Winslow was unusually impatient. He was ready to sip another bottle of fine French wine and load his bags with as many bottles as he could carry. The only impediment to his leaving the very next morning was the delay until his replacement arrived. He prayed it would be soon.

"Out with it, I said."

Wesley gulped, "Sir, only one lady went into the Consulate and she, well, that is…"

"That is, what? Spit it out, soldier."

Wesley nodded. "Yes, sir. She bolted the door from inside and me and Rollin here couldn't get the blasted door open." Wesley pointed to Rollin right next to him. At that moment Rollin wanted to wring Wesley's neck then disappear.

Winslow waved to Rollin to stand. Rollin reluctantly did and stood next to Wesley but cast his eyes downward. He didn't like attention, especially the scrutiny of the top commander of the troops. Winslow peered at Rollin. "Well, what do you have to say? He telling the truth?"

Rollin nodded repeatedly. "Yes, sir. Wesley's got it down pretty much. We tried to beat down that door and even shoot the lock open but it wouldn't budge."

The soldiers in the pews snickered and whispered among themselves until Winslow cracked his whip again. The two soldiers stood trembling in Winslow's sight until Winslow laughed. Then Captain Adams cracked a smile and the soldiers relaxed. Winslow said, "Well why didn't you say so? We'll just send more troops down there to help you do your job. And do you want us to wash your nightshirts too?"

Wesley, a bit thick-headed, answered, "Much obliged, sir."

Winslow cracked his whip. "What did I say? What did I just say? What have I been saying the entire time I have been in command of this fort?"

Rollin and Wesley looked at each other, then at Winslow. They were at a complete loss for words.

Winslow's words thundered throughout the church. "I said each of you has a job to do and you must do it, come hell or high water. I care not if you have to burn that woman out of the Consulate, you get that door open and you follow her every move. And you listen to everything she says. Do you understand your mission now, soldiers?"

Rollin and Wesley stood there, trembling. Captain Adams yelled at them, "Soldiers? Did you hear what Lieutenant-Colonel Winslow asked you? If so, answer him this instant."

The two soldiers nodded and said in unison, "Yes sir. We heard, sir."

Adams got the signal from Winslow and motioned the two soldiers out. "Get going and get that door open, soldiers."

Winslow looked around the room. The troops didn't move their eyes as Wesley and Rollin ran down the center aisle and out of the church. Winslow cracked his whip and left the altar, entering the rectory by the altar entrance.

When the commander was gone, Captain Adams looked around at the soldiers. "Does anyone have anything else to say?"

No one dared move a muscle. They all shook their heads.

Captain Adams grunted with satisfaction. "If you hear any talk of an escape or a resistance plan, make sure you talk to me as soon as you learn of it. I care not if that is day or night, or the middle of the night. Am I clear?"

The soldiers all nodded their assent.

"Dismissed."

The troops rushed out of the church, leaving Adams to blow out the candles and saunter out of the front door.

*

In front of the French Consulate, Wesley and Rollin beat on the door. They peered through the downstairs window but the thick curtains closed off any view to the inside. Rollin stepped back and looked at the second-floor windows. He saw flickering candlelight shining through the curtains of one room.

Rollin grabbed Wesley and pointed to the window. "There she be. In that there window. We got to knock this door down." Rollin picked up an axe and hacked away at the door. Wesley fired his rifle into the door. The first one hit the metal lock and ricocheted, whizzing past his ear. Wesley dropped the gun like a hot potato and turned to Rollin.

Inside the Consulate, Christine was awakened by a loud noise below.

"We need more help. I'll bring some men back," said Wesley.

Christine peeked out of the window to see Wesley running away from the building and Rollin hitting the axe against the front door. Rollin grunted and continued to swing the axe at the door, hoping to crack it. But the thick wooden door did not budge.

She quickly changed into some of René's trousers and her woolen sweater, then ran through the hall downstairs to the kitchen. She picked up René's gun and loaded the bullets. Brandishing the weapon, she slowly approached the door.

Rollin continued to hit the axe on the door and drag the pick down the door. He had barely made a mark on the thick wood. Christine opened the peephole and saw Rollin sweating, furiously swinging the tool at the door.

Christine pointed the gun through the peephole and yelled out as loud as she could. "Get away from that door. This is French property and I will defend it to the death. I have a gun pointed at your head at this very moment. Run fast before I pull the trigger."

Rollin tossed the axe and scurried away without looking back.

*

As Captain Adams jumped onto his horse, he looked all around to see if anyone was watching him. The soldiers had all retreated to their assigned homes. Adams slowly walked his horse through town. When he passed the Consulate, all was quiet, so he figured Rollin and Wesley had gained entrance. The Captain trotted after passing the fort, and nudged his horse downhill through the trees to the beach, then dismounted.

He knelt in the sand, bowing his head penitently, "Lord, forgive me for having any hand in this Exile. I must do my duty to my King but my heart breaks with every violent act against the wretched Acadian. Is it their fault they were not born into the one true religion?"

He waded into the water and dragged onto the beach the floating corpses of two women and the little girl who had been killed by his soldiers. Loading the bodies onto his saddle, he walked the horse into the woods. There, he took a shovel and a pick that he had hooked to his saddle. He began to dig through the frozen ground and wiped tears from his eyes.

*

Kitok and his Mi'Kmaq braves pressed Evangeline to continue moving forward to the base of the mountain after running through the empty fields. Kitok pointed to a peak. "Our family winters up there."

Evangeline was exhausted. She slumped to the ground, wiping her brow with her neckerchief. "How much longer, Kitok?"

Kitok grunted. "As long as it takes."

Evangeline was too exhausted to be angry with his response. He offered his hand to help her up. She too hold and stood, weary but determined to continue the trek. "I know I am not safe until we reach your family. We must go." She began the final leg of the trek uphill.

After walking for hours, Kitok signaled they would stay for the night in a small cavern he had located in the mountain. It was a day's journey to the Mi'Kmaq camp but this would do for the night. Soon, a fire blazed in the center and Evangeline sat in a circle around it with Kitok, Running Bear and Sitting Fox. They each had a bowl of cooked rabbit. Sitting Fox took his time telling the story of how he had trapped it on the mountain path. By the time he finished his tale, everyone had finished their dinner.

Evangeline listened respectfully, but her thoughts were elsewhere. She said quietly, "I shall never abandon my search for Gabriel or my promise to meet him in New Orleans. I must find a way to do so."

Evangeline snuggled under blankets and a thick bearskin, quickly falling asleep. Running Bear doused the fire, and the Mi'Kmaqs slept soundly under bearskins. In the morning, Sitting Fox brushed the footprints from the dirt with tree branches as if it had been uninhabited for years. Kitok tied ropes around Evangeline's waist and led her, followed by the braves, single file along the steep path up the mountain to the Mi'Kmaq encampment.

During the trek, Kitok worried how he could tell his father Prince Mahtok that his good friend Consul Le Blanc had been exiled to an unknown destination.

*

In the woods, Captain Adams stood and wiped his brow with his military scarf. He had dug a hole six feet deep in the frozen ground. He walked to his horse and respectfully carried the three bodies one at a time to the grave. He laid them carefully and covered them with dirt. Fashioning a cross from a tree branch, Adams knelt and said a prayer.

"Have mercy on their souls, and mine, O Lord. In Your infinite wisdom, accept them and me into your holy kingdom."

Winslow's speech had convinced Adams to do the right thing. He lay down in the shallow grave next to the bodies and pulled out his gun. Pointing it at his head, he pulled the trigger. The sound of the gun echoed through the woods and carried out over the water. Several birds in the trees flapped their wings and flew over the woods.

In town, the reveling troops guzzling beer and eating hearty Acadian food heard only the sound of their own drunken laughter.

CHAPTER 49
Sabotage

Atlantic Ocean

The long line of vessels crammed with Acadian men and boys sailed out of Minas Bay. Most sailed south to Bostontown, New York, the Carolinas and Georgia, but two transports headed east for England. The first was the ship carrying Gabriel and the young men destined for Westminster Gatehouse. The second was the old hull with René and the elderly Acadian men, including Marc's father Benoit de la Tour Landry, Jeanne's father Jean Lambert and Yvonne's husband Alain Poché.

René had been warned by Christine that the old hull had been sabotaged by English soldiers. She learned of Winslow's plan to cut holes in the boat and nail the Acadians shut in the hold before transferring the crew by rowboat to another ship. But he and the elderly Acadian men had been forced onto the boat before they could develop a plan to escape.

As the two ships reached the open waters of the ocean, the crew on the old hull abandoned ship. Rowing and boarding the ship headed for the Gatehouse prison, they left the old hull to toss about. Huddled in the hold below, René and the Acadians were unaware of what had transpired.

*

The commander of Gabriel's ship, Captain Burgess, defied Captain Turnbull in an argument the entire crew overhead. Burgess stated, "This ship is under my command. You and your prisoners are subject to my orders. They shall climb on deck every day to breathe in fresh sea air."

Turnbull said in no uncertain terms, "I control the prisoners. They stay in the holds for the entire voyage so they cannot escape."

"Into the freezing sea? My compensation is based on the number of living souls I deliver. Too many shall die in the hold with the stale air and cramped conditions you forced upon them." Turnbull gritted his teeth, but knew he had no authority.

Burgess ordered his crew to bring the first group of Acadians on deck, including Gabriel and Marc. Gabriel noticed Turnbull was monitoring them, so he spoke in a very low voice, "We could take over the ship if we have the help of our militia in other parts of the hold."

Marc nodded. "How can we speak with them?"

Gabriel shook his head, "We must find a way."

The Captain ordered the crew, "Get these prisoners below and bring up the next group." At that point, the sailors broke up their conversation and herded them toward the stairs down to the hold. As Gabriel climbed below, he turned to look at Turnbull, still glaring at him. The sailor pushed Gabriel down into the hold and both men disappeared from view.

*

A blinding storm erupted on the ocean, tossing the old hull from one wave to another like a child with a plaything. The ship bobbed up and down on the large Atlantic waves while the Acadian men were locked in the coffin-like hold.

The hull was so small and riddled with holes that the British did not bother to convert the one large hold into multiple smaller boxes as they had the other transports. René looked around at the men squeezed into the hold so crowded that only a few could sleep on the hold floor at one time. The others had to sit, kneel, or crouch in the remaining cramped space. Half were dying of pneumonia due to the freezing cold air that filled the hold. The other half were living without hope.

Squinting through a crack in the side of the creaking boat, René saw that the approaching waves in the distance were huge. The sight both astounded and frightened him. He realized it was only a matter of time before the water engulfed them.

René tried to stay as calm as possible, under the circumstances, but his words were pointed as he spoke to the other Acadian men. "A series of enormous waves is coming towards us. With the holes in this ship, we will be drowned. Help me open the hatch. We must climb up to the deck."

The Acadian men who could hold their heads up listened attentively to Lord Le Blanc who was the leader they admired and respected. René turned to Alain Poché, Jean Lambert and Benoit de la Tour Landry, the father of Gabriel's best friend Marc. They seemed to be the only healthy men in the hold.

Poché said, "Tell us what we can do. How can we break it open?"

René inspected the animal troughs that were still affixed to the side of the boat. He kicked one of the boards, which broke loose. Kicking again, he broke off more wood. "Let us pry the door open."

Poché, Lambert and Landry each grabbed a piece of wood. Their hands quickly became splintered, but they did not stop. They followed René's direction and wedged a piece of wood into the door, trying to pry it open. Alas, each of the pieces broke. Not to be deterred, they used the smaller pieces and again tried to open the lock.

Enormous waves rushed toward the boat, like huge sea monsters reaching for them. One gigantic wave broadsided the old hull. Water poured into the hold through the cracks and holes in the ship. A rush of water burst open the hatch door which landed on top of Alain Poché and pinning him down to the floor, now being quickly flooded.

René yelled to Benoit and Jean, "We must pull the door up. Ready?" They heaved the heavy door off the drowning man below even as the water level kept rising. When they were able to pull Alain out of the water, he had already died.

René pointed to the men huddling in the corner of the hold. Despite the rushing waters, they seemed frozen in their fear. He cried out, "We must help them get out." Sloshing through the incoming sea, René, Jean and Benoit were able to pull some of the men above the waterline and push them onto the deck through the opened hatch. The two men repeated their efforts until they had pushed all of the feeble old men onto the deck.

As that was being done, two elderly Acadien men kicked at the side of the ship as the water line rose up to their chins. Though the men were elderly, the wood was weak from having been cut by the crew before the ship set sail. The ship's timbers cracked from continued pushing and kicking. More water gushed in, forming a gaping hole in the side of the ship. The two men in the wake of the surging waters struggled to swim out of the hold to the surface of the icy waters. Jean swam over to help them but the incoming waves overwhelmed all three of them and they quickly drowned.

The ship began to list from the amount of water it was taking on. René knew the hull would sink in minutes and everyone still on board would be lost. The few old men left on deck held on to ropes and railings -- anything affixed to the boat. Some of the men tied themselves to the rigging hoping they would not be swept overboard, but would end up floating on a piece of wood.

René saw one remaining rowboat strapped to the side of the ship. He and Benoit frantically tried to untie the ropes but they were hopelessly knotted and waterlogged.

René slowly made his way from one end of the boat to the other, holding on to rigging and the ship's rail. He searched in vain for a knife or tool that he could use to cut the boat free but was knocked down by another wave. When he turned back, Benoit had disappeared, presumably swept overboard. "Benoit?" René shouted out, but he received no response.

Another large wave hit the ship, cracking the rigging and tossing the Acadians tied to it into the sea. René looked down and called out to them, "Michel? Robert? Where are you?" But he saw only churning waters below. No bodies at all, living or dead.

The next wave hit with such force that it ripped the ropes of the rowboat, tossing it into the water. René held out his hand to the old men that he and Benoit had rescued from the hold and brought on deck.

"Jump with me. We shall be safe."

The men shook their heads in terror.

"It will be alright. I shall help you," René urged.

They refused again just as a third huge wave swept them from the deck down into the dark sea. René peered down but saw nothing except waves and the rowboat bobbing up and down on the water.

Not seeing another living soul, René jumped off the rail and swam the short distance to the rowboat. He clambered into the small craft, grabbed the oars and rowed as fast as he could away from the ship, searching for other Acadians as he did so.

As the remaining hull of the ship sink, he continued to look for survivors. As he searched, the rains began to pour, blocking any view more than an immediate circle around the boat. He rowed in all directions near where the ship sank, desperate to find other men.

Fighting all of the elements took its toll on him as the waves pounded the small vessel and the rains beat down on him. Despite his exhaustion, René kept rowing and searching for other Acadians. He was their leader and he was responsible for them. He could not let them die alone in the deep. But, try as he might, his efforts were to no avail.

The rain let up and he searched as far as he could see, but no bodies turned up and he heard no cries for help.

Disconsolate at losing his friends and drained of his strength, he doubted that he could force his fatigued arms to row any more. He prayed, "Lord, please lead my craft toward land…." Then he dropped the oars and collapsed into the well of the little boat.

CHAPTER 50
Women

Grand Pré

T
he sounds of construction at the charred English fort could be heard far down the road in Grand Pré. Lieutenant-Colonel Winslow had galloped from town to the garrison several times a day every day this week to check on the progress.

He had a renewed spirit because he had received his orders confirming he was recalled home and would be replaced by Captain Osgood. Winslow had breathed a sigh of relief, praying aloud, "Thank you with all of my heart and soul, dear Lord, for removing me from this disagreeable business. I stand ready to obey our holy King's orders in Your name but am eternally grateful that I am being removed from such a pit of human misery and chaos."

Today Winslow changed his routine. He did not ask his aide to saddle a horse. Instead, he strolled from his rooms in the warm rectory past the church and along Main Street. Not that there was anything to see. Stores were closed. Houses were shuttered. No one dared walk the streets. Absent were the armed soldiers who patrolled the streets during the day whom Winslow usually passed on his way to the fort. No doubt they had settled down to warm meals and bottles of beer or wine in the homes of their Acadian "hosts."

The Acadian women, children and the elderly who had not yet been exiled were under informal house arrest. Soldiers quartered there watched their every move and reported back to Captain Edwin Fossett, newly-promoted by Winslow to fill the late Captain Adams' shoes.

Even Christine had lost her solitude when Rollin and Wesley finally broke down the door and moved into the Consulate. When they had first arrived, Rollin asked Christine, "Where be the other missy that lives here?"

Christine lied, "I fear she must have drowned. Or perhaps she ran away. I have not seen her." She had watched Evangeline slip into the water and swim toward Gabriel's ship. When Christine was herded back to town, she turned hoping to catch a glimpse of Evangeline, without success.

Christine prayed for Evangeline each night after she slid her dressing table against the door. Without locks on the doors, Christine worried that one – or more – of the soldiers would attempt to have their way with her. What did they have to lose? She knew they were going to force her onto a ship to an unknown destination. She had no redress for that horror nor any rights to complain against the troops whom she felt were her jailers.

She needn't have worried. The soldiers knew their duty was to eavesdrop on Christine's conversations with the Acadian women who visited her. They were not authorized to take advantage of her vulnerability.

The soldiers allowed the women to move from their houses and visit neighbors if they were escorted by the troops. The soldiers were required to report what they saw and heard. Of all the people in town, Christine was the person visited most often by the Acadian women. She was the source of information and of inspiration. Despite the adverse conditions, Christine gave the other women hope and the courage to continue.

Christine and Béatrice met and spoke without ever referencing their plan to disappear into the woods. They did not ever talk about the Mi'Kmaqs but rather reminisced about gathering their favorite flowers in the woods and talked about their favorite clearings. The references were too subtle for the soldiers to understand as anything other than womenfolk talk. But the two women fortified their plan to escape into the woods the following night.

As Béatrice was leaving, Christine hugged her friend and whispered she would wait for her and her mother Anne the next night at midnight in the clearing. They both knew that area of the woods quite well. Béatrice loved walking in the woods, talking to the trees as had her father, Thomas. She missed him and thought of him each time she saw his favorite tree. She rued the day she had asked Winslow for mercy for her father, who had lost his mind and had been ordered hanged by Lieutenant-Colonel Winslow after refusing to attend the reading of the King's Edict.

Christine visited the woods daily in search of herbs and roots with healing properties. She also sought the special plants that she ground to make a powder which induced deep drowsiness and sleep when stirred into a glass of wine. She smiled, remembering how the Mi'Kmaq medicine woman White Bird had taught her how to boil, dry, crush and mix the plants into the cures which Christine kept ready for anyone in town who needed them.

When Béatrice left and Christine closed the door, Rollin appeared and prevented her from bolting the front door with the huge plank. Christine turned away and trudged up the stairs to her room. She followed her routine of dragging her heavy armoire against the door, then changed into her nightgown and brushed her hair over and over. She knelt at her bed and prayed with a great sigh.

"Lord, send me a sign that my love René and dearest Evangeline are both alive and well. And one more thing. Bless our escape plan. Let us take as many Acadians as we can with us tomorrow night."

When dawn broke, Béatrice slowly looked around the room, the last time she would see the only home she had ever known. Anne slept soundly on her blanket near the hearth. The soldier who usually slept near the fire was gone. The door to the back room with the only bed in the house was ajar. Béatrice wrapped herself in a blanket and crept toward the door, then peered inside the room. The bed was empty. That soldier was gone too.

She found it odd that they had departed without a word, and could not imagine why they had left so early. She shivered and stepped outside to grab some of the few remaining pieces of firewood. What she saw struck her like a bolt of lightning. Soldiers streamed out of other houses and moved into formation under Captain Fossett's orders. Winslow was nowhere to be seen as the troops lined the main street of town.

Suddenly, Béatrice knew what it meant. She made the Sign of the Cross as she entered the house and shut the door. "Mother," Béatrice called out. "Mother, the soldiers are going to take us away. We must pack quickly." Anne looked up at her with one eye, then rolled over and went back to sleep. Béatrice shook her mother until Anne finally rose. "Put on all your warm clothes." Béatrice rushed into the back room and pulled out woolen skirts, sweaters and socks.

Anne looked blankly at Béatrice, who started putting on one layer after another until she looked like a small elephant. Anne pointed to her daughter and laughed aloud. "Vixm. Churlitby."

Béatrice nodded and started dressing Anne. "That's right, Mother. We are going to play a game. Shall we see how many sweaters we can wear?"

Anne played along and let Béatrice finish dressing her. Anne clapped her hands when she looked down to see herself looking as big as Béatrice. "Dbletney sivmil. Vixm!"

"Yes, we are going to be very warm on our trip. There you go. We're ready. Now let's pack some food. Fetch the bread."

Anne scurried to the hearth and grabbed the remainder of a loaf and stuffed it in her sweater, then looked down and giggled. Béatrice filled a sack with all the sausages, bread, dried apples and other edible items she could find, and tied it around her waist like a belt.

In another part of town, Yvonne Poché knitted for her husband Alain. "He shall be in need of new gloves when he greets me at the dock. I shall finish this pair and then work on a new sweater. It will be the dead of winter when we see each other again. I must have these ready." She spoke to herself, ignoring the two soldiers who walked out of the door gorging themselves on the dried beef they had found in her cellar.

In the Consulate, Christine was wakened by the noise of the soldiers trudging down the stairs in their heavy boots. Suddenly, all was quiet. She quickly dressed and peered into the hallway. Seeing no one, she flew down the stairs but the front door was unlocked. They had disappeared. She ran into René's office and peered through the window. The street was quiet outside. Rushing upstairs, Christine looked through the top window of the house in Evangeline's room. She gasped.

She saw rows of soldiers lining up, checking bayonets and muskets. "Mercy, no. They are not going to exile us by ship. They plan to kill us all," Christine cried aloud. She ran into her room and grabbed her travel bag of clothes. She headed into the kitchen and stuffed a sack of food and medicinal herbs into the packed bag.

She went to the back door of the Consulate and slipped into the stable. But the horses were gone, no doubt confiscated by the soldiers for their own use.

"I must head for the woods," Christine encouraged herself aloud. "I will be safe and can hide waiting for Béatrice and any others to show up tonight at midnight." She tried to calm herself as she scurried through the stable and pushed open the door. A familiar face stared at her.

"Jest where do you think you be going, missy?" said Rollin with an evil grin.

"I need some water," Christine replied thinking quickly.

"Methinks you cannot hold water in a cloth bag filled with women's things." Rollin clutched his bayonet.

"Well, perhaps I can wait until later." With that, Christine slammed the stable door and ran back into the house. She did not stop running until she reached the safe haven of her own room with the armoire blocking any entry into her space.

Outside the stable, Rollin laughed. "Stupid woman. You will get yours soon enough later today."

*

Captain Fossett rode up and down the lines of soldiers, shouting orders. "You there, adjust your jacket. Soldier, clean your bayonet. The two of you, cease talking immediately." Rollin and Wesley shut their traps immediately.

Without warning, Winslow trotted up to Fossett. He halted his horse and called out, "All troops, attention!"

Winslow reviewed the soldiers and nodded with satisfaction. "Captain? It is time. Carry out the orders so this business so disagreeable to my nature can be disposed of."

"Yes, sir. Right away, sir."

Winslow rode his horse back to the side of the church and dismounted, then entered the rectory and slowly closed the door behind him, saying, "May Lord have mercy on the souls of the heathens."

Captain Fossett watched as the troops marched throughout the town and entered one home after another. They led all of the Acadians into the church, where they sat in pews with pure fright on their faces. When Acadians resisted leaving their homes, whether women, children or the elderly, soldiers dragged them out by their arms or their hair. They were pushed into the church and directed to sit in the pews.

The Acadians in the church questioned one another in low whispers. Jeanne asked Madame Poché, "Do you know what they want?" All Madame Poché could do was shake her head and weep.

When Béatrice and Anne were seated behind Jeanne, Béatrice leaned forward. "What have you heard?"

Jeanne shook her head. "They have not said what want of us. Have you seen Christine?"

Béatrice replied, "We plan to head into the woods tonight at midnight. Perhaps she left early."

Jeanne said ruefully, "I believe they mean to keep us here as they did the men before shipping us out."

Béatrice shuddered. "Or worse. I watched them sharpen their bayonet blades. They cannot mean to kill us, can they?"

Anne interrupted, "Kekmerna sprub?"

Béatrice absentmindedly patted her mother's hand which contented Anne for the moment. Then Anne concentrated on a loose thread pulled from her sweater.

Jeanne shed a tear. "Surely the English could not be that cruel. They claim to be so pious, reading their King's Bible and such."

Yvonne Poché, overhearing their conversation, added, "It would be a blessing, not a curse, to die today. I would finally see my Alain again even though I do not know if he is alive or not. I feel nothing. What if everyone on that old ship died?"

Béatrice gasped. "No. It cannot be. Consul Le Blanc was forced onto that old hull."

Jeanne wiped her eyes, now red from tears. "My father boarded that ship, too. We must believe they are all alive – that all of our men are alive -- and that we shall meet again. I, for one, shall never give up hope of meeting my Marc again. Never."

Béatrice grabbed Jeanne's hand. "Yes. I pray for that daily. They are all alive and shall be waiting for us when our ships arrive."

Jeanne smiled at Anne. "Madame, it looks like you are dressed warmly for the trip."

Anne looked up and smiled. Jeanne was always nice to her. "Blixney traub delawim." Then Anne turned her interest back to the fascinating loose thread.

Béatrice asked Jeanne, "Were you able to pack clothes and food?"

Jeanne shook her head. "I had planned to do it tonight when the soldiers were sleeping. They have stuck to me like glue since they moved in. They said they were there for my safety. But we all know differently."

Béatrice wondered, "I do not believe anyone would have told the English of our escape plan, do you?"

Jeanne shook her head. "No. At least, not willingly. But if a soldier threatened my baby – that is, if I had a child-- I would have gladly told them anything they wanted to hear."

Béatrice nodded, realizing the gravity of the situation. "Yes, I would have done the same if they promised to harm my mother unless I spilled my secrets."

Jeanne replied, "In any case, we are here now and shall soon find out the reason for it."

At that moment, Rollin came in with Christine and strong-armed her up the aisle to the front row. Béatrice and Jeanne tried to touch Christine's hand in a show of support as she walked up. Rollin saw them and roughly slapped their hands away.

Fossett and Winslow appeared at the church entry doors and marched up to the altar. Fossett hit his musket on the wooden floor several times. "Attention, Acadians. Quiet! Lieutenant-Colonel John Winslow has an announcement and wishes to speak to you."

Fossett stepped to the side and Winslow took center stage.

"I must say I am feeling a bit of deja-vu. The Acadian men of this community sat in this very church not a month ago. In the same seats where you are today. And as I told them, I am telling you. You have nothing to fear if you obey my orders. You shall not be hurt. My troops were warned that they were not to harm a hair on your head, not to abuse you in any way, not to take advantage of your hospitality other than food, a warm hearth and a place to sleep. I have not heard a complaint from any of you thus far."

Winslow took a deep breath and stared at Christine for a long minute, then turned his attention to the other Acadians sitting in the church.

"Have any of you been forced to do things you did not wish to do?"

The Acadian women put their heads down, or shook them or otherwise refused to respond.

"Very well. I shall take that to mean you have all been well-treated in your homes during this period of reflection. I wanted to give you a period of time to think about how you would handle yourselves when you are shipped out. I cannot underscore the importance of obeying the orders that are handed down. We do not want a repeat of what happened at the shore, do we?"

When no Acadian dared a response, Winslow said impatiently and loudly, "You shall not be insolent and disobey orders as many did last time, shall you? Answer me. Now!"

The Acadians answered in one loud voice, "No, sir."

Anne looked up and shouted out, "Dwemney flikso."

Winslow peered down at Anne, then looked at Béatrice and shook his head as a warning. Béatrice quickly grabbed Anne's hand and whispered, "Mother, this is a game to be as quiet as a mouse. Okay?"

Anne nodded and put her finger to her mouth to shush herself.

Winslow harrumphed and spoke to the Acadians again. "The Royal Edict orders you to be exiled from these lands. Your homes, land, cattle and other animals were already forfeited to the King."

The women were expecting the words but still stifled sobs or cried quietly. Winslow ignored them and continued. "Within the month, new ships will arrive in Minas Basin and you shall be marched to the beach. Anyone who refuses, or creates chaos, or tries to escape will be shot without hesitation."

The Acadians gasped audibly at the threat to kill them.

"Does everyone understand? With God as my witness, if you obey my orders, and those of my troops, I shall not hurt any of you."

The church was suddenly as quiet as falling snow. Béatrice whispered to Christine, "Our fate was in his hands all the time. We should have known we could not trust a follower of the false religion."

Jeanne replied tersely, "Have faith. It will surely save us."

Christine added in a quiet voice, "Wait until we are locked in the hold of a cattle boat, as Winslow's orders say. I read them but it was too late to take any action. No water, no privacy, rotten food, if any at all, and corpses for shipmates."

Béatrice was afraid, "We are going to die, aren't we? I shall never see my brother Pine again."

Jeanne asked, "Do you trust in God, Christine?"

She nodded and whispered, "Enough to pray for deliverance. We must have faith but also watch for any opportunity to escape into the woods."

Turnbull and his soldiers gazed over the ground, watching for sudden movements. Winslow raised his Bible in front of the Acadians. "Go back to your homes. Remember your animals are property of the King. Death to anyone who touches them."

Béatrice stood defiantly. "But we shall starve without the meat from our cattle. And we have no men to hunt in the forest."

Christine stood defiantly. "Winter is upon us. If we feed our remaining food stores to the soldiers, we shall have none for ourselves."

Winslow shouted out, "Silence! You have no rights here. You are still expected to cook meals for your military escorts every morning and night. If you do not have enough for yourselves, perhaps a little hunger shall teach you to respect our holy King and the one true Church of England."

Christine stood bravely and responded, "Lieutenant-Colonel Winslow, I believe I speak for every Acadian here when I said that we understand exactly what you are staying. I can assure you that you will not have any trouble from any of us. We are all ready and anxious to board the ships and reach our final destinations."

Winslow nodded with satisfaction. "Good. That is very good." He remembered what it felt like to touch Christine's glowing flame hair, her soft white shoulders, and -- then his dream faded into reality.

He seethed with anger that she had teased him so. He knew she had drugged him with a concoction until he fell asleep so that she could steal from him. He never found anything missing, but he knew in his heart she had stolen something.

Christine looked at Winslow, angry at him as well. She believed he had never learned she drugged him to read his secret military documents about the British plan to exile the Acadians. With the information, she warned René, Gabriel and the other Acadians. But even armed with that knowledge, the Acadian men were too late to plan an escape or a battle. The English had outsmarted them by imprisoning them in the church until they were led to the beach and onto the ships that exiled them forever from their homes.

Christine tried to use her feminine wiles once more with Winslow. "Pray tell, where are we going and when do we leave?"

Before he could respond, Jeanne called out, "What is to become of us when we arrive?"

And Béatrice added in a strong voice, "How can we join the men you have taken from us?"

Winslow fired his musket at the ceiling. The church went deadly silent except for the cracked ceiling plaster falling onto the altar. Winslow raised his Bible in front of the Acadians and addressed them in a solemn voice.

"You may pack one satchel. Anything more and you will suffer instant death for stealing from the King. Ye shall reap what ye sow. The troops will march you to the shore when the boats are in the harbor."

The women moaned and cried out, but Winslow responded impatiently. "You should have signed our oath and worshipped in the one true church, that of our holy King."

Christine defied him. "You know we are still subject to the peace treaty that your own Queen Anne signed in 1713. That guaranteed that we are neutrals and have the freedom to practice our own religion."

Winslow's voice grew cold. "Be ready to leave on a moment's notice. When the soldiers order you to move out, you shall have no time. Captain Fossett shall be in here directly with more instructions." Winslow stormed to the back of the altar and into the rectory and bolted the door loudly behind him. He beat his breast and prayed for the fortitude to continue this disagreeable mission until his replacement arrived.

The women covered their faces with their hands and wept. Christine took action and began praying the Lord's Prayer, trying to comfort the grieving Acadians. "Our Father Who art in heaven."

Other women, old couples leaning on each other, and even the children joined in until the church was filled only with the whispered prayer.

"Hallowed be Thy name...."

Before they could finish their prayer, Captain Fossett marched noisily up the main aisle, avoiding eye contact with the weeping women. He issued an order, "Everyone is to return home. You shall be escorted by the soldiers quartered with you. Exit from the front of the church into the center aisle, one row at a time." Fossett signaled his troops and they waited at the doors for their charges.

"You there, go first." Fossett pointed to Christine, who dutifully stood and led her row down the aisle. Other rows of Acadians followed in order. When Christine passed Béatrice and Jeanne, she mouthed, "No" to let them know it was too dangerous to escape into the woods.

As they walked silently down the center aisle, the Captain added, "Captain Osgood shall take over this part of the operation, so stay in your homes until he sends for you. God be with your heathen souls."

Jeanne nodded slightly, but Béatrice was defiant. Christine gave her a knowing look not to disobey, then exited the church doors. Wesley and Rollin escorted Christine back to the Consulate and disappeared inside, where she sighed in resignation and began to prepare a meal for her unwelcome guests.

When it was Béatrice's turn to exit the church, she rose and lifted her mother, holding her hand all the way home. The soldiers followed the two women without a word as they entered the house. Within minutes, smoke curled from the chimney as a fire roared within the hearth.

Likewise, all the other Acadians were walked to their homes by their troop escorts. It seemed as though all hope had slowly been drained from their hearts. For many, loss of hope was as good as death.

Indeed, the Acadians already subsisting on low food stores had to share with soldiers and felt like walking death. Those would turn out to be the lucky ones, dying before they boarded the ships or expiring on board. Those were the ones who escaped the untold pain and suffering that the survivors would endure.

CHAPTER 51
Osgood

Grand Pré

Captain Phineas Osgood stood on deck of *Goodson* and peered out at the coastline blurred by the fog. The ship was on course as it sailed north from Bostontown headed for the Nova Scotia Province, the Bay of Fundy and its eastern inlet known as Minas Bay, where he would become the commanding officer at the fort in Grand Pré.

Osgood patted his jacket over the pocket that held his orders from Commander-in-Chief William Shirley. He relished the idea of ridding the province of the heathen Acadians. He shared his thoughts with his aide.

"If the winds continue in our favor, we should reach our destination within the fortnight."

"Yes, sir," the young soldier obediently replied.

Osgood continued. "Look yonder. See that ship heading south down the coast?"

"Yes, sir," said the aide, squinting to see the vessel.

"That is the first transport of Acadian prisoners removed from our province."

The aide squinted into the mist at the small ship flying the British flag. "Where they be heading, sir?"

"The port we just embarked from. Bostontown. The plan is brilliant. Those romanists will be marched off the ship and sold for cheap labor right into the fields."

"But, sir, don't they got laws against them popist people in Bostontown? What meself hears, they can't even get work or rent a room. They is outlaws, what meself hears."

Osgood nodded. "True, the heathens are forbidden from getting paid for work. That is why they are ordered to do hard labor. Them and those dozens of children they have."

"How is that so, sir? They work without getting pay?"

Osgood smiled grimly. "Upon their arrival in port, they are sold as slave labor for the plantations and farms in the Colony. Bostontown has a thriving business."

The aide nodded slowly, though he was still confused. "But, sir…."

Osgood cut him off. "All you need to know is we have our orders. We shall clear out the town of those people, as you say. We must make it ready for new English planters to arrive next year."

"Yes, sir."

Within a matter of days, not weeks, the winds had picked up so much that the ship sailed straight through the choppy waters of the Atlantic to the entrance of Bay of Fundy off Nova Scotia.

Osgood knew they were getting close to the Grand Pré inlet when he saw the tall rock cliffs in the distance. From there, it would not be long before he met Lieutenant-Colonel Winslow and took command of his troops.

"Brrr," Osgood shivered aloud. His aide handed him a pair of heavy leather gloves, which Osgood absentmindedly pushed onto his fat fingers. "Ask the cook for a bottle of his finest brandy. I want to celebrate the moment."

The aide saluted and quickly disappeared. After standing in the blustery winds for a near-eternity, Osgood watched the aide return with an awkward look. He explained, "Begging your pardon, sir, but cook said they don't got no brandy. Just this."

Osgood turned and saw the aide hold up a dusty bottle with a thick cork in the top. Osgood took in a large breath and blew the dust off the label, reading "Vin Français." Osgood smiled. "How appropriate. Drinking their wine as we rid our lands of the French themselves."

He bit the cork out of the bottle and took a long swig. "Just what I needed to quench my thirst to be in command again." He raised the bottle as the ship lurched forward on a fast-moving current in the choppy sea. Osgood nearly dropped the wine as he stumbled, but he managed to grab the ship's side railing and hold onto the precious drink all the while. The bumbling aide did nothing but stumble and fall onto the deck.

Osgood ignored him as the aide pushed himself up and grabbed hold of the rail. "Anything else, sir?"

Osgood gulped down the liquid. "Prepare my cabin for the night and pack up what you can. We shall be going ashore at dawn on the morrow."

The aide nodded and said with another salute. "Yes, sir."

Osgood waved him away and focused on the land ahead as the ship rocked back and forth. He failed to notice that the aide continued to fall, get up and fall again on his way to accomplish Osgood's orders.

*

Winslow woke before dawn, eager with anticipation to finally leave this backwater. He longed for the lights of the big city of Bostontown, which he planned to visit many times after returning to his home and family. Peering through the thick curtains of his room, he grunted with satisfaction. "No snow. I should hope today is the day I finally hand over the reins of this dreadful outpost to my successor. If so, it shall be a very good day, indeed."

A hard knock at the door roused him from his bed. Wrapping his woolen dressing gown about him, Winslow padded to the front entry and opened it. Captain Fossett saluted.

"Good news, sir. The transport for Major Osgood has been seen anchored in Minas Basin."

Winslow was about to clap with glee, but contained himself, "Thank you, Captain. Stay for breakfast with me if you will."

Fossett nodded quickly. Winslow sat at the dining table with his bedclothes still on. Captain Fossett waited patiently until the cook had brought out a tray laden with meats, fruits, cheeses, hard breads and a bottle of wine. Winslow motioned for Fossett to take a seat at the table.

When they had both filled their plates and Captain Fossett was about to dig in, Winslow folded his hands and bowed his head.

"O Holy Lord God, be merciful to us, your lowly servants. Thank you for answering my prayers to re-assign me back home. I pray that You give Captain Osgood the strength to carry out the mission. And bless Captain Fossett as well. Amen."

Fossett echoed him with, "Amen" before waiting for Winslow to take the first bite of the meal. Once Winslow had a mouth full of food, Fossett started shoveling in the food. He did not know how long he would be allowed to stay at table, since Winslow had a habit of eating quickly. But Fossett had nothing to worry about today. Winslow took his time and mused about his time in Grand Pré as if he were talking to himself.

"Finally, I am absolved of this dreadful scheme. I know the heathens deserve what they get, but I still feel a certain guilt in bringing it about. Better that a younger officer with unquestionable loyalty do the deed."

Suddenly, Winslow looked up and stared at Captain Fossett. "What did you just hear me say? Did I speak my thoughts aloud?"

Fossett answered prudently, "Only that you have served our King and Commander Shirley with honor and distinction. You have earned your transfer back home."

Winslow nodded, and quickly finished the meal. Fossett was shooed out of the building with a mouth full of food. When he closed the door behind Fossett, Winslow scuttled about his rooms gathering his few belongings. He packed them into a large leather bag then knelt at the prie-dieu in his bedroom.

He beat his breast as he prayed, but could hardly contain himself, murmuring his delight. "Finally the time has arrived. Just one more day in this wilderness and I will be freed."

Winslow dressed quickly and mounted the horse that had been saddled and waiting for hours. He rode past shuttered shops and curtained windows of Acadian homes without so much as a glance. He was a man on a mission, nearly finished with the part he played in the disagreeable business of exiling the Acadians from English land.

Winslow soon arrived at the fort embroiled in construction chaos. Troops continued to clear debris from the fire on one end and rebuild the outbuildings on the other. They had only recently completed the main quarters for Captain Osgood. They were as anxious as Winslow to meet the incoming officer who would lead them to complete their undertaking.

"At last, I am saved from having to fight my conscience every day to follow my good King's orders. And I shall be back in the civilized world in short order," Winslow told himself.

Trotting through the entry gates, Winslow called out to Captain Fossett. The young officer had filled Captain Adams' shoes better than expected and was quite talented in overseeing the fort's reconstruction. Winslow had appreciated Fossett's initiative in commanding the troops, allowing Winslow to read his Bible and sip French wine in the rectory.

"Captain? Is your man ready with the horses? I am off to meet the incoming commander."

Fossett stopped the work and pointed to his aide, a young soldier named Will, waiting with two saddled horses. "Follow the Lieutenant-Colonel." Fossett turned back to Winslow. "We prepared the quarters for the new commanding officer in the main house. I trust it shall be to his liking."

Winslow waved his hand, cutting him off while waiting impatiently for Will to walk the horses up to him. "Anything will best a ship's journey in the winter which arrives earlier each year. But an extra bottle of brandy or rum would be welcome about now."

Captain Fossett saluted Winslow and nodded. "Yes, sir, Lieutenant-Colonel." He rushed into the main building.

Alone in the blustery wind, Winslow reminisced about his life and the choices he made. He was a proud descendent of the Pilgrim Edward Winslow and had reaped prestige and financial benefits of being in one of the Colonies' leading families. With his family ties to Governor Shirley,

Winslow obtained a commission in the English army. He felt he had served faithfully long enough. He anticipated returning to his warm house, fawning wife Mary and three sons, Josiah, Isaac and Pelham. And he was anxious to supervise the work of his slaves and to see if they had made any progress on his fields.

Will trotted up, pulling the reins of a second horse. The soldier saluted Winslow. "Sir. Ready when you are."

"No hurry, soldier. I await your Captain. He has a prize for me, I believe."

Fossett walked up and handed Winslow a sack filled with several bottles of French wine and brandy taken from the Acadian wine shop in town. With a nod, Winslow guided his horse down the hill through the beautiful trees to the edge of the beach. Will dutifully followed him with the horse in tow. Winslow peered at the large ship anchored in the bay.

The fog was still thick, and he was hesitant to rejoice until he reviewed the goings-on through his spyglass. When the fog began to lift, he observed a contingent of sailors lowering bags and boxes from the ship down into a rowboat.

Only then did Winslow breathe a sigh of relief. "Finally, Osgood has arrived. And not a minute too soon for me. I feared I would lose my sanity in this remote hamlet."

Winslow stared at a man of immense proportions who was lowered from the large vessel onto the small craft. Winslow could hardly contain himself and waved at the incoming boat. Then he remembered himself and immediately drew his hand down. But he needn't have bothered. Captain Phineas Osgood was too concerned about maintaining balance in the over-loaded rowboat to even see Winslow's sign of exuberance.

"Drat it, men, pull harder," Osgood shouted tersely.

Osgood had long ago lost patience with the dimwits who served in the English navy. They were mostly second and third sons of lower nobility who would inherit no lands and chose the sea over a life of the cloth in a small English church parish. Osgood himself could hardly wait to touch ground after the arduous journey from Bostontown which should have taken only days. The unpredictable weather had caused the ship to veer off course, which cost additional days.

As a man, Osgood stood a head taller than the average soldier. He was a true ox of a man who could put fear in a man's eyes if he willed it. The sailors over-exerted themselves rowing madly onto the shallows of the beach so they could rid themselves of the burden of Osgood as well as the heavy load of his personal belongings and weaponry.

When the boat hit the snow-covered beach, Osgood stood and rocked the boat. All his packages fell into the water. Sailors jumped into the icy wetness to retrieve and deposit them on the sandy ground by Winslow.

Winslow dismounted and greeted Osgood as a long-lost friend, though in truth the two had met only once, which was several years earlier. Winslow reminded Osgood of their encounter.

"Captain Osgood, welcome. My gratitude to the Crown for sending a replacement in haste." Then he added, "You look no worse for the wear of your journey. And as fit as you were when we met in Bostontown with Governor Shirley."

Osgood shook hands quickly and presented his orders. Winslow reviewed the official document and nodded. Osgood replied, "Lieutenant-Colonel Winslow. I must return the compliment. Since our Governor became commander-in-chief of our colonial forces, he has made quite impressive changes in our military. I am sure you would agree." Winslow nodded as Osgood looked all around. "No carriage at this outpost I see."

Winslow led Osgood to the waiting horse. "Once we climb that hill yonder through the trees, we are nearly at the fort. A carriage would be a waste of the King's coin."

Osgood remembered Winslow's reputation as a penny-pincher. "Of course. We must always be watchful of the royal treasury."

As they urged their horses up the snow-covered hill, Osgood turned to Winslow. "Have you prepared the Acadians to be exiled or is that my duty?"

Winslow waved him off and smiled. "No need to concern yourself with that. The Acadians know their fate. They have accepted it and will be obedient lambs going to their ships."

Osgood posed more questions. "And what of the ones to the slaughter? Have you made preparations to that effect?"

"I assure you, per the Commander Shirley's orders, I appointed a special force to hunt down and punish any Acadians who do not board the ships. Whether by refusal or by attempted escape, they shall all be captured and hanged before long."

Osgood asked, "When will you herd the prisoners down here?"

Winslow warned, "Winter is coming early and it promises to be harsh. Many will die here on the shore without shelter if they are marched here too early."

"That would leave more food for the others on the ships." Osgood continued, "I am informed that all passenger ships are in use and that the firm of Apthorp & Hancock shall send animal cargo boats. They should arrive in several days. Or weeks, at most."

Osgood peered at Winslow. "Well, that settles it. Since you have wrapped up this mission in a neat bow for me, I trust you have edibles in this forsaken territory?"

Winslow smiled, "I shall let you decide for yourself after you taste of the culinary temptations our cook has prepared for your luncheon."

Osgood nodded with satisfaction. "Let us get on with it."

Winslow kicked his horse who galloped up the hill, with Osgood right at his heels. Both men were eager to eat a hearty meal but for different reasons. Osgood was a big man who was always hungry and could spend hours at a meal, sipping his favorite wine or sharing war stories for hours with fellow officers or family members.

Winslow usually ate hurriedly for the sake of filling his belly. He thought food should be simple and pleasant enough to the taste, but always in large quantities. He had experienced too many military campaigns that left him hungry due to a shortage of food for the officers, much less the soldiers. His plan was to rush through the meal, say his goodbyes and set out for the rowboat that awaited him at the shore. He wanted to return to the colonies as soon as possible.

In the end, the fort's cook had piled food so high on the dining table it groaned under the weight. Naturally, Osgood went about telling stories as Winslow ate rapidly. But by the time Winslow had grabbed and tasted every dish, they had spent three hours at table.

Captain Fossett was given the responsibility to make sure Osgood was settled in his quarters. "This way, Captain." Fossett respected the military hierarchy although he and Osgood held the same rank.

Following Fossett into the adjoining great room that also served as an office, Osgood left the table and settled into a huge leather chair before the roaring fire.

Fossett entered the bedroom and lit a fire in that room as well. Returning to the main room, Fossett queried Osgood. "If there is nothing else, sir?" Osgood waved Fossett away as he would a fly on a wine glass. "Very well, Captain. I shall take my leave."

This time, Osgood ignored him. Fossett turned on his heels and strode out, firmly shutting the heavy wooden door behind him.

Winslow left the dining table and shook hands with Osgood. "I trust you have all the information you need, but if you desire further details about this place, you need only write me."

Osgood abruptly interrupted Winslow. "That shall not be necessary. I know what I wish to do."

Winslow nodded and quickly disappeared outside where his aide waited with two horses laden with Bibles, weapons and overstuffed bags. The two men made their way out of the fort, down the road and through the trees, descending the hill to the water's edge.

As Winslow walked toward the shore, the sailors beside one rowboat stood at attention. They assisted Winslow into the small craft. His aide unburdened the horses and handed off Winslow's possessions to the sailors. They filled the rowboat with the bags then quickly pushed away from shore and rowed to the large boat anchored in Minas Bay.

The aide took one last look at the rowboat rowing up to the large ship. He wanted to make sure Winslow made it onto the ship and did not return.

"Good riddance," the young soldier said. "'Tis my hope the new commander does not force us to work dawn to dusk in the freezing cold every day like he did. We got Frenchies for that. Let them heathens find wood in the snow and cook us supper."

From the ship, Winslow peered back towards shore with his spyglass. Through the trees, he saw the English flag fluttering on top of the sentry tower. The beach was dotted with shadows of leafless trees hovering over the snowy sand.

He surveyed the scene until fog enveloped the ship and felt both sad and relieved that his part in the "Great and Noble Scheme" had ended. But his attention quickly turned to the thought of the onion pies Cook was so famous for. His mouth watered, dispelling all thoughts of Grand Pré and the Acadians from his mind. "To Bostontown," he shouted like a madman. This time, he did not care who heard him nor what they thought. He was going home.

CHAPTER 52
Quakes

*Lisbon * Boston*

On the other side of the world from Grand Pré and Bostontown, an event occurred of which not a soul in the New World was aware. On November 1, 1755 the earthquake to end all earthquakes hit the city of Lisbon, Portugal in mid-morning. Between the earthquake and fires in the city and a resulting tidal wave, the estimated death toll was up to 100,000 souls and the destruction was unimaginable.

Only seventeen days later, in the morning hours of November 18, 1755, another earthquake occurred. This time, it took place off the coast of Cape Ann in the Massachusetts Bay Colony. Unaware of the Lisbon earthquake, the Bostonians would never know the earlier quake could have been the cause of the utter devastation in Bostontown. Hundreds of buildings were ruined and fires erupted everywhere, burning hundreds more. More than 800 chimneys were destroyed, and over 1500 windows were shattered.

The quake was so strong it sent shocks along the coast throughout the southern colonies down to the Carolinas, and north of the Massachusetts Bay Colony up to Nova Scotia. The transports delivering Acadian exiles to the Colonies were particularly affected. They encountered huge waves that blew them off course or dashed them into the rocks. Ship captains reported feeling the ocean move so dramatically that they thought they had run aground.

Every ship carrying Acadian men and boys from Grand Pré to the Colonies experienced enormous whitecaps crashing over the deck and beating the sides of the ship. Water poured into the top level of the hold and seeped through the loosely-built planks for the additional makeshift holds below, drenching men and boys on the lower levels and drowning many of them. On deck, deafening waves crashing in all directions seemed a never-ending nightmare.

As for the crew on ships transporting Acadians to the Colonies, many fell to their knees and kissed the deck once they had docked in their designated harbors. Young Acadian boys who survived the terrifying voyage would remember for a lifetime their fear of being swallowed by a sea monster whose bellowing sounds seemed to continue forever, though the deafening waves lasted only a short while.

For the Acadians arriving in Bostontown, hell on earth was just beginning. They had undergone a terrifying voyage in the cramped ship's hold. And now they learned they would be sold into servitude without reprieve for the rest of their lives. What was worse, they would be forced to speak English rather than French, to anglicize their names and to abandon Catholicism which was outlawed in many of the Colonies.

Much of the misery the Acadians endured would never have occurred had William Shirley hired honest shipbuilders to deliver a sufficient of ships on time for the Acadian population. Instead, Shirley had been determined to remove the heathens by his fixed timetable, requiring the retrofits that exacerbated the Acadians' despair and pain.

*

In Grand Pré, the Acadians who were about to be exiled felt the ground shaking beneath them. The timbers of their houses shook and the roofs of the taller buildings collapsed. At the garrison, the newly-built sentry tower came crashing down, killing the young guard on duty at the outside gate.

Béatrice grabbed Anne's hand and rushed out of the house crying, "Help! The roof has dropped into the house!" They were joined by other women and children who darted into the main street, screaming in fear.

Christine dashed out of the Consulate, trailed closely by Rollin and Wesley. She chastised them, "Do not stand idly by. I am fine. Go to the other homes and rescue those who cannot get out themselves." When they looked at her with blank stares, she added, "Go on. Now!"

The two soldiers were confused, but they hastened to the large shop with the owner's house above. The windows had fallen and the chimney bricks were strewn all over the ground. As they tried to enter the shop, they felt tremors under their feet which tossed them flat on their backs. Fearing being killed if they went any further, the two men bolted and ran towards the fort.

When the soldiers ran off, Christine dashed into the shop and found the owner's wife and five young daughters cowering beneath the shop counter. She brought them out and rushed them into the Church. It was nearly filled with Acadians and soldiers alike, all of whom prayed together in the singular sign of respect and tolerance the Acadians would receive from the British in their lifetimes.

After that quake, the residents of Nova Scotia and the Colonies experienced a religious fervor unlike any they had known before. This was the first of several spiritual surges throughout the Colonies known as "The Great Awakening."

*

Thirty miles from Bostontown in the town of Marshfield, Winslow was enjoying his evening meal and writing in his journal. Without warning, the floor under his feet shook. The pot on the hearth swung to and fro. Fine ceramic dishes he had imported from England crashed onto the floor and large pots clanged loudly.

His wife Mary screamed, "Mister Winslow! The sky is falling. We shall all be dead."

Winslow grabbed his wife's hand and led her across the moving wooden floor to a chair. But the quake shook the entire house. Winslow's sons tried to clamber down the stairs from their bedroom loft but the wooden steps creaked and cracked, tossing them rudely down onto the floor of the main room.

"Father," said his son Pelham, 'What is happening?"

His other son, Isaac, cried out, "What can we do?"

Winslow yelled at them over the din of glass and ceramics breaking. "Climb under the dining table and stay with your mother. All of you. I shall return shortly."

Winslow unsteadily made his way to the door. He saw the ceiling sway precariously above him. Running outside, he surveyed the damage to his beautiful brick house, but he was one of the lucky ones. Other than losing several chimney bricks that had loosened and fallen on the ground, it looked to be sound.

Winslow heard sounds of panic from the small animal shed next to his house. His horse neighed and kicked the doors of the stall trying to escape. Winslow was able to calm the beast and walk it out into the street. When he mounted the horse and trotted slowly down the road, he was aghast at what he saw.

Many of the houses on his street were reduced to rubble. Brick chimneys had been tossed down onto the dirt road below. Several small fires had started. A neighbor and his wife and two children crawled out from under their cart, safe from danger but cut and bleeding profusely.

The road was eerily quiet and empty, save a neighbor gingerly directing his horse around the destruction. He nodded to Winslow as they passed. Winslow asked solemnly, "Anyone missing?" The first man shook his head. "My family is safe, but very fearful."

Winslow nodded, "No one was injured in my home but how could we have known this would happen? How could we have better prepared?"

*

The following week, on November 24, 1755, Winslow walked out of the military headquarters in Bostontown. A paperboy called out the latest headlines, "Read all about the quake. Buy the *Boston Evening-Post*."

Winslow queried the boy. "What does it say?"

The young man shook his head. "Can't read meself, sir. How about ye buy a paper and see fer yerself?"

Winslow handed the boy a coin and tore into the paper. He started reading it aloud. "Last Tuesday morning, we were surprised with the most violent shock of an earthquake that ever was felt in these parts of the world, since the arrival of the English. There was a rumbling noise like low thunder, immediately followed by such a violent shaking of the earth and buildings, as threw every one into the greatest amazement, expecting every moment to be buried in the ruins of their houses."

Soon, Winslow's thundering voice drew a crowd of onlookers and curious gawkers who hung on his every word. He continued, "This violent tremor continued for about the space of one minute, though some say two. During said time, the tops of a great number of chimneys were thrown down, and the roofs onto which they fell caved in."

"Much damage has also been sustained by the destruction of glass, china, earthen ware and the like, which was shook from shelves, and broke. And some vessels in the bay under sail, though 'twas very calm, were so agitated, that the men could not keep their legs; and 'twas the same with the vessels in our harbor."

The crowd had grown to fill the street surrounding Winslow. He relished the moment and continued in a booming voice. "I would recommend to inhabitants, that they would employ proper persons to sweep and examine their chimneys. Though they appear to be no ways damaged, they have actually received a great deal. A little inspection may be a means of preventing their fall by high wind and of many houses from being consumed by fire."

With that, Winslow folded the paper and waved at the crowd. "That is the gist of it, my good fellows. I must be on my way. Good day to all."

The paperboy eagerly offered his papers to the townsfolk, but there were no takers. Soon he was alone again, hawking his papers. "Buy a paper. Read all about the fantastical earthquake."

As Winslow galloped toward his comfortable home with his ingratiating wife, the boy's shouts faded and completely disappeared. In Grand Pré he had dreamed of doing nothing but reading his Bible each day and eating onion pies. He would never have imagined he would become disillusioned with his quiet life and answer the call from William Shirley to gather another provincial army. Nor that he would suffer bitter defeats against the French, retire from the military and delve into politics in the Marshfield legislature instead.

But today Winslow, had no knowledge of his future. He rode contentedly towards his home.

*

While the chaos caused by the earthquake ensued on terra firma in Bostontown and Grand Pré, the situation at sea was one of utter fear. No captain or sailor had ever experienced an earthquake or its aftershocks at sea, or on land for that matter.

The ships heading out of Grand Pré carrying the Acadians were undermanned, prompting the captains to release the Acadians from their holds so they could work on deck. The exiled men helped with the ropes, assisted with the sails, or formed bucket brigades to empty the deck of the constant streams of water.

When the waves had subsided to normal levels, the crew of one ship observed that the fish swam up to the surface of the water in great schools. The sailors clapped and shouted at their good fortune. Forgetting about the Acadians on deck, they jubilantly dipped their nets into the waves and caught the fresh fish.

One of the Acadian men seized the opportunity while the crew members were preoccupied. Francis Hébert, the shipbuilder who had been beaten for assisting a group of Acadians to escape their transport, took control of the ship. He and his friends jumped the sailors and the captain and cast them off in the rowboats. With his mastery of sailing, Francis taught the other men to set the sails and use the compass and sextant while he read the captain's maps.

He asked the men and boys on board, "We cannot sail back to Grand Pré for the English shall surely capture us again. Shall we sail to Santo Domingo or head for the Gulf waters and reach the Louisiana Territory?"

The Acadians gave the resounding cheer, "Louisiana!"

Francis laughed and responded, "To the port of New Orleans we go," as he set a southerly course for that destination.

*

The vessel carrying Gabriel, Marc and the other Acadian militia prisoners headed toward London on the Atlantic Ocean. After the earthquakes, Gabriel's ship had been hit with waves from every direction. Captain Burgess held on to the wheel for dear life. He knew he needed all hands up on deck in the tempestuous seas, and he decided to bring the Acadians up to assist the crew.

But when Turnbull explained what a rebel Gabriel was and how he had formed a secret militia against the English, Burgess was persuaded to keep the Acadians below deck. He could not risk Gabriel leading the other Acadians to pirate the ship and cast captain and crew onto the seas or, worse, put them down below in the holds.

Gabriel was not at all certain he would walk out alive from his destination, the Westminster Gatehouse prison. He was not sure how he would find Evangeline. But he knew he wanted to live only for her. As Gabriel was confined in the fetid hold, he believed his faith would strengthen him. He prayed quietly, "Lord, please protect my Evangeline and keep her safe. I know with Your guidance we shall meet again, as we pledged, in the French territory of New Orleans."

His prayer was interrupted by his fellow militiaman Marc who asked, "How do you propose to get out of the Gatehouse? I overheard some of the Captain's men say it is impossible to escape."

Gabriel shook his head. "How would they know? Have they ever been inside? I refuse to give up. No one can keep me from finding Evangeline. No one. I hope you feel the same about Jeanne. We shall find them and make them our wives."

Marc said dubiously, "I wish I had your fortitude. I want to believe that I can find her. I just cannot see past the death sentence Turnbull threatened."

"You know as well as I do that Turnbull was demoted when he was assigned to this ship. He thought he would supervise the exile of our Acadian women and children. He is angry about it and has to taunt us to make himself feel better. In his viewpoint, he was given nearly as bad a punishment as we were. We must try to avoid him when we are on deck and just enjoy the fresh air while we can."

Marc added, "I hope Winslow will be kinder to them than he was to us."

Gabriel spoke softly, "We must have faith, though I fear he will grant them no kindnesses, so determined is he to remove everyone. For all of his Bible reading, he has shown no mercy on his fellow man."

CHAPTER 53
Waiting

Grand Pré

Sunday morning dawned in Grand Pré like all the previous Sundays since the day the men and boys had been exiled. Snow flurries sprinkled the houses and dirt paths. The women, left defenseless without weapons and hungry without food, rose early to root around in the snow for berries and loose branches for the hearth. At least the fire would warm the family members during the day after huddling together all night.

With her two soldiers always at her side, Christine was unable to carry out her plan to escape into the forest. And she intentionally avoided any overt discussion of escaping with Béatrice when they passed each other on the street as her two guards followed her closely.

Christine gave a knowing look of caution and said politely, "Béatrice, you look well today. How is your mother Anne?"

Béatrice nodded in understanding, replying equally politely, "We are both well, thank you. And yourself?"

Christine forced a smile. "I must find more herbs in the forest as my supply has nearly run out. Perhaps we shall meet there tomorrow?"

Béatrice understood the coded message and was about to respond. Suddenly, she was pushed rudely forward by the soldier. "I hope so," was all she could manage before disappearing from Christine's view as snow flurries swirled around them.

Christine picked up a handful of broken branches and headed back to the Consulate. The soldier followed closely behind. Christine did not have anything but hope that she could help Béatrice and Anne escape into the woods. As soon as she entered the building, the soldier followed and locked the door behind her.

"Captain Osgood wants to see yer on the morrow."

Christine shook her head. "What did I do? Why does he want to meet with me?"

The soldier shrugged. "I gots me orders, is all I know."

Christine managed to stay calm as she prepared a simple meal of potatoes with forest mushrooms. The two soldiers lapped up their bowls of food. Wesley settled in René's bed for his usual nap.

"Rollin will be watching yer, so no need to get any ideas."

Christine nodded as Rollin escorted her to her room. When he bolted her door from the hallway, Christine cried out through the door, "Is that really necessary? You know I have no place to go."

The soldier ignored her and took his position on the floor. Within minutes he was snoozing loudly.

Inside her room, Christine tried to open the door but the bolt was firmly in place. She opened her travel bag and threw in another potato that she had hidden in her apron after their meal. She took a long look around the room and rushed to the window. It pushed up easily enough, but the shutters were closed. When she tried to open them, she discovered they had been locked from the outside too. "What do they think I am going to do? Escape into the woods? Of course I shall. Just watch me."

*

Kitok had successfully led Evangeline, Running Bear and Sitting Fox into the mountain camp of his family. Kitok had walked off with his father Chief Mahtok to share the sad news about his friend and ally, Consul René Le Blanc, who had been exiled to an unknown destination.

While the men spoke privately in one part of their cave, Mahtok's wife Princess Singing Bird and the other women welcomed Evangeline into the Mi'Kmaq family as the daughter of their chief ally and the honorary daughter of the First Nation.

Evangeline never asked for any special treatment. Instead she willingly did the same work as the other women – washing, cleaning, cooking. But her skill in making the red river paste that she had learned from White Bird was one of the talents most valued by the tribe as it healed wounds and stopped bleeding, which occurred often to the braves on their hunting trips.

Every day at dawn, Evangeline rose and stoked the fire in the cave. She looked at the Mi'Kmaqs sleeping under their bearskins and she wrapped hers tightly around her. Sitting by the fire, she and White Bird ground up more ingredients for healing creams and poultices. Evangeline wanted to have a sufficient amount of white paste for the daily hunting parties. The job took nearly all day as Evangeline diligently worked with White Bird.

In the large cave, other Mi'Kmaq women began to awaken and prepare the first meal of the day. Soon, the smell of hot flatbread and sizzling lamb from the last kill woke up the late sleepers in the cave. Chief Mahtok and

Princess Singing Bird took the places of honor and were served before anyone else.

Kitok and his braves entered from their cavern in the back of the main room. They bowed to Mahtok and Singing Bird, then squatted by the fire, eating quickly. When they stood, they motioned to Evangeline. Under the critical gaze of White Bird, Evangeline applied the paste to their arms, chest and legs before they wrapped themselves in bearskin fur capes and put on their heavy deerskin gloves. Gathering their weapons by the door, they exited the cave.

Each day, Kitok led the braves on daily hunting treks into the mountains. Since the day Evangeline had arrived, the hunting party had brought back several deer and an elk. Winter food was scarce because many mountain beasts climbed higher at this time of year. Bear, mountain goats, coyotes, mountain lions and wolves were scarcely seen, but the Mi'Kmaq usually saw elk, bighorn sheep and deer. Yet Kitok and his braves always seemed to bring home a big kill, to the delight of all the Mi'Kmaqs.

Evangeline smiled, remembering the tall hunting tales shared around the fire the night before by the old-timers in the tribe. But while they joked and ribbed each other, the members of the First Nation hoped their braves would bring back a fine kill tonight. Everyone's mouth watered at the thought of the feast the women would prepare of a big animal.

At dusk, Kitok pushed through the blanket covering the cave's entrance, blowing on his hands to warm them. He was followed by Running Bear, Sitting Fox and four other braves. They carried two slain deer tied by their hooves to fresh-hewn logs.

Seeing the freshly-killed animals, the women let out whoops of joy. They knew the animals would provide food, boots, blankets, candles and oil for the lanterns that hung on the walls of the cave. The elders and the children joined in the cheering, knowing there would be a great feast.

And what a feast it was on the night once a year when unmarried braves and unmarried girls chose their mates. Tonight, the single braves, dressed in their finest furs and necklaces, danced themselves into a frenzy in the firelight, showing off their strength and physical prowess with jumps, leaps, tumbles and flips. The unmarried girls watched them carefully. Each giggled to their friends and hoped to catch the eye of the man who attracted her.

As for White Bird, after she ate a supper that could only have satisfied a bird, she crept back to her cave alone. No one paid attention to the old woman as they continued to celebrate.

Evangeline was enthralled with the dances and the courtship rituals. Out of the corner of her eye, she watched the old medicine woman leave the circle.

After a respectable period of time, Evangeline went into White Bird's habitat. She found the Mi'Kmaq woman, pale as the snow, lying motionless on her bed of skins and furs.

Evangeline rushed to her side, grabbed her hand and checked to see if she was still alive. The woman was barely breathing and flush with fever. White Bird grabbed her arm slowly and said, "Do not tell them until after I am gone. Our young girls must find their husbands on this night. I do not want anything to hinder them from doing so."

Evangeline pulled her pouch of herbs from her skirt and placed some of them on the woman's forehead. Evangeline knew they would reduce the fever and said softly, "What can I do for you, White Bird? You have been a true mother to me all this time. Please, let me help you."

White Bird weakly pushed the herbs off her face and shook her head. "I must die this way. Take this, then leave me."

White Bird pulled a beaded necklace from around her neck and held it out. Evangeline ruefully accepted it and put it on. Then White Bird winced, clearly in pain and shut her eyes.

Evangeline was in a quandary. Should she stay? Was it proper for her to go while White Bird was clearly on her deathbed? Distraught but filled with emotions for White Bird, Evangeline was resolved to stay.

Sounds of the dancing and celebration continued for hours until all those of marriageable age had settled on a partner. Evangeline remained at the old woman's side throughout the night. When she thought White Bird was asleep, Evangeline re-applied the herbs but the medicine woman opened one eye and tossed them away.

As the noise and songs from the Mi'Kmaqs in the other cave began to die, Evangeline's eyelids grew heavier. She dozed off. When her head dropped to her chin, she woke her quickly and checked on White Bird. The old medicine woman had gone to higher ground.

Evangeline respectfully covered her long-time mentor in bearskins and animal furs and held her hand until daybreak. With a heavy heart, she slipped out of the cave to deliver the distressing news.

The medicine woman's death was not entirely unexpected by the Mi'Kmaqs, but, nonetheless, the entire tribe went into mourning. They gave White Bird a majestic burial ceremony including a funeral pyre. However, ever wary of English armies finding their camp, the Mi'Kmaqs set the fire in an empty cave. After the flames burned out, Chief Mahtok tossed her ashes into the wind from the edge of the mountaintop.

When the Chief declared the mourning period had ended, Evangeline wrapped herself in her bearskin rug and requested to meet with Chief Mahtok and Singing Bird. Evangeline had devised a solution to an ongoing problem the tribe experienced every year. The Chief accepted the proposal, and Evangeline put her plan into action.

She invited the young Mi'Kmaq women who had not been chosen during the mating selection to join her in meeting the unmarried Acadian men who lived down the trail. They had escaped their imprisonment in St. Charles Church through the tunnel and had made their way up the mountain. Mi'Kmaq hunting parties had discovered them lost in the mountains and had offered them shelter. Chief Mahtok had declared them friends, which meant they could live in the vicinity of the Mi'Kmaqs, but not in the same encampment. Also, the men were not invited to be a part of the First Nation daily activities and culture.

Evangeline chatted and shared memories of Grand Pré with the Acadian men in their cave. They had been members of Gabriel's militia but had not been identified and had luckily escaped being shipped to the Gatehouse prison. They reminisced about Gabriel, which brought a tear to Evangeline's eye. She changed the subject and introduced the men to the young Mi'Kmaq women. They whispered among themselves about how handsome the men were. The men smiled at the girls, and soon Evangeline noticed sparks of interest on both sides.

When one of the men chose a young woman to court, Evangeline tutored him in the Mi'Kmaq courtship ritual necessary to gain acceptance by the parents as partners for their daughters. In the weeks that followed, the Acadians received the parents' blessings and married the girls they had courted.

When the weddings took place, Chief Mahtok and Princess Singing Rain welcomed the grooms into the family. At the marriage ceremonies, Evangeline felt elated for the couples. But she also grieved because she could not share such joy with Gabriel, whom the Mi'Kmaqs knew and greatly respected.

From then on, the married Acadians were accepted as members of the tribe. They dressed and lived like Mi'Kmaqs, learned to speak the language fluently and integrated themselves into the Mi'Kmaq world. Some of the Acadians joined Kitok's hunting parties. Others served as lookouts for British troops who continually searched for runaway Acadians.

Not long thereafter, the new husbands received word that Acadian refugees who had escaped the Exile had built a thriving community on Île Royale. The Acadian men became restless and realized their future, and that of their native brides, would lie with other Acadians. Everyone knew that one day soon they would leave the Mi'Kmaq camp for the French island.

Thus, no one was surprised when they left, as their stoic wives accepted their fate and the men anticipated their new life with their countrymen.

*

At dawn, Christine was woken by a loud pounding on her door. Wesley, one of the English soldiers assigned to her home called out, "Get yerself up, missy. Cap'n is waiting on youse."

Christine rubbed her eyes and realized it was dark. She had slept all afternoon. She muttered, "Captain? What? Oh, yes, the meeting with Captain Osgood."

She climbed out of bed, straightened her dress and peered into the mirror. Her hair was a fright. She took out the pins, brushed her long locks and rearranged her. The beating on the door started again.

"Please do not pound on the door. I am coming."

Before she knew it, Wesley had opened the door and grabbed Christine's arm. "Youse coming with me, missy. No more waiting, or Cap'n will have meself's hide."

Christine pushed his hand away. "No need. I am ready to go."

She grabbed her warm cape from the hook and swiftly descended the stairs, followed closely by both soldiers. Wesley and Rollin marched her along the main street past shuttered houses and empty shops, past the church and around the corner to the rectory where Père Rivière had lived before John Winslow occupied it. She had overheard Wesley and Rollin talking about building him a new house in the fort, but she realized the Captain must have moved into the rectory instead.

As Wesley knocked on the door, a gruff voice called out, "Enter." Christine shivered. She sensed a foreboding presence that chilled her to the bone. She instantly felt that Osgood was a man not to be trusted before she even met him.

Rollin opened the door and pushed Christine through it. She pulled her cloak tightly around her and looked around the room. It looked the same as when Winslow was there. Sparse furnishings, a thick rug, a desk, large wooden chairs and a blazing fire in the main room. She glanced over at the adjoining room and saw the large rough-hewn dining table laden with plates of food and bottles of wine.

At the other end of the room was the doorway to the bedroom. She remembered how she had spiked Winslow's wine with a special forest herb that put him to sleep immediately. She looked at the stack of papers on Osgood's desk and wondered if she would be able to duplicate her plan.

Osgood's eyes followed hers and he smirked. "No, you shan't get your eyes on my private papers, woman. That is not why I called you here." He pointed to the fire. "Sit here and warm yourself."

Christine turned red, realizing Osgood knew what she had wanted to do. He was dressed in full British uniform. The buttons on his red jacket were polished, as were his black leather boots. She nodded and took a chair next to the fire.

"Thank you," she said as she warmed her hands over the hearth, appreciating the heat.

Osgood filled two glasses of wine from an expensive crystal decanter. He handed her one. "Drink up, missy. You will need it with what I am about to tell you."

Christine had never touched wine in the morning but she gladly gulped the drink with a stronger sense of foreboding. "Just why have you brought me here, Captain?"

Osgood waved her off as he sipped the wine appreciatively. "Sipping a fine wine brings out the taste of it. Slowly. No need to rush. You shall not go anywhere unless I order it."

Christine was raised to be polite in polite company, but these were unusual circumstances. She wanted to scream and relieve her anxiety. Instead, she restrained herself to ask, "Pardon me, but please tell me what you have to say. I would like to return home. I must try to find some food to cook for my military escorts."

Osgood stared at her. He understood why Winslow had been attracted to her, although he had enjoyed a big belly laugh when Winslow recounted how she had put a sleeping potion in his wine. Osgood had been astounded that an Acadian wench had the means to drug an officer to sleep while she snooped through his official papers. After that, Osgood had lost respect for Winslow and had been relieved when the former commanding officer sailed back to Massachusetts.

Osgood placed his glass on the table. "Very well. If you insist, I shall tell you now."

Christine put down her glass and leaned toward Osgood. She did not want to miss a word.

Outside the rectory, Christine's two guards chatted. Wesley said, "What is he gonna do with the wench?"

Rollin responded, "Methinks there is only one thing the heathen is good fer. Don't know why he would think about nothing else."

Wesley nodded, his eyes wide. "Why did Cap'n order us to leave the hussies alone?"

Rollin agreed. "They deserve it. Hope we get to have our way with them soon."

"Yeah, before they're gone. 'Twould be a shame to miss out on it."

The door opened and Christine stomped out into the rectory yard, now covered with snow. She pulled the hood of her cloak over her head, avoided the soldiers' gaze and trudged forward. The two soldiers saluted Osgood then fell in behind Christine.

Christine's tears flowed like pearls down her cheeks. She shook her head, praying that what she heard was true. A smiling Osgood watched her leave and shook his head with glee, "Winslow was right. These Acadians are as naïve as they are heathen. Tell them what they want to hear and they shall be docile as lambs."

Christine practically ran to the Consulate, and rushed inside well before the two soldiers arrived. She went straight to her room, not bothering to knock the snow off her boots or to close the door. She knew the soldiers would bolt it shut behind her.

In her room, she locked the door on her side and fell to her knees beside her bed. She bent her head and clasped her hands in prayer.

"Dear God, I pray that Captain Osgood's words were true. If so, my heart is leaping for joy at the thought that we shall be reunited soon with our men. Halleluiah! We are going to their destinations. I pray for your protection during our exile."

Christine fell asleep and woke to the shouts of Wesley and Rollin and more pounding on her bedroom door. She wiped her eyes and piled on layers of warm clothing before she grabbed her packed bag. When she unlocked the door on her side, the two guards roughly grabbed her and nearly pushed her down the hall and down the stairs.

Rollin grabbed her arm and pulled her toward the church. Wesley nodded to the guards at the front door who removed the plank barring the door and opened it. Christine was pushed into the dark building where she saw groups of women and children huddled together or kneeling in prayer. Occasionally an elderly woman raised her eyes up to hers and nodded sadly. Christine waited until the heavy doors were locked again before standing and addressing the other Acadians.

"Friends, we must have faith that we shall soon be with our family. Do not despair."

Jeanne stood up and asked, "How do you know that shall happen? What have they told us yet that is true?"

Other women nodded their heads, murmuring in agreement with her.

Béatrice rushed from a pew and ran up to Christine. "I tried to go into the woods last night but was caught. I poured an entire bottle of wine for the two soldiers, but this time I mixed your special herbs in their wine. You were right. They fell right asleep. I dressed mother and we quietly crept out. I thought we were going to make it but at the edge of town a guard spotted us. Alas, he marched us back home. We were spared a beating by the soldiers assigned to us only because they were too drunk to stand."

Christine nodded, "I had hoped we could slip away, but this is our destiny now. Let us light some candles and lead the others in prayer."

Béatrice nodded and they searched for the candles on the altar. They lit them and spread them on the windowsills throughout the church. The soft glow created such calm that even distressed children stopped crying.

Christine walked to the center aisle to instill hope in her friends. "The Captain told me we are to be sent to the same destinations as our men."

The women shouted in thanks, but Christine held up her hands. "But I do not believe a word of it. I want to, but I do not. I believe they want us to be submissive and meek, believing their lies as they take us to the ships. You know what is about to befall us. We shall be separated and shall not be sent to the same ports as our loved ones. But we must stay strong and have faith. We shall help each other. We shall find the way to our family members. We shall survive, And we shall once again flourish in new homes."

Old Yvonne Poché cried out, "But how will I ever find Monsieur Poché? Where has he gone?"

Béatrice rushed over to her and held her hand. "We shall find him together. I will help you."

Other Acadian women nodded as they looked to Christine for guidance and strength. Christine knew she must not allow doubt to creep into her voice as she began a prayer, "Our Father," she said in a strong voice that hid her pain.

The other women joined in. "Who art in heaven...."

The voices of Béatrice Gaudet, Yvonne Poché, Jeanne Lambert, her mother Lorraine Lambert, Henriette de la Tour Landry, and many others joined together in prayer with a shared hope that they would, indeed, find their families at the end of their voyage.

How could Christine have known that Captain Osgood had lied to her? She had prayed the night before and as she slept, she had a dream of Osgood as a lion wearing a woolly lambskin over his mane. That was enough of a warning for her. Yet, even armed with the truth, what could she do? She knew about the tunnel but knew it had been filled in to prevent additional runaways from using it. She was locked in the church and knew she would not be able to escape. So she tried to help others accept their fate.

*

The soldiers kept the women and children locked in the church for the rest of that day and night, and it was not until the next morning that the doors were opened. More troops abruptly marched into the church and Captain Osgood stepped out onto the altar from the backdoor entrance into the rectory where he was living.

He addressed the Acadians in a stern voice, "Like your men before you, all of your possessions save what you can carry with you, are property of our good King George. Gather what you can and fall into a line. You shall be escorted down to the beach until the rowboats arrive. Then you shall be put on ships and sail to the ports that have been chosen for you."

At that, Madame Poché stood up and cried out, "Where is my husband? Am I to meet him? Where was he sent?"

Béatrice joined her, "Yes, where are our families? How do you know which towns they are living in now?"

Jeanne Lambert rose and spoke up. "Captain, my fiancé Marc de la Tour Landry sailed on a vessel heading for London – Westminster Gatehouse. Which of your ships will take me to him?"

Captain Osgood ignored all of them. He signaled Captain Fossett, who fired his musket up into the ceiling of the church. "Silence," roared Osgood.

Children whimpered with fear as their mothers held them tightly with love and reassurance. Christine immediately fell back into her seat and clutched her most prized possession, a gold cross encrusted with pearls, rubies and other precious stones, hanging around her neck. Her eyes clouded remembering the gift from René's wife Lady Eugenie on her deathbed. Eugenie had recounted how her father had given her the cross belonging to her mother when she was six years old, just after her mother's death. Christine heard Eugenie's voice as clear as day. "Care for my husband and my daughter as you did for me. Please do not leave them and return to France. They need you." In the intervening years in the French Consulate of Grand Pré, Christine had grown from a young midwife into much more. She had been a healer, a cook, a housekeeper, a teacher, and a substitute mother for Evangeline. But she never anticipated she would fall completely in love with René, become his fiancée, and then be heartlessly torn apart.

Her thoughts were brutally interrupted by Osgood, who admonished the Acadians, "You have a choice to make. Leave alive now or stay and perish. My troops will shortly burn this place to the ground, with or without you in it. I trust I shall see you at the boats soon enough." He turned on his heels and returned to his warm rooms in the rectory through the door at the back of the altar.

*

The soldiers forced the Acadians to trudge through the streets to the beach. Fortunately, the weather was crisp and cold, but not windy or snowing. Those who could stand the weight of a travel bag carried it. Some aided the elderly with their packages, so they could bring their few possessions with them. Many had filled bags with their family Bible and extra woolen clothes. Some wrapped themselves in blankets. Others grabbed what little food they could find.

The ragtag Acadians were herded into a semblance of a line and marched out of town. They passed the fort which had been completely rebuilt, then found themselves descending the hill through the beautiful trees towards the beach and the ships that would remove them forever.

The English troops escorted rows of Acadian women, many with babies in their arms down the hill. Children clutched their mothers' skirts. Dogs followed them and barked at snow flurries beginning to fall. The elderly walked very slowly and British soldiers barked threats to whip them if they did not move faster. Yet that was not enough to make them pick up their pace. Many fell to the ground, or sat on fallen stumps in the woods, then remained there stone-faced as snow fell onto them.

As Christine and Béatrice plodded through the trees, they grabbed berries, roots and edible plants along the way and stuffed them into their cloaks. Christine looked around at the other Acadians, but most had resigned themselves to accept their fate and slogged down to the beach. Jeanne was nowhere to be seen but Christine knew she must be in the crowd somewhere. She shuddered to think of what would happen to her if she had refused to leave the church or had tried to hide in the woods. She would never see her friend again.

Christine said a quick prayer, "Father, watch over all our friends and our families, and help us in our hour of need. Amen."

Captain Fossett galloped through the woods down to the beach where the first of the Acadian women had arrived. Fossett peered through his telescoping glass at the horizon. He saw no sailboats entering the Bay. Rather, he saw raging whitecaps all along the horizon.

On the beach, the Acadians huddled for warmth as the snow continued to fall. Christine and Jeanne joined Béatrice and Anne at one end of the beach. They squinted at the water but no ships came into view.

Christine uttered a sigh. "I thought the boats would be here."

Jeanne nodded. "I do hope they come soon."

Béatrice voiced the thought on everyone's mind. "How do they expect us to stay here very long? Winter is here."

Christine nodded. "I managed to pack some food and wine. But I don't have enough for more than a few people. And then, for only a day or two."

Jeanne opened her bag, revealing a bottle of wine and a loaf of bread. "As did I. But there are so many of us."

The three women shivered as they turned around. Small groups of women sat together on the beach. As they huddled, the clutched their children to their bosoms. Some of the younger ones slept beneath their mothers' cloaks.

Christine felt the pain and fear on the faces of her Acadian friends and neighbors. She said, "We must find wood to make fires. Those women cannot leave their children alone, but if they sit there too long, they will all freeze to death."

Béatrice looked around. The soldiers stood in a line and stared at them. "Maybe that is their plan. There never planned to board us onto ships at all. They want us to die here."

Jeanne shook her head quickly. "Even the British would not be that cruel. I agree. I think we should go now."

Christine nodded. "They will not stop us from trying to stay warm."

Béatrice said, "Not if we each go in a different direction."

The three women quickly separated and scurried along the beach. Each kept one eye on the soldiers while heading for the woods. For the moment, the troops were content to joke among themselves, occasionally casting an eye toward the Acadians. Christine managed to grab an armful of fallen branches before being chased back to the beach by a soldier.

Jeanne scuttled to the edge of the beach near the high cliffs. She meandered around the cove and saw the cave where Evangeline had been revived by Kitok and his Mi'Kmaq braves. Slipping into the cave, she found the remnants of the fire. She stuffed small logs and branches into the apron of her overskirt. She exited and moved along the beach, gathering up more bark and pieces of wood. It wasn't long, however, until she heard a soldier calling out to her from down the beach.

"Youse there. Back to the beach. Do not make me chase after ye, missy."

Jeanne kept picking up broken branches and driftwood until she saw the soldier run toward her. Then she made her way as quickly as she could back to the center of the beach. She dropped the load of wood near a large group of Acadian women and children, and started a fire. Soon the wood was ablaze. The soldier who had been following Jeanne lost interest in her once he realized she was not trying to escape.

Jeanne opened her bottle of wine and handed it to the woman nearest to her, who took a big swig, then handed it to the next Acadian. When they had all taken a chug of wine, the bottle was returned to Jeanne, who refused it and handed it back to the first woman. The woman gratefully accepted it and the bottle made the circle again.

Osgood galloped up on the beach and ordered a handful of troops, "Time to bring the old-timers down to the beach. They have stayed there long enough. If they refuse to move, make it their permanent resting place."

The soldiers checked every Acadian in the woods. Most were already dead. Those who were barely alive died instantly when the troops finished them off.

Along the beach, a series of fires glowed brightly. Christine, Jeanne and Béatrice held their outstretched arms over the fire in front of them. Anne drooled silently, her head in Béatrice's lap. Occasionally Anne sat up and clapped at the flickering fire and the dancing embers, then she lay down and fell asleep.

Osgood nudged his horse over to Fossett, who expressed concern, "I thought the ships were to arrive today, Captain."

Osgood shrugged. "So I was told."

Fossett asked, "Should we march the heathens back up to their homes?"

Osgood shook his head. "Too much chaos. That would require more troops than we have. And I fear many would slip past the soldiers into the woods."

"I assure you our troops would keep the women and children organized. Most of the older Acadians have died. They were the stragglers. Without them, the others will be easy to keep in line all the way to town in a relatively short period."

Osgood stared at Fossett, "What did I just order?"

Fossett saluted. "Yes, Captain. They shall remain here until the ships come. I shall make preparations to stay here as long as it takes."

Osgood grunted and turned his horse to return up the hill.

Fossett called out. "Captain Osgood?"

Osgood turned impatiently. "What is it now?"

"Captain, what about feeding them? No doubt the children are hungry. And they have no wood to add to their small fires."

Osgood retorted, "That is no concern of mine. Do what you will. Send a report to me when you see the ships on the horizon. Do not bother me otherwise." Without waiting for a reply, Osgood kicked his stirrups and his horse bolted up through the woods.

Fossett watched until Osgood disappeared, then called his troops over to him. He divided them into groups and issued orders to each of them. To the first group, he commanded, "Form a brigade of soldiers here at the woods. Do not let any Acadians break through and escape. Anyone who fails this mission shall answer to me with twenty lashes." The soldiers nodded and stepped into formation, fixing their bayonets to their guns and standing in a line.

Fossett grunted his approval, then turned to the second group of soldiers. "Go to the fort and bring back food and drink. Enough for all the troops and the Acadians for several days. And bring pots that the women can use to cook over their fires. Distribute them to the women, no matter whose house you found them in."

As the men lumbered off into the woods, he ordered the third group of soldiers, "Dismantle the tent city and bring the largest ones here for the troops. I shall also need a tent for myself."

Two soldiers named Binner and Jasey were in this group and they grumbled to themselves. Binner turned to Jasey and asked, "Tents? What

Captain makes troops sleep in the snow in a tent with them warm houses just up the hill?"

Jasey agreed. "Methinks the discomfort shall be but a limited number of days. It would not do to suffer out here for weeks on end."

Binner nodded. "Just when me bones got used to that soft bed."

Jasey questioned him. "With or without an Acadian in it?"

Binner looked at him in horror. "They slept on the floor. Youse wouldn't sleep with a heathen?"

Jasey shrugged his shoulders and grinned slyly. Binner understood.

Fossett pointed to the fourth group, "Gather up firewood, branches and anything else that will burn. Be prepared for greater snows and cold." The men saluted and separated into small groups to search for firewood in the forest.

Fossett ordered the remaining troops, "Bury the dead bodies. Be respectful." The soldiers grumbled but left to do their duty, but not before they ripped wedding bands and gold chains with crosses from the dead, stuffing their uniform pockets with the jewelry.

At Fossett's insistence, the troops took cloaks, hats and bags from the bodies and tossed them into the empty carts, leaving them for the Acadians on the beach. Then they returned to the woods to bury the bodies, but not before a large wake of buzzards circled overhead.

The shivering Acadians were hesitant to disrespect the dead by using the clothes left in the carts. But Christine knew they had to protect themselves as best they could. She insisted, "We must pray for the souls of friends we lost, but I know they would not want us to freeze, especially the children. Distribute the clothes and any food you find."

Béatrice and Jeanne pushed the carts to the groups of women. Béatrice placed hats on the heads of the shivering women and children, while Jeanne handed out cloaks.

She encouraged them, "Do not lose your faith. We shall find our men again. Pray that the ships arrive tomorrow."

None of the Acadians refused the additional layer of clothing as the snow began to fall in earnest.

At the edge of the woods, soldiers set up tents and built blazing fires. Standing in a line in front of the newly-assembled tents, armed soldiers continued their watch.

The Acadians in turn watched the troops while huddling closer to each other in front of their waning fires. Every so often a woman reached into the nearby pile of branches and tossed a piece of wood onto the fire. The embers danced above the fire but even the children were not entranced by the sight.

Jeanne and Béatrice settled in front of their fire. Béatrice bundled up her mother Anne, who sat silently in the cold.

Christine plodded to the other end of the beach to the temporary tent Captain Fossett had set up. Guards crossed their muskets and blocked her entrance into the lean-to.

Undeterred, she called out. "Please, Captain! I must speak with you."

A voice from within the tent responded, "Let her pass."

The guards uncrossed their guns and stepped back. Christine slipped through the tent opening. Fossett sat at a small makeshift desk in front of a blazing fire. He offered no seat and looked up questioningly.

"Well? Are you here to thank me for the food?"

Christine was polite but direct. "Yes, Captain. For all the women and children, you have my greatest thanks. For the clothes and the firewood."

"So, what is it?"

"We would like permission to have a funeral service."

"What are you saying?" growled Fossett.

"May we say prayers at the gravesite for relatives and friends who died?"

Fossett shook his head. "Out of the question. It is a feeble excuse to escape."

Christine realized he saw through her ruse but acted innocently. "We simply wish to pay our respects."

Fossett waved his hand for her to leave. "I said no. In any case, you shall be exiled no matter what you do."

At the opening in the tent, Christine turned and asked, "When are the ships due to arrive? I expected them to be waiting for us."

He shrugged. "They cannot come too soon for me."

She added, "If the snow continues to fall this hard, you shall see many more deaths."

Fossett stood angrily and shook his fist at Christine. "Woman, I did more than any other officer would have done for you. You have food, winter clothing and fires because of me and my men. Apparently, that is not sufficient for you. Enough! Out of my sight. Guards!"

The two soldiers immediately entered the tent and saluted, their other hands holding their muskets.

"Captain, what can we do?" said the first. The second nodded.

Fossett pointed to Christine. "Escort her back to the beach. Do not let anyone else near this tent. On your life!"

They nodded and pushed Christine out of the tent. As they exited, several buzzards swooped by, as the tent was near the gravesite. Christine picked up some rocks and hurled them, chasing the birds away.

As night fell, the snow fell harder. All the troops except the night guards filled the tents. All was quiet on the beach, except for the occasional snap of firewood cracking. Christine, Béatrice and Jeanne moved swiftly throughout the groups of Acadians.

They set up small lean-to shelters near the fires by covering branches with several cloaks, then bundled the freezing women and children inside the makeshift tents. By morning, the Acadian lean-tos were covered in snow but the women and children, and even the elderly, were still alive.

The soldiers exited their tents and stretched. Soon the smells of their breakfast cooked over their open fires wafted over to the Acadians. As small children cried out in hunger, their mothers tried to comfort them with bits of hard bread from their small stock. Any baby wanting to suckle found no milk in her mother's breast.

Walking near the woods but always watching the guards, Christine and Béatrice quietly set out some small animal traps. They had made them from leftover branches tied with leaves and torn clothing. Christine whispered, "Let us hope we will catch some of those scurrying rats you said you saw."

Béatrice agreed. "At least they will help us feed the others."

Christine added, "Captain Fossett promised us more food but we cannot rely on him. British officers do not keep their word." The two women quickly made their way back to their lean-to, where Jeanne watched over a sleeping Anne.

Shortly thereafter, the soldiers finished their breakfast. Surprisingly, some collected the leftover food and bottles of grog and distributed them to the Acadian groups. The women snatched the food and divided it into small portions so that everyone had at least a bite to eat and a sip of grog.

Everyone knew that would be the only food they received that day, so they tried exceptionally hard to divide it into three small meals per person. But there was never enough, especially for starving children.

At the end of the day, pairs of soldiers tramped through the snow on the beach to check on each group of Acadians. The first time they did, children screamed and women begged for mercy, fearing they were about to be executed.

When Jasey and Binner approached Christine, she gathered the children behind her back, believing the soldiers were going to hurt them. "Stay away! What do you want?" Christine was defiant.

Binner tried to calm her, saying, "No need to be afeared, missy. Just checking for dead bodies. Got any in there with yer?"

Christine shook her head. "We are all alive. Hungry but alive. Did Captain Fossett give you more foodstuffs? We have many to feed."

Binner raised his hand, about to slap her. Christine dodged his movement. "Shut up, woman. Be thankful ye get anything at all. All of youse heathens deserves what ye get."

"When will the ships arrive and take us out of here?"

Binner shrugged, but Jasey answered, "No one knows fer sure. They keeps telling me tomorry, So, maybe tomorry it will be."

Binner nudged his fellow soldier. "Nothing to see here. Cap'n told us keep moving."

As they joined other groups of soldiers, they peered under the lean-tos. Occasionally, troops took out their muskets and knocked women's legs or torsos, checking for signs of life. The Acadians who moved after the soldiers hit them were left alone. Those who remained motionless were either already dead or soon would be from a bayonet thrust through the gut. A squad of soldiers followed the troops with a death wagon. The dead bodies were loaded onto the wagon and dumped in the grave in the woods.

This was to be the life of the Acadian women, children and remaining old folks for six long weeks, until the ships arrived in December. As snow fell and turned to ice, the Acadians became colder, hungrier and weaker. Many of the elderly simply died in their sleep.

Christine, Jeanne, and Béatrice continued to give hope and assistance to the other Acadians, who relied on them to survive. Christine and Béatrice devised a system where one served as a look-out or created a diversion with the soldiers while the other checked the traps they had hidden in the trees.

Occasionally, they found rats, squirrels and other small forest animals had been caught. With the animals, they were able to cook a gooey soup by cooking the critters in a broth of melted snow. By adding additional snow to the pot, they increased the amount of soup they had which fed more Acadians.

After several weeks, Christine and Béatrice were successful in supplementing the meager mush, bread and grog that the soldiers begrudgingly distributed to the women. But even with the occasional squirrel or rat cooked on the open fire, the Acadians barely had enough food to sustain them. Mothers that fed the largest portion of their share to their children became weak and sickly.

Christine collected herbs and plants when she was not being watched. Her know-how enabled her to make poultices to heal them of their illnesses or to give them a bit more strength, but some simply lost the will to live. She knew not how to save them from despair.

CHAPTER 54
Cornhandle

Bostontown

T he Governor of the Massachusetts Bay Colony was a powerful man, not just throughout the Colonies but in the halls of power in London as well. William Shirley was so well-connected to the controlling authorities that he was never questioned on the lucrative arrangement he had made with a notorious Bostontown auctioneer named Jonas Cornhandle.

Cornhandle, a squatty little man with beady eyes, was well-known as the premier slave trader in the province. He was the type of man who would sell his mother for a price, just as his cousin Timothy from Grand Pré would have, given the chance. Birds of a feather they were in the Cornhandle family.

But Jonas was smarter than his relative. He could devise a way to make money from any type of transaction. He ingratiated himself to the city fathers in Bostontown and soon became their indispensible middleman. When they needed to deliver a bribe for a favor, Jonas was the courier. When a certain official wanted to purchase a gift for his mistress without his wife learning of it, Cornhandle was the one who bought it for him.

He told a state assemblyman, who had need of buying trinkets for several women, "Naturally, I am happy to do that for you. For a fee, of course." He made the same speech hundreds of times until his coffers overflowed with his fees.

At first, Cornhandle's wife Prudence objected. "Just when we are gaining some social standing in the city and have a comfortable life, it appears that you have women all over town. The shopkeepers must think me a fool."

Cornhandle said nothing, but showed her his ledger of accounts. "Do you see this figure?" She glanced at it, then put on her spectacles. Her eyes nearly bugged out of her head at the number.

Cornhandle continued with more than a twinge of pride in his voice, "That is how much money we have made from my favors to important people, not only in Bostontown but also in the Colony. I even do work for the politicians now. Think of how many of them there are. We shall be rich!"

He handed her a stack of notes which she promptly spent in the finer shops in town. That was the end of her protests.

It was when Jonas decided to jump into the slave trade that his fortunes rose dramatically. He had imported laborers for the farms and plantations throughout the Colony, but he longed to expand his business. To do so, he knew he had to include the highest levels of government. Otherwise, a competitor could step in and take the business he had worked so many years to build.

Cornhandle spent a tidy sum for a private carriage to the Governor's house. Of course he could have walked, but he knew the servants would not have given him the slightest bit of respect. As with any wealthy family, servants gave visitors the once-over before the official even deigned to welcome them into his home.

When Cornhandle stepped out in his new set of finery and top hat, the doorman outside the Governor's house treated him as if he were a gentleman in Bostontown high society. Cornhandle tipped the valets, nodded to the pretty housemaids and hoped their internal system of communication would be his advantage when he finally sat in the lobby awaiting Shirley.

Within a short period of time, the entire house knew an important man had come to see the Governor on "very urgent business." Positive comments about Cornhandle flew up the servants' hierarchy until they reached the ear of Malcolm Sheepstiffel, chief assistant to the Governor.

When Sheepstiffel announced the important visitor to see the Governor, Shirley had no idea who Cornhandle was. But when he realized the shrewd businessman had cut through the red tape and managed to see him without an appointment, he had to meet the man for himself.

Cornhandle decided to be brief and to the point. "Your Honor, Governor, sir," as he was unfamiliar with the proper address for a man in Shirley's high position, "how would you like to make an unending stream of funds without doing any work?"

Shirley's face reddened and he stood with his fists clenched, "Sir, I accept no bribes from anyone." Of course, that was a bald-faced lie, since everyone knew that all high officials in the Colony took bribes right and left.

Cornhandle lowered his head in submission. "Not a bribe, Governor, not anything remotely looking like such a thing. I know you to be too honorable to accept a bribe and I, sir, am no fool."

Calmed by Cornhandle's sweet talk, the Governor retook his seat. "Why have you come to see me? Be quick about it. I am a busy man."

"Yes sir. I am a merchant and an auctioneer. But more than that, I am a trader, of all sorts of merchandise. I understand you have loaded ships with Acadians lately removed from that territory. And that some of those transports are on their way here. Imagine the sea of humans that will arrive and the reaction of the townspeople."

Shirley's interest was piqued. His information was good, maybe too good. How did he come to know this confidential military intelligence? If he could trust him, even slightly, it was possible he could do some business with the man after all.

"And how do you come by this information, presuming it is even correct?"

"Ah, your Governorship, my cousin Josiah Cornhandle had a successful shop in that Acadian town of Grand Pré. Sold to the English, and a lot of the hussies in Miss Hetty's pleasure palace. But the commander there told him to close his shop. He packed up but a vendor bought all his stock before he left and so that's how he came to live with us. That's my wife Prudence and meself. But don't you know it, he had caught himself that disease. Fisilus, I think was what the doctor called it."

"Do you mean syphilis?"

"That's it. Philisus. Yep. He up and died just like that. But before he did, he told me that officer at the fort, Winslow or some such name, told him they were shipping them heathens here to sell for slaves."

"Lieutenant-Colonel Winslow informed him that the Acadians were to be shipped out?"

"Something like that, sounds right."

"Anyway, suppose it is true. What do you propose?" asked Shirley.

"I shall take them Acadians off your hands and sell them as field hands and house help. And for your generosity in naming me your exclusive representative, I should bestow on you one-tenth of the profits. Not as a bribe, of course, but as a commission."

"So, we send shiploads of Acadians to you. In return, you agree to sell them all to owners of farms and plantations in my Colony. Is that correct?"

Greedy Cornhandle instantly acceded to the deal, "Absolutely, sir."

Shirley had another demand. "And you shall pay me one-fourth of the price you receive."

Cornhandle screeched aloud. "Sir! My costs shall be steep. I must house them, feed them, pay for water to bathe them. My profit is not even one-fourth of the total sales price. No, sir, it is not possible."

Shirley was not amused. "It is just as easy for me to send them to Philadelphia. I know a reasonable auction house there."

All of a sudden, Cornhandle was compliant. "Well, sir, let us not be hasty. What if I do you this favor and you assure me a continuing supply?"

"I knew you would see it my way. One-third of the price is my fee," Shirley held out his hand. Cornhandle was caught in his greed, but he shook his hand, "Agreed, Your Excellency, sir."

They both nodded and as Cornhandle left, each man was confident that the agreement would reap a considerable sum for him and that he had gotten the better part of the deal.

Naturally, Cornhandle was always ready to make his coin off the sales and please his customers. But before the first ships arrived, Shirley's men had bribed city fathers in Bostontown to pass laws against the Acadians. They made it illegal to practice the Catholic religion and to receive payment for work. That meant that any Acadian men who were not strong enough, or women who were not attractive enough, to be sold into slavery could work only in exchange for food, clothing and shelter.

Within days of making the deal, Shirley advised Cornhandle of the arrival of the first vessel from Grand Pré. It was November, 1755 and the transport was filled to the brim with Acadian men and boys.

Waiting at the harbor with bated breath, Jonas Cornhandle sat in the passenger seat of a horse-drawn cart designed like a cage, with wooden slats and a locked door. The driver tried to calm the horses which neighed and snorted impatiently. They knew this route would lead them back to a warm barn stall filled with fresh hay, and perhaps even an apple or two if their master was feeling generous.

Cornhandle muttered to himself, alternating between congratulating himself on his political connections and berating himself for not being able to buy a monopoly on the Acadian exiles.

"When will they empty that ship? My coffers are running low. Missus Cornhandle buys more silks and handmade shoes and jeweled necklaces than any woman I have ever seen, counting even the hussies in Madam Taylor's brothel. I must charge a pretty penny for every one of them Acadians. Yes, they will fetch enough for me to satisfy the woman of my house and the ladies in their plantation mansions."

Within minutes, the ship captain waved to the gathering crowds on shore. He peered down at the crowd and then saw the man he was looking for. Cornhandle croaked with glee as he waved excitedly with both arms.

"Ahoy, Captain. Send me some good strapping lads and some dainty beauties. I am certain to have the buyers."

Soon, small groups of young Acadian boys were pushed off the ship first and made to walk the gangplank to the wharf. The older Acadians who had protected them on the journey were held back by the sailors and soldiers on board.

Cornhandle and a bow-legged assistant that everyone just called "Bow" rushed up to meet the boys. Feigning niceties and speaking an anglicized version of French enough so that the young boys could understand, the boys were quickly roped and chained together and led toward the cart.

One young boy saw the cage and tried to run, but he succeeded only in falling when the other boys stopped, and he tripped. Bow slapped the little boy on the head until he got up crying and rejoined the line. They climbed into the cage and Cornhandle locked it. Then he turned his attention back to the wharf.

The other Acadian males on board, the older boys and men, proceeded down the gangplank. When the boys in the cage saw their relatives and friends, they shouted to them.

"Uncle Bertrand, over here."

"Cousin Vincent, please get me out of here."

The crying boys were soon comforted when the Acadian men they knew were led by soldiers into the cart. The cage was soon filled with shivering and sickly Acadian boys and men who were cold and hungry from the journey. Cornhandle handed the head soldier a stack of coins.

"For this load. You did well, cousin Jack. Keep the best of the others for me and you shall receive double."

The soldier named Jack nodded and bit into one of the coins with one of his few remaining teeth. He grinned from ear to ear, satisfied that his profits from this endeavor would allow him to court the daughter of the blacksmith in town.

"Ye needn't ask me twice. Ye knows I aim to help ye, cousin."

Cornhandle grunted. "Where will you keep the others?"

Jack replied, "They is staying on the ship a few more days, but ye gots to get all of them by then er cap'n turns 'em loose on the dock. Them will be freemen and nobody can pay for 'em."

Cornhandle shook his cousin's hand and laughed. "I want to get them as much as you want the money for tossing them out to me. Meet me tomorrow and I shall pay for another load."

Jack grinned again as Cornhandle drove off the dock and turned the corner then headed out of town. The cart jostled and bounced along the muddy roads, tossing and turning the Acadians inside.

Within the hour, Cornhandle had stopped the cart in front of a large storage shed. He unlocked the cart and he and Bow dragged and pulled the Acadians out and into the shed. Within the building was another cage with bars. The men and boys were forced into it and the door to the small building was locked.

One Acadian man named Giroir pleaded with Cornhandle. "Please, sir, we have had no food or water for three days. The ship's crew said they had nary a bite or drop for us, though we did hear them singing, drunk from grog and no doubt with their bellies full."

Cornhandle looked at the motley group of Acadians. They were, indeed, filthy. In fact, they stank. And some of them looked too skinny to be of any use for farm work.

A young boy named Jean cried out, "I am hungry. And cold."

Then the other young boys took up the chant. "Hungry and cold. Hungry and cold."

Cornhandle was so exasperated that he cracked his whip. Sudden silence in the shed. No one wanted to be striped with such a weapon. Cornhandle feared they would not bring the prices he needed to refill his strongbox. He realized he had work to do on them to make them presentable on his auction block. Cornhandle turned to Bow and handed him some coins. "Buy them bread, cheese and grog. When you return, those that took a bath shall get the eats and drink."

Bow asked, "Young-uns gets a man's part of grog and cheese?"

Cornhandle thought a moment and replied, "Half a portion. Each man is to have a full part."

Bow nodded. "Yes sir, Mist' Cornhandle. I'll be on my way, sir."

When Bow left, Cornhandle addressed the Acadians. "Anyone attempting to escape will be shot on sight. No questions shall ever be asked about it. I know the Governor and the Army Commander-in-Chief." He wanted to impress his importance on the Acadians. They did not need to know it was the same person, reasoned Cornhandle.

Cornhandle pointed to several large barrels and basins filled with water. Lye soap was on the floor next to each container. Wooden shelves were filled with blankets and wool clothing in the same style and color, as a sort of uniform. Straw mattresses were stacked neatly in rows.

"Take a bath and change your clothes. Then set out the mattresses and take a blanket to stay warm. You shall be fed later."

The Acadians at this point were too tired, cold and hungry to argue. Instead they nodded or whispered, "Yes, sir." The thought of a bath, food, and clean clothes was such a blessing for some of the men who fell to their knees in thanks or broke down and cried.

Cornhandle observed the scraggly lot of Acadians. He was angry that Jack had not taken enough care with the prisoners to keep them in good health. But then again, his cousin was young and had no idea that wealth could be built on keeping men alive and fed during transport. Now Cornhandle knew the necessary protocols he must follow to build up his wealth.

He muttered under his breath, "Drat my Missus. She has to go on a shopping spree each time a new merchant ship arrives."

As he walked out of the shed, he turned back to see that the Acadians were following the directions of a "leader" who had already organized the mattress and blanket distribution. He had set up an assembly line where mattresses were handed off until they were laid at the farthest point from the water basins and filled in to the edge of the cage.

Closing the shed door, Cornhandle shook his head. "I do not understand the patience and forgiveness of these papists. They have been exiled, their goods were stolen, they were starved for days and they had no warm clothes or blankets to protect them from freezing. How do they survive in such a state? How do they not turn into a mob on a killing spree?"

When Bow arrived with the food, he was surprised to see every Acadians freshly scrubbed and clothed in the new uniform. Each man and boy waited patiently on a straw mattress awaiting the first food they had seen in three days.

Bow almost felt sorry for them. "They is just poor lambs that Mist' Cornhandle will lead up onto the auction block," he mused to himself. "Tis only just that they be rightful fed before that. Many's the one who will journey for days to their new home in the plantation fields." He decided then and there what to do.

Calling out to the older men, Bow said, "Ye men, come here for a full ration and bring another whole part to a child near ye. That way I know all of youse is fed."

Bow sidled up to the cage and began passing out bread and cheese through the wooden bars. Instead of greedily rushing up for the food, the Acadians held to their assembly line passing the food from the front to the back of neat rows of mattresses. The grog was dispersed in the same manner. It was all very orderly. Not the chaos that Bow expected.

Bow scratched his head, partly out of wonder and party because of the lice that had comfortably settled into his thick locks. He blurted out, "Let me know if any of youse did not get something to eat."

Dishing out fresh-baked bread and chunks of ripe cheese that cost Cornhandle a bit, Bow did not feel guilty in the slightest. After one look at the malnourished Acadians, Bow knew he did the right thing in buying extra foodstuffs. Cornhandle would thank him when he got a better price for healthy-looking menfolk.

When Bow passed cups through the bars and dipped his ladle into the grog, the men shouted with joy.

Giroir was the first to speak up. "Thank you, sir. We began to think there was no mercy in any Englishman but you, sir, have made up for the crew on the ships."

Pierre said, "Your kindness will be rewarded, sir," as he gratefully sipped his cup of grog and retreated back to his mattress. The other Acadian men and boys stood in line for their share, down to the youngest boys of nine. When Bow had filled every cup, he left the remaining grog next to the cage bars with the ladle. "Don't let none of this drink go to waste," he cried out.

Pine Gaudet yelled back, "We shall not forget you. Bless you, sir."

Bertrand walked up to the cage. For a moment Bow felt afraid, as the man stood head and shoulders above him. The giant held out his hand through the bars. Bow did not know what to do until the Acadian grabbed Bow's hand and shook it. With tears in his eyes, Bertrand said, "You have my eternal gratitude, for me and the boy, here. My nephew."

Bow shook his head. "No thanks due, but youse are going to be put on the block tomorrow."

The Acadian was aghast. "What block? For what reason?"

Bow quietly replied, "Youse is Mist' Cornhandle's property. He sells slaves to the farms and plantations in the region. Slave sales is a big business for me boss-man. Big."

The Acadians looked at each other. Slaves? Bertrand reminded them, "Consul Le Blanc said they sent Père Rivière here and that they sold men into work." The adults nodded, dreading what future would hold.

*

The next morning at dawn, Cornhandle and Bow drove to the dock. Cornhandle reviewed the improvements made by his construction laborers to a large elevated wooden stage. They had repainted the stairs and hung a banner reading, "AUCTION TODAY."

Cornhandle whistled as he drove the cart around the harbor and through the town. He called out, "Fresh off the boat from Nova Scotia. Strong men and boys on the auction block at the port. Take your pick in one hour."

He wanted as many people as possible to see the merchandise. People stopped on the brick sidewalks to gawk at the Acadians. Shoppers peered through shop windows or walked out of stores onto the sidewalks to stare at the strangers in the cart as it drove by.

Cornhandle repeated his refrain. "Fresh off the boat. Acadian workers for sale. Auction is in one hour at the port."

CHAPTER 55

Ships

Grand Pré

D awn broke early as the sun peeked through the grey mist. A line of armed soldiers stood outside the tents at the edge of the woods. Everything as far as the eye could see was covered with inches of snow, from the cliffs to the trees to the soldiers' tents to the beach dotted with lean-tos filled with huddled Acadians.

Strong Acadian women like Christine were forbidden from seeing the Captain again. Without someone able to convince the Captain of better conditions, more food and proper shelter, the weakened Acadians became even more sickly. As a result, many died. The death cart was nearly full every few days as the soldiers verified which French Acadian neutrals were alive and which were gone.

Captain Fossett made note of the deaths and revised his estimate of the amount of ships needed to exile all of the Acadians from Grand Pré. After his calculations, Fossett realized he could exile them on far fewer ships than originally planned.

Fossett recalled that Captain Osgood had warned, "Apthorp & Hancock shall send only a limited number of animal cargo ships retrofitted to fit triple the usual number of bodies on board. Still, Lieutenant-Colonel Winslow grossly underestimated the population to be exiled. With a smaller number of vessels, you shall be capable only of loading a portion of the prisoners. You shall then guard those who remain to be exiled until they are able to drop off their cargo and return. This could take months to sail even to Bostontown and back."

Fossett remembered his dismay at the thought of staying in the frozen wilderness away from his beloved Bostontown. He had dutifully responded, "Captain, I am here to execute your orders."

Fossett shook his head as if to rid his mind of thoughts of that day so many weeks ago. Today, he was ecstatic. There was no need to stay longer after he emptied the beaches of Acadians onto the boats. Fossett checked his calculations to make certain he was right. He had to squeeze several thousand onto a few boats, which he was confident he could do.

"I shall be going home soon. And Captain Osgood should be as thrilled with the news as I am," he gleefully said aloud. "Indeed, he shall surely promote me for this."

Fossett jumped on his horse and headed for town. Galloping down the deserted main street, he reined in his horse at the rectory. Every evening since Osgood had put the Acadians in his charge, Fossett reported to his superior. Fossett figured sunset would be the perfect time to approach his superior.

It was well-known that Osgood followed a strict regimen. At sunset, he sipped wine or another liquor and partook of a hearty dinner. Generally Fossett found Osgood at table stuffing himself with meats and breads and cakes and anything else cook could round up in the now-empty town. The routine always put Osgood in a good mood, usually good enough to invite Fossett to dine with him.

As Fossett jumped off his horse, Osgood's aide Grimer stood in the doorway. Fossett held the reins of his horse and lifted them up expecting him to take them. But tonight, Grimer shook his head and left Fossett holding them himself.

"Captain Osgood said you was to wait here, Cap'n sir." Grimer shuffled his feet and blew into his hands to warm them.

Fossett was confused. "Did he give you a reason? I have news that I must share with the Captain immediately."

Grimer shook his head as he continued to block the entrance. "Cap'n don't tell me much, sir. He ain't said nothing to me. Just to keep the likes of youse outside whilst he finished his dinner."

"Drat," Fossett muttered to himself. "I passed up the troop's mush to get here. Probably won't get supper at all now."

Out of the blue Grimer said, "Goose."

"What's that?" Fossett asked him curiously. "Goose?"

Grimer nodded. "Yep. Cook gave me a piece. Not so's big that Cap'n would notice, but not so's small that I don't still have the taste on me tongue. Right tasty that goose was."

Fossett stomped off the entry porch into the snow, cursing his bad luck. "Goose? That has always been my favorite supper. My soldiers never spotted a goose around these parts. How did I miss out on goose at Osgood's table tonight!"

Walking from his dining table to the fireside, Osgood licked his fat fingers. He loved the thick grease of the well-cooked bird his hunting team had shot in the woods behind town. He took a seat in a comfortable stuffed chair and called out, "Now, Grimer."

Suddenly Grimer called out, "Cap'n sir? Cap'n said he's ready to see you now." Grimer scampered down the steps of the porch and took the reins from Fossett.

Fossett nodded and took the steps two at a time to arrive at the rectory door. As Fossett opened the door, he adjusted his eyes to the dim light. No candles were lit, but a fire was burning in the hearth. Osgood sat by the flickering flames and sipped a fine cognac. He handed the bottle to Fossett. "Pour a glass and join me. What news today? Have we lost more of that cargo we need to ship out?"

Fossett gladly poured a glass and chugged it, then quickly refilled his glass before handing the bottle back to Osgood. Fossett asked, "Sir, I have good news."

Osgood laughed. "As do I. Some ships will be here on the morrow. Governor Lawrence's runner came in this morning from Halifax. They overestimated the number of boats needed to exile the heathens in that part of the territory. So he sent the leftover vessels to us."

Fossett gave a long sigh of relief. "The ships are not coming from Bostontown at all? So we shall not have to wait."

Osgood took another sip. "Aaahhh. How I love a good French liquor. That is the only thing I shall miss here." He took another sip. "And your report? What is the number today? How many do we still have to ship out?"

Fossett smiled. "I have good news, too, Captain. We lost a large number in the snowstorm last night, mainly old women. Now we can fit all of the remainers into far fewer boats than we thought when we marched them to the beach weeks ago."

Osgood licked his lips, as much to taste the greasy bird as to display his delight at the sound of fewer boats. "Fewer ships means more funds left in my coffers," he muttered to himself.

Fossett discreetly ignored what Osgood said aloud. He remarked, "Who knows how many will be left on the morrow to board the ships?"

Osgood scoffed, "That will mean more food for the crew."

Fossett added, "I am ready to stuff those boats with heathens and move on to my next assignment, wherever and whatever that shall be."

Captain Osgood grunted his approval. "When you have loaded all the ships, send for me. I want to gaze on the vessels taking those heathens away from our good King George's lands forever."

Fossett nodded and clicked his heels in a salute. "Yes, sir, Captain."

Osgood grabbed the half-empty bottle of cognac and filled his glass to the brim. He waved Fossett away with a curt, "Dismissed."

Fossett quickly exited the building and grabbed the reins of his horse from Grimer. The aide saluted, "See yer tomorry, Cap'n?"

Fossett leaned down to Grimer and smiled, "Not if I can help it." He galloped off through the town, past the fort and through the woods. He slowed his horse as they descended the hill and voiced his thoughts aloud. "The Captain taught me a valuable skill. Overestimate your budget, then skimp on every single expense to put more in your own coffers. That is a commanding officer to look up to. And one that I aim to be."

Fossett's aide Jeremy took the reins from Fossett who dismounted.

"Where is my supper? I am starving!" Fossett tore into Jeremy who cowered. Fossett's temper was well-known.

Jeremy was taken aback, saying, "But, sir, you never ask for food after your meetings with the Cap'n."

Fossett glared at the young man. "I'm asking now, ain't I?"

Jeremy nodded rapidly. "Yes, sir, Cap'n. Right away, sir."

Fossett stormed into his tent and reached into his trunk for a bottle of wine. He bit the cork off and chugged directly from the bottle. Within minutes, Jeremy had appeared with a large bowl.

Fossett looked at it with disdain. "Mush? You expect me to eat this?" He tossed the bowl onto the dirty boards serving as a floor.

Jeremy rushed back out. He ran to Christine's camping site and begged her. "Missy, the Cap'n ain't one to eat mush. I seen yer and the girly there catching critters near the woods."

Béatrice looked up, afraid that he was there to hurt them. Jeremy pointed to her and asked her, "Do yer got any meat left? I mean, enough so's I can make up a bowl for the Captain?"

Béatrice shook her head and tried to hide the squirrel roasting over the fire. Too late. Jeremy saw it. Christine looked from Jeremy to Béatrice and Jeanne, then back to Jeremy. She slyly asked, "What will you give us for it?"

Jeremy shuffled his feet and shook his head. "Don't got nothing much."

Christine asked him, "How important is this to you? You want to please the Captain, don't you?"

Jeremy brightened and nodded. "Course I do, missy. Course I do."

Christine nodded as she cut a large portion of the squirrel and put it in a bowl. Jeremy's nostrils smelled the delicious aroma of the stew and knew he had to have it for his superior.

Christine asked, "What would you say to getting information about the destinations of our ships from your Captain?"

Jeremy shook his head. "Can't do that, missy. He would never give it to me."

Béatrice picked up on Christine's plan. "All you have to do is borrow the papers in his desk when he is sleeping tonight. He would never know."

Christine added, "Bring them to us and we will return them to you in an hour." She held up the cooked squirrel. It smelled so delicious that Jeremy knew he had to have it.

Jeremy agreed. "Done, but yer get a few minutes, not an hour. If Cap'n finds out it's twenty lashes for me. Maybe a hanging. Gotta make it quick."

Christine, Béatrice and Jeanne nodded in unison. Christine spoke for all of them. "Done." She wrapped the squirrel in some leaves and handed it to Jeremy.

He nodded. "Be back late tonight." Jeremy rushed back to Fossett's tent and filled a bowl with mush, then laid the roasted squirrel on top. He took a deep breath and entered the tent.

Fossett was quite drunk by this time. But not too drunk to smell the aroma of fresh meat. When Jeremy handed it to him, Fossett tore into it and soon had emptied the entire bowl. Jeremy asked, "What can I do, Cap'n? Clean your desk so's you got room to work tomorry?"

Fossett laughed. "No need. You'll be aiding the troops to clean up the entire camp tomorrow. The ships are coming."

Jeremy shook his head in disbelief. "They arrive tomorry? Well, that is good news, Cap'n."

Fossett waved Jeremy out. "Get your sleep. Spread the word among the troops that we shall send the heathens away on ships in the morning. Wake me at dawn then rouse the troops. The heathens will be gone by day's end."

Jeremy nodded. "Yes, sir!"

When Jeremy exited the camp, he noticed Christine and her friends were watching him. He ignored them and ran into the woods, then slipped into his tent.

Christine turned to Jeanne and Béatrice. "He lied to us."

Jeanne nodded. "We should have known. They have not told the truth from the first day we arrived."

Béatrice added softly, "Remember when Lieutenant-Colonel Winslow promised to pardon my father, but hanged him in the main square instead?"

Anne fidgeted in her sleep. She muttered, "Pine, where are you? Where is my beautiful little boy Pine?"

Christine and Jeanne looked at Anne with surprise. But no one was more shocked than Béatrice, who whispered, "That is the first time she has spoken anything but gibberish in years." She returned to the subject, "I have never forgiven that man. Winslow is pure evil."

Christine shook her head. "We must never forget. The time will come for us to rejoin our families and friends, and we must be strong. We must have faith."

The women nodded to one another. They knelt on the cold hard ground and bowed their heads. Suddenly Anne woke and grabbed Béatrice's hand. Anne surprised them all by praying, "Our Father who art in heaven...."

From the woods, the armed guards watched the makeshift tents of the Acadians. There was no movement as the women and children huddled together under layers of cloaks and clothing. As temperatures dropped, the guards left their line to gather around a roaring fire, the sole way they could keep warm. The soldiers in tents slept under heavy blankets. Fossett snored himself to sleep, his belly full of Christine's stew. Of everyone on the beach, the Acadians were the only ones who either slept fitfully or could not sleep at all.

Before the sun rose, Fossett and his troops had readied themselves into formation at the trees and along the beach. As Osgood was promised, the ships had arrived and were anchored in the Bay. Sailors lowered rowboats from the larger vessels and prepared to launch them into the swirling waters below.

Fossett knew it would not be long before he would accomplish the final steps of his task. He barked an order to Jeremy, "Advise Captain Osgood the ships are here. Then escort him here to the beach."

Jeremy jumped on a nearby horse and nodded, "Yes, Cap'n." Within moments, he had galloped up through the trees on his way to town.

Fossett rode the length of the beach behind the lean-tos. None of the Acadians had woken. "Excellent," he said to himself. "Soon I shall rid our lands of them forever."

By dawn, the snow had stopped. Rowboats manned by sailors were pulled onto the beach by troops. Fossett oversaw the operations on horseback and directed the troops to guard the rowboats.

Béatrice slowly woke and peered out of the lean-to at the Bay. She rubbed her eyes, then looked again. She exclaimed with surprise, "They are here! The ships are finally here!"

Christine woke to her shouts and stood up, looking in the same directly as Béatrice. Seeing the outline of ships, they hugged each other.

"Thanks be to God. We are saved," Béatrice cried. She reached down and pulled up her mother, Anne, still sleepy.

"Mother, the ships have arrived. We are going to see Pine very soon."

Anne drowsily repeated, "Pine. See Pine." Then she slumped back into her little corner of the lean-to and clutched the pile of cloaks around her. She fell back asleep repeating her son's name, "My beautiful son Pine. Pine."

Christine walked out of the makeshift tent. It was then that she saw the rowboats and the soldiers and sailors waiting for them. Fossett watched her closely. Just then, Captain Osgood rode up to the water's edge, following Jeremy and Grimer.

Fossett grinned as he spoke, "Captain Osgood, we are ready, when you are, sir."

Osgood snapped. "Stop wasting time and get on with the job."

Fossett wiped the grin off his face, "Yes, Captain." He turned to his troops and issued an order. "Fill the boats!"

Soldiers began to march up to the lean-tos and wake sleeping Acadian women and children. Babies cried and children screamed, afraid of the soldiers. Mothers tried to soothe their children, but there were so many that they were unable to comfort all of them at the same time.

Béatrice looked over at the other lean-tos. Most of the Acadian women and children were too cold and exhausted to move. The women held tightly onto the hands of their children, fearing the soldiers would separate them as they had sons from fathers.

Soldiers Will and Jasey pointed their muskets and bayonets at Acadian groups.

By one of the lean-tos, Will shouted, "Get yer arses up!"

To another group, Jasey ordered, "Get down to the beach and into that there boat."

When no one came out of the little tent, Jasey knocked the Acadians' legs or torsos with his musket. He wanted to make sure he put all living heathens aboard the ship. The dead, well, they could fend for themselves. Dust to dust, he thought.

Will reached into the lean-to. When the young woman did not move with Jasey's not-so-gentle nudge of this gun, Will ripped a gold chain and a wedding band from her still-warm body.

Fossett rode up to Christine and ordered Jasey. "Put her on my horse here."

Christine objected loudly. "Stop it. Where are you taking me?" She tried to fight off Jasey who slapped her and lifted her onto Fossett's horse.

Fossett galloped down to the other end of the beach. "You are going to a special place, missy. I picked out a boat just for you. Courtesy of Colonel Winslow. Said he don't like herbs."

"But I want to go on the boat with my friends. Please. It costs you nothing to let us stay together."

Fossett shook his head. "Animals have no choices. You do as I tell you to. I know you to be the troublemaker. With you out of the way, the others will obey."

He reined in his horse near the two soldiers that had been her guards, Wesley and Rollin. "Put this woman in that boat yonder. Away from her friends. Don't trust her. I think she's a runner."

They roughly pulled Christine off the horse and physically stuck her into a rowboat. She stood up and looked for her friends. "Béatrice? Jeanne?" Before she got out another word, Wesley yanked her back down.

"Sit there, yer heathen. And shut yer trap." Wesley's temper was boiling. "We gots to get all youse heathens in the boats so we can go home. Do like I say. Sit down and shut yer trap."

Christine looked frantically toward the shore, even as her rowboat was making its way to a large ship anchored in the Bay. "Jeanne? Over here!" Christine shouted.

Jeanne saw her and tried to run in her direction, when a soldier grabbed Jeanne by the waist and put her in a rowboat. Soldiers grabbed Béatrice and Anne and herded them down the beach toward another boat.

Béatrice stood and called out. "Christine? Where are you?"

Christine yelled back, "Béatrice. Remember the plan."

Béatrice put her head in her hands and cried. Anne reached over and patted Béatrice's hand. She understood. Béatrice held her mother's hand. "It's alright, Mother. We shall be alright. We shall meet Christine and Pine in New Orleans."

At the sound of her son's name, Anne clapped. "Pine. See Pine."

Before she said another word, she was pushed forward into a crowd of Acadians and she let go of Béatrice's hand. Béatrice went into a panic. "Mother? Where are you?" Béatrice searched the beach but did not see her mother.

The Acadians were forced into small, crowded rowboats. When the sailors wanted to load more bodies into a boat, they threw the Acadians' possessions into the water or confiscated bags and packages before the boarding began. The exile was, for many Acadians, a forced exodus with only the shirts on their backs. All of their worldly possessions were left on the beach or tossed overboard.

Jasey pushed Béatrice into a line, but she resisted. "Please, sir, I must find my mother. She is old and feeble-headed and cannot even feed herself."

The soldier's heart was as cold as his musket chilled by the winter winds and snow flurries. "Get yerself back in the line, missy, er else."

Béatrice started to run after an old woman who looked like Anne, but Jasey handily knocked her to the beach with his gun. "Don't yer make me repeat it. In the boat and yer live. Refuse and yer go into the deep," he growled as he pushed her into a line monitored by Rollin. Then Jasey headed for the treeline to find anyone who might be hiding to escape their fate.

Béatrice's forehead was bleeding. She held her head and slowly moved in line toward the water. She looked right and left for Anne but still saw no sign of her.

Rollin pushed Jeanne into a rowboat with a group of young Acadian boys and girls who had been separated from their mothers. Anne was sitting in the boat sucking her thumb. Jeanne sat next to her and whispered, "It is alright, Madame Gaudet. I am a friend of Béatrice and Pine." At the sound of her son, Anne dropped her thumb and cried out, "Pine, my beautiful boy, Pine." The children cried relentlessly, yet not even their wails touched Rollin's heart.

From his position on the treeline at the top of the beach, Captain Osgood adjusted his telescope. He remained motionless watching the procession of Acadian heathens forced into boats then pushed, pulled or prodded from the boats onto ship decks. Soon they would cast off and be out of his sight and out of his mind forever.

Osgood reflected on what he saw, speaking softly to his aide Grimer. "They have embarked very sullenly and unwillingly. The women seem to be in great distress carrying their children in their arms. Others carry their decrepit parents in their carts with all their goods. I cannot understand why, for there is not even enough room on the transports for themselves. Why is there great confusion? Why do the heathens appear such a scene of woe and distress? They knew they had it coming to them, so stuck were they on modifying the oath we required. All they had to do was swear complete allegiance to our King George and our true religion. But they refused, so this is their destiny."

Grimer dutifully responded, "Yes, Cap'n, truer words were never spoke."

Osgood stepped away from the telescope. He had seen enough. "Soon I shall move on to a new assignment," he told Grimer. "And I should like to take you with me."

The aide nodded with a perfunctory, "Would be my honor, sir." Grimer clasped his hands together and blew his frosty breath on them in futility. But that made them colder, so he started rubbing them together.

Under his breath he muttered, "Drat those ratballs Rollins and Wesley, stealing my gloves. Them-uns knowed very well I had me only the one set. And me with outside duty all day today instead of warming me hands by the fire in Cap'n's office. Drat them both."

*

Under the sharp orders of Captain Fossett, soldiers filled one rowboat after another. By day's end, as Fossett had predicted, the beach was completely empty of Acadians. Yet signs that they had been there were everywhere. Lean-tos, bags, carts and other possessions were strewn all along the snow-covered beach.

As snow flurries spotted Osgood's new jacket, he waited just long enough to see the last rowboat shove off into the water. He saw Christine's red hair fluttering in the wind and nodded. "At long last. My mission is done." He looked at the sunset and motioned to Grimer, "Time for dinner." Osgood waved to Fossett and, escorted by the aide, returned to his temporary home. He indulged in food and drink, ordering Grimer to leave him uninterrupted for five days.

As the ships prepared to set sail, the women, children and remaining elderly Acadians stole a last glimpse of the one home they had ever known. To their shock, they saw dark smoke and the glow of fires rising above the trees coming from the direction of the town.

Standing on the decks of the transports, the Acadians realize the English had set fire to Grand Pré. They knew that their homes, their businesses, their possessions would soon be ashes. Everything they had built over a lifetime, and for some, over generations, would be lost, except the memories and the few belongings they carried onto the ships.

That was when the Acadians realized all they could look forward to was one breath at a time. Many sucked in the fresh air on deck one last time before being pushed down into their holds. There they were to face misery, disease and the fear of never seeing their loved ones again. Many would wish to die and would accomplish their goal, but the survivors were doomed to live their fate.

*

The lead vessel carried Jeanne, Anne, and other young female Acadians toward Bostontown. There, they were destined to be auctioned in the slave markets, although none of the Acadians had been informed of that. They were to experience a rude awakening in Cornhandle's slave auctions to Bostonians.

The ship that Christine and Yvonne had boarded was a cargo vessel belonging to a one-eyed captain named Swillingham, who also headed for Bostontown. Most of the other Acadians on that boat were elderly women so, rather than force the women to climb the rope ladder, he hoisted the rowboat up and unloaded them onto the deck. As Christine later found out, Swillingham did that do not out of the goodness of his heart, but because he would be paid only for passengers who arrived at the destination alive and well.

Béatrice had been loaded onto a ship without her mother Anne. That ship set a course for France. Shirley planned to let King Louis XV know the power of the English navy to ship their own citizens to their enemy's country. Béatrice called out to the other ships, "Mother, where are you?"

Panic set in when she saw Anne being pushed up the rope ladder on a nearby ship. Béatrice waved to her. "Mother! Mother, look up at me!" But Anne's eyes were dully fixated on the knotted rope and froze on the ladder. The woman beneath Anne on the ladder was Evangeline's good friend Jeanne.

Glancing at the ship nearest hers, Jeanne saw Christine's red hair. But before Jeanne could call out to her, Christine was pushed down into the hold by a young soldier and disappeared from view. Looking up, Jeanne realized Anne was motionless on the ladder. She moved up several rungs until she could hold one of Anne's hands on the ropes while gently pushing the old woman upward.

When Anne reached the top of the ladder, a sailor roughly pulled her onto the deck. Anne's body shook with fear but the sailor just walked away, leaving her alone. Jeanne climbed onto the deck and protectively wrapped her arms around the old woman.

Béatrice continued to call out from her ship, "Mother! Here I am."

Anne's head turned to the direction of the voice but was confused. Jeanne moved her to the edge of the deck and pointed to the adjacent ship. "See there, Madame Gaudet? Béatrice is waving to you."

Anne recognized her daughter and cried out, "Bea! Pine! See Bea! See Pine!" She clapped with glee.

Jeanne patted her hand and said, "Yes, Madame Gaudet, we are going to see Béatrice. And we will meet your son Pine when we arrive."

The other transports loaded with Acadians headed for more southerly British Colonies, in keeping with Shirley's scheme to separate the Acadians in as many different territories as possible to prevent them from reuniting and returning to overpower the British in Nova Scotia.

As the Acadian women settled into the cramped quarters of their respective holds, none knew their final destination. Most had devised a plan to meet in the future in the French territory of Louisiana, but none of the women had any idea how that goal would be accomplished.

*

On his ship, Captain Swillingham leered at Christine with his one good eyeball. He leaned over the ship to see her voluptuous breasts heaving as she was hoisted up alongside the ship from the rowboat. He licked his chops when she passed. She scurried away from him, gathering as many Acadian children in her arms as she could.

Yvonne Poché was already on the deck when Christine arrived. "Thank goodness, it is you. I can withstand anything if you are here with us," Yvonne said as she hugged Christine. They joined a circle of the other Acadians aboard, hoping for a last glimpse of their home before they were rudely dispatched to the cargo hold.

*

From her ship, Béatrice caught a glimpse of Jeanne and her mother on the deck and waved. Anne clapped again, but a group of soldiers approached her and she hid behind Jeanne, clutching her skirts.

Jeanne took Anne's hand, "Do not fear. We shall follow these men. Come with me and we shall be fine." The head soldier led them to the hold.

Anne started crying when she lost her grip on Jeanne's hand. Tears ran down Anne's cheeks and she moaned to comfort herself. Jeanne reached out and grabbed Anne's hand again, then hugged the old woman to her breast but Anne pulled away and looked back at the other ship. She caught a last glimpse of Béatrice waving and blowing kisses. Only then did Anne stop crying and follow Jeanne.

As Anne and Jeanne descended into the hold, other Acadian women and children ascended the rope ladder to the deck. Most all of them moved up the ladder without incident. However, one young woman refused to climb. She gazed down at the swirling waters then up at the deck, as if she wanted to weigh her options.

An impatient soldier leaned over the railing and shot her without warning. She fell off the rope into the black waters of the sea. After that, the remaining Acadians on the rope climbed with renewed energy and arrived on the deck before being cruelly pushed into the hold.

*

When Osgood had recuperated and sobered himself the week after the women were exiled, he penned a letter to William Shirley.

"My Dear Governor,

"I have the pleasure to acquaint you that I have shipped off the remainder of the French inhabitants you left here. They were docile women and children with a few old hags and feeble elderlies who managed to stay alive in the recent snowstorm enough to board the transports. How they will fare is up to themselves now. Godspeed to you.

"Your loyal servant, Phineas Osgood – Captain."

Osgood wanted to scream to the four winds that he finished his mission and was ready to escape the isolated wilderness. Instead, he directed his troops to ransack every store, warehouse, cellar, cupboard and well in town, as well as all storehouses on the outlying farms. They packed crates and sacks of food, grog and, of course, the exceptional French wine he had been drinking the last week non-stop.

He was ready to leave, but knew he must await formal orders before making a move. And, unfortunately, that would be in Shirley's good time, not his own.

*

Weeks later, Béatrice stood on deck staring at the Bostontown harbor on the horizon. She overheard two sailors talking when they brought her to the deck with a group of five other young Acadian women. The chubby man said, "Cap'n says winds were unusually strong. Us will get to Bostontown at least a week before schedule. He's a-giving us the extra time in port."

The tall wiry one, a mere boy, replied, "Methinks me shall drink to that. Me paw sailed the oceans before me. He used to say wine and friendly port women was the cure-all fer his long weeks at sea."

"How did yer mom take it?" Chubby asked.

"She was just glad he came home. Ye died at sea? So did yer wages."

Chubby added, "This is me first time to Bostontown, but me gots an earful about them slave auctions. The auction man strips them girls to the waist so's the masters can get a good look at them bubbies."

He stared at Béatrice and licked his lips. Wiry grinned in understanding. They would get an eyeful up on the slaver's stage. And that was good enough.

Béatrice cringed at the conversation and turned away from them. She inhaled deeply, then coughed at the cold blast of air in her lungs. Still, she did it again. It felt good to be alive. She turned to Josephine Gotro, a Grand Pré neighbor standing next to her and whispered, "At least Christine warned us of the slave markets. We must impress the slaver to arrange for us to be in the main house. I should hate to be sold to work in the fields."

Josephine responded, "Surely they value cooks and seamstresses. Your soups were excellent, and I can sew. Every plantation needs these skills."

"We must communicate this to the auction master," Béatrice replied.

They both leaned into the whipping winds and breathed deeply despite the frigid air to experience their last moments of freedom.

Their plans were rudely interrupted when two sailors dragged a group of women and children up from the hold. They were sweating profusely from illness. The sailors tossed them in the corner of the deck like old rags, then tied their hands to the railings to prevent them from infecting anyone else.

A young woman begged for mercy. "Please let me go back. My little boy is in the dark, alone and afraid. I must find him. Please, sir."

The first sailor jeered, "Youse be quarantined here until you die."

Béatrice ignored her own safety and rushed up to the young women. "Your son died yesterday. Do you not remember? He is with God now."

The woman refused to believe it and continued to cry out. "Henri?"

The two sailors laughed as they walked away and joined Chubby and Wiry. The sickly Acadian women wrapped their untied arms around the young children on deck with them, most of whom they did not know, trying to keep them warm. The poor children would shiver, then sweat, with no end to their suffering.

Suddenly a young woman dropped to her knees, kissed her infant daughter, and dropped it to the deck. The two sailors grabbed the baby and tossed it overboard. Béatrice leaned down to her, "You miss your baby girl. Have faith. You shall be with her soon. I shall pray for you." The woman nodded and within moments, she collapsed. The sailors tossed her as they had her baby.

Part VI

Scattered to the Winds
1756 – 1758

Now, God be pleased, that to believing souls
Gives light in darkness, comfort in despair.

- William Shakespeare

CHAPTER 56
Karaztyev

Île Royale

Milosh Karaztyev was a crusty, wizened French gypsy who had first met René Le Blanc in 1738 when the gypsy tried to rob René's caravan of carriages on the dangerous road from Versailles to Le Havre. However, René had outwitted the gypsy leader and thwarted his plans of breaking into his carriages and getting rich by offering his family a banquet of wine and food. As René used to tell it, "I earned the respect of the wily man only after his family was too drunk to assist him in robbing me."

What René did not know was that Karaztyev and his family stowed away on the French ship *L'Acadie* which René and his bride Lady Eugenie, sailed to his new post in Grand Pré. The gypsies had remained hidden until, during the chaos of unloading and loading cargo, they slipped off the ship in the port of Île Royale perched in the Atlantic, north of Nova Scotia.

The family patriarch Milosh announced, "We shall stay here. But instead of being exposed on the flat beaches, we shall build our homes in the rocks and hills. See those shadows above?" The gypsies squinted at the hills, turn looked back at their leader quizzically. Milosh explained, "They are entrances to caves hewn in the rocks. Clear them of wild animals and we shall be shielded from public view but still be able to watch activity at the harbor." The "harbor" was merely a natural inlet cut into the beach, where Milosh planned to construct a port.

A year later, the area had been completely transformed. The gypsies had built homes into the rocks and mountains and devised a set of walkways and rope bridges with checkpoints. Since the gypsies had been born in France, they spoke the language fluently and blended in among the residents despite their looks. The islanders respected their privacy and avoided their beach they called "Karaztown," of which Milosh was proud.

They built a family business on procuring items non-existent on the island. If a merchant wanted a certain bottle of French wine for a special client, Karaztyev obtained it. When the local priest needed silks for new vestments, Karaztyev provided them. Other residents never knew exactly how Karaztyev was able to procure unavailable goods, but they never questioned the premium price he charged. Within a few years, Karaztyev had become known as a prime "fixer" of the island.

Their business expanded when an abandoned boat washed up near the shores of Karaztown. Milosh and his sons repaired it and began to ferry passengers and goods from Île Royale to nearby Île St. Jean and to Nova Scotia. With the profits, they bought goods and resold for greater profits than the ferry fees. The family's status on the island rose as did its profits.

*

The Karaztyev family business continued to flourish over the next three decades and his four sons joined him. One day at dawn, in the dead of the winter of 1756, Milosh and his sons finished their supply rounds of the islands. Manfri, his eldest son, skillfully navigated the boat into the small harbor. His siblings Barsali, Ferka and Ruslo tied up the boat at the dock and unloaded goods and sacks of coins they had obtained on this run.

Milosh looked on with pride. He had raised four fine sons, and was gratified that his wife had borne twin daughters after the quartet of boys. He announced, "It is good to be home. I enjoy these trips, but staying away for weeks is not for an old man like me. Not anymore."

His sons gathered round, clasping his arm or his shoulder and murmuring. Manfri spoke up first, "Father, you have taught us well. I agree it is time that you enjoy the fruits of your labors."

"Yes, Father, we know the business and all of its ins and outs," said Barsali, the blue-eyed, quiet one.

"He is right. You should take life easy now," said his happy son Ferka, who wiggled his oversized ears that protruded like an elephant.

His youngest son Ruslo added, "You have all the money you could ever need. Why not stay here with Mother and enjoy it?"

Milosh could always count on Ruslo to say a kind word, despite Ruslo being born with a deformity, a stump for a hand. Yet he had figured out how to row a boat, sharpen a knife, whittle a whistle, split a log and, hopefully, one day he would learn how to satisfy a wife. Those gypsy women were insatiable, thought Milosh, as he had a lewd daydream about his wife.

The sun rose in the sky, lighting the beach as they walked from the harbor towards the road leading to their homes. On the way, they noticed an unusually large piece of driftwood half-buried in the sand. The remains of a splintered British rowboat had washed up on shore. Underneath it was a half-dead figure in tattered rags, shoeless and barely breathing -- René.

After what had seemed to him like months but was merely days without food and water, René woke to find himself partially submerged in the sand. Not knowing where he was, he cautiously peered out from under the boat. He was nearly dead of thirst and could barely breathe.

His eyes met the steely gaze of Milosh Karaztyev himself. The old gypsy leader peered closely at the man lying in the sand. The man rubbed his eyes, believing he was dreaming. The last thing he remembered was a seagull flying overhead. All the man could think about was praying to reach land and a friendly people. And now, he looked up at someone who looked vaguely familiar. How was it possible?

Karaztyev's sons helped René clamber up and seated him on top of the boat. René leaned on Manfri for support as he mouthed the word "water." He managed to say in a small voice through his parched lips, "Thirsty."

The gypsy snapped his fingers and Barsali produced a bota of smooth animal skin filled with liquid. René guzzled the refreshing drink, though he did not know the taste.

Karaztyev was the first to speak, "Lord Le Blanc? Is it truly you? I have not seen you in years."

Nodding René asked. "Where am I? Karaztyev? How are you here?"

The two men shook hands, but Karaztyev broke protocol to hug René. "My Lord, you are in my own little paradise on Île Royale."

Le Blanc nodded and murmured, "So it is French territory, not British."

Milosh agreed. "You are safe here. We have much to talk about later. First, we must get you shelter and food."

The French Consul nodded weakly, stumbling and holding on to Karaztyev for support. "Thank you so…." René fell to the sandy beach.

Karaztyev smiled. "Ahhh, my lord, you cannot hold our Romani liquor so long. It has a kick quite missing from French wine." He and his sons lifted René and sat him down on the boat again. He told his sons, "Bring the carriage and carry him to my house. Treat him as you would a king."

The three young men nodded and sprinted toward the hillside overlooking the beach. "Yes, Papa," they spoke in unison.

By that time, more gypsies had gathered to fill the beach, curiosity-seekers all. Karaztyev looked around and grunted with pleasure. "It is good to welcome my old friend." The gypsy leader sought out his wife. She rushed forward to his side and Milosh introduced her to René. "Florica, my wife, prepares a feast like no other. I present you to Lord René Le Blanc, the emissary of our great French King Louis."

Florica curtsied to René. "Welcome to our home, my Lord."

René nodded, "It is my honor, Madame."

Milosh called out in a booming voice, "Where are Lela and Lolli?"

Two strikingly-beautiful twin girls of sixteen shouted out in unison, "Here, Papa!" Within seconds, they had joined him and bowed.

He patted them on the head and ordered, "Arrange a dance to honor our guest of honor at the feast."

They curtsied and replied obediently, "Yes, Papa," the disappeared into the crowd. Milosh's four sons arrived with a horse-drawn cart filled with soft furs. They wheeled René up the beach to a large cave home in the mountain and settled him into a room in the cave, lit a fire for his comfort, then left him alone with their father.

It was then that René remembered the story of his voyage. "The British hacked holes in the hull of the transport that took me and many older Acadian men out of Grand Pré. On board, we were told we were to be sold in the slave markets of Bostontown. But the ship became eerily silent and sat in the water. We later learned the sailors had abandoned ship with the rowboat. They must have boarded another transport."

Milosh blurted, "The British have never been friendly. Not the entire time we lived in France, and not here."

René nodded grimly. "Out of calm seas came chaos. The ship was tossed and turned by huge waves. We lost all balance. Without warning, a wall of water rushed into the hold. I made it up to the deck with some of the others, but they were swept overboard. I had no choice but to jump into the water and made it to the boat you found on the beach."

Karaztyev was enthralled. "What happened after that?"

Le Blanc obliged him. "The last thing I remember before waking up on your beach was rowing hard against a terrible storm. I cannot recall what happened or how I got here."

The gypsy wanted to hear more about the adventure. "How did you survive? The water is deathly cold. The clutches of the deep drown many a good man at sea."

René began to nod off. "Sorry. So sleepy." He dozed off and Milosh crept away quietly.

 Hours later, René woke up, covered in a thick bearskin in the darkness. He rubbed his eyes and looked around. Milosh sat by a small fire.

"Well, my friend, at last you have rejoined the living," said Karaztyev.

René tried to sit, but was too weak. "Where am I?"

Milosh gave a hearty laugh. "In my home on Île Royale. Where else would you be?"

René sputtered out his confusion. "But I was put on an old ship that sank. I rowed for days. Leastways, I think I did. How did I get here?"

The gypsy said kindly, "You let me return the gift you gave me so many years ago."

René shook his head. "Gift?" Then he remembered the cloak he had given Milosh so many years ago. He shook his head. "What I gave you was yours to keep."

"I meant trust. A gift freely given. It made me the man I am today. Your trust in me."

René nodded. "It is I who must thank you –"

Milosh waved him off and asked, "Are you hungry? I know you are. Come with me and let us dine and celebrate."

René followed Milosh through a winding hallway lit by torches affixed to the cave walls. Soon they arrived in a cavernous room with a large table in the center. He saw it was loaded with platters of food and bottles of wine until the table looked like it would collapse under the load. René's mouth watered when he gazed upon platters of meats, shellfish, tureens of soup, cakes, breads, cheeses, fruits, herbs and a bottle of wine. Karaztyev and his family staged the banquet in René's honor, giving him the tribute and treatment he deserved.

"Eat now. My daughters Lela and Lolli have prepared the food for you under my wife's watchful eye. They are learning the required skills before we betroth them to men who deserve their beauty and talents. Of course, that shall not be until they are fifty years old, eh, my friend? Eat now. Eat your fill. We talk after."

With that, Milosh vanished into the wispy smoke of the fire burning at one end of the room. As the shadowy figure exited the cave, René turned back to the table. His senses were bombarded with the aromas, colors and textures of the meal that Milosh's wife and daughters served. They insisted he taste every dish before Milosh returned with his sons.

The entire family joined René at table. Soon, the cave was filled with voices, laughter and the joy of being with family. René's heart was filled with longing for Christine and dread for Evangeline and Gabriel.

*

Joseph "Beausoleil" Broussard and his brother Alexandre were instrumental in helping hundreds of Acadian families escape the Exile. Just before the Edict was to be read, over a thousand French neutrals from settlements not far from Grand Pré escaped through the woods and traveled swiftly past the British fort before heading north to the coast.

Though the group was divided as to their final destination, everyone wanted to reach the safety and security of French territory. Many of the families decided to go to the French island of Île Royale, and some chose Île Saint-Jean, to the northwest. The remainder headed for Quebec. They agreed to travel together northward until they reached the coast, where they would diverge and cross the isthmus to separate islands. They hid in forests and avoided the muddy main roads where English soldiers, merchants and carriages traveled. In doing so, the Acadians added months to the journey before arriving at the isthmus across from their chosen island.

Neither the Broussard brothers nor the Acadians knew what lay ahead for them. But they did know that Île Royale was French territory, which meant they would avoid exile by fleeing English territory.

Upon arriving at the coast, the Broussards divided the families into camps and hid them in different parts of the woods. They reasoned that a small fire built for a few dozen Acadians in separate areas of the forest would be less obvious than one large bonfire to cook for hundreds.

Under cover of darkness, the brothers confiscated a nearby boat from the harbor and carried the first boatload of Acadians across the isthmus. Throughout the night, boatloads of French families crossed onto the beach below the Karaztyev's hillside domain.

After dropping off the last passengers, Beausoleil rowed the boat back to the Nova Scotia harbor. He managed to traverse the isthmus by propelling himself forward on a piece of floating wood. When Broussard arrived onshore, Karaztyev and his entire family were marching from their hillside perches toward them. The French Acadians trembled at the sight. Neither Broussard brother nor any of the Acadians knew the history of the gypsies with their French Consul, nor if they were friends or foes. In fact, they were the first people the Acadians had seen on the island.

Karaztyev himself stood out from the gypsies. Short in stature and covered in animal furs decorated with painted shells and rocks, he looked every inch an indigenous king adored by his subjects who stood behind him. He held a shell-decorated staff and wore a tall headpiece of animal tails which shook as he walked.

Broussard was taken aback, as were the other Acadians in his party. He was certain they had arrived on a French island but did not recognize the gypsies. He murmured to his brother, "This is without a doubt the French island of Île Royale. So who are these people?"

His brother replied quietly, "We could be in danger if we misread our navigation instruments. These appear to be natives."

Beausoleil nodded and added, "They do not look French in appearance or in dress. But clearly, they have staked out this territory for their own. We must be prudent and consider this their territory rather than our King's."

Broussard chose to give a mark of respect to the leader, Karaztyev, who had not uttered a word. The entire group of gypsies stared at the Acadians as if they were never-before-seen creatures like dragons and wolfmen.

Beausoleil made a sweeping bow with his hat and said in a loud voice in English, "We are Acadians from Grand Pré, Cobequid and Annapolis Royal, in Nova Scotia seeking shelter and protection. May we enter your territory?"

Karaztyev stared at Beausoleil, whose back was breaking as he continued to bend while awaiting a response. Taking the gypsy's silence to mean a lack of understanding, Broussard repeated his request in French.

The gypsy patriarch stared another full minute. Then he turned to the four young men behind him and the busty, rotund woman next to him. They huddled together and soon emitted guttural and strange sounds within the group. Then Karaztyev turned around and lifted his staff. "Welcome to the island of Karaztyev."

Broussard lifted his back which creaked with pain. "Have we not landed on the French territory of Île Royale? Our instruments guided us here."

The gypsy puckered his forehead as if in deep thought. After a moment of silence, he signaled his understanding. "Ah, yes, Île Royale. But of course, in a manner of speaking, you are on Île Royale. But this part of Île Royale is known as Karaztown on Île Karaztyev. The other islanders respect our piece of the island and we do the same for their part. We have lived here happily for decades because we have lived separately but together."

Alexander Broussard interjected, "Now I understand. We are most grateful for your hospitality. Thank you for welcoming us."

Milosh grinned from ear to ear. "Oh, we have not yet decided to welcome you. That will depend on the bargain we strike. If we agree, we can provide all that you seek. But first, we sit and determine the price."

The portly woman had set a blanket on the beach. Milosh positioned himself on one side and he motioned for Broussard to sit on the other side. As he did so, Beausoleil asked simply, "What is it you seek to provide us? We desire food, shelter and protection from the English."

Karaztyev was cagey. He would not be bated into settling for too little without knowing what the Acadians had. He retorted, "You ask much, my friend. That will cost a tidy sum. What do you offer in payment?"

Broussard turned to his brother Alexandre and the nearby men in the party, rounding them together. They formed a huddle away from Karaztyev's blanket and whispered among themselves. Broussard began, "What do we have that we can pay for our needs? Keep in mind that this may not be the final home for many in our group."

His brother Alexandre said, "Agreed. We must keep our highest-value items for bribes if the English get uncomfortably close."

Beausoleil added, "And we will need our muskets for protection. We know nothing about these gypsies."

Giles Rivette, one of the Acadian men, added, "Perhaps they do not want any of our weapons. I see no arms on any of the men."

The Acadians all turned quickly to gaze at the gypsies. Sure enough, not one appeared to have a weapon of any kind. But most of the men were covered from head to toe in animal fur tunics. The women had long gowns made of animal skins. Any of them, or all of them, could have hidden anything underneath their clothing without anyone being the wiser.

Alexander stroked his beard, asking, "What do they consider valuable?"

Broussard pulled a blanket from his sack and tossed it on the sand. He tossed a gold coin on it. "What can each of you offer?" Alexandre put a hunting knife on the sand. Giles added a gold piece. The other Acadian men each contributed to the pile of valuables and weapons. Soon, the blanket was full. Broussard tied it and walked over to Karaztyev. "My name is Broussard. I speak for our group. We offer you our tokens of respect."

Karaztyev snapped his fingers and two of the young men grabbed the blanket from Broussard's hand. They emptied the items onto the sand.

The gypsies eyed the offerings with pleasure, edging out others and elbowing some to get closer to the pile. Karaztyev looked over the items first. "Of course, gold and jewelry are our first choice. But we can use weapons." He snapped his fingers, and all the men pulled out knives or metal implements from under their animal skin robes.

Broussard, Alexandre and Giles looked at each other in relief. They had chosen wisely. Broussard nodded. Karaztyev snapped again and a free-for-all ensued. Gypsy men and women clawed and fought at each other to grab an article. When each clutched one of the offerings, they quickly darted up the beach and headed to their homes in the hills.

When the rest of his family was gone, Karaztyev nodded and smiled. He offered his hand in friendship. "I am Karaztyev. Follow me. We shall provide you with shelter and food and anything else that you shall need."

Broussard clasped the gypsy's hand. "Thank you for your hospitality."

Karaztyev laughed. "As you will see, we give nothing without payment. You paid, so you get what you bargained for." He motioned to the Acadians. "My sons shall show you the way." The gypsy and his family members scurried quickly through the sand up the beach. Passing by a clump of bushes, they climbed the winding road that had been built into the hill. Karaztyev and his immediate family soon arrived at their main cave.

Milosh's sons Ruslo and Manfri waited for the Acadians on the beach. The Broussard brothers organized the Acadians into pairs to drag their bags and carts up the hill. Those not carrying the Acadians' possessions helped the elderly climb. At every checkpoint on the road, gypsy guards let them pass. Once the Acadians had climbed part of the way up the hill, Ruslo and Manfri assigned several large caves to them.

*

The Acadians quickly settled in and made the caverns their homes. The gypsies taught them where to find the best fishing spots, how to spot berries and edible plants, and favorable locations to trap animals. Though they lived without fear of capture by English troops, they realized the gypsies would never accept them as family and needed to take care of themselves.

They set up their own governing council to resolve disputes and agreed on a few simple rules. All Acadians over age nine would vote for three men and two women to serve on the Council for a year, when a new election would be held for new Councillors. The five Councillors would elect a chief to preside over a monthly Council meeting. Anyone age nine or older with a grievance could present it in front of the Council, and each Acadian would have the same stature when the Councillors decided the resolution. The decision by a majority of the Councillors was final and binding.

With those decisions made, the Acadians held the first meeting. When all the Acadians had gathered, the Councillors appointed Alexandre Broussard as their Chief. Alexandre accepted the position but avoided eye contact with his older brother Beausoleil, who felt slighted as he was the organizer of the Acadian odyssey. Alexandre called the Council to order. They sat in a circle in the middle of the cave, surrounded by the other Acadians, and decisions were made that affected lives and kept the peace.

At the last meeting of the year, the Council met as usual. Alexandre lit the great fire in the center of the Council circle. The spectacular blaze pleased young and old who laughed aloud. Alexandre stood tall among everyone else seated in concentric circles around the Councillors. He cleared his throat. Was it a sign of nervousness? Or something in his gorge? The Acadians wondered what the gesture meant. They would soon find out.

Alexandre began, "Tonight, our case is one we have never before heard. Will Mary Daigle and her father step forward please?"

A young teenager of sixteen and a short, stubby farmer stood and made their way through the crowd as the Acadians moved to open a pathway in the sea of people.

Alexandre nodded. "Please tell us your complaint."

The girl nodded. "Your brother, the one they call Beausoleil, lay with me ten moons ago. This is his daughter, Louise Marie." She lifted an infant to her waist. A collective gasp ran through the entire cave. The child had thick dark hair just like Beausoleil. Everyone was thinking the same thing. Her claim must be true!

Mary's father, Louis Daigle, added, "He should not have taken liberties with my daughter, but we ask as his punishment that he pay enough to support the child and book passage to France for our entire family. My wife and I will help Mary raise the child and live our lives away from him."

Alexandre was clearly struck by the man's words. He was to be the child's uncle, but he would never see his niece again. He nodded, "You may return to your seats. Next, I call Beausoleil Broussard."

When his brother appeared, Alexandre sat next to the other Councillors. Beausoleil looked at the seated Acadians surrounding him. He noted their grimaces at him. Could it be that they took the silly girl at her word? He looked around the room and pleaded, "You know me. I led you to safety here. You have lived with me, talked with me and taken meals with me and my wife and seven sons. You know I would never take advantage of this young girl. I did not do this. I could not. You must believe me." Beausoleil nodded to his brother and the Councillors, then he took his seat.

Alexandre announced, "The Council shall leave to decide this case." The Council members wandered down into the depths of the cave. Their voices were heard as echoes, at times loud with anger, and other times calm.

At long last, the Councillors re-appeared in the main cave. Alexandre began softly, "This is the most difficult case we have had to decide here. I did not vote, as I clearly have a familial interest. But I do agree with the result. The Council casts Beausoleil Broussard to pay full passage to France for the Daigle family and an additional year of support for the child."

At that, Beausoleil stood and shouted, "I am innocent of this charge. But I respect our Council as the authority to decide our disagreements. Monsieur Daigle shall receive payment as ordered. Then, my family and I shall leave this place and make our home elsewhere. It is impossible for me to continue living among you. You did not believe me, despite the fact that I risked my life to protect you from the English. You doubted my sincerity, although I negotiated with the Karaztyevs for your security. I bid you good-bye."

A month later, Beausoleil, his wife, seven sons and Alexandre took their leave of the island. A few Acadians met them at the beach and thanked them profusely. Some cried as they were ferried to the nearby Île St. Jean.

From a distance, the Daigle family and their friends looked with scorn upon Beausoleil. They believed he had ruined Mary for life. One man said, "Wherever he goes, his name shall be tainted." A woman added, "Let us hope the people in his new town lock up their daughters."

But Mary chided them with a grace and compassion that stunned everyone, "I have forgiven him. And although I can never forget, I am joyful at the thought of making a new home in our mother country. My daughter shall know only happiness, not the pain we experienced here. Let us refrain from wishing Monsieur Broussard ill."

Her parents and their friends felt rather sheepish. A young uneducated girl had shown them how to love their neighbor.

But they still believed that Beausoleil had not paid enough for Mary and her baby to live in comfort in France. The man who spoke against Broussard took off his cap and passed it around as a collection plate. Every Acadian there placed a coin in it for mother and child.

CHAPTER 57
Fugitives

Nova Scotia

Despite the adept leadership of Lieutenant-Colonel Winslow and Captain Osgood, the English military in Grand Pré did not actually rid the territory all of the Acadians in ships in 1755. Claude, Adèle and Pauline Arnaud were among the fugitives who had planned their destiny and acted on it.

They had finally arrived in Quebec City, months after beginning their trek in the woods beyond Grand Pré, by hiding in the wagon of one of Adèle's vendors during the treacherous overland trek to Quebec City.

At the harbor, the Arnauds looked for Captain Boucher. But without knowing the name of his boat, they were at a loss. Being early spring, many captains were directing crew to work on their boats and prepare them for the sailing season. However, the gangplanks were raised.

Claude despaired and wondered how he would ever find the Captain. Then he found the small shed of the harbor master. "Sir, could you point me in the direction of Captain Boucher? We have traveled quite a long way to see him and we believe he should be expecting us."

The harbor master cared not a whit about who Claude was or why he was here or even if he was expected. But he had been given a handful of coins to be on the lookout for a certain French Acadian family. By Claude's accent, he knew they were not local. "Ye wouldn't happen to be the Arnaud family, would ye?"

Claude nodded with relief. "That is precisely who we are. I am Claude Arnaud ---"

"Why didn't ye say so in the first place? Ye was right. Cap'n is expecting ye. Has been expecting ye for quite some time. Months if I recall correct."

"Yes," admitted Claude, "It was quite a feat making the journey from Nova Scotia."

The harbor master had heard enough. He pointed out the Captain. "That big man over there. That there is Cap'n Boucher. Tell him Bublée sent ye."

Claude nodded, "Thank you, Monsieur Bublée. I certainly shall."

Claude escorted Adèle and Pauline to the ship. "Captain Boucher? Permission to come aboard?"

Boucher was a tall bear of a man. He shouted out, "Who goes there? What business have you on my ship?"

Claude announced, "I believe my brother Lord Laurent de Rochefort has been in communication with you…"

Before Claude could finish, the Captain interrupted and sent two crewmates to lower the gangplank. "Monsieur Arnaud? Welcome, welcome to my humble ship. Of course, I have communicated with your brother. Most generous he is, too."

Boucher was quite relieved to see Claude so he could set sail. Further delays would cause him to lose a substantial cargo and, with it, a large profit. Of course, he had received a substantial overpayment from Claude's wealthy half-brother, Laurent, the acknowledged son of Duke Charles de Rochefort. Laurent had wanted to assure that the ship would be waiting when Claude and his family arrived and offered to pay for lost profits if the ship had to delay past its usual sailing time.

Claude and his wife and daughter climbed up and reached the deck, where the Captain graciously welcomed them. Crew members were there to carry their boxes and bags except they had no travel bags at all.

After prepaying the passage for Claude and his family, Laurent had not stopped there. Not only had he purchased the largest private cabin on the ship, he had also arranged for the Captain to deliver Claude a purse of gold, new clothes and more food than they could eat on their journey. And, knowing Claude's penchant for French wine, Laurent had made sure the ship was fully stocked with a wide selection.

Claude knew the risks of a sea voyage, but he realized Laurent had tried to make it as comfortable a sailing as possible given the long trip they faced.

*

After what seemed like a lifetime of traveling, the Arnauds had finally arrived at Le Havre. They descended the gangplank from Captain Boucher's ship onto the dock. Now that they were in France, they found it hard to remember the long, cold nights in the woods and the times they had to ration berries and roots to survive.

Feeling safe for the first time in months, they all felt their long journey was but a bad dream. Their months of suffering and hardship had paid off, and they were in their new home at last.

Claude hired a carriage driver to take them to the Highpoint boarding house at the top of the hill above the port. Adèle was jumpy during the ride, not knowing how to anticipate the reaction of her sister Claire and her husband Michel Broussard, the owners of Highpoint.

Claude tried to calm her. "She will be so pleased to see you. And to meet our daughter."

Adèle nodded as Pauline held her hand. "Maman, do they know we are coming?"

Adèle looked at Claude, and then shook her head. "We left too suddenly to write."

Claude agreed. "We were lucky that the Captain delayed the sailing date until we arrived. At first, I feared the weather would delay the boat or cause the ship to cancel the trip altogether. But thanks to Laurent, Captain Boucher had been paid handsomely to wait as long as it took for our arrival."

Adèle agreed, "We owe our lives to him."

When the carriage rounded the bend and pulled up in front of the house, Claire and her husband Michel Broussard waited on the front porch. Michel called out to the carriage, not knowing who would exit. "Welcome to Highpoint."

Claude stepped out of the carriage first and assisted Pauline to step out, followed by Adèle. Claire broke into tears as Adèle ran up to her. The two sisters hugged each other tightly. Their kisses muffled their expressions of love and missed opportunities for so many years.

Michel clasped Claude's hand and slapped his back. "How many years ago did you serve with me in the King's Horsemen?" asked Michel.

Without missing a beat, Claude responded, "The same number as your wedding anniversary and mine."

They both laughed heartily. After the introduction of Pauline to her aunt and uncle, the family retreated into the Inn. They shared a meal and many bottles of wine, after which they regaled each other with stories until the wee hours of the morning.

When his wife and daughter were asleep, Claude re-read Laurent's letter that had convinced him to leave Nova Scotia and return to France. Claude had received it a year after it had been dated, and read as follows:

"Dear brother,

"Whispers are growing loud and spreading quickly throughout Court that England plans to declare war on our King and country. If that happens, the powerful English navy will set up blockades and prevent any French ships from crossing near their territories. Now is the time to leave. It is my most urgent plea that you bring your family to live with me here in Provence.

"I have arranged and prepaid passage for the three of you with Captain Boucher, whose ship docks in Quebec City. He has agreed to take all of you on his next departure for France after you meet him in the port. I beg of you, leave the wilderness of Grand Pré for a civilized life in France.

"Join me, dear brother. Bring your daughter and your other children, if you have them by now, for our large château always welcomes the sounds of more children. Come home, Claude, come back home to France. And come live with me.

"Of course, you shall serve as my valet, as you promised all those many years ago. But it shall not be a difficult service. I actually think it might bring back fond memories of our service to His Majesty at Versailles Palace."

"Your devoted brother (half-brother),

"Laurent."

After silently blessing his brother for providing the motivation, although albeit also a threat, Claude needed to leave Grand Pré he penned a letter to his brother:

"My dear brother Laurent,

"Should I still call you my brother? We are actually half-brothers. And although you are a wealthy noble now, I still consider you my family. I hope you do, too.

"I was unable to respond to your letter for two reasons. First, the letter took a year to reach me. Second, shortly after I received it, I was called by the Lieutenant-Colonel Winslow to present myself in our Catholic Church for a reading of an Edict by the King of England, George II.

"Much happened since then. The English commander locked all the Acadian men and boys over the age of nine in the church although we were promised it was just for a reading. The Edict declared us disloyal to the King, a fabrication, of course, as we had all signed an oath of allegiance to King George II. But the King authorized the troops to seize our homes and any possessions we could not carry or wear on our backs, and condemned us to be separated from our families and shipped out to unknown destinations.

"We presumed most of the Acadians were to be shipped to the English Colonies, but Lord Le Blanc had learned that our parish priest, Père Rivière, had been sent to Bostontown and sold into servitude to work on one of the plantations there.

"As you had warned me, the English are not to be trusted. I took you at your word and I had sent my wife and my daughter to hide with the Mi'Kmaq tribe before they left for their winter encampment. I could not risk their being sold in Bostontown and being separated from the ones I love so much was unimaginable.

"At least I knew they were safe then. I would never have gotten out of the church except to be boarded on a ship but for the strategic genius of our Royal Consul, Lord René Le Blanc.

"You do remember Lord Le Blanc, don't you? You met your wife Lady Véronique at the banquet celebrating his wedding to Lady Eugenie de Beaufort. That was the same banquet where you and I were in service.

"Lord Le Blanc organized a group of us imprisoned in the church to dig a tunnel from the cellar into the woods. He allowed all the single men to escape. He refused married men because Lieutenant-Colonel Winslow had threatened to hang the family members of any man who escaped from the church.

"I would not risk hurting my family, but I talked with Lord Le Blanc and convinced him that they were out of reach of the English troops and that we had a plan to go to Quebec City. That was your plan, my dear brother.

"After many missteps and a grueling journey to reach a French fort, we were able to contact one of the suppliers to Adèle's couture shop and he hid us in a false bottom in his wagon all the way to the Quebec City harbor. That is where we met your Captain Boucher, a delightful gentleman who took extremely good care of us on board his ship.

"The long and short of it is that we have arrived safely in Le Havre but not after the most harrowing experience at sea. My daughter Pauline declared that she saw a huge sea monster about to swallow us whole. But Captain Boucher deftly steered the ship out of its path and we landed safely at Île Royale.

"We watched from afar as the "monster" destroyed everything in its path, though it turned out to be a whale-sized wave. The Captain said he had never seen a sight like it before. As we disembarked onto the wharf, it trembled and shook so hard we fell down. We laughed and cried and did not know what to make of what happened next.

"The oddest group of miniature-sized islanders welcomed us. The greatest surprise of all was to find their leader was Karaztyev, a gypsy I had caught stealing Lord Le Blanc's wedding gifts on the route from Versailles to the port of Le Havre.

"That was seventeen years ago but it seems like yesterday. I had married my beautiful bride Adèle whose mother owned the boarding house Highpoint where we had rested before we set sail on *L'Acadie* for Grand Pré.

"We never could have imagined the adventure that awaited us then, nor the adventure that we embraced to meet you.

"I must confess I did not want to leave our home. Adèle had a thriving couture shop and our daughter Pauline was happy with her friends. But the English betrayed us and exiled the men and boys over the age of nine, separating them from their families and scattering them throughout their Colonies. We shall talk more of this distressing subject when we meet.

"For now, we are grateful that you had previously arranged passage for us, as many Acadians were not so fortunate to escape that fate. My family and I are at Highpoint at present with Adèle's sister and her husband. I await word as when you would like us to travel to your estate.

"I respectfully accept your offer to let my family live on your estate, but I would never assume to live in your château with your Lady and your children of nobility. If you can spare a servant's cottage and a small plot of land to raise vegetables, I will pay you every penny of the passage and the rental of the little property once I can get my affairs in order.

"Again, my dear brother, I am in your debt. I purposefully never acknowledged that I lost our wager those many years ago, as I never thought we should meet again. But even if there had not been a bet, I shall be your humble servant forever for the priceless gift of freedom and security you have given my family.

"Your eternally grateful brother (half-brother),

"Claude."

The next morning, Claude walked down to the port and handed the letter to the coachman bound for Paris. As he watched him drive away, he knew not how the letter would reach his brother. But what he was certain of was that the nobility were known far and wide. The de Rochefort name was one of the oldest, most powerful families in France. He did not fear that the letter would arrive at its proper destination. What he worried about was how Laurent would react to it when it was placed in his hands.

Every morning thereafter like clockwork, Claude walked to the port watching for new ship arrivals. He hoped other Acadians had been able to escape the exile, although he knew it was most likely impossible. Each day the port clerk answered the same, that no Acadians other than his family had disembarked the ships. And each day, Claude thanked the clerk and walked back to Highpoint rather than hiring a carriage.

Today, on Claude's walk back up the hill to Highpoint, he realized weeks had passed since he had handed his letter to the coachman. He wondered why he had not heard anything from his brother. Perhaps today he would receive a response. He hoped so. He was anxious to introduce Laurent to his family and to meet his brother's wife and children.

But Claude was most eager to start his new life in France, away from the threat of insecurity and English violence. He looked forward to a new life in the countryside of Provence. Though he had never been there, he imagined the life of a noble there to be one of peace and tranquility. He hoped a noble's brother – half-brother—could have the same life.

Walking the road up to the inn, he noticed a handsome and costly carriage sitting outside the building. As he strolled past the fancy horse-drawn coach, he heard a male voice call out.

"Claude? Is that you? Is it really you?"

Claude whipped around to see a lean male figure garbed in brocade and furs exiting the carriage. His jeweled rings sparkled in the sunlight. He wondered what such a wealthy man could want and how he knew his name. Soon he realized the only logical answer and shouted, "Laurent? My brother? Yes, it is you. Brother!"

Claude gave his younger brother a bear hug as the two men laughed and cried simultaneously. The reunion of the two brothers was enough to bring a tear to the toughest eye. They walked arm-in-arm into Highpoint and ordered the cook to fill the table with food and drink. They began talking at once, each trying to outdo the other with stories of their youth.

Claude recounted, "Remember when the rat appeared in the dining room at Lord Le Blanc's wedding dinner. Such pandemonium. That was...."

Laurent interrupted, "The night I met the Lady who became my wife and won the wager for me. Do not tell me you have forgotten?"

Claude shook his head ruefully. "How could I? You reminded me in each correspondence you sent."

Laurent clapped with glee. "Then you agree to be my valet as soon as my carriage drives you onto my estate?"

Claude nodded and quickly changed the subject. "Of course, but do tell me about Lady Véronique. And your children. Tell me everything that has happened to you in the last seventeen years since we last saw each other."

Claude was as ravenous for information as he was for the delicious dishes that arrived. Platters kept coming out from the kitchen and the brothers partook generously of everything that was served.

The two brothers talked through the night and were still reminiscing in the morning when Pauline and Adèle entered the dining room for their breakfast. At that point, another great reunion ensued.

CHAPTER 58
Disembarkation

British Colonies

The long trail of corpses floated behind each transport within a few short weeks after the Acadians were transported out of Grand Pré in October 1755. Many had died of smallpox and malaria before they even reached their destination. The bloated bodies indicated the dwindling Acadian population on board, and deaths were so commonplace on some of the ships that the crew called working on deck a "death watch."

Despite the tragic demise of many exiles, Winslow and Governor Shirley believed the Acadians should have left of their own accord. Shirley had already advertised for English planters to resettle the former Acadian province and expand his Massachusetts Bay Colony farther north. And, of course, with additional colonists, he could generate greater taxes and more revenues to put into his pocket.

Winslow felt nothing but relief to have washed his hands of this disagreeable matter. The distasteful part was having to force the Acadians to board the transports unwillingly. But Winslow was especially pleased that he had rounded up most of the young Acadian militia, including the ringleader, Gabriel Mius d'Entremont. He thought the decision to send the resistance fighters to Westminster Gatehouse prison was a brilliant resolution to those troublemakers.

After being at sea for several weeks, the ship carrying Gabriel, Marc and the other Acadian militia had been struck by a powerful gale. Furious waves and torrential rains battered the ship and inundated the crew with floods on deck. The craft lurched and pitched as if it were a cat's toy.

Sailors and Turnbull's soldiers valiantly tried to protect the sails and ropes, but the storm intensified and thwarted their efforts. The winds ripped sails to shreds and tore the ropes free to whip around wildly and knock down many a good sailor. Waves crashed so hard on the bridge that the Captain was thrown onto the deck below. The storm did not relent and continued to deluge the crew while still surging over the sides of the ship onto the deck.

Locked in the multi-level holds below, the Acadians were not prepared for their feelings of helplessness as the ship tossed and rocked on the huge waves. Gabriel shouted above the howling winds and pelting rain that pounded the sides of the ships and echoed loudly in the holds. "Acadians, have faith. We have worked together well against the English and we shall do the same now. We must do more than merely survive. We must take this ship. Watch for any opportunity. If you can hear me, spread the word to the others."

As Gabriel was stirring up the passions of his militia in the hold, on deck Turnbull was mourning several soldiers who were swept overboard. He did not particularly care about the men themselves, but was concerned about the loss of manpower. He urged the ship captain, "The loss of sailors weakens the ability of the remaining crew to remove all the water pouring over us. I approve the use of the prisoners."

Amidst the noise of the storm, the Captain agreed. "We should make do with the group from the top hold alone. No need to risk a rebellion." He shouted an order to two of his crew, "Get the men in the top hold and give them buckets. But chain them to each other. Give them no opportunity to escape or overpower our men."

The taller sailor, Ebenezer, grumbled, "Ain't no bodies gonna jump in that churning sea."

Franklin, his chubby shipmate replied, "Lessen they got themselves a death wish. Nary a man can make it alive through them waves."

Ebenezer added, "Them men will be lucky to stay alive in the face of them incoming waves. They is prisoners but no bodies deserve to die like no drowned rats."

The two men dragged the Acadians from the top hold onto the deck, with Gabriel and Marc leading the pack. Once Franklin and Ebenezer chained Gabriel and the others together, the Acadians formed a bucket brigade to empty the decks of the never-ending waves spilling everywhere.

A young Acadian man standing near the side of the ship was swallowed up by a huge wave that pulled him over the side. Gabriel went into action. He called out to the Acadians closest to the man being pounded with water that enveloped his entire body.

"Pull him back, men. Pull. All together. Pull! Pull" With concerted effort, they managed to land the man back on deck. Yet, despite Gabriel's attempts, the young man had swallowed too much water. His face was ashen and his lips were blue. He was gone.

When Gabriel saw it, he shouted out to Ebenezer, "Unchain this man. We must bury him at sea."

Ebenezer ignored him but Franklin taunted, "Get on with yer work, prisoner. Don't give no never mind to them that's gone. Nothing can be done fer him now."

Gabriel was undaunted. He shouted to Turnbull, "Captain? We need to release this man from his chains."

Suddenly, another set of huge waves pounded the deck.

Turnbull aimed his rifle at Gabriel and shouted, "Back to work or you shall join him in the deep."

The crew refused to unchain the Acadians, whether dead or alive. All hands frantically scooped pails of water from the deck and dumped them in the sea, only to find more water had swept over the deck in the meantime. As the Acadians worked harder than the crew to empty the deck of water, the ship was blown off-course.

After what seemed like an eternity, the Captain was able to adjust his course and sail out of the violent tempest. To everyone's surprise, he navigated the ship to Île Royale.

When the transport sailed toward the eerily-quiet harbor, Gabriel thought he saw a family of strangely-dressed people staring at them from cave-houses built into the rocks above the beach. Indeed, Karaztyev and his sons Manfri, Barsali, Ferka and Ruslo watched the ship from their perches along the mountainous road.

Gabriel blinked and looked again, but the men had disappeared. Gabriel could not have imagined that his future father-in-law, René Le Blanc, was recuperating at that moment inside Karaztyev's cave from his own harrowing experience at sea.

*

Karaztyev and his sons descended to the wharf. The ship anchored in deep water but was near enough to the harbor that the Karaztyev family could hear the voices on deck. Likewise, those on the ship overheard, but could not understand, the guttural French uttered by the gypsies.

The ship captain assigned Franklin and Ebenezer to guard the Acadians on deck as soldiers rowed Turnbull ashore. Stepping onto the dock, Turnbull held up a thick sack of coins, then opened it, spewing gold over the wooden planks. At the sight, Karaztyev's eyes sparkled like the coins. Turnbull walked up to the gypsies and announced, "I am a Captain in the British Army heading for England. I need fresh provisions. Have you any to sell?"

Karaztyev stared at Turnbull, grabbed the sack of gold and queried, "What cargo are you carrying?"

Turnbull scoffed. "Animals. Heathens called Acadians. Filth of the earth."

Milosh nodded to Turnbull. "My sons Manfri and Barsali will sell you whatever you need." He barked orders to the two young men, "Fill the cart. with venison, dried fish, bottles of wine, bread, apples, shellfish. And cakes. Bring many cakes." His sons rushed down the beach as Turnbull watched.

Gabriel observed the activity on the beach with curiosity. While still chained on deck, he was happy to be breathing fresh air, despite the winter chill. The little old man directing the young men looked somewhat familiar. Gabriel closed his eyes and tried to remember when he had heard French spoken with such an accent. It had been years ago. Aha! He remembered meeting the man hiding on the ship when Gabriel had sailed with his father Henri to the New World. Gabriel remembered his name. Karaztyev.

Risking the wrath of Turnbull, Gabriel yelled out, "Monsieur Karaztyev? Do you remember *l'Acadie*?" At the sound of his name, Milosh jerked his head around in the direction of the ship. He knew the name of the ship very well where he and his family had stowed away rather than pay the expensive passage to the New World.

"I am Gabriel Mius d'Entremont. You knew my father Henri? And our French Consul Lord Le Blanc?"

At Gabriel's shout, Turnbull tried to shout to the captain, "Put the prisoners back in the hold." But the captain was below in his quarters, waiting for Turnbull's return. Turnbull turned to his soldiers and issued a stern order. "Row back to the ship and tell the crew to put the prisoners back in the hold."

Turnbull's soldiers jumped, ready to obey. But one cocky young sailor, who reported not to Turnbull but to the ship captain, retorted, "If we do that, we shall not have time to return for you. Hear the winds?" Turnbull and the soldiers cocked their heads and listened. They heard the wind whistle where before it had been silent. "They are starting to blow. We should set sail very soon."

Turnbull grumbled, "Then let us get on with it."

Manfri and Barsali returned with a cart loaded with foodstuffs. While Turnbull directed his men to offload the supplies onto his rowboat, Milosh scampered down the wharf, bidding his sons Ferka and Ruslo to follow.

With a sly grin, Milosh announced, "We shall go to the ship." They jumped into one of their rowboats. In no time, his sons rowed to the anchored ship out of Turnbull's view. The three men shimmied up the rope ladder and came face-to-face with Gabriel. Milosh and Gabriel recognized each other although many years had passed. Though Gabriel was in chains, Milosh gave him a warm bear hug.

"You are young Gabriel? The boy on *L'Acadie* so long ago?"

Despite his grim situation, Gabriel chucked, "Not so young anymore."

Milosh continued, "I owe you my life for not revealing to that Captain where my family and I were hiding."

Gabriel grinned, "It has always been our secret. I have never spoken of it until today. And shall never talk of it again."

Karaztyev stroked his long beard and said, "I must repay you for your silence." As his sons spoke with Gabriel and Marc, Milosh sought out the captain of the ship. He spotted him climbing up on deck. Before he went to the bridge, Karaztyev caught up with him and asked, "How much do you want for that man's freedom? I have gold. The captain just paid me."

The ship captain hesitated. The thought of that much gold was tempting. But he knew these men were gypsies and had no intention of paying him anything. For all he knew, they would promise the gold, take the prisoner back with them and then disappear in the mountains. Then he would be out both his payment and a prisoner. No, he could not take the risk.

He shook his head, "I regret, but I cannot, sir. He is under the charge of Captain Turnbull, the very one on the dock buying vittles from your men."

Milosh looked at the wharf. Turnbull was still loading food onto his rowboat. He nodded to the captain and rushed back over to Gabriel with a riddle. "You must guess who is in my house at this moment."

Gabriel gasped. "Is it -- can it be -- Evangeline is alive? My fiancée?"

The gypsy leaned forward saying, "You are very warm. Almost hot."

Gabriel frowned, "Who could it be?" All of a sudden, he realized, "Consul Le Blanc is alive? How wonderful. I thought for certain the old hull that took him away would have sunk."

Karaztyev shook his head vehemently, "It did, but he rowed and ended up on our beach. When we found him, he was very ill indeed. Still, my wife and daughters are better than physicians. They have cared for him these past weeks. He is getting stronger every day."

Gabriel squeezed his eyes. He suddenly felt very sad and did not want to shed a tear. Not on the boat. Not in front of his militia. He said quietly, "Tell him I am being sent to Westminster Gatehouse Prison in England. And if -- when -- he sees his daughter, Evangeline, tell her my heart belongs only to her. If I am released, I shall travel the world to find her. But I hold little hope."

Milosh apologized profusely, "I tried to buy your freedom. Alas, that captain refused. He must have figured I would not pay him. But I would have. I would have paid a lot of gold for you. I am sorry."

He clasped Gabriel's hands, though his wrists were locked in chains, and slipped him some gold coins. Out of sight of the captain, Gabriel put them into the pocket of his pantaloons.

Ferka saw Turnbull and his crew finish loading the stores in their rowboat. They cast off and were heading for the ship. Ferka tapped his father's shoulder and said, "We should go, Papa."

Gabriel and Milosh nodded a goodbye as the gypsy and his sons scampered back down the rope to their boat. Before Turnbull knew they had been aboard, the Karaztyevs had rowed swiftly around the other side of the boat and had landed on the shore.

As Turnbull directed the soldiers to unload the food supplies, the gypsies scampered up the road to their caves, where Milosh's other two sons waited with their cart, now empty. In the blink of an eye, all the gypsies disappeared from view.

The Acadian prisoners were sent back to the holds and the captain charted a course again for London. As they sailed away from Île Royale, Gabriel and the other Acadians prayed that each would survive the trip and yet somehow escape their fate at Westminster Gate.

CHAPTER 59
Colonies

Bostontown

Ships carrying Acadians destined for ports other than Boston had been blown off course after the earthquake and storms. They had sought shelter in Massachusetts Bay and had to remain there until the harbor master determined that ships could once again sail safely out of the harbor.

The Acadians had been locked in their holds for weeks as the ships anchored in the port. Many became too sickly to continue traveling. These were dumped on the docks of Boston Harbor.

Jonas Cornhandle was called on by the city officials to inspect the pitiful specimens. He passed on each one of the Acadians. He told the council members, "These men are too old, too sickly or both to do any work. I know of no plantation owner who would pay a penny for the lot of them."

The officials mulled over the situation amongst themselves. In the end, they decided to do nothing. Without food, blankets or shelter in the freezing weather, many of the Acadians died soon after they arrived, solving part of the problem for the city councillors.

But the issue of the survivors remained. The councillors did not wish to pay the costs of these men. Instead, they hired Apthorp & Hancock to furnish a ship and crew to send them to the North Carolina Colony. The Acadians appeared weak and begged to be left on deck to breathe healthy air. The crew fell for the ruse, and as soon as the ship was out of sight of the harbor, the Acadians overpowered the crew, set them off the ship in rowboats and sailed to French Louisiana.

*

After many weeks, the British transports carrying the Acadians who were well enough to travel were finally authorized to set sail for their designated Colonies of Pennsylvania, Virginia, Maryland, the Carolinas and Georgia. The ships found themselves with a lighter cargo after removing the dead bodies from the hold and tossing them into the harbor. As they sailed away from Bostontown, the crew watched as discarded bloated corpses that had not been properly weighted with stones rose to the surface, to the horror of Boston inhabitants.

The Bostonians passed laws against the Acadians, partly because of their religion and partly because they were French. Those that were too weak or ill to be sold by Cornhandle, had to beg for work to survive. Though not many found employment, those who did were often mistreated by their employers and ignored by the authorities when the Acadians lodged protests.

One young boy was apprenticed to a furniture maker. The man was not happy with the boy's work, so he beat his arm so badly he could not work for a month.

Two Acadian brothers worked a month at a factory and when they asked for their wages on the pay day, the factory owner refused. When the brothers threatened to report the owner to the council, he beat them to within an inch of their lives and fired them without any compensation.

An Acadian who complained that he did not receive money for working for a business was given old clothes and animal fat, then he was beaten with a poker until his face and mouth bled for days.

An elderly man was given an old house with no roof, but no materials to build a new roof and no job to pay for one. When it rained and the house flooded, the man complained to the council but was told to build a boat and float in it.

So many other Acadians were mistreated, abused and lied to by the shopkeepers and employers in Boston that they began to dream of escaping. The council passed laws preventing Acadians from moving from one town to another. But still, some of them succeeded in getting away.

*

Lieutenant-Governor Phips sent a letter by his fastest courier to the Governor of New Hampshire. When the Governor received it, he perused it carefully, reading it aloud to his staff.

"Dear Governor,

"It is with the utmost urgency that I plead with you to take some of the Acadian prisoners exiled from our northern province. Other colonies have taken their fair share but cannot take any more. I beg you, sir, to help us fulfill the orders of our holy King.

"Lieutenant-Governor Phips."

Without bothering to take a fresh piece of parchment, the Governor wrote a cursory note on the back of Phips' missive.

"Lieutenant-Governor Phips,

"In receipt of your request this day. I am not in a position to assist you. Any ships sent here shall be returned forthwith."

The courier was not literate, but he was a good judge of human nature. He knew he would have to brace himself when he returned with the short response, knowing full well his superior would not be happy with it.

Staving off the inevitable, the courier took to the local tavern and drank himself to sleep, hoping an accident would befall him before he arrived at Phips' mansion. Unfortunately for him, he survived the trip only to be severely beaten by Phips with his cane upon reading the Governor's note.

*

Governor William Shirley received a copy of The *Maryland Gazette* dated December 4, 1755 from that Colony's Governor. He read it aloud to his aide, Stratford, becoming angrier with each sentence.

"Sunday last arrived here the last of the vessels from Nova Scotia with French neutrals for this place, which make four within this fortnight who have brought upwards of 900 of them. The poor people have been deprived of their settlements in Nova Scotia, and sent here bare and destitute for some political reason. Christian charity, nay common humanity, calls on every one according to their ability to lend their assistance and help to these objects of compassion."

Shirley exploded. "Who do they think they are? Mary Land is a British Colony just as Massachusetts. They owe allegiance to His Majesty. They dare not question our King's removal orders. Besides, this Colony is quite rural with much open land. How can they possibly understand our overcrowding and the demand for factories and manufactured goods? The northern territory is essential for growing crops to feed our expanding population. The other Colonies may not experience these problems for decades to come. I shall write the Governor and tell him that they shall receive more ships of Acadians since they are such a welcoming Colony."

Stratford always agreed with his superior, who held Stratford's career in his hands. He was pleased to report that unlike "welcoming" Mary Land, more ships carrying Acadians had landed successfully in Virginia and Georgia after they implemented a proposal that Shirley himself had devised.

Shirley wrote letters to other Colonial Governors, citing with pride his proposal that the two Colonies had put into operation, saying:

"They separated the Acadians upon arrival, dispersed them throughout each Colony and ordered them to remain in the assigned towns and villages or suffer punishment. All other Colonies should consider this successful plan."

But Shirley caught wind that some Colonies had rejected the Acadians. He barked to Stratford, "Investigate the reasons for refusing the delivery of the French. I shall bring their insubordination to the London Board of Trade, that reports to the King. Or perhaps I shall write to His Majesty personally."

Stratford scrambled to get the information for his boss. When he had all of the information, he was hesitant to deliver his report that Pennsylvania and Delaware had both rejected the Acadians.

Shirley wrote to officials in Philadelphia the next day, stating:

"Pennsylvania is known to be a Colony with a strong affirmation of religious tolerance. Your religious beliefs as Quakers are proof of this. All the Acadians want is to practice their religion in peace, though we know that religion is heathen."

The Pennsylvania Governor was piqued, sending a huffy statement:

"If your western border was the French territory of Louisiana, you would refuse to allow any new Frenchies from entering. What happens if they invade us from within by joining with their brethren next to us?"

Shirley argued forcefully in his reply:

"These Acadians have not been French for generations. They have been loyal to England and are most likely unaware of French territory in any case. You shall accept them now."

Shirley did not receive a reply. Embarrassed by the lack of response, he turned his attention to Delaware. Stratford's account stated that the Colony's reason for refusal was a rumor of several shipboard cases of smallpox.

Shirley's directive to the Delaware Governor was short and concise:

"Disembark the Acadians onto a dock and lock them in an old building that can house them all. Take away their shirts and socks and burn them. Do not provide them with additional clothing or blankets. Finally, set armed guards at all entrances and let no one escape for food, wood, or any other purpose. Force them to remain inside until those with the pox are dead."

The Governor followed Shirley's suggestion. In short order, only a few Acadians remained alive in the building. They were placed in squalid, broken-down barns until the roofs had caved in from the weight of the snow.

In July 1756, Governor Lawrence received correspondence from the London Board of Trade disputing his belief that all the Acadians ended up in the colonies. Lawrence had no idea that the letter had been generated as a result of a communique from Shirley months earlier. The letter read:

"Governor Lawrence,

"We are informed that two boatloads of French prisoners you exiled from Nova Scotia have newly arrived in London. The officials in South Carolina and Virginia have refused the heathens entry into their colonies.

"Now our work houses are overflowing. Should you wish to retain your command and the luxuries accompanying your title, immediately assert more forcefully that each Colony must accept the Frenchies without protest.

"If you are unable to do so, we are confident another officer will. This is the end of our communication on this matter."

Lawrence was furious and lashed out at his staff. "The pox on you for not using a heavy hand with those ship captains. They are hired to do our bidding. My bidding. His Majesty's bidding. Going forward, each of you shall travel with a ship and supervise dumping all cargo onshore. I care not if you must empty the holds yourself and throw the heathens into the harbor, but assure that the captain leaves them in port and sets sail immediately thereafter."

The staff grumbled but knew Lawrence was right. The heathens needed to stay where they were deposited.

*

In Bostontown, the city fathers were in a panic. They had been kept in the dark by Shirley as to the boatloads of Acadians who had arrived in the harbor and were moved outside the city. Were the Frenchies planning to take over the town? Were they gathering forces to rob the treasury and build new lives for themselves? Being ignorant of the lucrative agreement between the Governor and Cornhandle, they imagined the worst.

Since the Governor knew they were in no danger of any takeover by the Acadians, he remained oblivious to the consternation of the Boston officials. His focus was in attracting English planters to the newly-vacant homes and fields in Nova Scotia. When the officials tried to contact him, he responded in a brusque letter:

"You are quite capable of handling your local affairs. We concern ourselves with the broader concerns of the entire colony. The offices of Jonas Cornhandle will provide the remedy to your problems and relieve any burdens you imagine. Allow the plan to work itself out."

The correspondence infuriated the townspeople of Boston, who grew angrier and more resentful at the thought of overcrowding their beautiful city. They wrote to Governor Lawrence, but his response was curt:

"I had no apprehensions that it would occasion any considerable charge to the provinces, or that it would be disagreeable thing to have those people sent there. I am sorry that it is likely to prove so burdensome but I have it not in my power to support them at the charge of the Crown."

*

Governor William Shirley's attempts to assert his power against colonial authorities was largely ineffectual. Shortly after the Acadian Exile, he lost the respect of his peers and, with it, his positions.

Later, he was charged with treason and sent to England for his trial but was eventually exonerated. He received another appointment, this time as Governor of the Bahamas Islands. When his term expired, he returned home to Massachusetts, where he died a broken man.

CHAPTER 60
Jeanne

Massachusetts Bay Colony

The lumbering ship with Jeanne Lambert, Anne Gaudet and other Acadian women sailed toward Boston and the slave auction to be held shortly after their arrival. The two women were on deck for their daily walk in the salty air. Today, huge waves crashed over the sides and pelted them with water. The captain tied them to each other with ropes. He did not want to lose any silly women overboard. He knew Jonas Cornhandle would reduce the bribe if he lost even one.

The ship arrived in the harbor under an awning of dark winter clouds. Cornhandle greeted the captain by shoving a pile of gold coins in his hands. Satisfied with the bribe, the captain directed his crew. "Men, empty the holds. Make certain everyone makes it down the gangplank."

Jeanne held tightly onto Anne's hand as they managed to descend the slippery plank. "Madame Gaudet, stay with me at all times. I promised Béatrice I would watch over you." Anne nodded, seeming to understand, as she gawked at the tall warehouses at the dock. "Blerksep tindel," she cooed.

Cornhandle was careful not to harm his merchandise so he offered his hand to the women to step into his large horse-drawn carts. He lifted crying children into the wagons and patted their heads, to no avail. Impatiently he called out, "Quiet yer little ones or ye shall see the lash when we arrive."

Jeanne asked politely, "Where are we going, sir?"

Cornhandle grunted as he sat next to the lead driver, "Ye shall see."

The carts rolled through town carrying hundreds of women and children. Couples on the street and in shops stopped to watch the wagons, but not out of surprise because Cornhandle paraded his wares whenever he had them. The men stared at the pretty women hoping to afford one as a mistress. The women looked for homely girls to work as maids and hoped their husbands would not want to take them for themselves.

Anne stared at the dazzling women dressed in the latest fashions and the men resplendent in their brocade jackets and breeches. She recognized they presented a fine sight but then turned her attention to tall brick houses that lined the streets. She pointed them out to Jeanne, "Chlinsing, revnim, soomler." As always, Jeanne nodded pretending to know the words, but this time she understood Anne's awe. "Yes, Madame, soomler, soomler."

After passing rows of shops and houses, Cornhandle's wagons exited the city and traveled on the dirt pathways to arrive a warehouse in a field. The women were shocked and dismayed to be unloaded in the rude building.

Jeanne spoke up, "Sir, we were told we would be given our own houses and would be employed. We must buy food and clothes. And medicine."

Cornhandle snorted with derision at the thought of those straggling heathens living amongst the wealthy town folk of Boston. Cornhandle turned to Jeanne, ready to slap her. But she was too attractive. If he bruised her, she would sell for less. He gritted his teeth and said, "Thank your lucky stars you are a pretty sight, missy. You escaped a good beating, you did."

Cornhandle pushed the dawdling women and children through the narrow door into the old building. The women woefully entered the very place where their husbands, brothers, fathers and sons had stayed before their auction. He surprised them with his next statement. "Divide up the stuffed bedding and blankets amongst ye. Find a spot and get some sleep. Ye have a big day ahead tomorrow. Then is when ye shall go to yer houses."

The women sighed in relief. A young Acadian woman of twelve, Cecile Roy, whispered to Jeanne, "So the crew members did speak the truth. Thank goodness. I would not want to stay here. It is filthy."

Cornhandle's assistant Bow left sacks of hard bread and dried meat and water jugs by the door. "Eat your fill. Ye get another share on the morrow."

Jeanne turned to Cecile, "At least they thought to give us food. If I am hungry, the children must be starving. Let us distribute these stores." They handed out the food and drink to each group that had formed. Suddenly, Cornhandle shut the door, casting the place into darkness. Children whimpered and cried as the women who had become their new mothers held them for reassurance. Gradually the Acadians' eyes adjusted to the moonlight streaming through the cracks in the roof and the barred windows.

Carrying food and a jug of water, Jeanne and Cecile half-led, half-dragged Anne to the back of the building. They fluffed the pine needle beds so they could lay on them. Jeanne pounded the bed to remove the dust. A small piece of wood popped out. It was carved with some letters and numbers that Jeanne read in the moonlight. "Jean-Luc Pellerin. 1755."

Jeanne called out, "Is anyone from the Pellerin family here? Jean-Luc was brought here. He carved his name and the date in this memento."

A young girl sitting with an old woman called out, "I am his sister here with our grandmother." Jeanne carefully scooted between the beds to deliver the wood to them. The girl clutched it to her breast. "My older brother. That means he is still alive." The grandmother hugged the girl and wept. "He is in Bostontown. I shall see him again before I am gone. Praise the Lord."

*

The next day, the Acadian women were loaded into Cornhandle's carts and driven to the wooden stage set up for the auction. They climbed down from the carts and were pushed assembly-line style past a water trough. They had been allowed three minutes to wash their face before they were lined up outside Cornhandle's cart. He personally inspected their hair for lice, their mouth for loose teeth and their blouses for stuffing.

If anything was amiss, that female was sent back inside the storage building where Bow personal inspected every orifice to make sure no owner could accuse Cornhandle of selling false merchandise. Jonas was a slave trader, a cad, and an obnoxious little man, but he prided himself on being honest with his customers. What they saw is what they got.

When Cornhandle had auctioned the Acadian men a month earlier, he had ripped their shirts off to show the muscles rippling in their backs and arms. Today was the first auction of Acadian women and girls, and Cornhandle had decided to do something similar. No one would accuse him of cheating or faking physical attributes auctioned to the highest bidders, so he did a hands-on inspection of each one before loading the carts.

"If Cornhandle touches me one more time, I promise I shall bite his fingers off," Cecile whispered to Jeanne.

Jeanne's reply was terse. "Shush. He will just hurt you worse. Forget him. Smile when you get up there. Perhaps we shall end up together."

"But how ever shall we escape and make our way to Louisiana? You know that is where our families and friends promised to reunite?"

"Have faith and be watchful. We shall each find our own way."

Bow walked up to them and said abruptly, "Auction is starting. Hush!"

Cornhandle walked up to the solid wood podium he had paid a local Bostontown carpenter to build. His performance on the auction block was not just to intimidate the Acadians who were lined up awaiting their turn. He wanted to impress the hundreds of colonists from near and far who had gathered to watch the latest lineup of Acadians.

Jonas had built his reputation throughout the Colonies because he had "the eye" for selecting the right workers for fields as well as main houses. But he always had more buyers than the number of Acadians shipped by Governor Shirley to Boston. Due to the industrialization of the region, colonial plantation masters were in dire need of cheap labor. They looked to Cornhandle to solve their dilemma.

And solve it he did. He loved to pound his gavel indicating a sale and the solution to the owner's problem. He licked his lips and nodded to Bow to start the show. Bow helped Cecile and Jeanne up the stairs to the wooden stage raised above the level of the gawkers below.

Cornhandle did not allow anyone to touch the merchandise. He had no way of knowing if they were potential buyers or simply young men starving for affection. Months earlier, an energetic young colonist had pulled a young girl down from the auction block to kiss her, and he had broken her arm.

Cornhandle had to refund part of the price when the owner's wife complained about the girl. "She can't even carry a heavy pail of water or walk with a load of washing till her arm heals. She is not worth full price."

After that, Cornhandle had hired a former soldier armed with a musket who stood at the stage glaring at the audience. No one broke the rule again.

Cornhandle proudly announced the next sale. "Take a gander at what we have here. No finer, lovelier ladies I assure you have ever been seen."

Bow hissed at Cecile and Jeanne, "Give them a big smile and show those pretty white pearls. Sign of good health. And Cornhandle gets more fer ye. Remember what I learned ye? Do yer turn in the middle then move back. And don't talk. Men don't buy women that talk all the time."

First, Cecile walked to the center of the stage and whirled around. Cornhandle walked up to her, unhappy that she was not smiling. He grabbed her mouth and pulled her lips apart, showing shiny white teeth. The crowed oohed and aahed. She was a healthy one, for sure. Then he lifted up her skirts and the slip she wore, displaying her nether region for all to see. Cecile turned red, and pulled her clothes down, then walked to the side.

Jeanne walked up after that, smiled widely at the audience, displaying her teeth. She did not want Cornhandle's dirty hands all over her, so she did a little dance and raised her skirts a time or two, enough to give a hint but not a clear picture of her privates, then moved next to Cecile.

Bow helped several older Acadian women after. Jonas was ready to force their mouths open, but every one of them smiled. He sighed in relief that this first group all had good teeth. Anne clomped up the stairs and ran across the stage with her hands in a halo about her head. The audience began to laugh, which scared her. She dropped to the floor of the stage and spoke her nonsense. "Brudlimy tromler." More laughter from the gawkers.

Jeanne danced over to her and helped her up, whispering to her, "It is alright. Just stay with me, Madame Gaudet. You will be fine." Anne followed her to the end of the stage. She sucked her thumb as she did so and turned away from the audience.

A tall and homely plantation owner, Marcus Fieldstone, was on the front row of buyers next to the stage. He nodded approvingly to Cornhandle. Cornhandle tipped his hat to Fieldstone. A good customer, that one.

Cornhandle called out from the podium. "Do I hear fifty pounds to start?" He pointed to Cecile." Twelve years old. Pretty teeth. Fifty?"

Fieldstone called out, "Done. Cook needs a scullery maid."

"Not so fast, Mister Fieldstone. The auction is not yet over. This one is a bargain at fifty, so who shall offer seventy-five?"

Another buyer in the audience called out, "Seventy-five here."

Cornhandle nodded. "And one hundred? Any takers for one hundred for this pretty little lass?"

The buyers talked among themselves but none were willing to pay the price. Cornhandle could not risk letting buyers become restless so he pounded the gavel. "Sold for seventy-five pounds to Mister Ichabod Millenwhist.

The buyer handed the notes to Cornhandle and Bow escorted Cecile off the stage and into the colonist's carriage. Cecile waved sadly to Jeanne, who smiled and waved back. Then Jeanne walked to the center of the stage. Jeanne wanted to choose her buyer but in the sea of faces staring up at her she saw nary a smiling one. She guessed that Fieldstone would be a kind master so she smiled directly at him and did another little dance.

Cornhandle was impressed. He started the bidding high. "One hundred for our dancer. One hundred pounds anyone?" Fieldstone was tired of the game. "One hundred fifty if you close this sale now."

The gasp in the audience was audible. It was unheard of to offer such a high price so early in the process. Most buyers made an entire day of the spectacle. They brought a picnic lunch and sat on a blanket at the intermission to discuss what they had seen, if the prices were too high or too low and such gossip. They were disappointed that they would not see the woman dance again.

Cornhandle looked around but could not afford to lose this one so he quickly banged the gavel. "Sold. Mister Marcus Fieldstone. One fifty."

Bow tried to help Jeanne down the stairs but she pushed him away and climbed down of her own accord. She did allow Fieldstone to assist her into the carriage. Fieldstone joined her. "Sit next to me, my dear," when Jeanne tried to sit on the seat opposite the man who had paid a small fortune for her.

"I should not like to inconvenience your comfort, sir," she said in English. He motioned for her to sit next to him, and she obeyed. She could not afford to upset him. Not in her situation. She needed time to find out how to ingratiate herself to him and explain that she was engaged and only wanted to marry the man she loved. She hoped he would understand.

That surprised the wealthy man, who took her hand and caressed it. "I expected to speak French with you, though I must say your English is ten times better than my speaking your language."

"We are all educated women, sir. I helped my parents run their boarding house by ciphering the accounts as well as preparing the meals."

"Ahh," he was pleased, "So you can cook."

"I am told my cooking skills are excellent, sir, but you shall be the judge of that." She discreetly pulled her hand out of his. He did not seem to notice.

"I am happy to hear it." He then looked off into the distance through the carriage window.

"How far is your plantation?"

He looked at her briefly, as if being pulled back from a dream. "Quite far. We shall be riding for hours. But we shall stop at an inn along the way for supper. Are you hungry?"

She nodded. "That would be most appreciated, kind sir. Thank you."

He nodded and gazed off again. He said nothing until they reached the inn. He assisted her out of the carriage by putting his hands on her waist. It took everything she had not to grimace, but then he offered her his arm.

When they entered the inn, he escorted Jeanne into the noisy dining hall. They sat on rough-hewn benches and the innkeeper's wife handed them each a tray filled with beef, potatoes and bread. She soon returned with two mugs of grog.

Fieldstone dug into the meal without saying a word. Jeanne ate as fast as she possibly could lest they take it away. He finished and stared at the drunks and farmers in the hall. "I lost my wife last year," he said simply.

"I am so sorry to hear that. I shall pray for her," Jeanne replied.

"Ready? We still have a long ride before we get home." He stood abruptly and offered his arm to her.

"Yes, sir." She gladly leaned on him to avoid the lewd men ogling her.

He left a coin on the table that the innkeeper's wife quickly snatched up. When she saw how much it was, she followed him all the way out, "Thank ye, sir. Can I get ye something else? Use of the bed upstairs for a roll or two?" He glared at her and she whimpered back to the bar.

Once back in the carriage, Jeanne fell asleep. Without realizing it, she leaned against her new master, who put his arm around her to steady her as the carriage hit potholes and bumps in the road. More than once he leaned over and smelled her hair, then leaned back and closed his eyes. She reminded him of his wife. Poor sweet Lily.

The next morning, Jeanne awoke in a comfortable feather bed in a large bright bedroom. A servant girl drew the curtains open and brought her a tray of food.

"Hungry, Miss? Master Fieldstone says to make sure you eat a good breakfast. He is a-taking you riding today with Mistress Fieldstone."

Jeanne rubbed her eyes. Was she dreaming? She had imagined the worst but prayed for the best. Was this to be her life here? He had told her he was a widower, had he not?

"Mistress Fieldstone? Where is she?"

"She got the big rooms down in the other wing all to herself."

"You mean they don't stay in the same room? Master and Mistress?"

"Heavens, no, Miss. They ain't married. They is brother and sister."

"I see. Thank you for the tray. What is your name?"

"Lizzie I am, Miss."

"Thank you, Lizzie."

"If I make ye late, I'll get the hide beat out of me. When the Master wants something, ye gots to do it or you pay fer it."

"I shall remember that."

Lizzie droned on, "The last girl he brought listened nary a bit."

"Where is she?" Jeanne was a bit worried.

"Gone. Nobody knows where. Just up and left. That's what the Master said. Just gone. Yer riding clothes is laid out in yer dressing room."

Jeanne looked around. She saw many doors leading in and out of the bedroom but did not know where to go. "Where is it? This dressing room?"

Lizzie pointed to the third door on the left wall. "There it is, Miss. Hurry, Miss. When the clock strikes the hour, ye best be downstairs."

"Of course." Jeanne looked at the clock. She had about twenty minutes. She grabbed the tray and rushed into the little room. She gobbled her food, she washed it down with a lemon-flavored liquid. She tore off her dressing gown, thrust her legs into the riding garb and slipped into the leather boots. She wondered how he knew her size and why he insisted she go riding.

She presented herself exactly at the appointed hour downstairs and Marcus took her hand and led her out to the stables. There, he had the stable groom assist her up onto her horse and Marcus took off. "Keep up with me, Lily," he called out. Jeanne was confused, but knew that she had best do what he says. He owned her now and as Lizzie had explained, she did not want to get on his bad side.

When they finished riding, he bade her goodbye. "Your uniform is on your bed. When you change come downstairs and serve tea."

Jeanne quickly changed and ran back downstairs. In a maid's uniform, she served tea to Marcus and his sister, Eliza, who squirmed uncomfortably.

Eliza said, "I need the girl to help me in town with my packages."

He disagreed. "But my dear sister, I have plans for her. We shall play cards. I am lonely and want her companionship."

"Jeanne, wait for me in the wagon," Eliza said.

"Do not move, girl," Marcus ordered.

Eliza glared at her brother intensely. After a moment, he backed down and walked over to her, holding up a hundred-pound note, a small fortune. "Give this to Cornhandle. I owe him for – something. I suppose I shall have to amuse myself alone today. You are a selfish old hag, Eliza."

Eliza angrily jerked Jeanne by the arm, half-dragged her out of the house to the carriage and shoved her in the coach. When it was rolling, Eliza screeched, "Hussy! Seducer! You are trying to take my brother from me."

"No, madame. I am doing nothing of the sort. I am your servant and his. I do not wish to come between you. I only wish to do my job."

The carriage careened around the corner and halted in front of Cornhandle's office. Eliza stormed out, muttering, "I shall show you and him both." She stayed in the office for a goodly two hours and exited on Cornhandle's arm back to the carriage. Eliza stepped into the carriage and smoothed the folds of her silk dress she took her seat across from Jeanne.

Cornhandle called out to Jeanne, "Come into the office, dear. Miss Fieldstone asked me to speak with you."

Eliza smiled at her, so Jeanne followed him into the office. But Eliza's coach sped away. Jeanne looked askance, "What is to become of me?"

He smiled, the sunlight glinting on his gold tooth. "Do not fear. Jonas Cornhandle shall take care of you." His wife Prudence waddled out from behind the curtain. He handed her the hundred-pound-note and whispered instructions. She gave Jeanne the once-over, pinched her waist and cupped her hands around Jeanne's breasts. Jeanne was speechless. Prudence finished and shuffled out. "Care for some tea?" Jonas leered at her.

Jeanne shook her head. "The mistress of the house has left me alone with you, your wife has felt my private parts and you ask me if I want tea?"

He nodded. "And some bread and cheese? You look like you could eat."

Jeanne had to admit she was. "Frankly, I could eat a horse."

"That is more like it," he retorted. By the time Jeanne finished the food and drank the tea, Prudence had returned. She handed a stuffed travel bag to her husband and disappeared behind the curtain. Cornhandle pulled some papers out of his desk, dipped a quill in ink and signed the documents with a flourish, then rolled the blotter over the ink before handing them to Jeanne. "Your travel documents, your passage, warm clothes, food and a few coins."

"But where am I going? I need to bring Madame Gaudet with me?"

"Forget the old woman. After you left, she ran into the street and was hit by a carriage. As for you, missy, Mistress Fieldstone wanted me to send you far away. To New Orleans. Your ship leaves in one hour. Do not miss it. Goodbye and good luck to ye."

Jeanne was both elated by her good fortune and saddened by the news of Anne Gaudet's fatal accident. But Jeanne was going to Louisiana where she was certain Marc was waiting for her.

CHAPTER 61
Proposal

At Sea

While Jeanne and the other Acadian women were learning their fate in Cornhandle's auctions in Bostontown, a storm was blowing Christine's ship far away from the same destination, unbeknownst to the Acadians on board. Captain Swillingham, a grossly overweight little man, cursed the storm under his breath. "Dad blast them winds. They done blowed me so far south of Bostontown there ain't no way I can get there now."

Swillingham boasted an eye patch and a beard so thick and unkempt his face was nearly entirely covered in hair. The moustache he sported was spotted with particles of bread and meat partially buried within. He cursed louder, oblivious to whoever might hear him. This was his ship and he would do as he pleased. He yelled his anger over the powerful winds blustering on deck. "Dad blast 'em. Now I gots to find another port to sell me cargo and for good money. Dad blast them all."

In the hold below deck, the Acadian women were cramped and miserable as the ship tossed and turned in the tempest. Yvonne Poché wept in a corner. "I will never see my beloved husband again. Never. How can I live without him?"

Christine scooted over to her as other Acadians cleared a pathway for her. "We are all going to make a new life for ourselves. Let us make the best of it and help each other. We do not even know our destination. Surely, we shall all feel comfort once we learn where we are going. Monsieur Poché might already be there. Come now, sleep for a while." Christine wrapped her arms around the frail little woman who cried herself to sleep. Christine adamantly refused to abandon her positive outlook. "I shall speak with the Captain. Then we can make a plan."

The other women murmured their agreement, confident that Christine knew what to do. A young girl, Isabelle Cormier, blurted out, "We are so fortunate that you are here. You understand these matters after working for our French Consul for many years. We would be lost without you."

Christine responded, "And I without you. We are all now a family. We shall stay together and survive to tell our grandchildren about this. Let us pray for strength." They bowed their heads and Christine led them in prayer, interrupted ever so often by Yvonne's soft snores.

When the winds subsided, Swillingham ordered his aide, Dinkleson, "Carry up a handful of them women. Be sure to bring that one with the flame-colored hair."

When Christine and the other women breathed the fresh sea air on deck, the winds picked up and the women had to hold onto ropes to steady themselves. They heard the Captain's shouts but could not understand him with the winds blowing.

Christine wanted to take advantage of the Captain's consternation. She huddled with the other women and proposed a plan. "If I can get close to the Captain, perhaps I can receive a dinner invitation and learn our destination. At least that will relieve the fear of the unknown."

Yvonne Poché leaned forward and said, "Yet we may be more afeared of what we come to know."

"I have thought of that. I have a small bag of herbs tied under my apron. If I mix it into the Captain's wine, he will fall asleep yet remember nothing the next day. While he sleeps, I can find out look at his maps and charts and learn more than he wishes to tell us."

A young Acadian girl named Martine Broussard asked, "How can you get close enough to poison his wine? If you do, who shall command the ship? We shall be lost at sea. Woe be to us!"

Christine tried to reassure her. "These herbs do not kill anyone. They cannot even hurt him. They merely lull him into a deep sleep."

Martine believed her. She had to or she would not be able to sleep at all.

Yvonne Poché added, "You certainly do not mean to join that man in his cabin? You are an engaged woman. And you have no chaperone. It is scandalous!"

Christine assured her, "These are times that call upon us to do things we would not ordinarily do. But I must confess I did the same thing to Colonel Winslow. Whilst he slept, I read his orders and found out about the Exile."

Madame Poché held onto Christine as she felt faint. "What did our Consul say to that?"

Christine replied, "He was imprisoned in the Church, so he knew nothing. I had to do something. Evangeline agreed, and I took the risk. How could I tell the man I love that I would be dining with another man, even for the right reasons?"

Yvonne, ever the cautious one, nervously coughed and cleared her throat, though she knew Christine had acted properly. Christine continued, "Because of my actions, our men were released to their families for a few nights before they were exiled. If I had done nothing, we might never have spoken to them again before they were forced onto the ships."

The women murmured silently in agreement. They waited to hear more as the wind began to howl about them. She continued, "I know men like this Captain Swillingham. He, like the Lieutenant-Colonel, all want the same thing when it comes to a woman."

Isabelle asked, "But what if he is married? Surely, he has a wife at home. If so, the plan is doomed to failure. We need an alternate plan."

Christine pooh-poohed her. "Married or not, a ship captain away from a wife months at a time is like a military officer at a post far away from his family. If a man has an opportunity to be with a woman, he will jump at it. Do you trust me to do the right thing for us?"

She waited until the other women nodded their assent, which they did, though some more reluctantly than others. They had no choice and they knew it. At the ship's railing, Christine cautiously watched. Swillingham took notice of Christine's glossy red hair and descended down the narrow steps from the bridge to the deck.

Christine spoke first. "Thank you, Captain. For letting us breathe the air up here. At least for a while."

Swillingham came on strong in his response. "I ain't doing it for me amusement. I gets me more money if I drop off healthy females to the main slaver in Boston. What I hear flame hair is in demand. Ye could fetch a pretty penny for Cornhandle. Yes, a pretty penny indeed."

Christine felt panic swell up in her throat. They were to be sold? It cannot be! It took her entire might to calm herself and gaze into his eyes. She was not about to allow herself and her friends to be sold like cattle.

The Captain was entranced by her hypnotic eyes. He looked cautiously around, even on his own ship, then whispered, "Supposing you convince me to sail to another port. What say ye to that?"

"What would become of me? Where would I go?"

"Go? No, missy. I wouldn't want no harm to come to ye. Ye would stay in me quarters, with me. I give nobody permission to go in, not even my aide Dinkleson there."

Christine looked in the direction the Captain pointed. Dinkleson was a mere lad of thirteen or fourteen, hardly someone to know what it meant to have a woman in the Captain's cabin.

Christine pouted. Swillingham wanted to grab her and kiss those plump, red, juicy lips of hers right then and there. But even though it was his ship, he had to respect decorum around his men. He asked her quietly and politely, "Think of what it's worth to ye. Shall we discuss me plan over dinner tonight?"

Swillingham licked his lips, then hesitated. He would have been paid handsomely by that scoundrel Cornhandle for bringing the Acadians to Bostontown. But to keep the beauty with him, he would change his plans. He was too well-known in the Colonies. And sometimes those blasted port officials inspected every nook and cranny on a ship for diseased passengers and stowaways. He would have to find a new port anyway, since he was too far south of the original destination. But she did not know any of that. This gave him bargaining power to keep her on the ship and offload the others with his goods.

Swillingham would tell the lady at supper tonight. "Dear Madame, how may I call you?"

Christine smiled. She had him where she wanted him now. "I am Mademoiselle de Castille. But please, sir, call me Christine."

"Ahh, I thought all youse Frenchies was married."

Christine lowered her eyes demurely but said nothing in reply.

"Me dear Christine," he whispered, "I shall send Dinkleson to fetch you this evening."

She curtsied, "With pleasure, Captain."

He clumsily grabbed her hand and kissed it. Christine sashayed back to her friends on the deck. The Captain gazed at Christine until she turned back to look at him and smiled. Swillingham motioned for Dinkleson to take Christine and the others back to the hold. The aide herded the women below and locked the door in place before returning to the deck.

Invigorated by his new plan, the Captain practically flew back up to the bridge, taking the steps two at a time. He checked his compass and his charts looking for something. A port where he had customers who would pay double for his goods. There it was! He would head for the Caribbean island of Santa Domingo. Merchant ships did not stop often at that port despite the rich islanders. He himself had not been there in five years. Swillingham knew if Lord de Mendez were still there, he would pay a tidy sum for his goods, maybe the entire shipment. And he might even pay for delivering the Acadian women. The winds blew him straight into a fortune!

Just then, he realized his stores would run out before they reached the port. Instantly, his solution was to direct his crew to fish now that the weather was better. Dried salted fish would get them to the island before they starved. And he would reduce the water and grog rations by a half. Yes, they would all make the trip and end up alive at the end. Or so he hoped.

Christine settled in the hold with the other women, who clamored for news. Acadians told the others what they had just witnessed.

"What happened?" queried one.

"Did you succeed?" asked another.

Martine replied, "Of course she did."

Isabelle added, "The captain is smitten. He kissed her hand."

Yvonne announced, "Christine was right. About everything. She shall fix our plight."

Christine raised her hands to shush them before revealing her plan. "Yes, he invited me to dinner tonight. He also said that he had been ordered to take us to the slave markets of Bostontown."

At the mere sound of the word "slave" the women gasped. The women huddled around her, their faces frozen with fear. Madame Landry unconsciously twisted her wedding ring. Other women held on to the gold crosses on chains around their necks.

"Do not worry. He shall not allow us to be sold as slaves. He is willing to take us to another port for a price," Christine said adamantly. "What valuables did you bring?" She opened her apron and placed in it the bejeweled gold cross given to her by Evangeline's mother Eugenie on her deathbed.

Isabelle pulled a gold chain and cross from her neck and laid the jewelry in Christine's apron. The women looked at their wedding rings. The gold bands were their most precious possession. No one wanted to give them up. Many tugged at their necks and handed over their gold crosses and chains. Lorraine Lambert and a few other women pulled coins from under their skirts, sadly adding them to the pile of jewelry. Martine tossed a gold bracelet into the apron.

Christine noticed their distress. "I know it is very difficult to forego personal items, but they are just material things. Is not our freedom worth more?"

She turned to Henriette de la Tour Landry, Marc's mother, who stared at the ring on her crooked finger. "It is all I have from my Benoit. I lost my cross when I tried to join him on the shore," she wailed.

Christine gently said, "If we are sold to plantation owners you shall never see him again. How would he ever be able to find you? Please, Madame, we need as much as we can give to buy our freedom. I shall ask him to drop us off at a different port so we can make our way to New Orleans."

Henriette shed a tear, then twisted the ring off her finger and gently placed it in the apron. Christine hugged her as she continued to sob quietly.

Madame Poché asked, "Do you actually think the Captain will let us go for some a few gold chains and coins? Would he not be paid more by a slave trader?"

Christine shrugged. "That I cannot say. But if I can make it worth his while, he may be willing to help us escape our current fate. So, does everyone agree to the plan?"

The women who were able to speak assented. The others were sleeping children and sickly old folks who were either too young or too old to know what was happening, or to care.

Dinkleson opened the hatch door and yelled down into the hold, "Missy Christine? Time to come up." Christine climbed out and disappeared from view of the Acadians in the hold below.

In the Captain's quarters, Christine feigned drinking the wine offered by Swillingham. The table bowed under the weight of many dishes but Christine ate sparingly. She was more interested in her mission and needed a diversion. She pointed to the map on the wall, "That looks fascinating. What is it? A map of your travels?"

When Swillingham ambled over to the wall and took down the map, Christine stirred in some of the herbs from her bag. Swillingham returned to the candlelit table, his gold tooth shining as he grinned.

"Indeed. I have visited many exotic places."

Christine recognized the Louisiana territory on the map and pointed to a large "X" marked at one particular place. "I would give a dozen gold rings to visit the city of New Orleans. Do you know it?"

Swillingham leaned back and guffawed. "Know it? I was borned there. But I ain't no Frenchie. Me maw was a brothel maid. Way she told it, she had a special man, a richie from Boston who squired her around the town. Bought her lots of pretty dresses and baubles. Came time for him to leave, he took me up north to his wife who couldn't have no kids. But I have a little spot in me heart for French folks. Like you, me dear."

Christine pulled a tied-up scarf from her apron and opened it. She held up several gold wedding rings that sparkled in the candlelight. She poured out the contents onto the table. Swillingham's one eye widened at the sight of the dazzling offering in front of him. She held up a jeweled ring and her encrusted cross to the candlelight as he pored over the pile of the Acadian women's jewelry, necklaces, chains, and a heart-shaped pendant.

Christine said, "Take our payment and set us free in New Orleans. Do not take us to the Colonies, I beg of you."

Swillingham chortled loudly. "We been long blown off that course. My ship is going to Santo Domingo, the French island, yer people."

He eyed the gold, picked up some of the jewelry and raised it to his one good eye, then put it down and shook his head.

"No, Missy, this ain't worth enough to let all ye Frenchies go fer free. My goods will sell for a hunnert times this but I have to think of what I can get for the lot of youse. There's sugar plantations down there. They might just need more workers for the fields."

He held her chin and twisted her face to the right and then to the left. "And youse would make the right kind of housemaid for the master, don't ye know?"

Christine feared what he meant but led him on. "What could we possibly have of enough value for you to let us go?"

Swillingham grinned evilly and rubbed his hands. "Ye lets me get me hands in that red flame of yours. And not only up top. Me wants the down below, too."

Christine smiled although she was completely disgusted with him and the stink his hands left on her face. She nodded, "Of course, Captain. I understand. One night with you. Tonight. You set all of us free in Santo Domingo and let us keep our valuables?"

Swillingham stood up quickly and clapped his hands. "That is the bargain, missy. Let's get to it." He stumbled trying to reach her chair to pull it out. His mouth opened but no words formed. His one eye rolled and suddenly he crashed onto the thick carpeting on the cabin floor. Christine checked his breathing. Yes, he was alive, but out cold.

Christine had successfully repeated the deed she had done on Winslow. That seemed a lifetime ago, yet it had been barely over two months. She dragged Swillingham to the bed, undressed him and put on his dressing gown, mussed his greasy hair and rumpled the sheets on the empty side of the bed. She covered him with the linens and spilled some wine on his pillow so he would wake thinking he drank too much again.

Christine had to work as fast as she can. Swillingham was a big man and she did not know how long the herbs would make him sleep. She packed as much meat, bread and fruit as she could in her apron pockets and tied bottles of wine with scarves to her underskirts. She looked chubbier, but most of the crew members were too young to detect the difference.

When the Captain started moving in his bed, she feigned dressing in front of him. His one bleary eye recognized her and reached out to grab her. "One more roll in the hay."

Christine tied her scarf to her head and wrapped her shawl around her. "Captain, I expect you to be a gentleman and tell no one of this encounter. I thank you for agreeing to free us when you dock the ship."

Swillingham put his hands over his face and nodded. "I's a man of my word. It's just I don't reckon I remember a thing."

Christine smiled, "You very much enjoyed yourself, Captain. You told me yourself. Good night and thank you, sir."

She unlocked the door and waved the lantern. Dinkleson hopped over ropes and bales and rushed to escort her to the hold.

Back in the cabin, Christine distributed the feast. The elderly and the young children ate and drank heartily for the first time since they had been forced onto the ship.

When the little ones and the old folks fell asleep, Christine met with the women who had given up their jewelry. To their amazement, she returned their highly-valued possessions to them. They lovingly put on their jewelry and hid their coins back under their skirts.

Christine quelled their curiosity. "The ship is heading south to a French island, not a British Colony. We stand a much better chance of working to earn money or finding a benefactor to send us to New Orleans, where we can hopefully reunite with our families."

Madame Poché shuddered. "The thought of getting farther away from my family causes me great fear. What if we cannot get a ship and we are bound to live on an island forever?"

Christine nodded, "The island is much closer to the French territory of Louisiana, though I understand it is difficult to accept. But it will be our sole chance to take control of our destiny. I would rather risk everything I own for that opportunity than to be stuck as a slave under English rule. René was told they sold Père Rivière into slavery. And many of the other women were probably sent to Bostontown to be sold. What makes us think we would be any different? We are French and Catholic. The English hate us, and have for a hundred years."

Yvonne said quietly, "Tell us what you want us to do."

The other women nodded and Christine said, "Be ready to run once they get us off the ship. It is our best chance. Stay together in small groups in case the Captain changes his mind and sends his crew to recapture us."

Martine understood the plan at once. "This way, they will not be able to catch all of us at once."

Christine smiled gratefully at her support and told the group, "Choose your partners now."

Henriette ruefully asked, "What about our sickly old friends sleeping over there? Who will go with them?"

Christine patted her hand. "I shall. If they are alive at the end of this journey, I promise I shall help them to freedom."

CHAPTER 62
Prison

Westminster Gatehouse Prison

Madness! It was sheer madness at the docks. London was a major trading center where ships from throughout the world sailed into the crowded harbor. Pushing his way down the gangplank through the sea of humanity, Turnbull led his Acadian prisoners in irons toward a big horse-drawn cart, where a cage with wooden bars was affixed.

The Acadians did not glance back at the ship that was their prison for the last five months. Crew were swabbing the decks, anxious to clean off the stink of their heathen prisoners.

Gabriel leaned back to his friend Marc behind him, "At least this is better than the ship."

Marc replied dully, "We cannot even guess the horrors that await us at the Gate." The "Gate" was Westminster Gatehouse prison, which some shortened whenever they referred to it.

Gabriel and Marc led the group of Acadians into the cart. Once a dozen men had climbed in, the line halted. Turnbull cracked his whip, angrily seeking the culprit. He strode to the back of the cart and found one of the prisoners was dead. His leg irons blocked men behind him from climbing up into the cart. Turnbull was furious and whirled around seeking a scapegoat. He focused on one man in the cart.

"Gabriel Mius d'Entremont! This is your fault. You should have told me this traitor died. He would have been buried at sea."

Gabriel was at a loss for words, not knowing his fellow Acadian was gone. Despite Gabriel's hesitation, Turnbull was not about to let him get a word in. Turnbull had to show control in this chaotic scene.

"Cut these chains. You and your fellow traitor there. Cut this man loose." He ordered the two soldiers standing nearby, Ebenezer and Franklin, "Unlock their irons. And be quick about it!"

Gabriel's and Marc's legs were close to the cage's bars so the soldiers made quick work of opening the irons. The two Acadians maneuvered their way out of the cart through the pile of other men, most of them sickly or near death.

Turnbull motioned to the two soldiers. "Give them your knives. But train your musket on them after you do. If they hurt anyone or try to escape, you will be shot before I even take care of them."

Ebenezer and Franklin handed over their rusty weapons to Gabriel and Marc. The Acadians were repulsed at their task, but the guns aimed at their heads convinced them to comply with Turnbull's order. Their friend's body was still warm. What if he were alive? How could they do the unthinkable? Yet if they did not, they would find themselves like him, dead as a doornail. A warm doornail, but dead none the less.

Turnbull screeched out his order. "Do it now. Cut those irons off and pull him out of the line. We must get to the prison today, of all days. It is market day. The streets shall be overcrowded. We must arrive before the Gatehouse closes its gates tonight. Do whatever you must. Saw and hack away. But get this done now!"

Turnbull muttered under his breath, "Market day! What bad luck. Perhaps this is an omen. I should never have requested a promotion. I should have stayed away from London. How can I return to the wife tonight, after all this time? If only I had written Jane of my trip here. If only I had gotten an inkling of whether she wants to see me."

Turnbull told himself, "Wake up. You shall have no music to face. She has lived the life she wanted and you still rule the roost. She shall do as you say." Then he second-guessed himself, "I should have written more often. But she sent correspondence less and less frequently as well. Her last letter rattled on only about making a new friend and demanding more funds to redecorate our house. Well, she shall receive no more of my money. No indeed. The king has come home to his castle and she shall accept it as it is."

As Turnbull was immersed in his thoughts about returning to his home after so many years, Gabriel prayed under his breath, "Our Father, forgive us for what we are about to do to Etienne."

Gabriel looked at Marc, who nodded to him. Each took one of the dead man's feet and began to saw through it. Blood oozed everywhere and although the skin was easy to cut, the bone was another thing. The knife was too rusty to saw cleanly, so Gabriel grabbed Etienne's leg and slammed it against the cart. He repeated it over and over until heard the bones crack. Marc repeated the action on the other leg.

At long last, with the leg held together only by sinew, they were able to hack through the tissue that bound the leg to the ankle. After struggling to cut the cartilage, they were finally able to sever each foot from the leg at the ankle. The chains slipped off Etienne's feet. Gabriel cradled Etienne's body while Marc picked up the two body parts sawed off at the ankles.

Turnbull was dissatisfied with their slow progress. "What is taking you so long? Dump him in the river. You are causing delay. Warden Kettlebum will not be happy if we are late. And if he is not happy, you shall not be pleased when you are tossed into the dungeon."

Gabriel and Marc completed their gory task by taking Etienne's torso, hands and feet and tossing them into the river. When they clambered back into the cart, the remainder of the Acadians were squeezed on top of the men already there. They would have suffocated but for the openings between the bars, which was of no concern to Turnbull.

Turnbull jumped into the seat next the driver and shouted. "To Westminster Gatehouse with haste. We have dead men awaiting executions here."

From his vantage point atop a few men, Gabriel was able to look out at the water. Etienne's body had risen to the top. His blank eyes stared back at Gabriel. Gabriel quickly made the Sign of the Cross just as the cart turned the corner.

The Acadians were jostled, jolted and bruised as the cart hit large potholes and cobblestones. They crossed a bridge filled with gawkers staring at them. As the cart rumbled down the road, shopkeepers and customers came out of shops to stare. People peered through windows of their brownstones to catch a glimpse of the men the London journal had called "Heathen Traitors." British townspeople milling through the streets made way for the cart but kept their eyes glued to the men.

After what seemed an interminable period of time, the cart made its way to a sinister-looking building. The infamous prison loomed ahead, dark and forbidding. Built entirely of stone, the structure was solid but for tiny slits between some of the rocks. These served as windows through which rain poured more often than sunshine.

The prison's outside iron gates were open to the dirt road leading into the courtyard. Wagons and visitors that entered the gates were made to wait until the outside doors were locked and the inside fence was opened. Armed militia walked the ramparts above, scrutinizing everyone who walked near, ready to aim and fire their muskets. So thorough was the security of the Gatehouse that the Warden frequently boasted no prisoner had ever escaped alive.

Outside the prison, vendors hawked their wares to customers and passers-by. Today, the crowd was much larger than usual, seeking a glimpse of the rare cart full of prisoners. Public hangings and punishment of stocks or pillories had deterred most folk from theft and assaults, the commonplace crimes of the day.

The shoppers at the vendors' stands gawked as the wagon overstuffed with Acadians lumbered toward the prison. They had arrived early and waited all day till now, nearly sundown, for a glimpse of the strange foreigners. A few boys grabbed rocks from the road and pelted them at the Acadians, hitting a few squarely in the face or on the jaw. The boys hooted and hollered at their success in drawing blood and injuring the dirty, dangerous men in the cart.

As the cart rumbled toward the entry gates, Turnbull gaped at the armed guards starting to close the heavy iron gates. He stood and shouted, "Keep open the gates! We are here with the prisoners from the New World. Do not close the gates. We have arrived!"

The guards heard Turnbull's shouts but ignored them and continued to push the weighty doors closed. They moved clumsily as the swords and knives at their sides clanked and jangled.

Turnbull slapped the driver. "Hurry. It is nearly sundown. Drive into the center of the open yard. Hurry, I say."

The driver whipped his horses to move faster even as the large iron gates were halfway closed. Turnbull grabbed the reins in frustration and whipped the poor horses over and over again. The cart hit one large pothole after another but Turnbull would not yield. The whips continued harder and harder until the horses ran through the now-narrow opening in the iron gates into the yard. Only then did Turnbull release the reins.

He screeched at the guards, his face red with rage. "Who do you think you are? I am His Majesty's Captain. You are but lowly guards. When I order you to keep the gates open, you do it. Do you hear me?"

The two guards looked at him, then at each other and back to Turnbull. They both nodded and replied, "Yes, Captain." They locked the gates and walked into their guard house without another word.

Turnbull nodded with satisfaction then turned to the guards manning the fence. "Open up, I say. I have the King's business for Warden Kettlebum with these prisoners."

The two guards were younger than the ones at the entry gates and they obeyed instantly. They could not risk losing their positions when clearly this man was a powerful Captain.

Once the fence was opened, Turnbull maneuvered the wagon into the large dirt yard. The Acadians stared with dread at the walls inside the yard. At one end was a wall smeared with blood stains. They knew that meant firing squads had hit their targets there.

Marc pointed out the forms of punishment at the other end of the yard. A tall gallows stood against the wall. Beyond it were stocks and pillories, with holes just large enough for human heads to squeeze through. The edges around the openings were smeared with blood where men's ears had been nailed and ripped off when they were removed from the cruel devices.

"Surely that cannot be for us. We have not had so much as a trial."

Gabriel scoffed. "Do you actually think they care about the law here? The English are medieval. They took all our guns when we were at our church dance in Grand Pré. They tried to attack us and would have succeeded if we had not hidden weapons with our Mi'Kmaq friends. They arrested us during a time of peace. Then they violated the treaty between our two countries to exile us here."

Marc shook his head. "We can expect no act of kindness or mercy from the English. All I pray for is a swift death if that is to be my end."

They heard the locks clicking behind them and knew this was the moment. Turnbull unlocked the cart and gave the order. "All prisoners out now. Form a line in the yard."

Gabriel turned to Marc. "Have faith. This cannot be our destiny. I shall do whatever I must to stay alive and find Evangeline. I promised."

Marc nodded even as Turnbull's screams got higher-pitched in his anxiety to deliver the prisoners on time. "Out, I say. Out, out, out!"

"We shall help each other. I must find Jeanne. We cannot die here. We shall not. We must not."

Gabriel and Marc were pulled into the chain gang of Acadians, their leg irons clanking as they stood in a long line. Just then Warden Carston Kettlebum entered the yard. He tipped his hat to Turnbull, who did the same. "I say, Captain, this delivery was a bit of a mess, eh? I expected you this morning."

Turnbull stammered in front of the bear-sized man. Could it be that he was intimidated by the big jailer? Turnbull cleared his throat and managed to sound gruff. "We have a large load. Dirty business took longer than expected to get off the docks." He pulled out a crumpled parchment and exclaimed, "Shall we go to your office? I need your signature on the transfer."

Kettlebum roared with laughter. "You are telling me what you want me to do? Have you forgotten you work for me now? But being as though it is your first day today, you are dismissed when these prisoners finish with my presentation in the yard. I expect to see ye early in the morrow. On time."

Turnbull turned crimson with embarrassment. Gabriel and Marc exchanged glances. Gabriel whispered, "This is an opportunity for us. The Warden is his powerful enemy." Marc nodded in agreement.

Kettlebum issued a clipped order to the Acadians. "Remain in your line. We have a show you may particularly enjoy. Stay silent until you reach your cells."

As the Acadians waited quietly and Turnbull shuffled his feet, a giant bald executioner exited the main building. He was followed by two armed guards leading a male prisoner in arm and leg chains. The man dragged his feet so that the guards had to lift him and carry him.

They climbed the stairs to the wooden floor of the scaffolding. The guards led the man to the noose. The executioner pulled the noose around the prisoner's neck and said, "You have been judged and condemned to death by the gallows. What say you?"

The man wept and peed himself. "I did not steal the pig. I saw the thief who did, but the judge would not listen. Please do not hang me. I have seven mouths to feed. Think of my children. My wife. Have mercy, please."

The executioner placed a black hood over the man's face, then pulled a lever. Suddenly, the bottom of the floor fell out. The man dropped through the hole and swung freely, screaming and writhing in agony. After a short while, he was silent and his body was still. The yard was quiet except for the sound of the rope creaking as it swung.

Warden Kettlebum shouted his order, "Follow me. All of youse."

Turnbull drooped his shoulders in shame and took his place walking behind the Warden, followed by a long line of Acadian men in irons. They entered the ominous building that would be their home for the rest of their lives -- unless France and England agreed to a peace treaty.

After the last Acadian had traipsed through the door and the guards shut it, Turnbull climbed back on the wagon. He thought of the first time he had visited London. There, he had met Jane, the daughter of an admiral, and was so smitten he had married her within a fortnight. But she had lived her entire life in the city and when Turnbull had been assigned his post in Grand Pré, she had refused to accompany him, preferring to spend his salary in the fancy shops. He had tried his best to put her in the family way before he left, but had never succeeded. Nonetheless, she had been happy to remain behind.

Turnbull mused, "I made the right decision. I had a better life than most of the men posted in Grand Pré. After all, I enjoyed the comforting arms of women at Hetty's place without any of the guilt that usually accompanies such acts when an officer's wife is nearby."

Then he changed his tune and groaned, realizing his new post at the Gatehouse would bring him home each night hereafter. "Woe is me," he muttered. He could never have imagined what waited for him when he crossed the threshold of his home without giving his wife the slightest advance notice of his arrival plans.

The driver dropped him off at the stoop of his brownstone. It was located in an ordinary-looking part of London, where each of the row houses looked like every other one on the street. It was not the largest in the neighborhood, but he was not ashamed of that. His home was his castle, no matter what size it was.

As Turnbull knocked the excrement from his boots, he knew it was time to take back the helm from his greedy wife. He turned his key in the lock, but it did not work. After a moment of panic thinking she had changed the lock, he realized he had placed the key upside down. When he righted it, the door opened easily. His greeting was nonchalant, as if it were just another evening back home from his work. "Wife? I am home."

He crossed the entry foyer into the downstairs sitting room. He found it empty. The fireplace was filled with dying embers. He rushed upstairs into the bedroom and flung open the door. What he saw at once excited and repulsed him -- his wife, his property, in the arms and legs of another man. The two were too intently engaged in the throes of love to notice him.

Without saying a word, Turnbull rushed downstairs and grabbed the fireplace poker. He took the stairs two at a time and ran into the bedroom. He shouted, "Begone, you interloper!"

Turnbull beat the poor man with the poker until his body was filled with bloody welts. The man screamed and held up his hands to fend off the beating, but his arm bones cracked and blood spurted from wounds on his hands.

Jane screamed and covered herself with her handmade quilt. "Husband! What are you doing? This is Dunley, the new friend I wrote you about."

The man grabbed his clothes and climbed out of the second-story window, jumping down onto the street.

Turnbull peered out and yelled after him, "Do not let me catch you in here again!" Turnbull was infuriated. He grabbed the poker and tore the quilt off Jane. He raised the poker and was about to beat her but she held her hands protectively over her belly.

"Do not touch me! I am with child. I birthed two boys while you were in the New World, but they both died just afterwards. I shall not let this one die. I need someone to love me." She burst into tears and wept loudly.

Turnbull's cold heart and anger melted. "I could never say no to you, my love. I have missed you. Truly I have."

She shook her head. "You are cold and cruel. He gave us both a gift – a child for me and an heir for you."

Turnbull reflected silently and stared intently at her. "You are right. You need a child to keep you company. I am sure to be given another promotion, and I do not want you to be alone."

Jane squinted at her husband through her tears. "Do you mean as you say? You shall not put me out?"

Turnbull sat on the bed and tossed the poker across the room. "I shall keep you as my wife and the child as my own. But now you shall do your wifely duties for me."

He grabbed Jane roughly as he always did. She felt he was a bit too forceful now that she was to have a child, but he was going to acknowledge the child as his. And she was his property. She would let him take her however he wished.

CHAPTER 63
Domingo

Santo Domingo

"Ahoy, Cap'n. Port o' Santo Domingo straight ahead," shouted the sailor in the crow's nest. "About time," barked Captain Swillingham as he scratched his dead eye under his black eye patch. The trip had been much longer than anticipated, but in the end, being blown off-course was fortuitous. His coffers would overflow with many more gold coins than when he left. Since merchant ships docked on the island only once every few years, local merchants and rich landowners snapped up all the goods for wealthy plantation wives and daughters who spent small fortunes on imported goods.

The Captain commanded his crew efficiently, sailing smoothly into the harbor and tying up on the moorings. He ordered, "Release all of the women on board, then place on deck all the goods we have."

"Aye, aye, cap'n," crew members shouted and carried out the order.

Christine was the first to step out. "Free at last!" she cried and inhaled a large gulp of what she thought would be fresh air. Instead, the tropical heat nearly seared her lungs. She coughed uncontrollably and wobbled down the gangplank clutching her travel bag which, luckily, was not confiscated by the British soldiers in Grand Pré. The other women followed Christine onto the wharf, feeling the island heat burning their bodies inside and out.

Christine turned to observe Swillingham. He shouted orders, "Open the box of lace and ribbons. And the corsets. Bring those stacks of fabric. Don't forget the hats." The crew rushed off, eager to finish their work and spend their wages on grog and women.

"I owe him a great debt," she told the Acadian women with her who had escaped their ordeal.

Yvonne Poché nodded, "We had best get out of sight before he changes his mind." The other women in the group agreed.

A dark-skinned woman in a bright batik floor-length skirt and a puffed-sleeve white cotton blouse exited the carriage and cried out in colloquial French to several dock workers, "Want to work today? A coin to load our wagon." They agreed and lined up behind her as she marched up the gangplank and announced to Swillingham, "I am the seamstress of Master Boss' big house. He wants you to sell me the finest goods for the Missus." She opened her fist to show a pouch of gold coins.

Swillingham nearly jumped for joy. This was, indeed, his lucky day. He would get four, maybe five times what he could have gotten in Bostontown. And that was after he had been paid to deliver the women to Cornhandle for his auctions. The woman quickly made her purchases and left with workmen carrying boxes and packages for the mistress of the house.

Swillingham pocketed the coins and squinted at the wharf as an ostentatious carriage pulled up. The occupant, a white-suited Spanish gentleman with a perfectly-trimmed goatee, stepped out. He adjusted his white straw hat and colorful handkerchief and gazed at the melee. His gaze fixated on Christine, speaking with the other women across the road.

Despite her disheveled look and her long journey, Christine still was a strikingly attractive woman. She lifted her lengthy red locks to cool her neck and glanced over at him. He tipped his hat as he walked up the plank to the ship. Christine wondered who the obviously-wealthy man was. No one else in the harbor was so finely-dressed.

On the ship's deck, Swillingham shouted with glee, "Tis you in the flesh, Señor de Mendez. It has been a few years, has it not?"

Luca de Mendez retorted, "We both know you have been gone for five long years, Swillingham, you scoundrel. Why have you kept us waiting so long? You know I always pay a prettier penny than the traders. Our women have cried out for those lacy French delicates from New Orleans."

Swillingham hemmed and hawed, trying to dream up a credible answer. "These times are very uncertain. War is a nasty business, Señor."

Luca nodded as he stroked his goatee. "But it is the perfect time for risk-takers to increase their wealth. Join me for a drink in my carriage. We shall make an agreement where you import the goods and I finance them."

Swillingham was eager to rekindle his relationship with the rich buyer, but he knew he had to sell as much merchandise as he could now. "An inviting proposition, indeed, after you make your purchases from this shipment."

Luca interrupted him. "You know I shall buy all that is yet unsold. Stop fretting about pence when I am offering to feather your nest in gold."

Mouth agape, Swillingham replied, "You realize the bribes to pass through the blockades shall be quite handsome?"

Luca laughed heartily again. "That is not your concern. For my part, I shall simply write out the notes for you to spend. Just assure me you shall obtain boxes of ladies goods. Did I say boxes? I want shiploads full. They command the highest prices in Spanish Florida. My brother is Governor and assures me he can sell everything I send."

Swillingham shook his hand and crowed with delight, "Let us drink to that." He motioned for his crew to load all remaining goods into the cart behind the large carriage for de Mendez. As the workers sweated in the hot sun, Swillingham and Luca walked arm-in-arm down the gangplank to the carriage. The captain daydreamed about all the money they would make.

As de Mendez entered the carriage, he turned back to Swillingham and asked quizzically, "You did not bother to count my gold?"

The captain shook his head. "You always do me right, Señor. Now Brits, them's the kind would cheat a countryman or their mother."

On the wharf, Christine gathered the Acadian women. "Let us ask the port officer where we might find lodging." The women scooted along, dodging workmen and wagons until they arrived at the small, garish yellow building at the end of the long roadway. Christine swung around and ran into the man clutching his leather briefcase overflowing with papers.

"Kind sir? Could you please tell me where we might find an inn for the night? And a bath? But not too dear. We have little money."

The agent stared blankly, then spoke in French. "Can you speak our language? We are a French colony. Most do not speak other tongues."

Christine breathed a sigh of relief and repeated her query in her native language, "We are seeking lodging for the night. And a hot bath."

He pursed his lips and said, "Take the road into the jungle. You may find shelter with the croppers. As to baths, water is everywhere."

She was at a loss to understand him. "What are croppers?"

He laughed, "Farmers who rent land from owners and sell their crops."

"So there are large plantations here?"

The agent looked at her quizzically. "In fact, some of the world's largest sugar cane plantations. We ship sugar to France and French Louisiana."

Hearing that, Christine's heart jumped for joy. "Do you mean boats leave here headed for the port of New Orleans?"

The agent nodded as he rushed off. "Sometimes not for years, but every now and again. You are on island time now. No one is ever in a hurry here."

"Where is the jungle?" she called out after him.

He said over his shoulder, "Where the road ends." Then he disappeared.

Christine walked out as if she were on a cloud. She shared her newfound knowledge with the other women. "I thought Swillingham had lied to me. But ships really do sail to Louisiana from here."

Madame Poché was cross with her. "That is all fine and good, but we are here now. Where can find somewhere to eat?"

Isabelle and the Widow Laroche chimed in, "And sleep?"

Christine nodded, "Take this path and we should find what we need."

Around the corner, they found themselves in the middle of a market. Vendors sold squawking chickens, colorful scarves, handkerchiefs, floor-length skirts in bright batik prints or plaids, white chemises, a variety of vegetables and fruits, jugs of wine, herbs, candles, and much more. Women glided past them balancing large baskets on their head filled with goods.

The Acadian women spent some of the coins they had and filled a sack with food and jugs of wine. They even had enough to buy a new dress for each. Vendors prized French coins and the women were glad they had not buried everything in their yards in Grand Pré before being exiled.

The women walked down the dusty road until they saw an opening in the tall grass near the water. A well-worn path led to the sea where islanders took their baths. With a newfound sense of freedom, the women tore off their raggedy clothes and frolicked in the water, heated by the sun.

When they had refreshed themselves enough, they dried off in the sun. Finding a small tree that gave some shade, they had a picnic and shared in the food and wine. In their new dresses, they felt like new women. But the island gave no hint of what was to befall each and every one of them.

The women walked for hours in the sun on the dusty path until they came to the edge of the path. Straight ahead of them was the jungle that the customs agent had described to Christine. "This is it. We should find the sharecroppers nearby," she exclaimed.

They gingerly stepped into the overgrown mass of trees, vines, bushes and other plants in which only a narrow trail had been cut. Madame Poché trailed the women, looking at all of the foliage on either side of her. A bright spot of berries caught her eye and she veered off the path. Pulling the berries from the vines and eating them quickly, the old woman's eyes suddenly widened. She bent over and gagged, then vomited. But it was not enough to regurgitate the poison. She keeled over and died alone in the berry patch.

The women took a break, sitting on the path, and Christine looked for Yvonne. She double-backed and called, "Madame Poché? Where are you?" When she finally found her, they mourned the death of the old woman whose courage buoyed their hope. "I should have been with her," moaned Christine.

"You could not have anticipated that," Isabelle said.

"But I know roots and berries as well as I know my own name. I should have explained. I should have told her."

At that moment, a snake crossed the path and bit Henriette whose foot blocked in its way. She screamed and foamed at the mouth. But Christine's knife and attempts to suck out the poison could not save her.

As the day drew to a close, the Acadian women held a funeral for the dead women, praying that the rest would survive the hostile unknown world.

Walking deeper into the tropical forest, the women had to force their way through dense vines and knock branches out of their way. Finally they reached a small clearing filled with wooden huts built in a circle, where a large fire burned outdoors. The native women and children gathered firewood, chopped roots and berries or cracked nuts preparing their communal dinner. The men oversaw the cooking of several fat rabbits on a spit over the fire.

Christine led the Acadian women into the clearing. Before she could say a word, the women grabbed their children and hid behind the men of the village. She tried to calm them. "My name is Christine. We are French Acadians, from the New World, newly-arrived by ship. Would you allow us to sleep here tonight and share your meal? We can pay, of course."

A wizened old man sitting near the fire used his ornately-carved cane to stand. He hobbled forward to face Christine directly. Though he was small in stature, he commanded her full attention. No doubt the village chief.

"I am Turselon. This is my family." He waved his arms around the circle, and the women and children came out from behind the men to gawk at the Acadians. "You are welcome here. Eat with us and tell us of your journey from to our home. We shall talk of payment later."

As the Acadian women moved into the circle, many fell to their knees and praised God for the kind strangers. The sharecroppers and the Acadians stayed up far into the night exchanging stories.

Turselon explained, "We sit near three large plantations. The mistresses of these houses have many children. Maybe you can teach book learning?"

Christine asked, "Yes, perhaps. And what about a nanny?"

Turelson did not understand the word. He shook his head.

Christine asked again, "A woman to take care of the children. Or clean the house. Do they hire housekeepers?"

At that Turelson shook his head. "They have slaves for that."

Christine was surprised. She had not thought of slavery in a French territory, even though she knew that she and the women on her ship barely escaped their fate at the hands of the Boston slave masters.

Turelson continued, "But slaves cannot read. That is what the children need. Learn to read. Leave this place. Go to the New World."

Christine nodded, "Reading is very important in today's world. Children should be educated. All children, no matter if they are boys or girls."

The chief's face lit up as bright as the sun rising to the east of them. "That is your payment. Teach our children to read."

Christine and the other women were taken aback. They expected to pay in coin or jewelry, but not in education. She looked around at the group of women, who smiled and nodded amidst their yawns. "Of course, we shall teach your children."

Within a matter of days, the men of the village had built large lean-to shelters and huts in which the Acadian women slept. Each day, they went into the jungle, half with Turelson's wife Jatsur to hunt for edible plants and the other half with Christine to search for medicinal herbs. The rest of the Acadian women worked with the villagers in the fields. Some women talked to Turelson about becoming sharecroppers. The chief laughed aloud, saying, "But you are women! You cannot rent land from the masters. Only men."

When the Acadians cooked, Christine taught the children for an hour before they left to work the fields and an hour after they returned before supper. Every day was the same regimen. Eat, work, eat, sleep.

After a month, Christine reported to Turelson, "The children are fast learners. Most know their alphabet and the older ones can recite a poem and do some numbers."

Turelson grunted his pleasure. "Do not let them rest. They must learn."

One evening, some of the Acadias returning from working the fields vomited on the way back to the village. Still others passed out on the path before reaching the huts. The men did not understand what had happened. They carried the sick women into a big hut. Christine examined them to find white-striped tongues, red spots inside their mouths and red blotches on their skin.

Christine knew instantly they had the dreaded pox. She had seen it in France and on the ship. There was no cure, and no survivors. She told the other, "Do not enter here again. The sick women are quarantined."

She could not explain why did not become ill after tending the quarantined women all night. Exhausted, she left and walked past Turelson's hut. It was shuttered tightly but through a slit in the window shutter, she saw him and his wife smoking pipes. She watched them blow smoke onto human skulls in the middle of the main room.

Shivering uncontrollably, Christine dashed into her hut. She crawled into bed but remained awake, vigilantly watching the door throughout the night. Finally she fell into a deep sleep before dawn. A few hours later, she woke and remembered what she had seen. She hurried to Turelson's house and found the door cracked open. She peeked in to find it empty except for the skulls on the floor. Turelson, Jatsur and their family were gone.

She traversed the little village but the huts where the islanders had lived were all empty. The little schoolhouse where Christine taught the children was silent. Christine immediately felt a sense of foreboding. She ran to the other women and explained, "They have human skulls in their hut. It can mean only that they are cannibals. I cannot say what they are planning to do – wait for us to die of the sickness or plan an end for us that I dare not speak aloud. They are French, yes, but they live their lives according to their superstitions and their island rules, to which we are not privy."

Isabelle, always one to give everyone their say, offered a solution. "Perhaps they found the skulls. Or maybe they are long-dead relatives that they honor in that way."

Widow Laroche made no bones about anything. She asked bluntly, "Do you think they plan to kill us?"

The other women screamed at the thought. "No! Please not that!"

Christine shrugged. "Their survival is more important than we are. This illness spreads only if someone who is sick coughs or spits in your face, but they do not know that. I believe they see us as the enemy now and Turelson will destroy anything that threatens their family. The single certainly I know is that we must leave now. Get your belongings. Hurry, before they return."

As the women frantically packed the few possessions they had and grabbed food and water jugs, Christine checked on the dying women. All but one had died during the night. Lorraine was the last one alive. She begged Christine, "Water. Please. Some water." Christine picked up the water jug and walked over to the bed. But she had expired. Christine said quick prayers over all of the women and exited the hut, leaving them there.

She advised the other women, "The officer said the largest plantation is run by Lord de Mendez. If we traverse the jungle, we shall find it at the end. I shall ask him if we can work for him for passage to New Orleans."

The Acadian women nodded weakly and as they walked the narrow dirt path away from the Turelson family huts, they felt the heat of the steamy jungle.

By midday, though the women were sheltered from the sun, the jungle became a humid inferno that burned their skin through their sweat. Widow Laroche fell to the ground. Christine checked her pulse but she had died. Christine and some of the other Acadians dragged her off the path and dug a large, shallow grave in the dirt with their hands, then covered the bodies with branches, vines and leaves.

At sunset, the women stopped for the night, their bodies dripping with sweat and fever. More Acadians fell to the ground, some crying out in delirium, and others with skin icy cold or burning hot to the touch. Christine applied the herbs in her pouch to ease their pain until they died. Exhausted, the remaining women slept without finding any food or water in the jungle.

The next morning, only Christine and Isabelle were still alive. Christine had run out of her natural remedies and she was completely spent. Nonetheless, they buried the other women in a large grave and pushed on until they reached the end of the jungle.

Before them was a gentle sloping hill. Slowly making their way to the top, the two women saw fields filled with rows of sugar cane. The only sounds they heard were the cane stalks waving in the wind and the buzzing of the evening insects.

The fields were void of human activity, but Christine thought she saw fires burning outside a group of wooden shacks beyond the fields. It reminded her of the sharecroppers' village, which gave her a sudden chill.

Beyond the cane was a large plantation house where soft candlelight flickered. Christine thought she heard laughter and the tinkling of glasses.

She suddenly felt very sleepy. She shook her head several times as she and Isabelle walked slowly down the path through the fields toward the main house. She thought she saw skulls dancing between stalks of sugar cane. Was it a premonition, she wondered. Or perhaps she was delirious herself.

Her last thought was of René as she dropped to the ground.

CHAPTER 64
Île

Karaztyev Beach

"How much longer till we arrive?" Evangeline had been asking that same question of her friend and guide, Kitok, every few hours.

"As long as it takes," Kitok patiently replied each time she asked.

They had trekked overland from the Mi'Kmaq camp and waited on the beach for the Karaztyev ferry. They were anxious to leave Nova Scotia for Île Royale, and more specifically, Karaztyev Beach. The gypsies there were well-known to Acadians as sympathizers to their plight. Evangeline looked at the rough waters for a boat in the foggy mist. "You are certain they can help me get to France?"

Kitok nodded. He saw a hazy figure in the distance. "Ask him yourself. All I know is many Acadians traveled here to get back to France."

Once they were ensconced in the deep deck of the ferry boat, their captain, Manfri Karaztyev, inquired about his passengers. "Who might you be and what are you doing so far north?"

Evangeline proudly answered, "My name is Evangeline Le Blanc. I am the daughter of the French Consul at Grand Pré, Lord René Le Blanc. Have you heard of him?"

Manfri, the eldest Karaztyev son, nearly dropped his steering rod. "Heard of him? I met him in the flesh."

Evangeline screamed with joy. "Where is he? Please take me to him. My father is alive? Praise God."

The boatman shook his head. "Cannot do that."

She moaned. "No. Do not say it. He died?"

He shook his head apologetically. "He was alive when he left two months ago. Washed ashore on our beach after his ship was torn apart in a storm. My father and yours go a long way back. A beautiful story. They met when your parents had just married and were on their way to Le Havre to board *L'Acadie* for Grand Pré. My father stowed away and got off here."

Evangeline was incredulous. "Your father saved my father. Where is he now?"

With a shrug, Manfri answered, "We ferried him across this very canal. Said he was returning to Grand Pré to take you and a lady named Christine to Quebec then to France. He disappeared from sight once he left the shore."

Evangeline shook her head. "We planned to meet in New Orleans. I know Christine was exiled after the men because some Acadian fugitives stayed a while with the Mi'Kmaqs and had heard the story from others hiding in the woods. Maybe my father did travel there. I pray that he did. For that is where I shall go."

"There is more."

Evangeline looked at Manfri. What could he mean? She was all ears.

"I met your fiancé, Gabriel."

She jumped up and hugged Manfri so hard the boat rocked. He and Kitok steadied Evangeline as she took her seat once again. "Is he on your island? Please tell me he is. Is he alive and well? He was not sent to that horrid prison in London? Where is he? How much longer before we get to your island?"

She squinted at the horizon. Karaztyev's beach was coming into view.

Manfri said quietly, "A ship with prisoners anchored not long ago.

She blurted, "Gabriel was on a prison ship. Did you see him?"

He responded, "He talked about that English captain. Trimbell?"

"Turnbull? You mean Captain Turnbull?"

He nodded. "He had such dislike for Gabriel. When Turnbull went ashore for provisions, some of us sneaked up on deck and tried to buy your man's freedom. The Captain would have none of it."

"So the ship went to England after all? Now both my father and my fiancé are gone. Perhaps forever." Evangeline was distraught.

Kitok interjected, "Be thankful they were both seen alive. They survived the exile. You shall find them. You were meant to be together."

"You're right, of course." She did not want to think of anything else. "And now that I am sure of it, I can pursue a different plan to meet them."

Kitok asked, "What do you mean?"

"Instead of waiting here, we shall go to the islands farther north." She turned to Manfri. "Are St. Pierre and Miquelon still French?"

The boatman nodded. "They are. But our family has no contacts there."

Kitok had an idea. "Do you have another boat to take us there?"

Manfri roared with laughter. "How did we gain the reputation of procuring whatever a man needs here? Of course, we have many boats."

Kitok added, "When he learns the daughter of his famous friend Lord Le Blanc needs his help, how can he not?"

Evangeline was impatient, especially moreso today. She knew once she arrived in the islands that she would be on her own waiting for a ship to take her to France. St. Pierre and Miquelon had been a haven for French fishermen that hauled catch off their banks and returned with the fish to France. So she could find a boat heading to France there and would be that much closer to Gabriel. She continuously reminded Kitok, "Hurry! The sooner we arrive, the sooner I can book passage to France."

Kitok nodded and tried to calm her anxiety. "Not long now."

She nodded and said, "When I get to Versailles, my family will help me get to London. With my uncle's wealth, I hope we can buy Gabriel's freedom from the Warden at Westminster Gatehouse."

Kitok stopped in his tracks. "Family? You never spoke of this."

Evangeline gazed into the mist as if she were entranced. "My mother's twin brother. We never met, but I am certain he will do whatever it takes to help me find Gabriel."

Manfri interrupted their conversation as they drew closer to the beach. "Land ho. Take care when stepping off the boat onto the dock. That water is very cold."

Kitok jumped from the ferry boat onto the pier. He assisted Evangeline to step onto the wooden planks and escorted her to the beach.

Manfri tied the boat and ran to catch up with them. "This way to my father's house. He will insist on a huge feast to welcome Lord René's daughter. Be prepared. Dinner will take many hours."

Evangeline looked up at the cave houses which had housed the Karaztyev family for decades. "Your father is up there?"

Manfri laughed. "All of us live there. In many caves. We have a very large family."

As they walked up the cobblestone walkway toward the Karaztyev family houses, Kitok and Evangeline spoke in low tones about what to expect.

"When should I ask him to help me with passage to France?"

Kitok grunted in response. "Enjoy his hospitality. Meet his family. Listen to him tell stories of your father."

Evangeline moaned, "But that could take all night. I want to leave now. I am ready to go."

Kitok shook his head. "Manfri will have told his father everything about you. The patriarch shall decide when the time is right to leave. You are like his daughter now, and he will feel responsible for you until you leave."

She asked, "Are you certain he will let me go at all?"

He nodded. "He will want you to be with your father and with Gabriel. In that, I believe he is honorable."

"How much did you have to pay for the boat ride?"

He waved his hand. "He charged nothing. So the family will do right by you. They must owe Lord René a very large favor. These gypsies have the reputation of charging an eyetooth for their services. Then again, they are willing to take great risks. They could have been shot on board the ship if Turnbull had returned before they left."

She nodded in agreement. "That was quite daring. At least they were able to talk to my beloved Gabriel. It eases the pain to know that he was alive when he left here."

Manfri could not have been more truthful. Evangeline could smell the aromas of many different dishes wafting from the cooking room to where she was. When the feast had been prepared, Milosh escorted Evangeline into the main cave where an oversized long table had been set. All of the seats had been taken except four at one end of the table.

He led her to the place of honor sitting at the head, between him and Manfri. Kitok was seated next to Manfri. The other sons, Barsali, Ferka and Ruslo, had laid out a piece of parchment on the table. It looked like a map but only had a sketch of the beach where Manfri had guided the boat.

As Karaztyev's wife and daughters served them plates piled high with steaming, aromatic dishes, Manfri kept their wineglasses filled. Evangeline looked at Kitok and smiled. He nodded, happy that she was the focus of everyone's attention.

When they had eaten the first course of food, Manfri leaned over to Evangeline, "Tell me everything of your journey. How did you decide to come here?"

She replied, "I am on my way to France, but I truly need your help."

Kitok overheard her and glared at her. He tried to warn her with his eyes, but Milosh thought nothing of it. He simply waved her off. "That is for later. What was the trip like? Were there many soldiers? Where are the forts? How often do troop reinforcements arrive? Which ports do they use?"

Milosh fired off questions right and left, but Evangeline refused to be intimidated. She answered every query with as much detail as she remembered. Barsali and Ferka drew on the parchment with various symbols and markings that must have meant something to them.

Before long, Evangeline ignored the map on the table and concentrated on the tasty dishes and responding to every query by Milosh.

Her host was determined to find out where the British enemies were located in the land south of the island. Such valuable information would earn him and his sons substantial sums in carrying Acadian refugees out of harm's way. By knowing where British troops congregated, he could better prepare maps to send to his spies who served as guides in English territory. By leading Acadians to the island, Karaztyev's coffers would fill and grow.

At the end of the dinner, sunlight streamed into the cave. The family departed, leaving only Milosh and his sons with Kitok and Evangeline.

Milosh turned to Evangeline. "Now we talk. What is your plan?"

She turned to Kitok, who nodded encouragement to her.

"I must get passage on the next ship to France."

Milosh asked, "What port? France has many ports."

She shook her head. "I do not care. I shall go anywhere as long as I can get the next boat."

Milosh asked, "Where are you going in France? It is a big country, you know."

It was her turn to look confused. Kitok could not help her. Neither had ever been there. Evangeline lowered her eyes, trying to think of something that would help her get what she wanted. This man was outsmarting her at every turn. She was not used to that. And she did not like it.

Ferka sensed Evangeline's embarrassment and said, "Father, perhaps we could look at the ports to the north and northwest. Le Havre and Belle-Île-en-Mer, for example."

Milosh stroked his long beard, perfect groomed. His wife Florica kept her husband's shaggy growth expertly trimmed with the knife she hid in the belt of her leather dress. It was made from the hide of a deer she had killed and skinned herself. "Yes. That is a good plan. Yes, I think that will work."

Barsali asked, "We know of no ships coming this way."

Ruslo added, "There are winds of war everywhere."

Ferka piped up, "Do you think France will declare or do you expect England to act first, Father?"

Milosh raised his hand. Ignoring talk of war, he said, "If we expect no ships here, we must take our esteemed guest to a port to book her passage."

Manfri nodded, understanding his father very well. He looked at Barsali and Ferka. "Prepare the sloop." He turned to Ruslo, "Ask mother to prepare provisions for our trip. Our sisters can pack foodstuffs that will fare well on the long voyage to France." They nodded and slipped away from the table.

Evangeline smiled with deep gratitude. "I can never repay you."

Milosh nodded to Manfri. From under the table, his eldest son pulled out an animal skin sewn into a purse and tied with leather strings. He untied the purse and poured out a stack of gold coins.

Evangeline was stunned. "For me?" But why?

Milosh replied humbly, "We owe your father...and your Gabriel...a great debt. I only wish I could do more."

Evangeline jumped up and hugged Karaztyev, thanking him graciously. "I shall never forget you. My family shall remember you with fondness."

Milosh wiped a tear from his eye and stood. He cleared his throat and suggested, "Manfri will show you and Kitok to your rooms. Sleep as much as you can today. We leave tonight and sail under the cover of darkness. That way you will arrive at St. Pierre and Miquelon in the morning before the ships leave. If one is destined for France, you will be able to buy your passage and get away before the British find out where you are, as there are certain to be English ships there as well."

Manfri agreed. "You would make a very valuable prisoner. They might be able to trade you for your father and send him to the London prison."

Evangeline shook her head vehemently. "The English would do that?"

Milosh agreed. "You are valuable property. A double-edged sword. If they found you, they would not hurt you but would hold you for ransom, so to speak. They could get a boat of prisoners in exchange for your freedom."

Kitok was a man of few words, each of which he chose carefully. When he spoke, everyone listened. "No reason to ponder things that will not happen." He turned to Evangeline, "We shall see you set sail on a French ship. When you arrive, you have funds for private transport to take you to Versailles." Evangeline nodded, thankful Kitok would see her board.

*

Two weeks later, Kitok and Manfri escorted Evangeline onto the deck of a French ship. Manfri had negotiated the passage and also paid for a deck hand to guard the door of her little cabin below deck, bring a crock of fresh water and her meals each day and assist her to climb up to the deck for fresh air. Manfri had made sure the meals would be the same as what the Captain ate. But as a precaution, he also packed the bag of foodstuffs that his sisters had prepared that would last at least part of the voyage.

The ship arrived in the Port of Le Havre without incident. On deck, Evangeline took in the sight of the chaotic port that buzzed with passengers, horse-drawn carriages, handcarts and workmen. In the midst of the crowd, she thought she saw Adèle and Claude Arnaud. She called out, "Adèle? Is it you? Adèle Arnaud?"

The woman turned to look at her and instantly recognizing her, she waved and cried out, "Evangeline! How in the world are you here?"

Evangeline rushed down the gangplank just as a large carriage dashed along the wharf. The coachmen drove his team of horses past her, knocking her down onto the board road. The carriage rolled on without a second thought. The Arnauds fought their way through the crowd, calling out, "Evangeline!"

Evangeline was numb with pain, but her last thoughts were of her fiancé. She moaned, "Gabriel. So close. I was so very close to seeing you again."

PART VII

The Search for Paradise
1758 – 1760

"Sustain me according to Your word, that I may live;
And do not let me be ashamed of my hope."

- Psalm 119:116

CHAPTER 65
Luca

Santo Domingo

In the early morning light, two oversized women in colorful native costumes and carrying fruit-filled baskets on their heads found Christine curled up and unconscious on the path near the fields. They arranged for two burly field hands to carry her out of the fields. The men deposited Christine in a large bedroom in the main plantation home and went back to the fields.

Once Christine was in bed, the women removed her dirty, ragged clothes. They washed her, cleaning and refreshing her body. As they worked, their dark skin glinted with sweat in the sunlight that streamed in through the room's large windows overlooking the fields.

If Christine had been awake, she would have seen lines of workmen walking through the neat rows of tall sugar cane. She would have marveled at the grace with which they sliced the tall stalks with machetes and other tools, humming local songs as they did.

In the bedroom, each native woman was dressed in a white cotton blouson trimmed with colorful ribbons at the neck and sleeves. Each wore multiple skirts layered in bright batik patterns and wrapped her hair in multi-colored scarves. Neither had any other adornment but necklaces made of seeds and beads which tinkled softly as each of them moved.

They opened the armoire filled with garments. The taller woman pulled out a traditional island floor-length skirt and white cotton blouse. The shorter woman approved and fanned Christine with large palm leaves to keep her cool as the other female dressed her in the new garments, then they crept out of the room. Christine slept fitfully, tossing and turning all night.

The next day, Christine woke but did not open her eyes. First, she heard the sounds of two distinctly feminine voices speaking a garbled form of

French. Her body felt hot all over until the women's hands began to wipe her arms and legs with cool wet cloths.

When Christine did open her eyes, she thought the two women were so beautiful. But who were they? Where was she? Christine's head hurt, still foggy from her illness, and she felt like she was on fire.

One of the women touched her forehead and called out to the other, "Molina? Mo' water. Po' thin', she burnin' up again."

Molina replied, "Firs' thin' firs', Fina. Me gonna shut dem curtains." When she pulled the heavy drapes together, Christine was enveloped in near-darkness. She felt a little cooler. That was better. She sighed and closed her eyes again. Asleep in a moment, she never felt the women place additional cool wet rags on her skin. Nor did she hear the padded slippers of Fina and Molina as they quietly exited the room and closed the door.

Hours later, Christine opened her eyes. This time she saw nothing in the pitch-black room. Turning to look at the door, she notice a sliver of light from under the wooden entry. She listened carefully. Glasses tinkled and laughter and conversations were muted, but she was definitely in a house. Was this the plantation home she saw from the top of the hill? She did not remember getting here. And where were the other Acadian women? She shuddered to think what had happened to them. She prayed her friends were alive, too. Perhaps they were in this very house.

As her eyes acclimated to the darkness, Christine looked around the large bedroom. The drapes were still shuttered but she could see she was alone. Though the fireplace was filled with wood, it was cold. Not even dying embers. A small pitcher of water stood on the night stand.

As she tried to sit up and reach for it, her head started spinning and she knocked the pitcher on the floor. She fell back to the bed, thirsty. She knew she would have to wait for help but could not make a sound because her throat was so parched.

At the crashing sound, Fina and Molina rushed into the room. "Water, please," Christine managed to get out. Fina poured the liquid into a cup and lifted her head while Christine sipped it all. Her thirst temporarily quenched, Christine pleaded with the two women, "Please. Help other women. Fever."

Molina touched her forehead. "Po' thin', she still got de fever." She dipped a cloth into a bowl of water and patted down Christine's arms and legs again.

Fina dipped a cloth in cool water and touched it to Christine's lips. "Shush. Save yo breath. De fever very bad dis year." Christine nodded, curled up and fell asleep again.

The next day Christine woke feeling like a new woman, except for her hunger pangs. She sat up in bed and touched her forehead. No fever. No dizziness. She was fine. She was about to get out of bed and open the curtains when Fina carried in a tray piled with biscuits, meats, butter, honey, fresh fruit, and juices of all flavors. "Fever gone, Missy. Time to eat some vittles. Get yo strength back."

Molina waltzed in and pulled the heavy drapes open. Sunshine poured into the room. Christine smiled at them, "I am Christine de Castille and I owe you both a huge debt of gratitude."

Molina shook her head. "I am Molina, Missy. You don't owe nuttin'. Our boss man Señor de Mendez, said get yo anythin' yo want."

Fina said, "My name is Fina and me is here to help yo. Yo had a powerful bad fever, Missy."

Christine responded, "You are both too kind. As is Señor de Mendez. Did you find the other women? French Acadians that traveled on the ship with me? Are they feeling better?"

Molina and Fina looked at each other, then down at the floor as they shuffled their feet. Neither wanted to give their special guest the bad news. Christine deduced their thoughts.

"I see. They caught the fever, too. Have they been buried?"

Fina nodded quickly and spoke bluntly. "Dat fever powerful strong, Dat lady -- can't leave no body in the fields. Too many critters pokin' around."

Molina was a bit more diplomatic. "Señor waited but yo had the fever too long, so we…."

Christine nodded and brushed tears from her eyes. "Only one? Isabelle? Could you show me her grave? I want to pay my last respects."

The two women nodded. They were so curious about her, having heard her cry out names of people during her fitful sleep. But the name they heard most often was "René." They wondered if that was her husband. Molina knew it was not her place to ask, but Fina ignored the social customs and piped up. "Who is René, Missy? Yo called out to him in yo sleep. Dat yo man?"

Molina frowned at Fina's audacity but Christine understood their curiosity. Of course they would want to know more about the stranger they took in and cared for as if she was family. "He was – he is – my fiancé. But he was sent away on a ship by the British before we had the opportunity to get married. I am not certain where he is, but we plan to meet in the port city of New Orleans. Do you think Señor de Mendez could help me book passage to get there?"

She looked at the two women, who glanced at each other. Fina responded, "If de Señor wants to do it, he get it done."

Christine moaned, "I have no money. I hope he would trust me to send the money back to him after I was settled in the city."

Molina remained mum. She wanted no part of promises on the part of her boss. But Fina answered, "He so rich he can't spend it all. Sure 'nuf if he wants to help, he gonna pay."

Christine grinned widely. "Well, when can I meet my benefactor?" The island women had no idea what she meant. Christine asked the question in a different way, "Where is Señor de Mendez? I would very much like to express my thanks to him."

Molina nodded, "In his carriage now. Riding over all his lands and in de town. But when he at de house, he be on de veranda, Missy. Dat where de boss is ever' aft'noon if he be on de property."

Fina added, "Taking his 'peritif."

Molina corrected her, "Yo know de boss man calls it a-peritif."

Fina shrugged, "He loves dem toddy drinks, too."

Christine asked, "Shall you show me the way later today? After we visit my friend's grave?" Fina and Molina agreed.

They served her a light luncheon that Christine ate in its entirety. They returned to her room when she had finished, and they escorted her to the gravesite. A dirt mound had been set inside a low wooden fence. A hand-carved wooden cross sat at the head of the mound.

As she visited the grave, Christine asked, "Could we put her name on the cross? Isabelle Cormier. That was her name."

Fina said, "We get de carpenter to carve in de name of you friend."

Christine took both of her hands and shook them with gratitude. "And a funeral? We are Catholic and must have a funeral."

Fina said, "Señor is Catholic. So is me and Molina."

Molina shook her head, "Sorry, Missy. Priest be away from Señor Luca's lands till next month."

Christine got a faraway look in her eye and tears rolled down her cheeks. She briefly brushed them off, but more took their place. Looking out into the fields, she wondered aloud, "How big is this plantation?"

Fina proudly answered, "Far as yo eyes can see it, dat be for de Señor. He away on big business now. Back in some days. Don't know how many."

Molina added her bits of knowledge. "Nearly dis big ole island is for de Señor. He gots hisself sugar cane and coffee fields from de jungle to de port."

Christine showed surprise. "Coffee, too? No wonder he is always gone tending his business interests."

After the gravesite visit, Christine felt very tired. She went to her room and knelt by the bed with the drapes closed. "Dear Lord, I pray for the poor souls of the women who died. Forgive me for not knowing they were dying of the fever in the fields. I pray for René and Evangeline, and her Gabriel, too, that they are alive and under your protection and that we shall all meet again soon on this earth. And finally, I pray that you grant your courage to all of the exiled Acadians and that their faith will save them. Amen." Then she crept into bed and slept restlessly throughout the night.

At the end of the week, Fina and Molina led Christine around the manor house to the large covered porch they called the "veranda." It was filled with rocking chairs, settees and hammocks. The perfect way to spend a lazy afternoon, Christine thought. She settled on a hammock and stretched out as Fina fanned her with huge leaves. Before long, Christine fell asleep.

The large carriage that Christine had seen at the port pulled up in front of the manor house. Señor Luca de Mendez, the man who owned the carriage and who had seen Christine in the port, climbed down out of the coach and walked down the pathway to the veranda. There, Fina was fanning Christine and Molina was waiting with a tray of glasses and various bottles of liquor. She served her boss, who took a whiskey in a small glass.

As he sipped his drink, Luca gazed again at Christine and his heart melted. Sitting back in his chair, he watched her as she slept.

Christine cried out, "René! Eugenie is gone…I am here." She fell into a deep sleep, breathing heavily.

Fina commented, "She want take dat big ship to New Orleans. Gonna look for her man. He named René."

Luca replied, "Impossible. England has declared war against France, which everyone anticipated but it is now official. English naval blockades shall prevent all transports from crossing them on the high seas, fearing they haul money or weapons for the enemy. The lady must stay here as our guest."

Molina asked, "Señor got ideas for dis woman gonna stay here? Not go away on de ship?"

His eyes gazed upon Christine again. "I hope she stays forever." He was enthralled with the sleeping beauty in front of him. "She is mesmerizing. It would be a pleasure to sit across from her at every meal for the rest of my life. Yes, I should like that very much."

Christine slept through the afternoon. At sundown, Luca directed Fina and Molina to let her sleep undisturbed.

When Christine woke later that night, she was still on the veranda, covered with a quilt. Her thoughts were fuzzy and she thought she had been talking with René. When she realized it was but a dream, she wrapped herself in the quilt and made her way to the bedroom, where she promptly fell asleep.

The next morning, Christine was awake when Fina and Molina brought in her breakfast tray and opened the curtains. "Did Señor de Mendez arrive yesterday? I must have fallen asleep, but I did so want to meet him."

Fina responded, "Señor saw yo but tole us do not disturb yo. But he here today. He fo' sho' be on de veranda."

In the afternoon, Christine meandered over to the veranda, and enjoyed a refreshing drink with fresh mint leaves that Molina made for her. Fina said, "Me gonna fan you."

"Thank you, Fina, but that is not at all necessary. I really should like to speak with Señor de Mendez. I have encroached on his hospitality long enough. It is time for me to leave Perhaps he can arrange to take me to the port and book passage? You promised I would meet him today. So, where is he?"

At that moment, a tall dashing figure stepped onto the veranda. He sucked in his breath at the vision before him. Christine was aglow in the afternoon light glowing before sunset. "What a beautiful day!" He bowed to the waist, sweeping his hat at his side. "And a beautiful woman. I am your host, and your servant, Luca de Mendez."

Christine nodded. "Christine de Castille."

Luca nodded. "Ah, it seems from our name that we are both from the same part of Spain, my dearest Mademoiselle de Castille."

Christine blushed. "Yes, it appears so, Señor de Mendez. But you have shown me such kindness, I cannot hold to archaic notions of politesse. Please, call me Christine."

Luca bowed. "As you wish, but only if you call me Luca." He snapped his fingers and Molina handed him a whiskey in a small glass. He sniffed, sipped and approved. He raised his glass to Christine, who did the same.

"Here is to you and your miraculous recovery. You are looking quite well, my dear Christine." They both sipped their drinks.

Luca asked, "Do you have everything you need? Can we provide anything else for you?"

Christine nodded. This handsome man was kind and caring. Why was he not married, she wondered. "Quite. Fina and Molina have taken exceptional care and brought me back to the land of the living."

He nodded gravely. "Yes, you were very ill. Please accept my condolences on the loss of your friends. Terrible thing, this island fever. If I had not lived here so long, I probably would have succumbed to it long ago. But the longer you stay here, the heartier you become. Before long, you may even feel like riding. Would you like that?"

Christine's lilting laughter filled the room. "It would be my greatest pleasure. I do love to ride, but have not done so in, well, far too long. But I have imposed long enough."

"Nonsense. You want to ride so we shall do so. And Fina shall prepare the most delicious lunch for a picnic. When you are ready, just let her know and we shall make a day of it."

Christine said gratefully, "I so appreciate everything you have done. But once I am well enough to ride, then I should be seeking passage on a ship. I cannot stay infringe on your hospitality."

Luca looked anguished. "Not too soon, I hope. You need more rest. I have sent word to my physician who should arrive within the next few days. A ride can put color back in your cheeks, but it cannot give you the strength you need for a sea voyage. Besides, the fever is vicious and unforgiving. Sometimes we see it return with more vengeance than the original illness."

Christine looked horrified, but Luca was quick to reassure her. "My apologies. I did not mean to say that you would not be strong and healthy again. Not at all. I simply want to make certain that you have time to recuperate and enjoy the simple pleasures we have to offer here."

She nodded. "I understand. I do still feel weak and tired most of the time despite how good I feel today."

He nodded. "I am gratified. So no more talk of ships, agreed?"

She smiled. "Agreed. At least for the moment."

"I have not laughed like this since my Angelina left us, bless her soul. Surely you know you are a special woman, Christine."

They continued their small talk, all of which was overheard by Fina and Molina.

A few days later, when Christine was able to ride, Luca galloped alongside her and led her up to the hilltop overlooking his sugar and coffee plantations. There, they dismounted as he proudly showed off his land holdings.

As she looked over his properties, he descended on bended knee. Offering her a sparkling bejeweled ring, he asked, "Marry me and become Lady de Mendez. We are a perfect match. The same Castilian blood of Spanish nobility runs in our veins. Let me care for you and love you to the end of my days."

Christine felt joy and sadness at once, and clasped his hands in hers. She looked away. Should she? She did not know. What if René were still alive? Then again, what if he had died and she knew nothing of it? This man was kind and generous. What is more, he loved her unconditionally.

"All that I have is nothing without you, my dear," Luca pressed her.

"I do not know. I need time. Please, give me some time, Luca."

He continued as if she had not spoken. "I know not how it happened, but I fell in love the first time I saw you at the port. Then when you turned up here, delirious with island fever, I was overjoyed to do my small part in your recovery. You are but an angel to me. An angel that I have prayed for all these many years."

"Luca, you are so kind. You, Fina, Molina, everyone. You could not have been more welcoming and gracious to me."

"I understand. But there is someone else."

Christine hung her head and softly asked, "How did you know?"

Luca continued, "You cried for him to leave his wife."

Christine shook her head. "Things are not as simple as that. She died years ago. My competition has been a ghost. Everything changed in September when he proposed to me, but by then, our destiny had been set in stone by King George. He was exiled to a destination I know not. And I was to have been sent to Bostontown but ended up here." She wiped tears from her eyes.

He leaned forward and took her hand in his. She did not resist. He lifted her chin so that he could look directly into her eyes. She did not flinch.

"Captain Swillingham explained your courage and your ingenious solution that brought you here, for which I am eternally grateful."

"Nothing untoward happened on the ship, I trust you believe me."

"Of course not. The Captain simply admired your bravery, as do I. My only desire is to make up for the horrors that you have experienced. I want to make you happy. If you will let me," Luca said.

Luca leaned over to kiss her, but she pulled away at the last moment. She wondered what would have happened if she had not been thinking of René at that very moment.

Christine chose her words carefully. "It was such a traumatic experience that I do not know if I shall ever forget. But I am strong and I know I shall press forward."

Luca felt she was pulling away and asked, "Do you still love this man?"

She nodded, "With all my heart."

Luca sighed, "Then there is no hope for me. It makes me very sad."

"Luca, please forgive me. But I must find him."

He nodded, "My dear Christine, if you need anything, you have but to ask. If it makes you happy, I am your servant. I shall provide whatever you desire, even if it means you shall not be with me."

She chastely kissed his cheek, and he knew she would not allow him to express his affection so he withdrew from her. She explained, "I do need your help. To arrange passage to leave."

"France is out of the question. Captain Swillingham told me the English naval ships patrol the seas heavily. The war still rages on, as you know."

"The territory of Louisiana is not under a blockade, is it? I must find my family and my friends. We made a promise before, before we were...."

Suddenly Christine burst into tears. She wept uncontrollably. Luca offered his monogrammed handkerchief. Gratefully, she accepted it and wiped her tears as she leaned her head on his shoulder. He wrapped his arms around her and they stood in silence for a long while.

When Luca spoke, he said, "I would be pleased to help you. Louisiana is still French so ships bound for that territory can avoid the British. I have strong trade relations in the port city, so I can send a ship there to get you established properly. Captain Swillingham and I are in business and he can help you should you desire it."

He wrapped his arms around her, hoping to remember this as the moment when his love for her burned at its highest peak. She rested in his arms feeling at once relieved and excited about beginning her search for René.

They mounted their steeds and rode back to the house in silence. They had said everything they needed to say. And their silence told volumes more.

The next month, with her bags and boxes packed onto the carriage, Christine exchanged heartfelt goodbyes with Fina and Molina. The two women cried and loudly blew their noses with colorful handkerchiefs as Luca helped Christine into the carriage and climbed in after her. The women waved to her as she leaned out of the window of his carriage.

"Thank you so much. I shall miss you," Christine told them.

Fina cried, "Don' forget us here on de island."

Molina added, "Me and ever'body is gonna miss ye, Missy."

As the carriage drove away, Christine wiped tears from her eyes. Again, Luca offered his monogrammed handkerchief to her.

At the port, before Christine stepped out of the carriage, Luca handed her an intricately-carved box. He opened it and she gasped at the contents, gold coins, an emerald necklace and matching earrings, "They will look beautiful with your flame-colored hair, my dear."

He locked the box and handed her the key. "This will assure you of a good life in New Orleans."

Christine was speechless but finally found the words to express her gratitude. "I never expected...this is too generous, Luca." She handed the box back to him. "I cannot accept it. It is far too much."

He gently pushed it back into her hands. "I insist. Consider it a gift from a man who shall be your lifelong friend. Besides, it is quite a selfish gift. I shall sleep better knowing you have a roof over your head and that you are wearing fine clothes that attest to your beauty."

She brushed his cheek with her lips. "I shall never forget you, Luca. Never. Because of you, I shall find a way to locate and reunite the Acadians who have been scattered to the winds. I know that I shall. I must. It is how I shall find the way back to René."

"You must write me if you need anything. Promise me?" He asked.

She nodded, "I could not need more than what you have so generously given. I am overjoyed you came into my life. And that you gave me back mine. I shall miss you. And Fina and Molina, of course. But most of all, you, Luca. I should hope you can visit one day in Louisiana."

He escorted her onto the deck of the ship. He hesitated before taking her hand and kissing it, with a brief goodbye, "Safe trip, my dear. Write me when you arrive and from time to time, if you wish." He bowed and took his leave.

Christine mounted the gangplank and watched him from the ship's railing. He climbed in his carriage, waved at her one last time, and shut the curtains. He could not watch her sail away. It was too painful. Almost like watching his wife die in his arms of the fever. His carriage soon sped away. Luca realized that the only woman he loved as intensely as he had loved his wife sailed away from him forever.

After Christine's ship sailed, Luca returned to his mansion, empty but for his faithful servants Fina and Molina. He refused supper and retired to bed early.

The next morning, Molina opened the heavy curtains, letting sunshine pour into the room. "Morning, Señor. It is a fine sunny one again today.

On the bedside table, Fina set a tray with Luca's favorite breakfast. Hot biscuits dripping with butter and honey, and a large cup of piping hot coffee. "Your breakfast, Señor."

But Luca remained in his bed, eyes closed. The two women instantly knew something was wrong. He usually sat up in his bed as soon as he smelled the coffee or felt the sun on his face.

Fina leaned down next to Luca's face. She shook her head. He was not breathing. She covered his face with the sheet as tears streamed down his face.

Molina said what they were both thinking. "Dat man died of a broken heart two times now. First, Angelina. Den, Christine."

Fina wiped her face and nodded. "Dat kind heart of his couldn' take it no more. It just burst apart from giving out so much love."

CHAPTER 66
Provence

France

"Where am I?" Evangeline moaned as she tried to raise her head in the darkened room. Her vision was blurred, but she could see a uniformed housemaid tidying the room, adjusting fresh flowers in the vase on the bedside table, filling her goblet from the wine bottle.

"Hello?" Evangeline formed the words but no sounds came out. Her head felt like it was splitting and her throat was parched.

"Drink this, my Lady. Lady Véronique said it will help with your head pain." The young maid could not have been more than twelve years old, but Evangeline obeyed her. What happened? Who was Lady Véronique? She could not remember anything after seeing Adèle on the wharf. Try as she might, her mind drew a blank.

The young girl curtsied, "My name is Mylène. Ring the bell if you need anything – your clothes, your hair, a bath, anything."

"Thank you," Evangeline managed to utter before her head started hurting again and she fell back into the soft feather pillow.

The maid curtsied and scurried out of the room.

Several hours later, Evangeline woke but kept her eyes shut. It was too painful to open them. Adèle Arnaud entered the room, carrying an infant in her arms. She was followed by her daughter Pauline and another woman of Adèle's age, presumably the lady of the house. Mylène trailed behind her.

"Can anything else be done for her?" Adèle whispered.

The other woman shook her head. "Doctor Lezay said she needs rest and wine to bring the fever down. Let us leave her to sleep and return after dinner."

Adèle began to tiptoe out of the room. She was startled to hear Evangeline's soft voice. "Adèle? Is that you?"

Adèle rushed to Evangeline's bedside and clasped her hand on top of the hand-woven lace coverlet. "I am here, dear friend, with my daughter Pauline and my son Etienne."

Evangeline rubbed her head but expressed happiness for her friend. "Your children are simply wonderful. What happened?"

Adèle hugged her friend. "I am so happy we found you. Claude and I were in Le Havre visiting my sister Claire and her husband Michel Broussard when we saw you fall on the dock."

Evangeline was confused. She could see the view from her chamber out into the flower gardens, stables and fields beyond. "But this is a château surrounded by land as far as the eye can see. How did I arrive here from the port?"

The woman spoke up. "Lady Le Blanc de Verdure, welcome to the home of my husband, Lord Laurent de Rochefort. I am Lady Véronique."

Adèle explained, "This is my sister-in-law. She married Claude's younger brother, Laurent. Well, his half-brother. They have different fathers, as it turns out. It is a long story I shall enjoy telling you. Laurent and Véronique met at Versailles at the wedding banquet for your parents. Isn't that romantic?"

Véronique smiled. "I shall never forget my husband's courage. He rescued me from a rat that has escaped the secret passages of Versailles and was hungry for the scrumptious dishes at your parents' wedding feast. It was truly love at first sight, but my father opposed our union until he learned Laurent was the son of Duke Charles de Rochefort."

Véronique was the sole heir to the fortune of the Marquis Robert de Navarre and had been a Lady-in-waiting to Queen Marie Lecszinka, wife of King Louis XV. Besides receiving a most generous dowry from the Marquis, Laurent had inherited the Duke's château and more wealth than he could spend in his lifetime. Though extremely wealthy, Véronique and Laurent were generous to a fault with anyone who needed their help.

Adèle responded to Evangeline's query, "When the local doctor declared it safe for you to ride by carriage, we brought you here. Laurent's personal physician has been treating you ever since. How is your head?"

Evangeline winced as her head throbbed violently. "Painful."

Adèle nodded. "What would you have done if you were alone?"

Evangeline shrugged, "I was planning to go to Versailles. My uncle should be at Court."

Adèle looked at her quizzically. "What uncle? This is truly news. I thought when your mother died bearing you that she left only you and Lord Le Blanc."

Evangeline laughed softly. "Everyone says that. My mother's brother is here in France, though I know not where. Apparently, he is quite wealthy."

Véronique queried, "Do tell us his name."

Evangeline replied softly, trying to ignore the shooting pains in her head. "Guillaume. He is the twin brother of my mother, the late Lady Eugenie. He inherited the family title, so I suppose I should refer to him as Count de Beaufort."

Hearing the name, Véronique's eyes widened like full moons. "The Count is our neighbor. Just over that second ridge."

Evangeline turned to look where her hostess was pointing. It was but a floating image on the horizon. "It looks very distant. How long would it take to ride to his property?"

Adèle stopped Evangeline. "You are not near well enough to ride the lands here and certainly could not ride that far, at least half a day's journey."

"Could I pen a letter to him? Do you know him well?"

Véronique laughed. "All of those things are true."

Adèle added, "No one would have ever thought to connect you to him. Claude and I met your mother on the voyage to Grand Pré, but we never knew her last name, not being a member of Court. I only knew her as Lady Eugenie Le Blanc de Verdure."

Evangeline smiled. "How grand if he could meet me here."

Véronique replied, "He is rather a recluse. We see him rarely though I met him riding one day."

"Be that as it may, I must meet him before I leave for Versailles."

Véronique suggested, "I shall send one of our couriers to his château inviting him to dinner at the end of the week. Presuming Doctor Lezay agrees, of course. Does that meet your approval?"

"That should be enough time to recuperate, or at least to make a good impression on my uncle. It is important that he like me."

Adèle hugged her friend. "Of course he shall like you. You favor your mother in nearly every way, except your dark hair compared to her golden locks. He shall love you."

Véronique laughed with a lilt in her voice, "I have come to know the Count quite well since we have lived here. As well as he allows, in any case. He shall accept you with open arms. Of that I have no doubt."

Adèle offered Evangeline the goblet filled with wine, which Evangeline drank greedily. She managed to say, "Thank you both. I am eternally grateful for your kindness," before she nodded off again.

Evangeline remained in bed for most of the next day and the next. When she felt stronger, she walked to the window seat and enjoyed the view. Adèle joined her for lunch in her bedroom. They played cards and laughed and cried about old times in Grand Pré. Before long, Evangeline had fallen asleep and Adèle tiptoed out.

The following morning, with her breakfast tray, Evangeline found a small envelope closed with the red wax seal of the de Rochefort family. She tore it open and read it aloud.

"My dear Lady Evangeline,

"I write rather than to disturb your sleep. My courier returned early this morning and relayed that Count Guillaume de Beaufort is not in residence but has gone to the Palace of Versailles.

"We stand ready to provide a carriage and travel guards to escort you should you wish to travel there. We trust you shall await the Doctor's permission before you leave."

"Your new friend,

"Véronique, Lady de Rochefort."

Excited by the prospect of meeting her uncle and, hopefully, the King, Evangeline began to rebuild her strength. She walked a bit each day in her room, ending up by sitting in the window seat overlooking the stables. The stable boys took pride in their work brushing down the creatures after they had been ridden hard.

By the end of the week, Evangeline felt strong enough to write a letter to her uncle at Versailles, explaining who she was, how she came to be hosted by his neighbors in Provence, and asking to meet him as soon as she was well enough to travel to the Palace.

Véronique took the letter and assured her, "My rider shall leave at once. Trust him to deliver it into your uncle's hands."

Evangeline responded, "Thank you for all of your kindnesses. I do wish to travel to Versailles but when I am a bit stronger. It would not do for me to faint upon meeting him. I want him to see me as my mother, strong and independent. At least that is what I am told."

Adèle stood by her side and agreed, "She was, indeed, very much her own person."

Véronique added, "Then by all accounts, you are your mother's daughter. A weaker woman would not have recovered as quickly as you. We are, of course, willing to assist in any way we can."

Adèle grinned, "Claude and I have decided we shall travel to Versailles with you. Pauline shall care for Etienne in our absence. Claude has not been back since he left the King's service when he and I wed and voyaged to the New World. I have never had the pleasure of being in the Palace. It shall be much more fun if we all ride together, do you not think so?"

Evangeline seemed relieved. She might be independent but did not want to be foolish by traveling nearly across the entire country alone, even with guards. "I would welcome both of you very much. It should make the long trip much more enjoyable."

Véronique clapped her hands. "Then it is settled. When Doctor Lezay releases you, the three of you shall be on your way to Versailles. Now it is up to you to get well. We shall leave you to rest for now. If you are up to it, we dine at seven."

Evangeline nodded, "I shall be there with bells on. I have not even met my host yet."

Véronique and Adèle waved to her on their way out. Evangeline rang the little bell at her bedside. Mylène appeared at the door. Evangeline looked at her with glee. "I shall be dining downstairs tonight. You must choose a ravishing gown and fix my hair up."

Mylène curtsied and said with delight, "My Lady, you shall be the most beautiful one at table. I promise you that." She picked up a comb of pearls and began to stroke Evangeline's long luscious locks. "I think the blue satin encrusted with sparkling beads is the one for tonight. I shall return with the perfect jewelry for you."

Before Evangeline could object, Mylène slipped out of the room. The chambermaids and dressers knew what their mistresses owned and what they would be agreeable to loaning.

Mylène went straight to Véronique's head maid, Yvonne, with a proposal. "I have never requested any favor of you, but should you agree, I shall clean and fold all of Lady Véronique's laundry for two days."

Yvonne's curiosity was piqued. "Two days' worth of laundry is not insignificant. You must need something very badly."

"A pair of the Lady's diamond earrings for Lady Evangeline to wear tonight."

Yvonne shook her head. "Too valuable. My Lady's favorites."

Mylene disagreed. "Your Lady must have a dozen different pair of earrings. This is one pair for one night, tonight."

Yvonne countered the offer. "Wash and clean all the laundry for a week, not just two days."

"Done," replied Mylène with a smile. She held out her hand and Yvonne placed a silver monogrammed box it in.

"Make no mistake. I shall cut off your ears if you fail to return them in perfect condition to me tomorrow morning," Yvonne hissed.

Mylène waved as she glided out of the bedroom.

Evangeline's entrance that night elicited the desired responses from the four others waiting in the salon. Claude and Adèle applauded her as she walked through the door.

Véronique smiled welcomingly and whispered to her as she kissed both cheeks, "The earrings look lovelier on you than they ever did on me. Consider it my gift to you." Evangeline nodded in humble acceptance.

Claude introduced Evangeline to Laurent, who bowed and kissed her hand.

Before they struck up a conversation, however, the seven children of Véronique and Laurent entered to kiss their parents goodnight. A dutiful chorus of "Good night, Papa" and "Good night, Maman," was recited by their four sons and their three daughters. The de Rochefort children bowed to Claude and curtsied to Evangeline and Adèle before they rushed out of the room.

Pauline Arnaud, who was older than many of the children, carried Etienne for a good-night kiss from Claude and Adèle and curtsied to Evangeline and Véronique before slipping out of the room.

Evangeline exclaimed, "What well-mannered children! They must be a delight to you."

Véronique nodded while Laurent rolled his eyes. He spoke up, "They are always on their best behavior when guests are here. But before Claude and Adèle came, well, let's just say, they thought they were the owners of the house, not myself."

Everyone chuckled at the thought, then Véronique said, "Shall we?" The host and hostess led the way into the dining room. Claude escorted Adèle on one arm and Evangeline on the other.

Once they entered the large dining room, the women admired the gold candelabras emitting soft light and the table set with a profusion of flowers. Private stewards pulled out chairs and filled the wine goblets.

As conversations flowed, glasses were emptied and refilled. Laurent and Claude recounted stories of René and Eugenie at their wedding feast, and of René's relationship with King Louis XV at Versailles during their tenure there.

Evangeline turned the subject to one of her favorite pastimes. "We simply must go riding and have a picnic. It is one of my fondest memories with Gabriel."

Adèle responded, "You used to talk about your picnics on the bluff whenever you visited the dress shop."

"There is no finer feeling than the wind rushing through your hair, without a care in the world, thinking the future you envision will come true...." Evangeline's voice trailed off in a wistful whisper, "I hope and pray that he is safe. And that we meet again soon."

Claude reassured her. "I know him well. He shall not let anything sway his determination to reunite and make you his bride."

Evangeline nodded quickly. "That is why I must ride again. It gives me strength, which I shall need if I am to find my uncle and somehow get to England."

Laurent spoke up. "Whatever you need, dear Evangeline, consider it my honor to provide for you."

Evangeline attempted to retract her question. "I did not mean – I apologize, but I – I was going to ask my uncle to pay, not you."

Laurent waved his hand. "Nonsense. I would be happy to make all the necessary arrangements."

Adèle smiled. "You will need quite a bit more than just the cost of a private carriage. If you expect to enter Versailles, and be received, you shall need an entire new wardrobe. After all, your father was – is – the King's cousin, is he not?"

Evangeline nodded sheepishly.

"Then who better to design and sew the clothes you shall need to dazzle than I?"

Evangeline pooh-poohed the idea. "Surely you have too much to do here."

"Nonsense. I should love to keep occupied. It seems our family have so much money that they have hired everyone in the village for the work here. I cannot do one thing for myself. Not dress, eat, or even pour my own wine. No, I shall write to Paris for all the fabrics and trimmings for you. Since I have been here, I have studied the latest fashions and know where to acquire the best silks and satins, ribbons and bows, shoes and bags, laces and shawls. Naturally, nothing but the best for you, my dear friend."

Evangeline demurred. "Really, Adèle. Do not make a fuss. I would rather be invisible at court."

"You shall have no say in the matter. When I finish with your couture gowns and accessories, no man shall be able to resist your charms. The word shall spread and your uncle shall be at your side to fight away all the nobles battling for your hand."

Evangeline, "If you insist, then of course I accept."

Adèle added, "You are actually doing me such a favor. I have wanted to start another dress shop, but Claude," she looked at her husband who motioned for her to drop the subject but she defied him and continued. "My husband has tried to convince me to enjoy life with our two families. But embroidering a pillow is not at all the same as an elegant gown that will see enchanted evenings at one of the many balls held here in the countryside."

Evangeline embraced Adèle, kissing her on the cheek. "What are you waiting for? I cannot wait to see your sketches."

*

Within two months, Adèle had completed a custom wardrobe and packed it into a comfortable carriage for Evangeline's trip to Versailles. Pauline wanted to go with them, but Claude insisted that she wait a year until Laurent could arrange for her to presented at Court, something that the untitled Claude was unable to do.

The Arnauds climbed into the carriage with Evangeline. Laurent had thoughtfully provided all the comforts money could buy – thick pillows, beautiful draperies, a picnic basket, and bottles of wine. Their carriage sped away with the de Rochefort family and Pauline holding Etienne on her hip waving to them.

On the long journey from Provence to Versailles, Evangeline was often lost in her thoughts. Would her uncle be there? Would he welcome her with open arms as his niece? Or would he reject her as an upstart seeking the family fortune?

Despite Adèle's friendly banter, Evangeline stayed in a state of anxiety until she realized one thing. All she had to do was assure her uncle of her sincere motives to know him as part of the family. As a female, she could not, of course, inherit the title. But that was of no interest to her in any case. She wanted to visit the home where her mother grew up and own some of her mother's most precious possessions.

Once Evangeline had her plan, she remained calm and enjoyed the trip with Claude and Adèle.

CHAPTER 67
Ursulines

Paris

The British ship with its load of Acadians from Grand Pré was anchored off the island of Belle-Île-en-Mer near the small commune of Le Palais. Béatrice remembered how the Captain had dropped anchor, then unceremoniously tossed the rope ladder over the side of the transport down to a small rowboat.

He had forced the few remaining Acadians who survived the perilous journey to descend the rickety rope into the row boat. Two sailors rowed the small craft over to the pier. Once it got close to shore, they made the Acadians jump off the boat into the shallow, freezing water. When Josephine Gautrot did not jump, a sailor pushed her overboard, but she drowned. Béatrice was saddened at her death and prayed for her and the others who had died, then prayed just as hard for those who were alive.

Before the Acadians even knew what had happened, the rowboat turned around, heading for the ship. The Acadians dragged themselves up on shore, freezing like wet rats. By the time they were on land, the rowboat had been hoisted up to the ship and the Captain had set sail for England.

Belying her young age, Béatrice had assisted the other girls, even those older than she, onto the dock. They clung together, shivering in the cold, while Béatrice walked up the main road searching for blankets, food and a fire where they might dry off.

She staggered into the village linen shop, run by the mayor's wife, Madame Odette Trahan. She was shocked to see Béatrice's appearance like a wet animal, rather than the young woman that she was.

"My dear, what happened? Where have you come from?"

Béatrice cried as she replied, "We were exiled from Acadia by the British and left here. They wanted all of us to die to send a message to His Majesty. And many of my friends did pass away. The girls who are still alive are on the wharf. Please help us alive. Everyone is cold and hungry."

Odette pulled blankets, a wool dress, warm sweater, socks and boots from the shelf and gave them to Béatrice. "Dry yourself and change into these. Stand by the fire and warm yourself. Could you eat something?"

"We have not eaten for the last day, Madame. The sailors said the food was for their trip to England. But I must help my friends. They are quite hungry, too." Béatrice gratefully stood by the hearth and changed quickly.

Odette brought a plate of cheese and bread and a glass of wine insisting that Béatrice eat, so she quickly downed the meal. But the heat she felt from the woolens and the burning logs did not compare to the warm kindness she received from Madame Trahan. They piled stacks of thick sweaters and coverlets into a small cart near the door. She motioned to Béatrice, "Pull it down to the dock. I shall meet you there with others who can help."

Within the hour, Madame Trahan had gathered most of the families in the village who opened their hearts to the refugees. They wrapped blankets around them and gave them food to eat. Then each family took in at least one Acadian and welcomed her into their homes.

Béatrice was invited to live with Odette and her husband. When Béatrice told Madame Trahan that she was a seamstress, Odette immediately offered her a position at the linen shop. During daylight hours, Béatrice stitched linens for custom orders. At night, she enjoyed a late supper with the mayor and his wife, who recounted long stories of the proud history of the island. Soon, Béatrice felt at home in the small village.

Using a quill, ink and paper borrowed from Odette, Béatrice wrote to King Louis XIV. Her correspondence to His Majesty over a period of months always asked for the same thing. She pleaded for transport for herself and the other Acadians on the island to the French territory of Louisiana in the New World. But all of her requests had gone unanswered.

After nearly a year on the island, when she least expected it, several of the King's carriages led by a contingent of Royal Horsemen had appeared across the narrow inlet on the mainland. The Royal brigade dismounted and left their steeds with one of their aides. Then they boarded a small ferry that transported them to the island. When the Kings' men arrived, the mayor and his official delegation were waiting on the pier to greet them.

The royal representative announced that His Majesty ordered the Horsemen to escort the Acadians out of Belle-Île-en-Mer to their new home. Béatrice was overjoyed to learn the King had agreed to her request and had also provided a travel bag, new clothing and coins for each Acadian. She was disappointed, however, when she learned their destination was Paris rather than Louisiana. Her heart was firm in desiring to end up in that French territory, though she knew not how that would occur.

Hurried good-byes were exchanged between the island residents and the Acadians at the dock. Odette pleaded with Béatrice to stay Béatrice shook her head. "You have been more of a mother to me than my own, and for that I love and thank you. But I must follow my heart and leave today."

The Acadians and the King's Horsemen piled into the ferry, which took them to the mainland. There, the Horsemen mounted their steeds and the young women boarded carriages. They traveled for days, with brief stops only to change horses and drivers at inns along the way. The girls were given food at the stops, but there was no time for overnight rests, so they slept as best they could in the carriage which bounced along the muddy dirt road filled with stones and potholes.

Béatrice tried to determine how long the journey had been from Grand Pré to Paris. She knew the sea voyage had taken months, followed by many more on the island, and now many days' voyage by carriage to her destination. Retracing the journey was exhausting in itself, so Béatrice forgot about her calculations and willed herself to sleep.

*

Days later, the rhythm of the horses slowed to a plodding gait and jolted Béatrice awake. She peeked between the curtains at the approaching building that resembled a fortress. At the entry, large iron gates surrounded an open yard filled with trees bare of leaves. The sides of the building offered only tiny slits for windows.

As the coaches rode up to the building, a procession of nuns in black robes exited and waited by the front steps. Béatrice looked through the window and saw a group of women dressed in black approaching. Béatrice exclaimed. "A convent? We are to be locked up in a nunnery? Why were we not told where we were going? How shall I ever meet a man to marry me if I am here, even if I do not take the vows?"

The younger girls were confused, but a pair of twins seated opposite her in the carriage understood exactly what she was saying. One of the twins, Anastasie, commiserated with Béatrice. "We are doomed to a life of washing and cleaning. That is all the nuns do, isn't it? We would have been better off in a prison. That way, at least there would be guards we could have chatted up. Maybe one of them would have released us and married us. I would rather wash and clean for a houseful of babies than for the nuns."

At that, her twin sister Amelie laughed, as did Béatrice. The only good thing Béatrice could think of in the situation was the release of her fear of the unknown. "At least we shall no longer wonder what we shall do for the rest of our lives."

226 | M. M. Le BLANC

Anastasie retorted, "I shall definitely try to escape. Once I get a good night's sleep, that is. Anyone want to go with me?"

Amelie shook her head. "I will happily wash and clean. That is a low price to have more than one meal a day and a roof over my head."

An elderly nun at the head of the line waddled up to their carriage door and opened it. Clapping her hands for silence, she announced, "I am Mother Superior. You shall be living with us now. And you must do as I say if you expect to have food to eat and a clean bed for sleeping. All of you, come out now. Hurry. Follow Sister Marie and Sister Laure into the convent."

The girls exited and met the two younger nuns Mother Superior had introduced -- the squatty, stern-faced Sister Marie and the kindly, tall Sister Laure. It was Sister Laure who helped each girl down the stairs, only for each Acadian to be met with a haughty look from Sister Marie, who constantly barked orders. "Follow me. Quickly, girls. No time to waste."

The girls all obeyed the instructions, although it would have been hard to determine if that was done out of fear or fatigue.

Mother Superior repeated her orders after she opened every carriage door. The girls inside cowered at the thought of a life under her orders, but they all obeyed the instructions to the letter.

Once all the carriages were empty, Mother Superior thanked the drivers. They wasted not a minute longer to crack their whips on their horses and speed away. Béatrice held her two travel bags close to her entered the convent. She was awestruck at the silence as they walked through the long corridors, punctuated by closed doors. Nuns seemed to glide everywhere without making a sound as they passed the Acadian girls in the hallways.

Béatrice could not be certain if the nuns were told to ignore them or if they had taken a vow of silence. She knew not what to expect. But one thing was certain. They had to obey Mother Superior.

*

Time passed quickly at the convent. What a difference a year made to Béatrice. Though just a girl herself, she had become a teacher in the Ursuline convent school instructing very young girls. When not teaching, Béatrice sneaked out of the convent to walk along the Seine River.

Today she stopped at an artist's booth to admire a portrait he was finishing of a young girl holding a bouquet. The girl's mother smiled and paid the artist, then the girl skipped away holding her mother's hand.

"Very good likeness," she complimented the handsome young man.

He turned with a grin, showing perfect white teeth except for a gap in the front "Thank you, Mademoiselle. Paul Deschamps, at your service." What began as a brief conversation lasted all afternoon as he sketched her in charcoal. But he refused to give her the portrait. "You must do something for me if you want my work."

She was instantly leery of him, saying, "What would that be?"

Paul grinned slyly, "Have a coffee with me over there. Café de Paris."

She looked relieved. But she had been warned about not having a chaperone. She still did not know his intentions but she did have a coffee and a brief conversation with him before she returned at sunset to the convent.

When Béatrice walked in the building, Sister Laure was waiting for her. She directed her to Mother Superior's office.

Mother asked, "My child, I understand you have taken a long walk outside our walls. Is that so?"

Béatrice showed her surprise on her face. How in the world did she know about that. Still, she recognized it was best to be honest and replied, "Yes, Mother Superior."

"Surely you understand that it is not seemly for a young girl to walk unchaperoned, no matter if day or evening, but particularly this late?"

"No, Mother, I did not know, I mean, I did not realize. I used to walk here and yonder in Grand Pré, doing everything for my mother and my brother." Béatrice's eyes welled with tears.

The old nun drew Béatrice to her and wrapped her arms around her, waiting as Béatrice sobbed her eyes out. "There, there," said Mother Superior. "You miss your family, I understand."

Béatrice nodded, "Not knowing if my mother and brother are alive keeps me awake until the wee hours when I simply fall asleep exhausted."

The nun pondered Béatrice's words. "And you think if you could walk out of the convent that you might be able to resolve your loneliness?"

Whatever she said was fine with her. "Yes, Mother Superior."

"Shall we strike a bargain?"

Béatrice stared at her blankly, then nodded quickly. Whatever did she mean? What kind of bargain?

Mother Superior continued, "You have been a good and faithful teacher this past year. The girls adore you. But I must say, to my distress, I have heard the pupils say you make learning fun. You know, of course, it should be strict and regimented. Certainly not enjoyable."

"Yes, Mother. I mean, no, Mother." Béatrice was still confused.

"The point I am making," Mother Superior continued to drone on. Béatrice daydreamed about Paul and heard nothing the old nun said until she asked, "Do you?"

Béatrice said, "I must reflect on that, Mother," stalling for time to figure out if she even heard what was said.

Mother Superior became impatient. "Either you have a vocation to life as a nun, or you don't. Think carefully. Do you? Your answer affects my decision."

Béatrice swallowed hard and pretended to think about it. She was happy teaching the girls and happy in her life where she did not have to root around for food or bend over a hot hearth cooking, or even peel potatoes or bake bread. She knew the answer immediately. "I am certain that this is my vocation. I want to join the convent permanently. But I would like some time on my own before taking the vows."

Mother Superior grunted her satisfaction. "Good girl. Then I shall grant you permission to take a walk once a week, but only down the rue St. Michel to the Seine and back to our convent. You will find mainly artists and booksellers there, but do not dawdle. The purpose is to let you get a whiff of the air of Paris, with its smelly carriages and slop in the streets. You can even smell the nightsoil from chamber pots on that street. I am certain once you do that, you shall return at once to the cleanliness of our home."

Béatrice could not refrain from showing her excitement. "Thank you, Mother. Thank you so much," she exclaimed as she hugged the old nun.

"You may go now, child. Return to me after you take your next walk and we shall talk of what shall be required to fulfill your vocation."

The following week, Béatrice lingered over a delicious tiny cup of coffee with Paul, although she knew she had to return. "Alas, it is time for me to leave. Thank you for a lovely afternoon, Paul."

Paul paid the tab, including a customary centime as an additional tip for the waiter. He jumped up and escorted her back onto the street. "May I have the honor of walking you home?" he asked breathlessly. He had never seen such a beautiful girl, or even one who would speak to him. Good girls were always chaperoned; they were never allowed to speak to the likes of him.

She shook her head. "I think not. Perhaps we shall meet again if I walk the quay. If not, I wish you luck with your art." She bid him adieu, then began to walk down the street. Paul called out after her, "You never told me your name."

She shouted back, something that was accepted in Grand Pré but frowned upon in Paris. "Béatrice. My name is Béatrice Gaudet." She practically skipped all the way to the convent. She rang the bell outside the front gates and Sister Laure slowly made her way to the iron grill to open it. Béatrice was unaware that Paul had hidden behind a nearby tree after following her all the way to the nunnery.

But Sister Laure saw him. He shook his head warning her not to reveal his hiding place, not so hidden, to Béatrice. The nun nodded silently to him as she allowed Béatrice into the gates and shut them promptly again.

Béatrice dutifully presented herself to Mother Superior the following day. "Mother, I am waiting on a sign from God that this is my vocation."

Mother Superior nodded her approval but sensed some hesitation. "It seems you have more to say. Please, go on or I shall call Sister Laure in to tell me about it."

Béatrice sheepishly said, "I would like to be able to take another walk, perhaps even one each week. The air along the Seine rekindled my spirit and, besides, I met, I met someone on the quay."

Mother Superior leaned forward in an intimidating way and barked, "Would this have anything to do with your wish to return to the River?"

"I shall not attempt to deceive you. The person is a man."

Mother Superior said in mock horror, "A man? An old man? Was he hurt? Did you help him walk along the quay?"

Béatrice shook her head. "Not old. A young man. An artist. He sketched my portrait with his charcoal stick. He is excellent at his craft."

Mother Superior held up her hand for silence. "Return to me next week after your walk." She returned to reading her Bible in the candlelight. Béatrice remained rooted to the floor, afraid to move, afraid she imagined what she just heard.

The elderly nun shooed her away. "Say your prayers and get to bed."

Béatrice repeated the same regimen each week as did the nuns and students. She attended daily Mass, taught the girls in her class, ate supper at the communal table, said her prayers and went to sleep. The only variation was her weekly walk. But even that was a ritual. She walked to the quay, perused the stalls of the booksellers, walked by the artists then stopped at Paul's easel. Sometimes he gave her a pastry. Other days he shared a loaf of bread, a hunk of cheese and a bottle of wine. They chatted as Paul waited for commissions always ending the day with a coffee at the Café de Paris.

After each walk, Béatrice reported to Mother Superior, who always asked, "What are your intentions about joining the Ursuline Order?"

Béatrice replied today, as she did every other day, "I have a great desire to take my vows and join your Order. I am still waiting for a sign. Could I have more time before making a commitment?"

Mother Superior always nodded and said, "Yes, my child. I shall give you another week."

When the summer sun beamed into the convent windows on the last day of the class for the term, Mother Superior walked into Béatrice's class and took a seat in the back of the room. The old nun observed silently and waited until the class had ended. Once the students had left the room, the nun walked up to the front of the room and gave Béatrice a simple order. "Pack your things. You leave this convent on the morrow."

Béatrice was confused. "Mother, why are you sending me away? I love it here. My students, my sisters. This is my home."

On her way out of the door, Mother Superior stopped in the doorway. "I am sending you to our Order in New Orleans. They need a teacher for the children of the French aristocracy." Béatrice slid into her chair, so stunned was she at the directive. Realizing this could be the sign she had waited for, she felt joy at the thought of actually going to New Orleans. That is where the Acadians in Grand Pré pledged to meet each other. She cleared her desk, stacked the books neatly on the shelf and practically ran to her cell to pack.

The next day, Béatrice and two young women, Fleur and Lucette, who had recently arrived at the convent for their vocations, lined up outside the front gates, next to a hired carriage. Mother Superior checked to verify that each was dressed properly in a black habit with a black veil. "God shall forgive all of us for what I am about to do. But you shall be safer as you travel in these habits, though you have not yet taken your vows. And you must each wear one of these." She put a gold wedding band in the hand of each of the women, then continued, "Once you arrive at the convent in New Orleans, return the band and the habit to the Mother Superior there. You may not otherwise possess them before the final investiture ceremony."

Béatrice kissed Mother's ring and stepped in the carriage. The two other girls piled into the carriage and Mother Superior spoke to them before the door was shut. "Yours is an important mission. You shall educate young aristocratic girls for their lives as Christian wives and mothers, just as the sons are being taught by the Jesuits. Consider this a test of your vocation and you shall not fail. May God be with each of you. Goodbye."

Each of the young women was lost in her thoughts and almost failed to catch the old nun's last words to them. "Sister Laure shall chaperone you during your trip. And I have asked Paul Deschamps to provide assistance and assure you arrive safely."

Béatrice's head shot up as Sister Laure and Paul climbed into the carriage. Paul smiled at Béatrice and introduced himself to the other girls. "I am Paul Deschamps, at your service."

The youngest one, blue-eyed Fleur giggled, "Pleased to meet you Mister Deschamps." The tall blonde waif, Lucette, boldly held out her hand. Paul kissed it and winked at her. She blushed and averted her eyes.

To Béatrice, he nodded, "It's good to see you again."

Béatrice simply nodded and said, "And you."

As Sister Laure passed around a basket of breakfast breads, honey and butter, Paul knocked on the carriage ceiling. With an immediate jolt, they left for the Seine River.

On the quay, they would board a boat that would take them upriver to the port of Le Havre.

CHAPTER 68
Versailles

France

Tired and disheveled after the long journey from Laurent de Rochefort's château, Claude, Adèle and Evangeline poured out of the carriage and dragged themselves into the inn along the route to Versailles. Claude arranged two private rooms for them to stay the night so they would be refreshed when they arrived at court the following day.

In her small room, Evangeline enjoyed a tub which maidservants filled with hot water. As the steamy water clouded the candlelight, Evangeline dozed off. She woke to the sound of horses outside the inn, as several drunk soldiers dismounted and entered the inn seeking food and ale.

She quickly dried herself off and dressed in her day clothes. She did not trust the flimsy latch on the door so she managed to push the tub of water near enough to the door that she could just squeeze out, but a man could not get in. She lay in bed under the covers remembering why she had a fear that a man would break into her room.

It was the "incident" that seemed like it had happened many years ago. In fact, it had been less than two years earlier when the English Lieutenant Greenfield had grabbed her off the main street in Grand Pré and dragged her into an alley. True, he was drunk, but he was still stronger than she was. He had covered her mouth and ripped her dress, holding her down as she felt helpless. Tears flooded her eyes as she recalled how Gabriel rushed into the alley and pulled the soldier off her, then gently covered her with his coat.

Evangeline was surprised she still had such strong feelings about the matter and she shivered at the thought of it ever happening again. She calmed herself, remembering Lieutenant Greenfield his gotten his due and died when a snake appeared out of nowhere and bit him.

Evangeline dozed off thinking of Gabriel and woke only when she heard a loud knocking on the door. The chubby maid tried to enter to serve her breakfast but could not fit through the door, so she left the tray outside her room. Ready to continue on the journey, Evangeline jumped out of bed and pushed the tub out of the way. She enjoyed the hearty meal of breads lathered with butter, cheeses, fruit, jams and jellies, and steaming hot coffee.

She knocked on the door of the adjoining room where Claude and Adèle had slept. Her timing was perfect. They were packing their bags to leave, so they all descended the staircase at the same time.

Claude arranged payment of the bill and escorted them downstairs. Once they were settled in the carriage, Evangeline asked, "How is it that you are so comfortable going to Versailles after being away for nearly two decades?"

Claude laughed, his dimples now creased into those of a middle-aged man. "The wheels of change grind very slowly at the Palace. Everything revolves around the King, which means time often stands still until His Majesty agrees to see you, or dine with you, or even walk in the gardens with you. Prepare yourself that His Majesty might not see you today, or tomorrow, or even next week. There is no schedule, and you have no right to demand an audience. Keep that in mind. We must be at his beck and call. He may even invite us for a visit while he is in the bath."

Evangeline was shocked. "His bath? Must we join him?"

Adèle felt the same as Evangeline. "Are you saying we must get into the tub with him?"

Claude clapped his hands with glee. "Ladies, calm down. He stays in his bath drinking champagne, and he usually offers his guest a seat on his bed as his servants bathe him. It is all very civilized. You shall see."

Evangeline disagreed. "I see nothing civilized about the King sitting naked with ladies present. Nothing civilized indeed."

Claude reminded her, "King Louis is unpredictable. Did your father not prepare you?"

Evangeline shook her head. "He had made me promise on my sixteenth birthday that I would be presented at Court to eligible royal and noble suitors to remain in my station. That is all we discussed. But then, everything happened so fast with that soldier attacking me. Papa wanted to make sure I was protected and he almost sent me to France then. But I fell in love with Gabriel and refused to leave. After that, nothing else mattered."

Adèle patted Evangeline's hand. "Everything is going to be fine. Your father was a member of Court and you are simply reminding people of that. Besides, look at you." She adjusted Evangeline's hat and tied a loose ribbon on the bodice of her dress. "Anyone who sees you will fall in love with you."

Evangeline started to protest, "But that is not why I am here."

"I know, but it does not hurt to get the attention of the men. That will make you more attractive to the King."

The carriage traveled around a bend in the road and the Palace came into view. Claude smiled as he looked out of the window. "It shall not be long now before our beautiful Evangeline shall impress all of the men at Court, even His Majesty."

Adèle looked on her handiwork with pride. The long nights she had spent on Evangeline's gown was about to pay off. "Especially His Majesty," she said.

The carriage drove along the winding road and stopped in front of the Palace gates. Two burly men armed with swords, approached the coach through the gates and called out, "Who goes there?"

Claude stepped out of the carriage handed one of the guards his papers through the wrought iron gates. "I am Monsieur Claude Arnaud, formerly here at Versailles. My brother is Lord Laurent de Rochefort of Provence. We are escorting Lady Evangeline, late of Grand Pré, daughter of Lord René Le Blanc, the King's Consul and relation to His Royal Majesty."

The two young guards reviewed the documents, discussed the situation in low tones and nodded, opening the gates. "You may enter," said the taller of the guards, who returned the papers to Claude before he climbed back in the carriage.

The second guard reminded them, "Drive straight up to the main palace and enter through the large double doors."

The driver proceeded through the opening, when the gates closed behind them. Rolling towards the Palace, Evangeline was in awe of the fountains with sculptures spouting water, and the gold trim everywhere.

At the front door, two more guards, younger this time, stood at the double doors. Claude looked at them and reminisced. "There nearly two decades ago stood Laurent and myself. Where has the time gone?"

Adèle patted his shoulder. She had learned long ago to humor him when he remembered his childhood with his brother, who now had a title, had married nobility and had more wealth than he could spend in his lifetime. "At least your brother did not make you honor your promise to be his valet, my dearest."

At that, Claude let out a belly laugh that even surprised the two guards who heard him.

Evangeline had to restrain herself to recall the training that Christine had given her in Grand Pré. Remain a lady at all times. Do not rush as you walk. Others will wait for you, due to your station in life.

When Claude offered his arm to her and his other to Adèle, each lady accepted it and allowed him to set the pace. Claude was back in his domain.

He was going to prove that he could be as well-respected as his brother, even without a title. The trio was escorted up the stairs to the door, which the guard opened with a slight bow.

Evangeline smiled at him, but Claude shook his head and whispered, "Do not acknowledge the servants."

Evangeline asked, "Why? It doesn't seem right. They are very kind."

"It is considered in poor taste. Beneath your station. Just ignore them."

Adèle said in a low voice, "Do as he says, dear. We are here to find your uncle and hopefully to meet His Majesty. We must follow the rules and customs of the nobility in order to do that."

Evangeline nodded, "You are right, of course. Lead on and I shall follow."

Once they entered, they were left in the great hall, where Evangeline admired the portrait that her father had first seen long ago. The painting by Jean-Baptiste Pater entitled, "La Fête Champêtre," often referred to as, "The Garden Party," featured her mother as the central character.

Evangeline touched the woman's face. She felt so light-headed, giddy and nearly forgot her manners. An electric shock ran through her body. Was it an omen? A warning? A signal from her mother? She did not understand these things, nor did she wish to learn.

An aged attendant approached them and bowed. As was the custom, he spoke only to Claude, the man in their party. "Sir? I am Jules Martin, the Prime Minister's assistant secretary, at your service. What is your purpose and whom is it you wish to see at Court?"

Claude repeated his introduction. At the name of René Le Blanc, the servant's eyes widened. Claude added, "Lady Evangeline requests an audience with His Royal Majesty. She is also here to meet her uncle, Count de Beaufort."

The servant nodded humbly. "Yes, sir. Of course, sir. The Count is often at Court. I saw him recently playing cards. I should say working hard, because he is generally the winner. However, I am unsure if he is here at this time. But I shall be pleased to verify for you."

He turned to Evangeline and pointed at the painting. "Permit me to apologize, my Lady. I should have seen the resemblance. The woman in the portrait is your mother, no?"

Evangeline nodded. "I never knew her. She died birthing me. But you knew her, did you not?"

Jules nodded sorrowfully. "I was saddened to the core when I learned of her passing. She was very beautiful. You could say ethereal. Lady Eugenie was often painted by the King's Royal Artist, Pater. He was very fond of her. He even called her his muse and painted several portraits of her on the voyage to the New World after she had just been married."

Evangeline was thirsty for more details about her mother's life before she had married her father. "Was she well-liked at Court? Did she have a lot of friends?"

Adèle added, "On the voyage to Grand Pré in the New World, everyone on the ship adored Lady Eugenie. She could do no wrong in anyone's eyes. She was truly beloved."

The secretary shook his head. "I wish I could say the same in the Palace. But the ladies at court harbored strong feelings of jealousy and anger towards her. Still, the few that loved her were very powerful and they protected her. This is Court, after all. One must have strong, influential friends to survive in these vicious circles."

"Was her brother her protector?" Evangeline dared to ask.

Jules answered carefully. "At that time, the man who held the title of Count was Lady Eugenie's father, your grandfather. He rarely came to Court except on His Majesty's orders. Your mother explained to me one day her brother – your uncle -- had taken his share of the family inheritance and quit the family château, preferring to live in Italy. Venice it was, if I recall. This was some years ago, you know. My memory is not as good these days."

Evangeline was quite curious now. "So what happened?"

Adèle nodded quickly, enthralled by the story. "Yes, what happened next?"

Jules spoke directly to Evangeline. "When the old Count died, your uncle had to appear in Court with his papers, to confirm his noble birth. It was the only way the King would approve the official transfer of the title and ownership of the family lands and fortune. At least, I presume there is still a fortune."

Evangeline looked at the painting, then turned back to him. "Can you tell me anything else about my mother?"

Jules looked at the painting. It seemed to Evangeline that he was teary-eyed, but perhaps it was his age. "The Palace intrigue only got more complex the longer she stayed at Court. I always thought His Majesty had arranged her marriage to Lord Le Blanc and appointed him Royal Consul in the New World to remove her from the hate and spite of the ladies at Court. I loved her. She was always kind to me. She often acknowledged me, even thanked me. Not like the others at Court. They pretend you are invisible. But your mother was a true beauty, inside and out. And your father adored her. I have never seen a man more in love with a woman he did not know before he married her."

Evangeline thanked him profusely. "I owe you such a debt of gratitude. I hope I shall see you again. I should like to hear more about my parents."

The old man sighed. "There is something else. The King removed from the public galleries all the works that Pater painted of Lady Eugenie on that fateful trip. He locked all of them away. As far as I know, no one but His Majesty has ever seen the other paintings. This one is the only painting he allows for public viewing."

He turned to Claude. "I remember you too, sir. You were but a lad, but I remember you at the front door. You and your brother, was it?"

Claude nodded. "Laurent. He was legitimized by his father, Duke de Rochefort and inherited one of his many châteaus."

"I know that, but you were always the more interesting one. I see you married well, too." He bowed to Adèle. She smiled, instantly forgetting her own admonition to Evangeline.

Claude was getting impatient and became cross with the old man. "Could we get on with it? Lady Evangeline has business to attend to."

"Of course, sir. I shall make arrangements for your rooms. How long do you plan to stay?"

Evangeline sputtered, "Not long. Time enough to meet my uncle and speak with the King. How long will that be?"

The old man shook his head. "Oh, not the King. It is impossible. He refuses to see anyone. And even if he did, his physicians and bodyguards will not let anyone near him."

Evangeline was visibly disappointed. "No one talks to His Majesty?"

Jules replied, "Only his doctors. The assassination attempt is still fresh in everyone's minds."

At that, Claude, Adèle and Evangeline were shocked. Claude spoke first, "An attempt on His Majesty's life?"

The secretary spoke in a low tone and looked around as if the walls had ears. "A servant named Robert Francois Damien made his way into the back hallway. When the King walked through, he pulled a knife from his cloak and stabbed His Majesty in the side. He immediately went into shock and was taken to his bedchamber. The treasonous weasel was tortured and quartered then burned. Too good for him, if you ask me. If the assassin had not been taken down by the guards next to the King, I shudder to think of what could have happened. After all, the King's sons previously died, leaving only his grandson as the heir. And he is a mere child."

Evangeline said slowly, "Is His Majesty recovering? He is not going to…." She could not bring herself to say it.

Jules said, "He is getting stronger every day, though it is said that he fainted from the loss of so much blood when it happened."

"Do you think I could speak with the physician and give him a note to give to His Majesty? Under these circumstances."

The servant said, "My lady, I shall do for you what I would have done for your mother. Anything you wish, after I see you to your rooms. Once you are comfortable, I shall personally see to your other requests."

Evangeline interjected, "But…"

Claude interrupted her by touching her elbow. "We should like to be shown to our rooms."

The old man pulled a cord on the side of the portrait frame that no one had noticed before. A wall panel slid open and revealed a small room. Two young valets who had been sitting in the room until called stood and exited.

Jules looked at the valets. "Their luggage is in the carriage. Bring their bags to the east wing. I shall be waiting there."

The valets bowed and exited the great hall. The secretary led the way. "Follow me."

The four people walked silently through the Hall of Mirrors, just as René Le Blanc had done so many years ago. Their images reflected in the glass to infinity just as his had done when Cardinal de Fleury had escorted him to the chamber of King Louis XV. That is where René's adventure had begun. The monarch had appointed him as Royal Consul to Grand Pré to be his eyes and ears in that British territory. As a reward, Louis had arranged René's marriage to the ethereal Lady Eugenie de Beaufort which had been celebrated with an enormous wedding feast. Claude and his brother Laurent had directed the wait staff who served the wedding guests. The following day, the newlyweds had traveled in a caravan of royal carriages to the Port of Le Havre. Boarding *L'Acadie*, Eugenie had bid adieu to France, not knowing it was the last time she would ever grace its shores.

Evangeline, having seen her mother prominently featured in the painting in the great hall, felt an even stronger connection to her now. For years, Eugenie's portrait had hung on the dining room wall in the Consulate in Grand Pré, and Christine had told her stories of her mother at Court. Thus, Evangeline grew up knowing some things about her mother. But only when she entered the Palace did she truly feel her mother's spirit near her.

Overwhelmed by emotion, Evangeline steadied herself by leaning her hand against the gilted frame of the large mirror facing her. She was unaware that a pair of eyes peered through two obscure holes in the frame. If anyone had noticed the eyes at that moment, they would have seen them gaze upon Evangeline and fill with tears. And if anyone had been listening intently, they would have heard a barely audible gasp. But no one was paying attention to the mirror. They were concerned about Evangeline.

Adèle went up to her friend and gave her a shoulder to lean on. "Do you wish to sit or can you go to our suite?"

Evangeline shook her head. "I am fine. Just needed to catch my breath. Let us continue to the rooms."

After walking through the Hall of Mirrors, Jules directed Claude, Adèle and Evangeline into the large outer chamber. In other times, the vast room would have been a noisy, overflowing sea of wall-to-wall royal cousins, nobles and their ladies currying favor, rural Frenchmen seeking justice, and wait servants offering libations and refreshments to hundreds of nobles.

Today there were but a handful of diehard nobles who lived at court and came to the antechamber each day hoping to speak with the King. Alas, today was not going to be that day.

As Evangeline strolled by, they perked up. Lord Morlaix, dressed in blue brocade and red feathers leaned over to another well-dressed dandy. "Do you see what I see?"

Baron Faubert, standing next to him, nodded with approval. "Indeed. Not only fresh and young but methinks she is untouched. Look at her walk, her mannerisms."

Morlaix nodded as he leered at Evangeline. "Pure as driven snow. But I saw her first, so I shall have her first."

Claude called out to her as she dallied, admiring the opulence of the chamber. "Evangeline, please join us."

Faubert and Morlaix noted the name and gave each other a knowing look, silently mouthing the name "Evangeline." When she had passed, the nobles went back to their favorite pastime, watching the ladies at Court for possibilities of a brief dalliance.

Finally they arrived at their rooms. Evangeline and Adèle walked quickly through the palatial guest suite -- three bedrooms, two sitting rooms and a large common room with a dining table and chairs facing the large fireplace. Fresh flowers had been placed in vases throughout and the curtains had been pulled back to show the gardens.

Claude was impressed, "You have made your mark already, Evangeline. Only the highest of the nobility are given rooms facing the gardens. Others face the front entry or back porte cochere and hear carriages night and day."

The ladies chose the rooms they wanted and sat on one of the beds, chatting animatedly about what they saw. Adèle was elated, "Notice the beautiful fringe and trim on the draperies. That is all the rage now. I must remember to buy some to bring back to Provence. The local shops usually have very few of the latest fabric or notions from Paris."

Evangeline looked around the room. It was exquisitely furnished with expensive items – the bed, chairs, divan, rugs, candelabras and much more. But something did not seem right. She walked over to the armoire which was partially open. She opened it and noticed a loose board in the back of it. When she tried to right it, it fell to the floor, exposing an opening into a secret hallway. She waved to Adèle, whispering, "What does this mean?"

Without waiting for her friend, she stepped through the opening and found herself in a cavernous maze. Adèle stuck her head through the opening and tugged at Evangeline's skirts. "Not now. We must get ready for dinner."

Evangeline agreed and returned to the bed room, closing the armoire tightly. "I am famished now that I think of it."

Just as they returned from the tunnel, Jules knocked. "Enter," the two women said simultaneously. Jules bowed and said, "The valets are here."

Evangeline pointed to two bags, "Those are mine. Please put them over there," pointing to the racks near the armoire.

Adèle asked, "What time is dinner?"

Jules said, "Usually we begin at six and go as long as the King wishes. But due to the unfortunate circumstances, cook sends dinner trays to anyone at Court who desires it."

"Has the King forbidden the Court to gather in his absence?" Evangeline asked innocently.

Jules bowed, "No one at Court may sing, dance, dine or walk in the gardens until invited to do so by His Majesty, my Lady."

Evangeline nodded. "I should very much like some dinner. What about you, Adèle?"

Her friend nodded. "Yes, that would be wonderful. Thank you, Monsieur Martin."

Claude entered. "Could you arrange a meeting with the King's physician or other representative?"

"It has been done, Monsieur Arnaud. The Royal Notaire, Jean-Luc Delacroix shall meet with Lady Evangeline on the morrow in the great hall. Should I return here to fetch her and help her through the maze of hallways?"

At that moment, Evangeline entered. "What maze? No, of course not. I remember how to return there."

Jules bowed and crept out of the room.

As dusk fell, Evangeline looked through the windows of the suite into the windows of the opposite wing of the Palace. Lamplighters touched their torches to wall sconces and candelabras, which immediately threw the darkened halls into lovely soft light. The unique U-shaped design of the building allowed inhabitants on one side of the palace to see the goings-ons in the halls of the other wing. Such viewings never failed to be an excellent source of gossip for the noblewomen at Court and their ladies-in-waiting.

When dinner was delivered, Evangeline ate quickly while the Arnauds preferred to take their time and talk over nearly every morsel.

Evangeline was suddenly very tired, "Would you please excuse me. I have such an important day ahead of me."

Claude stood as Adèle kissed Evangeline's cheek. "Sleep well. We shall see you in the morning."

She walked into her bedroom and quickly fell sound asleep.

In the morning, Evangeline woke to find her breakfast tray by her bed. On it was a pot of a hot brown substance. She timidly tasted it and found it delicious. She wondered what it was as she walked over to her bags and opened them, only to find them empty.

She looked around the room, and a servant sitting in a chair in the corner quickly stood. "I hope you do not mind, my Lady. I unpacked your clothes. They are quite beautiful. And the drink is His Majesty's favorite recipe. He calls it hot chocolate. Only members of Court are allowed to enjoy it. I would much like a taste meself but I ain't allowed."

Evangeline nodded, "I see." She poured a bit of the chocolate into a deep saucer and handed it to the girl. "If you keep it our secret, you may have a taste."

The girl curtsied and lapped it up. She closed her eyes and thought for a moment she had gone to heaven and the Lady was an angel. "Thank you, my Lady."

Evangeline walked over to the armoire, but the girl ran ahead and reached it first. "If you please, that is my job, my Lady. I am your servant while you are at Court. Simply tell me what you wish to wear and I shall dress you. My name is Lianne."

Being independent, Evangeline did not want a servant, but she decided to allow herself this luxury as others at Court. "Very well, Lianne. Let us try the green one to highlight my eyes. Perhaps that will be a good omen. I am going to a very important meeting."

"Very good, my Lady."

The girl carried the green silk gown with its hand-embroidered lace to the bed and unbuttoned each button carefully, then helped Evangeline slip into it. But before she buttoned it, Evangeline looked at herself in the mirror and changed her mind. "No, the gold. My father always liked me in gold."

"Of course, my Lady." She brought forth the gold satin encrusted with pearls and assisted Evangeline into the dress. Evangeline turned right and left, admiring herself in the mirror. But that was not right.

Over the next hour, Evangeline tried on half the dresses in the wardrobe and finally decided to wear the first one, the green silk. Lianne did a marvelous job of combing and arranging Evangeline's hair above her neck, which highlighted her impressive décolletage.

"And the jewelry you prefer, my Lady?"

Evangeline, too embarrassed to say that she had none, shook her head. "I think none for today."

Lianne would not hear of it. Though a lowly servant girl, she had learned good taste observing the noblewomen at Court during the last two years in Versailles. She pulled some of the pearls from the bottom of the gold dress and cut a swatch of lace from the under-trim of the green dress that Evangeline was wearing. Stitching them together, Lianne created a sophisticated albeit inexpensive accessory that set off Evangeline's face and neck. In no time at all, Evangeline was enthralled with the elegant yet simple lace collar lined with pearls. She patted Lianne's hand.

"You have done well. Thank you."

Lianne glowed. "No one ever said that to me before, my Lady." I hope you shall let me be your servant forever."

Evangeline smiled and glided out of the door. On the way out of the suite, Claude and Adèle clapped with admiration.

"You shall get everything you want today, Evangeline," Claude said.

"You are more beautiful than ever," added Adèle.

"I shall never forget your kindness," Evangeline replied. Then she was gone in a swish.

Walking past the Hall of Mirrors, Evangeline calmed herself. She was meeting a Notaire, like her father. Nothing to be nervous about. Entering the Great Hall, she saw a tall, wiry man at the far end of the room. He wore a long day coat and stood admiring the painting of her mother. He coughed several times, wiping his mouth with his handkerchief. He saw a speck of blood on it and quickly hid the cloth in his pocket.

He turned and waited until Evangeline waked up to him and gave a sweeping bow, "Lady Evangeline, I was taken aback. For a brief moment I thought you were Lady de Beaufort. Your mother was the most beautiful woman at Court that I have ever known. You bear such a striking resemblance to her." .

Evangeline smiled. "Thank you, Monsieur le Notaire."

Delacroix coughed, wiped the spittle off his mouth with a handkerchief that he slipped back in his pocket, then offered his arm and escorted her to an anteroom just off the Hall of Mirrors but before the antechamber near the King's rooms.

He felt faint and quickly took a seat, out of character for a member of court to sit before a Lady did, but it could not be helped. He motioned for her to take a seat next to him. "Now how can we be of service?"

Evangeline responded, "My purpose in requesting an audience with His Majesty is for assistance in locating my father and my fiancé, Gabriel Mius d'Entremont. Both were in Grand Pré. Papa was the King's Royal Notaire, as you no doubt already are aware."

He nodded and looked at her pensively. "Of course, Lord Le Blanc de Verdure. Alas, you know His Majesty is indisposed and unable to welcome you."

"But I thought, since I came from so far away, and he knew my mother…."

Delacroix interrupted her, "Pardon me, Lady Evangeline, but I do have news for you. His Royal Majesty holds your father in the highest esteem and has obtained information on his whereabouts for you."

A glimmer of hope shot across her face. "You have found him?"

The Notaire shook his head. "We learned of his miraculous survival of the British transport and his arrival on Île Royale. He arrived in Quebec, but the ship he booked passage on to France was captured by the English."

"No, it cannot be true. He survived one exile only to be captured?"

"Not exactly. The last our informers told us was that he managed to escape when they were leading him and the other passengers to a prison in the Colony of Pennsylvania. Those rogue English troops have been hunting him ever since then. We believe he is in hiding."

"So he is still alive, then?"

"We do not know that for certain. Our only hope is that our men can find him and secret him away first before the English discover his location." Delacroix reached into his jacket and pulled out two pouches of gold coins and handed them to Evangeline.

"We have held his salary payments since the Exile. Since we cannot locate your father, I am authorized to transfer everything to you."

She sucked in her breath at the sight of such wealth. "This is the answer to my prayer that His Majesty would help me rescue my fiancé."

"Our relationship with England is quite delicate, with the ongoing war. But we do have spies in London. They say he is still in Gatehouse Prison."

"Praise God! He is alive. Can I see him or get a message to him?"

Delacroix replied, "It is much too dangerous. His charge is treason."

"But he did nothing of the sort. He saved the lives of the Acadians when the English tried to massacre them. In peacetime at that!"

"Our men are keeping track of Gabriel and the others in the Gatehouse. The English also threw many Acadian families into workhouses or just left them at the docks and they died, starving and penniless. We have many issues to resolve, but the Acadian militia prisoners are a priority for us."

Evangeline said simply. "If I cannot meet his Majesty...?

Delacroix shook his head. "Impossible, my Lady. At least now."

She nodded. "Please express my great desire to His Majesty for an audience when appropriate. I thank you."

Delacroix bowed deeply, "Your servant." He pulled out his worn handkerchief just in time and coughed. This time he saw more blood splatters, but folded it and tucked it in his coat pocket.

As Evangeline took her leave, she turned and asked, "About my uncle, the Count de Beaufort. What do you know of him? Has he left for Provence?"

Delacroix nodded. "True, you did just miss him. He prefers not to stay at Court on a permanent basis. It seems to be a bit too confining for him. He enjoys being the center of attention, which is not possible here, as you can imagine. But he is intelligent, witty and is excellent at cards. He never leaves the table without a stack of coins."

"Does he look like my mother?"

Delacroix looked at her curiously. "Whatever made you ask that? Yes, of course. They are identical twins. Many say he is the most handsome of all the nobles at Court. Of course, he does have that long knife scar on the right side of his face."

"A scar? That sounds like he is a dangerous man."

Delacroix nodded ruefully. "No one knows the entire story. Perhaps it was a jealous husband. Or an angry mistress. Then again, it might have been a fellow gambler. Surely, he shall tell you the story one day and you can relate it to me." They laughed, knowing full well if Evangeline ever got her uncle to divulge the origin of the scar, she would never reveal it. Some secrets should stay within a family.

As she took her leave with the sacks of gold, Delacroix observed her to the end of the Hall. He admired her ambition, not different from any of the young, beautiful women at Court. But he disapproved of her independent ways. She should be under the thumb of a man. She should be married.

Suddenly, his stomach growled a long, churning sound. He belched loudly and a distasteful smell filled his mouth. His eyes widened and he realized what was about to happen. He grabbed a chamber pot from an armoire and pulled a wall lever that opened into the stone tunnel. He rushed in and tossed his breakfast in chunks in the pot, then sighed in relief.

Evangeline entered the suite of rooms where Adèle and Claude were waiting. She said dismally, "My uncle is no longer in the Palace."

Claude said what they were all thinking. "Perhaps we crossed his carriage on the way over. I was not watching for it, though it is not a certainty that he would even be traveling in his own carriage. There are so many highwaymen along the roads now who swoop down on richly-adorned carriages, particularly with a royal or noble insignia."

Adèle looked at her husband. "Yet you did not think to tell me this when we stepped into your brother's luxurious coach?"

Claude took his wife's hand and kissed it tenderly. "You know I would never let such an incident ever happen. Not while I am alive."

Evangeline broke up the argument. "We arrived safely and you shall return with security as well. Perhaps the King's Horsemen can escort you? Does Laurent wield that much power at Court?"

Claude nodded. "The clout of my brother -- half-brother, that is -- never ceases to amaze me."

His wife chimed in, "He and Véronique have been exceptionally generous to us. Anything we have ever asked they have given."

Claude added, "To be fair, we ask for very little. But they are big-hearted, indeed."

Evangeline replied, "There is your answer. You should have the ability to request additional guards for the trip home."

Adèle asked, "Does this mean you are not returning with us? If so, they should all be so disappointed. Especially Pauline. She was so eager to go riding with you to your uncle's château."

Evangeline hugged Adèle, then Claude, and turned to her friends. "I shall meet my uncle at a future date. If you see him, would you explain and give him my love? But I must continue on my quest to free Gabriel from the Gatehouse Prison in London."

Claude warned, "Being at war with England, it is impossible for any French citizen to cross the channel. How shall you ever arrange it?"

Evangeline responded calmly, "I do not yet know. But I shall find a way. With Papa's funds that were entrusted to me, and the money I still have from Karaztyev, I want for nothing. I should be able to find the right man to bribe his way into the prison and leave a letter."

Claude answered matter-of-factly, "If the English jails are anything like the ones in this country, a substantial payment to a guard or the warden should get you anything you need, short of helping a prisoner escape. Sending letters to loved ones in prison is a universally-accepted custom."

Evangeline smiled broadly. "Then is it settled. I shall return to Le Havre and hire someone to carry my correspondence to Gabriel. I want him to know I am alive and waiting for him."

Adèle reluctantly said, "I should go with you, but you have assured me you wish to travel alone this time. And I do miss my children. At least promise me you shall stay at Highpoint, which my sister Clare and her husband Michel took over when my mother died. He is a former King's Horseman with whom Claude served. He may know the type of person you need. Let them help you and send them my love."

Evangeline promised, "I shall expect letters from you often."

Adèle hugged and kissed her again. "And I from you. Go with God, my dear friend." After Claude and Adèle departed, Evangeline felt a slight headache coming on. She slipped into the nearest chair and rang the bell.

Lianne quickly appeared and curtsied. "Yes, my Lady?" She noticed Evangeline looked peaked. She handed her a goblet of water that Evangeline drank gratefully.

"Have you any type of powder for aches? For an ache of the head?

Lianne nodded. "I shall ask, my Lady."

Evangeline shook her head. "No, on second thought. I am fine now. No need to stay." Lianne curtsied and scurried off.

When Lianne left, Evangeline notice an envelope being pushed under the door. She walked over and picked it up. Turning it over, she saw the seal and fell back into her chair. It was from the most notorious member of Court, the King's Chief Mistress, Jeanne Antoinette Poisson, Marquise de Pompadour. She was infamous, but she had His Majesty's ear anytime she wished, so trusting of her was the King. A person with an invitation from Madame to a meeting, luncheon, or one of her famous salons, was envied throughout the Court.

Evangeline rushed to the armoire and immediately started looking through her clothes. As she did, she noticed the wooden board in the back was loose no more. In fact, it was quite possible that the other armoire had been switched for a different one. She wondered why and what it meant.

*

The following week, Evangeline found herself in her gold satin gown covered in pearls sitting on a hand-embroidered pouf in the antechamber of the Marquise. So many questions ran through Evangeline's mind. What should she say? How could she enlist her help? She knew how powerful "la Pompadour" was and that she had precious little time to make an impactful impression.

While Evangeline was deep in thought, Madame was watching her through the eyeholes in the painting over the large fireplace in the room. Every once in a while, Evangeline turned to look over her shoulder. She sensed someone was there with her, but she knew better. She was alone.

Moments later, two dwarfs dressed in brocade uniforms opened the ornate gold-and-rose double doors into the richly-decorated suite of rooms belonging to the King's concubine. The two men bowed to Evangeline.

"Enter, my Lady," said the first.

"Follow us," added the second.

Evangeline nodded and did as she was bid, walking through a wide hallway covered with thick exotic rugs, interspersed with marble tables. As she walked past the tall stands, she enjoyed the perfumed aromas of hundreds of fresh flowers in crystal vases. She knew the Palace contained opulent rooms but she could never have imagined one such as this.

The dwarfs led her to a queen-like figure wearing silk robes embroidered with sparkling jewels. She was stretch on a velvet chaise longue. When she nodded to a nearby servant, he poured two glasses of champagne and offered one to Evangeline. Evangeline looked at Madame, who smiled at her, then she accepted the goblet.

"Come closer, my child. Let me take a look at you."

Evangeline compliantly responded, "Yes, Madame de Pompadour. Thank you for inviting me today."

Madame waved her hand as if the invitation were an everyday occurrence, though she knew she could make or break the reputation of any woman at Court. A meeting or a luncheon with la Pompadour could catapult a noblewoman to the top of the social strata, for which otherwise many women employed social, political and sexual skills to achieve.

Of course, Evangeline knew nothing of the hierarchy of power and greed at court. She only knew that the woman in front of her had the money and power to help her reunite with Gabriel and her father. She was also certain that the Marquise could arrange for her to meet her uncle or even encourage, if not coerce, him to return to Versailles.

Evangeline sipped her champagne to bolster her courage. The bubbles tickled her nose and she giggled, wondering why she had been invited to visit this powerful woman. She did not have long to wait for answers.

Madame leaned forward to inspect her. "Yes, you are certainly your mother's daughter as Pater painted her. She was quite beautiful, as are you."

"Thank you, Madame."

Pompadour clapped her hands. The dwarfs escorted a grand dame, Lady Louise, into the room. Louise accepted a champagne and gulped it down.

"This is Lady Louise, my dear. She was a friend of your mother."

Evangeline shook her head innocently, "I know practically nothing about my mother. She died at my birth so I never knew actually her."

"And your uncle," Louise cut to the chase, "How is Count Guillaume?"

"I have not actually met him. I was in Provence...."

Louise rudely interrupted as she felt was her right. "Whatever were you doing in the country? Nothing happens there. This is the honeycomb of activity for the Court buzzing around His Majesty."

"My host was the son of Count de Rochefort."

"Ahh, yes, the former Royal Guard. How fortunate his mother had an affair with Count Charles. Or he might be working in the stables now." Louise never failed to deride anyone not of noble birth who ascended to the level of Court where she and her family before her had been for generations.

Pompadour was amused at the little scene being played out in front of her. She was right to have invited Louise, always good for a conflict or two in any of her gatherings.

But Evangeline cared little of social status and the customs that the Court were expected to respect. She believed in standing up to powerful people. Lady Louise was nothing compared to Captain Turnbull.

"Lady Louise, I must tell you that Lord Laurent and Lady Véronique have been nothing but generous to me. Their personal physician tended me after a horrible accident. I owe them my life. His brother Claude and his wife Adèle were loyal friends of my father in Grand Pré. I appreciate their friendship."

Louise was taken aback at Evangeline's audacity to support her friends. She tripped on her words as she spoke, "Of course, my dear, of course, we must all have friends. I only meant that we are so pleased you chose to spend some time with us." She tried to sound polite, but the two other women knew better.

Louise barely camouflaged her contempt for Claude and Laurent who had served her in their lowly position. She believed that common lowlife should never rise above their station. She harbored bitter resentment toward Laurent when his benefactor, Cardinal de Fleury, had negotiated the contract for him to marry Lady Véronique with her father, Marquis Robert of Navarre. As a result, Lady Louise had lost a huge commission from an obscenely wealthy, elderly nobleman who wished to get his bony hands on Véronique's curvy parts. Louise touched her left hand to her right wrist where the emerald bracelet sat underneath her silk sleeve. She had been allowed to keep the incentive even without delivering Véronique's hand.

"And your father, dear, what do you think of him? Was there not a deep dark secret involved?" Louise's voice cracked slightly staring at Evangeline.

Evangeline shook her head. "I know nothing of that. I was hoping Madame would have news of his location now."

Pompadour took control of the conversation and the reason why she had invited Evangeline. "We have no additional details. But when I told His Majesty we were lunching together, he promised to advise me of any news."

Evangeline's eyes lit up. "Oh, could I meet His Royal Majesty? I want to thank him for everything he has done."

Madame shook her head. "Unfortunately, that simply is not possible with the ongoing war. No one gets a private audience anymore. Except me, of course. I shall be happy to relay your message."

Evangeline said appreciatively, "My eternal gratitude to you, Madame."

Madame turned to Lady Louise and gave her a knowing look. "My dear, it was lovely seeing you again. I am certain Lady Evangeline should love more discourse with you at another time, but for now, let us bid you a good afternoon."

Louise knew she could object but it would only come back to hurt her, so she graciously curtsied and said her goodbyes. "Of course, Madame. Until we meet again, dear Lady Evangeline," she said before turning on her heel and following the dwarfs out.

Pompadour turned back to Evangeline. "I want to help you, as I know your family. I often join your uncle at cards when he is here. He plays well."

"I do so want to meet him. But he had departed when I arrived."

Madame nodded, "Yes, the Count de Beaufort does stay here long, but he always returns. There are too many noblemen who cannot play cards always pleading for a game to win back their losses."

Evangeline smiled, "How soon do you think he might be here?"

"Sooner than one might think. When I heard you were here, I wrote Guillaume insisting that he needed to return urgently, for Eugenie's sake. He adored her, so I believe he shall return any day."

"Madame, I understand you are the most powerful woman at Court."

Pompadour loved hearing about herself. "Do tell."

"I hope and pray that you shall see your way to assist me. My fiancé, Gabriel Mius d'Entremont, was exiled and imprisoned at Westminster Gatehouse prison where I believe he is today."

Madame saw the entire picture. "You want me to manage his release?"

Evangeline nodded quickly. Thank goodness she understood.

"From an English prison during wartime? True, I have been known to accomplish the impossible, but this—this is madness. George of England does not fancy anyone trifling with his prisoners of war."

"But Gabriel was exiled when the peace treaty was in effect. King George ignored it and banished us." Evangeline's eyes began to water.

Pompadour's heart melted seeing her exhibit such courage and fierceness of purpose. Evangeline reminded her of herself years earlier. She promised, "I shall speak with some friends about this matter. Return to me in four weeks. Or I may see you at sooner if the Count deigns to favor us."

Evangeline grinned widely, "Yes, Madame de Pompadour. I shall count the days." She practically flew out of the room behind the dwarfs.

After Evangeline left, a tall nobleman entered the room.

Madame asked, "Well, Nivernais, did you hear all of it?"

The Duke of Nivernais nodded. "Every word. She is correct. But in the midst of this war, His Majesty is reluctant to negotiate a prisoner exchange for fear of reprisal from England. Our New World territories are at stake."

Pompadour whipped out her fan and fluttered it in front of him. It usually disarmed a man so that she could convince him to do her bidding.

"Louis-Jules, you know you have the contacts to get inside that prison and retrieve the poor girl's fiancé. Why should you not wish to do it?"

"The English are like petulant children, except powerful ones with gallows and muskets. If we pull out one, they might execute the others. But I could send one of my spies to bribe the Gatehouse guards. He could talk with Gabriel and observe the details necessary to launch a potential rescue."

"Very well. Do not bother His Majesty with this affair. You have my permission and my approval of any funds you need. Contact your spies and report only to me."

"Of course, Madame de Pompadour," said the Duke. He was dismissed.

CHAPTER 69
Tearoom

New Orleans

New Year's Day 1758 dawned quietly with a haze that covered the entire city of New Orleans. Christine wiped the frost off her bedroom window with her dressing gown and peered outside. The streets were empty. Quite the opposite of the wild revelry that had taken place during the festivities the night before.

She quickly dressed and hurried down two flights of stairs until she entered the large room on the ground floor. It was dark and cold, but it was early. Her staff had not yet arrived, so she grabbed firewood outside the door and stoked the embers on the hearth into a flame. Filling a kettle from the outdoor well, she hooked the kettle over the fire to boil water for tea.

While she waited, Christine took a look around. She was proud of what she had built in two short years. Luca had arranged her passage to the port of New Orleans. With the funds he had given her when they parted, she had purchased the small building.

Christine vividly remembered the day she had found her shop. She had taken her first stroll down the cobblestone streets of New Orleans, not long after she had found lodging in a boarding house for women. A spark of intuition struck her as she had passed a stationer's shop on rue Conti with a "FOR SALE" sign in the window. She had hesitated, peered in the glass, and decided to inquire within.

After a brief discussion with the owner, Christine had proffered a handful of Luca's gold coins. Moments later, the proprietor had removed the sign from the window and handed her the door key. He had walked out, leaving all of the furnishings and stock in the store.

She would always remember his parting words, "This city has grown too big for the likes of me. I need me the open air. Gonna travel west. Find me some land to graze some cattle, sit on the porch and watch the sunset till I'm too old to move my bones. Good luck to ye."

Just like that, he was gone. She searched in his stock for a quill and ink. Finding one on a nearby shelf, she scribbled on the other side of the sign and replaced it in the window. Her first decision had been to hire a painter to make the sign for the business. She never looked at the sign without feeling a sense of pride, reminding her of how she began her new life. It read: "SALON DU THÉ ACADIEN - ACADIAN TEAROOM."

She had decided to blend her idea of a small restaurant serving tea and refreshments with the writing utensils and beautiful papers left in the shop. She had moved the furniture away from one of the walls, and had written in large letters, "Have you Seen these Missing Acadians?" With that act, Christine had devised a plan to keep lists of all Acadians missing and known dead. Next to the shop sign, she added a small notice: "Acadian List Kept Here. Register and Find Missing Loved Ones.

Christine had then stacked paper, quills and pots of ink on a desk nearby. She had wanted any Acadian entering the Tearoom to be able to post a notice of the loved one they were seeking. She had started the list of the deceased, sadly writing the names of the dead Acadian women who had been exiled with her on the ship that detoured to Santo Domingo. As she wrote the names, she shed tears for Yvonne Poché, Widow Laroche, Lorraine Lambert, Henriette de la Tour Landry, Isabelle Cormier, Martine Broussard and many others whose deaths she sadly witnessed.

Aside from Luca's initial funding, Christine had run the small restaurant on a shoestring and had made a profit. Her simple plan had resulted in an unprecedented response and had attracted many patrons. She remembered the very first Acadian who had walked through her door. It was none other than Francis Hébert, the Grand Pré shipbuilder, who had pirated a British ship with other exiled Acadian men and sailed it straight into the New Orleans harbor. He and his sons and the men on board had saved an entire ship load of their countrymen, and were able to provide details on other the whereabouts of other Acadians who had sailed with them.

Other patrons of the Tearoom were Acadians who had made their way to Louisiana overland or by ship, as had Christine. Acadians whom Christine did not know who had been exiled from other parts of Nova Scotia also came in with more information to add to the lists.

Then, too, there were the local French citizens curious to meet real Acadians. By that time, years after the initial Exile of 1755, all the French territorial residents knew what had happened.

Within a short time, Christine had become one of the best-known persons in the City. Her Tearoom became a meeting place where Acadians could reunite and find long-lost family members and friends.

In addition to being an enjoyable afternoon tea spot, the Tearoom was the place that single Acadian young men and women met one another. Many continued the friendship through courtship and eventual marriage and Christine had provided the banquet after those weddings that had occurred from chance meetings in her Tearoom.

*

As the ship docked in the port of Le Havre, the trio of young women – Béatrice, Fleur and Lucette -- eagerly rushed off the boat and waited for Sister Laure. Paul arrange a carriage which took them up the hill to Highpoint.

At the entry to the boarding house, Claire and Michel Broussard welcomed them enthusiastically. Upon learning Béatrice was from Grand Pré, Claire peppered her with questions. "Did you know my sister Adèle Arnaud? Was she on the ship with you? How did you get to France?"

Béatrice nodded, "I knew Adèle well. In fact, I worked for her dressmaking shop. But I did not see her on my ship, or on the beach awaiting our transports, for that matter." Then she abruptly blurted, "Madame, could I please have something to eat. The ship ran out of food a day ago and I, we, could use a bite."

Claire apologized and put her arm around Béatrice's shoulder, inviting everyone inside. "Please, follow me. Cook always has something prepared. Our guests arrive at all hours of the day and night."

Michel and Paul carried in the travel bags as Claire directed the four ladies to the dining table. Claire left briefly and returned with the cook, both carrying trays of a variety of dishes. The girls, Sister Laure and Paul ate plates piled high with foods.

Claire continued her questioning, so anxious was she to receive news from her sister. But Béatrice could add very little to the conversation.

When the young ladies finally extricated themselves from the questioning over dinner, they dropped into their beds and fell fast asleep.

It was improper for Paul to sleep in the same building, so he stayed in the garçonniere outside, but he did not complain. The second-floor tower provided wondrous views of the harbor. Soon he had sketched boats in the harbor, sunsets and the town of Le Havre from his room on the hilltop.

The next day, Michel hired a carriage to drive Sister Laure and the three young women to the harbor where they boarded a ship bound for New Orleans. Claire wept when they left, but soon returned to the day-to-day business of running the boarding house.

*

Abandoned by the driver in the middle of the busy wharf in Le Havre, Sister Laure and the girls looked to Béatrice for direction. She was the resourceful one, unafraid to speak to anyone.

Béatrice noticed two sailors sitting on the steps by the harbor master's shed. The red-headed one winked at her. When she took the initiative to walk over to him, he grinned. She wanted to speak to him, but not for the reason he thought. When she stopped in front of him, a breeze blew open her long cloak, exposing her nun's garb.

The sailor's face turned as red as his hair. "Sorry, Sister. How was I to know you was a holy person? I just wanted to have me some fun is all."

"Sir, we are seeking the ship headed for Louisiana. Do you know it?"

He pointed to the large ship at the end of the harbor. "That there one over there. Them sailors just hoisted the French flag. See it?"

Béatrice followed the direction in which he pointed. She smiled. "Thank you." She turned to her friends, "We are on our way, Sisters. Follow me."

As Béatrice walked off, the red-headed sailor asked the other next to him, "Why are all the pretty ones in the service of God?"

In no time, Sister Laure, Béatrice, Fleur and Lucette had boarded a large merchant vessel bound for the port of New Orleans. They stood on deck as Paul waved to them from the wharf.

When the ship sailed out of the harbor, a young sailor showed the four ladies to their cabin. It was nothing more than a small wooden cell with four wooden cots nailed to the floor. But there, they began their new adventure.

*

Paul returned to Paris and most days he painted at his easel on the quay along the Seine. In the evenings, he mopped floors at the Ursuline convent to sustain himself.

Eventually Paul married a young orphan girl he met at the nunnery and he moved with her back to Le Havre. He gave up his art and painted and repaired ships at the harbor as he and his wife raised nine lively children and lived out their days.

*

The morning was colder than cold. Christine left the Tearoom and fought the bitter wind that blew hard, forcing her to wrap her cloak tightly about her. She scurried around the corner and down several streets until she came upon a two-story brick building with an iron gate at the entry. She rang the bell.

Sister Catherine walked up to the gate. "Good morning, Madame de Castille."

Christine smiled. "Good morning, Sister. I am meeting Sister Therese."

"Enter, please. She is expecting you."

Christine shivered as she followed the nun who ushered her into the kitchen, a small, freestanding structure in back of the main building. As she entered, Christine watched the nuns bustle around her as if they were bees in a hive. She searched the big room for the chef, Sister Therese and finally saw her at the other end of the kitchen. She was directing other nuns to peel potatoes, chop onions, press garlic and cut meat portions.

Once the food preparation was underway, Sister Therese motioned Christine to join her at the heart. She removed lids from simmering pots hung above the fires, one burning low and the other a roaring blaze. She dipped a large spoon into each pot and tasted the food. She grabbed jars of pepper, salt and other spices and tossed a dash into this pot, and a soupçon into that one until it tasted just right.

When Christine walked up, Sister Therese wiped her brow. "I must apologize to you. I have been so busy that I forgot about your cooking lesson today. Last night, a group arrived from our convent in Paris and Mother Superior asked me to prepare a welcome feast for tonight. Fancy a taste?"

Christine smiled, "With pleasure." She breathed in the unusual but delicious-smelling dishes being cooked. Pointing to the simmering pot in front of her, she asked, "What is this soup, Sister?"

The chef nun replied, "Gumbo. You have not yet learned to cook what is our local version of a French bouillabaisse with Spanish sausage, Indian vegetables, okra from Africa, and Caribbean island spices mixed together. Start with a roux of flour and oil. Once it is brown, toss in the vegetables, cook them down over a low fire, then add a little water and as much fish, shrimp or chicken as you like."

Christine looked confused. "How long does cooking them down take?"

Sister Therese shrugged. "As long as it takes. We do not rush our cooking nor do we dilly-dally. After that, toss in the sausage and add more water and additional spices. Once you have stirred it all in, cover the pot and let it simmer over a low fire so the spices penetrate the meat and season the soup. Last, pour it into small bowls and add a large spoonful of rice. I also add a large slice of bread for dipping so none of the sauce goes to waste."

Christine exclaimed, "If it tastes half as good as it smells, I am certain this will be a favorite part of the meal today."

Sister Therese dipped her spoon into the simmering soup and held it up to Christine, who tasted it and smacked her lips. "I must have the recipe."

The nun nodded, as she waddled past Christine to the other end of the kitchen. "I shall ask Mother Superior if I may give it to you. Try this." She pulled a fresh beignet from boiling oil and poured rich cane syrup over the puffed pastry. Christine gingerly bit into the hot treat and licked her lips.

Sister Therese turned to Christine and said, "Come next week and we shall make an etouffée. You will love that dish, too."

"Thank you. I shall meet you next week with great anticipation," Christine smiled as she exited the warm, cozy kitchen into the biting wind. She would never have suspected that one of the newly-arrived young ladies was a friend from Grand Pré. Neither she, nor the other Acadians who had been exiled, had any inkling that Captain Osgood had sent a ship to France. Had she known, she would have had a jubilant, albeit tear-filled, reunion with Béatrice Gaudet. But she was not privy to that information. Not yet.

In the main convent, everyone had woken early and had eaten a simple breakfast of bread, butter and jam. Afterwards, Béatrice, Fleur and Lucette had joined the rest of the Ursulines, of which Sister Laure was now a part, in the chapel. They attended the private Mass for the Order performed by Father Poirson, the priest at the Cathedral. When the priest departed and some of the nuns joined the kitchen workers to finish cooking, everyone else remained in the chapel to recite prayers and sing songs. After singing every song in their hymnals, they followed Mother Superior out in single file to their assigned tasks.

The new girls had not yet been charged with any duties, so they walked back to their tiny rooms which were called "cells." At the door of her cell, Béatrice Gaudet turned to Fleur and Lucette who had traveled with her. "Do you ever question whether you should take your final vows? I mean, have you ever, you know, been with a man?"

Young Fleur answered adamantly, "Never! From the time I was old enough to go to church and saw the nuns, I knew that is what I would do."

Béatrice turned to Lucette. "And you? What do you think about it?"

The girl replied sheepishly, "My older brother's best friend took me to our barn and kissed me once. I liked it so much, I kissed him back. Then we started doing more than kissing, but my brother caught us. After that, my parents sent me to the convent where I have been to this day. And I am happy, though I must say, I did enjoy it while it was happening."

Béatrice pressed her, "Could you do without it the rest of your life?"

She nodded. "I think so. I mean, that is what taking a vow means, doesn't it? You sacrifice one thing for something greater? Your love for God is more powerful and beautiful than a love for man could ever be?"

Lucette questioned Béatrice, "Does this have something to do with that man who traveled with us?"

Béatrice replied innocently, "Paul? He is just someone I met in Paris."

"He is an artist, after all. You know their reputation."

Béatrice shrugged, "He has always been a perfect gentleman with me."

Fleur asked, "How did you convince Mother to let him travel with us?"

Béatrice giggled. "That is the best part. I never asked."

The next day, Béatrice went into Mother Superior's office. Before she could say anything, the nun told her, "Mother Superior in Paris informed me that you seek news of your mother, who was exiled onto a different ship than you. Since you came to us in a roundabout way from Nova Scotia, I thought you would may be interested in speaking with a certain lady who operates the Acadian Tearoom on rue Conti. She keeps lists of Acadians and their whereabouts, as well as those missing and the ones who are confirmed dead. Please deliver this to her. You may leave now." She handed Béatrice a note fixed with the seal of the Ursuline Order.

Béatrice exuberantly took the note and hugged Mother Superior before rushing out of the convent. Hurrying down the cobblestone streets to rue Conti, Béatrice arrived at the Acadian Tearoom and peeked through the window. The restaurant was bursting with customers.

Béatrice was overjoyed to recognize Christine and hastened inside. From the counter, Christine saw a young woman at the door who resembled someone she knew in Grand Pré. But then, nearly every customer looked like an Acadian she knew. Members of the large French Acadian families had inter-married with each other for so many generations that not only were their names alike, but many of their faces were as well. Christine smiled, "May I show you to a table?"

"Christine de Castille? Is it possible? You are here? I am Béatrice."

"Béatrice Gaudet? It is you. I thought I recognized you," Christine looked closer at the girl who had transformed from the gawky Grand Pré teenager into the beautiful young woman standing in front of her. She hugged the girl like she was her daughter.

Béatrice nodded through her tears. "I am at such a loss for words. Finally, I have found a piece of home again."

"Do you have any news of Evangeline? Jeanne? Or your mother?"

Béatrice shook her head. "I was about to ask you the same." Béatrice nearly forgot Mother Superior's note. She pulled it quickly from her cloak and handed it to Christine. "From Mother in the convent."

Christine read it and clutched it to her breast. "She is giving me their valuable recipes. Come with me. I want to show you something." They climbed up to Christine's private apartment above the shop.

Christine pulled a satin box from the armoire and opened it. Béatrice gasped at the beautiful wedding dress and veil. Christine said softly, "I kept it all this time, praying Evangeline would wear it at her wedding to Gabriel. But I have heard nary a word as to their whereabouts. And nothing of René either."

"Surely you have helped many Acadians meet long-lost relatives and loved ones here," Béatrice commented.

Christine nodded sadly. "Though too many are gone."

"I pray each night that Evangeline and Gabriel are alive and are together at last, or soon will be," Béatrice said as she reached for the dress. "May I?"

Christine smiled. "Surely, she would approve."

Béatrice pressed the dress against her bodice. Perfect.

Christine asked, "Are you planning to join the Order?"

Béatrice shrugged. "I am still praying about it. They knew I was undecided when they sent me here from Paris to teach."

Christine nodded understandingly and walked her back down the stairs. They hugged each other and Béatrice slowly exited the Tearoom. On her way out, she looked back wistfully at the shop then strode to the Cathedral.

Inside, she lit a candle and knelt on a hard, wooden kneeler, made the Sign of the Cross and pulled the hood of her cloak over her head. As Béatrice prayed, she clasped the chain and locket containing Gabriel's portrait that was one of Evangeline's most treasured possessions.

Béatrice had not known when they were waiting on the beach at Grand Pré that she and her mother would be separated onto different ships. She gave thanks that she had taken the jewelry from Anne's apron and that the locket would keep alive the memories of life in Grand Pré. At least, until her friends and family met her in the very city where she knelt, which she firmly believed they would.

Béatrice promised herself she would remember everything about her life with the other Acadians. That was where she had grown up quickly, because she had been forced to do so. She recalled how handsome Gabriel was. And he was kind. He had bought all the flowers she was selling on the day they first met, which was Evangeline's sixteenth birthday. She had been thrilled that he had treated her as if she were a lady like Evangeline, instead of the young girl she was.

Kneeling in front of the altar, Béatrice prayed to meet a man with the qualifies of Gabriel. She planned to tell her own little girl one day about how she had lived in a convent. She imagined her story be quite a tale, but little did she know exactly how amazing her personal story would be.

Then she thought of how much she loved teaching the girls at the Ursuline school. The other nuns said she had become so important to the children that she had transformed their lives for the better. If she devoted her life to teaching at the Order, she knew she could make a significant impact on their lives, particularly as they grew older, married and raised children.

She debated within herself the importance of making a positive, lasting difference for other people's children or her own. She prayed silently about her life, her friends, her future and whether she should take her vows.

Then, as if she had been struck by lightning, she received the answer to her prayer. As the last vestiges of light trickled through the stained-glass windows, she tucked the locket back inside her clothes. Making the Sign of the Cross, she stood up and walked out of the Cathedral on her way back to the convent.

Her heart sung, floating effortlessly without the weight of a decision. She had made her choice.

At long last, Béatrice knew what she was going to do.

CHAPTER 70
Break

Aaargh! The bloodcurdling scream pierced the dawn and woke Gabriel with a start. He rushed to the wall and stood on a stone he had pulled from the interior of his cell. Peering through the tiny window with iron bars, though no one could slip through the little slit in any case, he saw fresh blood splattered on the wall of the yard. The guards called it the "execution wall" where they fired their muskets at a target.

Against the stained brick wall lay the crumpled body of Gabriel's fellow Acadian prisoner, Augustine Cormier. Warden Kettlebum had not bothered to put him on the gallows. Within a matter of seconds it was all over, yet his friend's screams still lingered in Gabriel's memory. The guards who carried out the execution walked away, leaving the body on the ground.

Gabriel stepped down slowly and fell to his knees. He silently prayed the soul of Augustine, the fifteen-year-old who had joined his secret militia in Grand Pré and had been exiled with Gabriel and most of the other militia members. He shook his head and muttered, "Was that only three years ago? It feels like a lifetime. I pray each day to strengthen my resolve to live."

He heard the shuffle of slow, deliberate steps down the corridor. As he heard the approaching sounds, Gabriel knew instantly that it was the elderly guard who would be serving their meal tonight.

The iron grate on the food chute opened and a tray with a bowl of mush and a mug of grog appeared. The old guard grunted but before he closed the grating, Gabriel spoke up.

"Pardon me, sir. I am Gabriel Mius d'Entremont and my friends in these other cells are Marc de la Tour Landry, Nicolas Darbonne and Bernard Guidry."

The old guard mumbled, "I know youse names. I check if they be on the execution list every morning when the Warden calls for a musket squad or a gallows man."

Gabriel continued, "We have been seeing each other for years now without speaking. Might we know your name, sir?"

The guard said, "Everybody here calls me Old Pinckney. Been a guard here since Kettlebum dropped out of his mum's legs."

Gabriel nodded, "Pinckney. Old Pinckney. What a fine name." He heard the scratching of the rats in the dark cell. This time they were near the chamber pot in the corner.

Pinckney spoke up, "If youse got any jewelry, give it to me. For safekeeping, shall we say."

Gabriel felt the outline of the gold wedding ring through his shirt. He had it ordered it from the goldsmith in Grand Pré for what would have been his wedding to Evangeline. For safekeeping, he had stitched it into his pocket before he was exiled. He was amazed that no one in the jail had found it when he first arrived. But they did not distribute new prison clothing to the Acadians. The Warden preferred that they stay in their rotting clothes, hoping that would also rot their will to live. Knowing he had the ring gave Gabriel hope. He did not know if he could give that up so easily.

"Suit youse own self. But them other guards been known to slice up some body parts looking for hidden gold. Best you turn it in. I promise youse can trust Old Pinkney. I never stole a thing in my life. And I been living a purty long one."

Gabriel ripped open his pocket and shoved the ring in the food chute. "If you truly keep this safe for me, I will reward you with more than you can dream when I get out."

The guard retorted, "This here is the death walk. No one gets out alive."

As the old man shuffled away, Gabriel shouted out, "I know you shall escort me out. And I shall be very much alive."

Pinckney grumbled aloud as he made his way to the end of the hall and closed the door to the cell block. He chided himself, "Youse rule is never get to know a prisoner on the death row. Never get up close and personal. Youse never have till now. Why did youse have to go and break youse own rule?"

Emaciated and weak from the lack of food distributed to the prisoners, Gabriel lay on the insect-infested straw pallet that the Warden considered a bed. He stared at the moonlight squeaking through the barred slit above.

Taking a small rock from under the straw, he tapped on the wall. He soon heard a knocking on the other side of the wall. Gabriel turned to the other wall and tapped the rock on it. Hearing a similar sound in response, he rushed to the door of his cell and lifted the food hole.

Carefully looking as far he could see through the food hole, he spoke in a loud whisper. "Is everyone still here? Was anyone else taken?"

He began to hear his longtime friends in response. "I am here, Gabriel," replied Marc. Next was Nicolas, "As am I." The voice of a third Acadian, Bernard, "I saw everything."

Gabriel asked, "Did Augustine try to escape?" The other Acadians awaited Bernard's response.

Bernard said, "Late last night at food time, he feigned illness and moaned loudly. I peeped through the door hole and saw Old Pinckney pull him out and try to help him. That was when Augustine pushed Pinckney down, grabbed the guard keys and disappeared. I could not sleep a wink last night hoping against hope he had made it out alive. The musket blasts at dawn gave me the answer."

Marc mused, "Old Pinckney seemed fine. Why did he not take the usual precautions with the boy? We know they are ordered to stab or shoot us through the opening if we stand next to the door at food time."

Gabriel agreed, "I must say that out of all the guards, I have respect for only Pinckney."

Marc interrupted, saying, "Gabriel, he is a guard like all the others. His mission is to make our lives miserable while we are in the cell and inflict the most torture on us when we are out of it."

Gabriel disagreed. "He is kind even when he has to carry out the Warden's cruel orders. Have you not noticed our grog and soup have no bugs in them? Well, practically none."

Bernard chimed in, "Mine had half a dozen last night."

Gabriel responded, "That is surely better than the three dozen every day last week, no?"

Nicolas suddenly blurted, "I am always so hungry I relish eating the grubworms. But I must tell you something. I prefer to die than stay another three years in this hell hole. It is agony not knowing if a guard's footsteps in the corridor mean I shall be sent to the yard like Augustine or not."

Gabriel said sadly, "I am of the opposite opinion. Each day we are alive gives our King more time to reach peace with England."

Marc objected, "How you remain untouched by the horror of this place is incomprehensible."

Gabriel replied quietly, "Faith, my friend. Faith in God and in Evangeline's love."

Nicolas was filled with consternation. He pulled away from the food chute and paced his tiny cell, kicking rats out of his way. He seemed agitated, not himself. He re-opened his food hole and mumbled, "First, we overpower Old Pinckney. Take the keys and hide in a vendor's cart outside the walls. Bribe the merchant somehow, or threaten him, to take us to the harbor and swim…where? We must swim somewhere, I forgot."

Gabriel admonished him, "Nicolas, it is not safe to speak such thoughts aloud. We would sign our own death warrant for certain."

Nicolas was incensed. "How many more years of this can you stand? Waking each day not knowing if it is your last? I think of it so often my head hurts."

Marc replied, "Even so, you must keep your ideas to yourself."

Gabriel agreed, "I for one plan to get out alive, but in a lawful way. Without hurting anyone. God shall take care of us and keep us safe."

Nicolas continued his pacing and muttering as if he had not heard the warnings of his friends at all.

Gabriel warned, "Quiet. Someone is coming."

The Acadians dove back onto their pallets, holding their knees to their chests and squeezing as far into the corner and as far away from the door as possible. They had been spooked by the conversation.

The rapid clip of the footsteps told them the guard was not Old Pinckney. Suddenly the food chute in Gabriel's door opened. Turnbull leaned down to look at Gabriel at the far end of the cell.

"Before I go home to my loving wife and sons, I want you to know that I still have no regret at shipping your fiancée away."

Gabriel glared at Turnbull. "Thanks be to God she is alive."

Turnbull continued his taunt, "She broke the law and laughed at my orders. I could not let that stand, could I? This very minute she is on the auction block in Bostontown being sold to some master who shall take liberties with her, then have her scrub his floors and cook his meals."

Without waiting for a response, Turnbull clicked his heels and strode out of the corridor. Gabriel was silent for a long while. He heard tapping from the Acadians on either side of him. Slowly he crept to the door and opened the food chute.

Marc said, "Evangeline is alive. He said it. And she has a roof over her head and food every day."

Bernard added, "We all pray that it is so. But I do not believe plantation masters are all that cruel. They could not be with Evangeline."

Gabriel nodded and slowly said, "Sometimes when I wake in the middle of the night and the moonlight streams through the window, I close my eyes and think I hear her calling out to me."

Nicolas asked, "What does she say?"

Gabriel answered, "Find me. Join me. I am waiting for you." Gabriel sighed and continued, "It seems so real. But in the morning, I realize it was but a dream."

Marc replied, "I wish I could say that about Jeanne. I think about her often but I cannot hear her voice. Or maybe I have already forgotten that sweet lilting sound of hers."

*

The day passed slowly as the Acadians kept to themselves in their cells. At the usual hour for their night food tray, Bernard warned, "Guard. Quiet."

Once again, the Acadians crept to the back corner of their cells, away from the door. This time, at the sound of the slow gait, the men knew it was Old Pinckney delivering their night meal. Gabriel heard the chute open, the grating of a tray being pushed through and the screech as the food drawer shut.

Arriving at Gabriel's door, Pinckney opened the food hole and shoved a pot of watery grub through, then slammed the hole closed. Suddenly, Gabriel heard a loud thud on the floor. He opened the hole again and saw Pinckney laying on the stone floor, clutching his chest.

Gabriel shouted, "Pinckney! Pinckney, are you ill? What is wrong?"

Pinckney nodded, "Chest hurts. Breathing hurts. Help -- me."

Gabriel tried to stay calm. "Pass your keys through the hole. You can trust me. I shall help you." He tried to stay calm as he watched the guard pull the ring of keys from his belt.

"Alright," Pinckney grunted in pain. He held out the keys at the food hole. Gabriel grabbed them, jumped up and unlocked his cell.

Gabriel loosened Pinckney's clothes and pressed his ear against the old man's heart. The guard was unconscious but his heart was still beating ever so slightly. Gabriel opened the cells for the other Acadians and called out to them, "Help me. We must drag Pinckney to the guard station. Hurry!"

Nicolas looked at him and shook his head in disbelief. "This is the chance I prayed for. Do you not see? God has given us a way out."

Bernard agreed, "With the keys, we can open all the gates and finally escape."

"And sign our death warrant," Gabriel reminded him.

Nicolas argued, "There is a warrant for each of us already. It is the waiting that is worse than death itself."

Gabriel started to drag Pinckney down the hallway. "I must help Pinckney. You must do as you see fit, but remember the Warden's warning. Anyone caught escaping shall be shot on sight. And do not forget he posts armed guards on the ramparts. Even if you do get out, they can shoot you."

Nicolas clasped Gabriel's shoulder. "Have no fear for me. As for my part, I shall always remember your friendship."

Bernard patted Gabriel on the back, saying, "Thank you for teaching us courage. I am going with Nicolas. Marc, shall you join us?"

Marc made a split-second decision to help Gabriel and shook his head, "Old Pinckney needs our help."

Nicolas looked at his two friends. "I will pray for you both. But now we must go." Nicolas and Bernard looked at each other, then ran down the row. At the door, Nicolas shouted to them, "I shall leave all the doors unlocked for you."

The two men climbed the stairs and were about to unlock the door when an armed guard opened it from the other side. The men used the element of surprise to overpower the guard. Bernard hit him with his own musket, and Nicolas tied him up. Then they ran out and disappeared into the hallway.

Marc and Gabriel dragged Pinckney the length of the corridor. Seeing the unlocked door on the landing, Gabriel put the old man over his shoulder and climbed up, walking through the door into another hallway. At the end, a lamp was burning in a small room. When they reached it, they saw that the guard had fallen onto his desk asleep. Nicolas and Bernard were nowhere to be seen. Gabriel hoped they had made it out alive.

Gabriel shouted, "Guard, please help Pinckney here. He is hurting in a bad way and needs a physician."

The guard jolted awake, recognized the two prisoners and blew his whistle. Marc and Gabriel placed Pinckney on the floor and checked his breathing. It was labored and unsteady. But he was still alive.

Within minutes, Warden Kettlebum and Turnbull arrived with armed guards that grabbed Gabriel and Marc. They locked them in leg irons and marched them back to their cells. Turnbull followed behind, gloating at the good fortune of finally ridding himself of Gabriel.

The Warden leaned down to Pinckney's face but heard no breathing. He put his hand over Pinkney's mouth but no breath came out. It was too late. Kettlebum directed the guards, "Take him to the morgue." They laid Pinckney on a table with wheels and rolled the body down the hall.

The guards tossed Gabriel onto his bed and threw Marc into his cell. Turnbull angrily spit his words at Gabriel, "You shall not get away with this. I shall watch you swing by a rope till dead. My prayers are answered."

Gabriel objected loudly, "I did not escape, nor try to. I was helping Pinckney, who was kind to me. He was ailing and he needed to be doctored. I forced Marc to help me. None of this was his idea."

Turnbull glared. "You two convinced Pinckney to unlock your door. Then you killed him, and used him as a shield from the guards' weapons."

Gabriel said vehemently, "No! Not true! We tried to help Pinckney"

Marc joined in, "We did not try to escape. We woke up the guard."

Turnbull contradicted them. "If the guard had not woken, you would have dropped Pinckney and escaped. And for that you shall be executed."

Turnbull slammed the cells and marched off with the guards.

When all was silent again, Gabriel and Marc tapped each other's wall and opened their food chutes.

Marc asked, "How can we defend ourselves? No one believes us."

Gabriel agreed, "If only Old Pinckney were not dead. He could vouch for our honesty and our courage to help him, knowing the guards would mistake our kindness."

*

The morgue was cold and damp, even moreso than the prison cells, if that was possible. Rats scurried around the room searching for food. The sheet rustled over the shapeless figure on a table.

An arm slowly inched out from under the sheet and pulled the cloth off the face of the "dead" man. It was Old Pinckney, and he was very much alive. He grabbed the sheet to his nose and blew into it, rubbing his nostrils until they were pink. "Ahhh," he exhaled, "Where am I?"

He raised himself to a sitting position, but felt so disoriented he lay back down again. Looking around, he saw the room was empty. He cocked his head toward the gloomy hallway, but he heard nothing except the scurrying feet of rats running to and fro in the dark.

*

Morning broke cold and gray. Gabriel was rudely awakened in his cell and dragged down the hallway in his leg irons by two burly armed guards.

Turnbull followed and taunted Gabriel. "Today is the day I get my revenge. You shall get your just reward and I shall never have to look at your sorry face again."

Gabriel ignored Turnbull as he was half-dragged by Marc's cell. Gabriel shouted, "Stay strong. Have faith, Marc."

Marc risked being punished by calling out through the food opening in the door. "He shall protect you, Gabriel. Believe in God's mercy."

"You should pray too, you killer," an armed guard spit through his teeth in anger. "Pinckney was like a poppa to all of us guards here. You shall pay dearly for killing him." The guard threw open Marc's cell and grabbed him, locked irons onto his legs and pushed him down the hall behind Gabriel, his guards and Turnbull.

*

Old Pinckney inched his way out of the morgue toward the prison hospital. Walking through the corridor, he peered out of the window that overlooked the yard. He was curious to see a flurry of activity.

"Firing squad? Who tried to escape?" he wondered aloud, watching the guards standing in formation with their muskets near the execution wall. Pinckney looked closer through the little window and gasped at the prisoners in the stocks. They were two of the Acadians in his cell block.

A senior guard cracked his cat o' nine tails on each man's back in succession, then reversed direction and back again. Bernard and Nicolas screamed in anguish as flesh mixed with blood flew in the air.

Finally the guard opened the stocks, brutally ripping each head from the pair of ears that had been nailed to the wooden form. Each man screamed again and prayed for a quick death by musket ball.

Pinckney watched as the senior guard marched the two prisoners to the execution wall. He locked their hands and legs in irons and strode back to the row of armed soldiers. The Acadians were helpless to save themselves, but each was thankful his remaining time on earth was short. They looked at each other and nodded between their tears of pain. Each experienced the others' pain and knew they had a camaraderie like no other.

The senior guard called the order, "Bayonets!" The eyes of the two Acadian men were as large as the sun. They realized they were to be stabbed to death rather than shot. They would feel infinitely more pain before they rested in peace.

"Charge," ordered the senior guard.

The firing squad rushed forward. They pushed their bayonets into the soft, weak flesh of the Acadians, then pulled out the bloody weapons and prepared to repeat the painful procedure.

"Charge," the guard ordered again.

Again the soldiers rushed toward the wall and thrust the sharp bayonets into the shoulders, abdomen, chest and groin of each man. Once the long knives had done their worst, they were removed. Twice was all it took.

"At ease. Well done, men." The guard tossed a few coins amongst the soldiers, who scrambled for them.

At the other end of the yard, another group of guards marched two prisoners, Gabriel and Marc, toward the gallows.

Pinkney could not believe his eyes. He tried to shout but his strength left him. "Gabriel? Not Gabriel. He saved my life. And Marc helped." He scurried as fast as his old legs could take him, but it seemed he had hardly moved an inch when he saw the guards lock Gabriel's hands into the chains on the wall.

Pinckney noticed that the Warden and Captain Turnbull had walked out of the building into the yard. They stood in front of the very window where he leaned behind the glass. Yet neither had seen him.

Pinckney muttered, "Warden will be calling for it anytime now. Must get there in time. Wrong to shoot those men."

Outside, Kettlebum ordered the guards. "Ready your weapons." Each guard obediently filled the barrel of his gun with a steel ball and stuffed it down with powder then raised the weapon preparing to fire.

Gabriel closed his eyes and prayed, "Dearest God, I accept Your will although I pray that You shall let the truth prevail and allow me to live. Please protect Evangeline if --- if anything happens to me. Amen."

Pinckney pounded on the window and called out in a feeble voice, "Stop. They helped me. Stop the execution. Those men saved my life."

The Warden heard the knock on the glass and the muffled voice behind him and looked back. He did not believe in ghosts but was shocked at the sight of Pinckney in the flesh. The guard was crying out and beating in the window. The Warden had to find out for himself how he came back to life, or if he was a real ghost that looked identical to Pinckney.

Kettlebum shouted, "Guards, halt! Stop this until I can get to the bottom of it all."

When the Warden disappeared in the building, Turnbull turned and recognized Old Pinckney. "Drat it all," Turnbull muttered under his breath. He issued his own order. "Guards, raise your weapons and fire at will."

The guards just stared at him, refusing to act.

"I said, fire at will. Fire! Fire! Kill that dirty heathen, Gabriel! And the other one, too. They tried to escape. The law demands this punishment. Fire now!"

Turnbull was about to grab one of the muskets and shoot the men himself when the Warden strode out accompanied by Pinckney. Kettlebum held up his hand. "Guards, remove the prisoners to their cells. Then you are dismissed."

Turnbull screamed at his superior, "You cannot mean what you are saying! Are you incompetent? The prisoners tried to escape. They must be shot. That is the law."

The Warden motioned to two guards, "Arrest Captain Turnbull. Take him to the hospital and see that he is tied to the bed. For his own safety. Send word to his wife he shall be kept here until I see fit to release him."

Turnbull turned beet red, realizing he had forgotten his place. "Warden Kettlebum, my sincere apologies, sir. I did not know what I was saying. I thought the prisoners had killed Old Pinckney and were to be punished."

The Warden ignored him and motioned for the guards to carry out their orders. "Captain Turnbull is relieved of supervision of the Acadians. Mister Pinckney shall assume his duties." The Warden gave Old Pinckney a knowing look. Pinckney took that to mean he could be kinder to the Acadians during their imprisonment and nodded in understanding.

The guards grabbed Turnbull roughly. He jumped and turned to them, "Unhand me. I can walk of my own accord." They only clasped his arms tighter as they led him toward the building.

The Warden turned to Turnbull and with a steely voice said, "Captain, when you have calmed yourself, we shall meet and speak of your future here." The guards forced Turnbull into the building and they quickly disappeared behind the heavy doors.

Pinckney spoke to Gabriel and Marc as the guards marched them past, "If not for youse, I would be dead at this moment. Youse have my gratitude."

Gabriel humbly nods. "It is I who is grateful, Mr. Pinckney, sir."

Marc added, "Thank you for saving my life, Mr. Pinckney."

The old guard apologized, "I am sorry fer yer friends that died. Them young guards was mean to use bay'nets 'stead of musket balls. Terrible mean," said the old guard.

Before Gabriel could reply, guards pushed him and Marc forward into the bowels of the Gatehouse to return to their cells.

*

In the hospital ward, Turnbull was flat on his back on a small bed, with his legs chained to the posts for all to see. He should have been mortified, but instead he considered it a badge of honor. "I shall show them all," he muttered to himself. The other patients ignored him, as did the burly guard.

Turnbull muttered to himself, "No one has overseen more executions of those filthy heathens than meself. And I am the only one here who follows the rules without question. I believe the Warden shall appoint me to a new position with a higher rank, maybe even Assistant Warden. If so, I shall bring down the rules hard on all prisoners and give no one a reprieve."

*

After Turnbull was removed from their supervision, Gabriel and Marc received markedly improved meals That night, Old Pinckney slid their food through the chutes and said, "Me wife is as grateful as meself. She promised to feed youse proper like. All I ask is that you not tell them other guards. I can't be having them think meself is a weak fool that owes youse me gratitude now, can I?"

The food trays he delivered overflowed with a supper that was not only edible, but scrumptious. Gabriel's eyes widened when he pulled off the lace napkin placed by Mrs. Pinckney to reveal a whole leg of lamb, vegetables, fresh-baked bread, a shiny apple and a pint of ale, not the usual, grub-infested crumble. Gabriel whispered through the food chute, "I shall be forever grateful to you and the missus, Pinckney." Then he sank his teeth into the juicy meat, the first he had tasted since before the Exile.

Pinckney teetered off chucking to himself, "A weak fool, indeed."

Gabriel and Marc were ecstatic at every meal, and cared not a whit about Mrs. Pinckney being the source of the food. All they knew is that they gradually grew healthier and stronger in their faith. They wholeheartedly believed their faith had protected them and that they would be released one day to search for, and marry, the women they loved.

*

To Gabriel, the weeks seemed to drag by until one day, out of the blue, Pinckney slipped a small parchment into the food tray and pushed it through the opening in Gabriel's cell. He whispered loudly, "Did you look at it?"

Gabriel picked up the parchment and carefully read it. "Is this the death list?"

"Yep. Meself cannot read but the head guard said them is the prisoners to be hanged before year-end." said Pinckney.

Gabriel perused the list, then traced each name with his finger as he read the list cautiously and carefully. "My name is not there. My name is not on the list, Pinckney," Gabriel sighed with relief. "Bless you! This is a greater gift than you can ever know. One cannot imagine how an unknown execution date kills a man's spirit and will to live."

Pinckney coughed. "Gimme back the list."

Gabriel pushed it back through the chute, adding, "Thank you for giving me back hope."

*

A few weeks later, in the prison hospital, two guards entered the ward and unchained Turnbull from the bed. "What is this? Am I finally to be released? Finally, the error has been corrected." The guard nearest Turnbull said, "Warden Kettlebum ordered us to take you to his office."

When Turnbull was delivered to the room, he saw the door wide open and the office empty. Puffed up at the thought of a promotion, he took the liberty of sitting opposite Kettlebum's desk in the tall leather chair reserved for high-ranking officers. He was certain he was right about a new position with a higher rank. After all, when the Warden wanted to see you, that could only mean a promotion.

The Warden entered soon after and sank into his regal, overstuffed chair behind the desk. He motioned to Turnbull, "The bench." The bench was reserved for prisoners, with irons affixed to the wood for clamping down on prisoners' wrists. The Warden wanted to humiliate this proud man in every way possible. Turnbull sheepishly moved from his comfortable seat to the hard, wooden bench so low he could not see over the massive desk.

After a long silence, the Warden finally spoke. "I understand your wife is with child and that you are in need of funds for your growing family. Is this true?"

Turnbull nodded "Yes sir, Warden Kettlebum, sir."

Kettlebum handed a signed document to him with an abrupt, "Your new orders. You have no time to waste. As soon as your wife gives birth, you and your family are expected in the Georgia Colony. You have a guard post at the prison there. He frowned at Turnbull. "Good sailing to youse." The Warden motioned for Turnbull to go away.

Instead, Turnbull wailed, "Georgia? With Jane and an infant? What shall I do in that forsaken wilderness? Nothing but English debtors and criminals too violent to put in here. What is the meaning of this?"

Kettlebum addressed him through clenched teeth, "You are dismissed."

Turnbull was stunned into silence. He was frozen to his chair and did not, could not, move a muscle. Kettlebum stared at him. "I said, that is all. If you refuse to go, I have been given the authority to send you to the madhouse. I truly believe you are touched in the head."

Turnbull sputtered and spit as he shook his head vehemently. Realizing he had no other choice but to leave, he marched out defiantly. Kettlebum wasted no time perusing the stack of papers on his desk.

*

Captain Turnbull had been home but a half hour, yet Jane had not cooled her anger at his pronouncement about his new position. After breaking half the dishes in the cupboard, she resorted to tossing her husband's new suit of clothing out of the window into the gutter.

Only a few minutes earlier, his wife had attempted to use her feminine wiles in a calm demeanor. "Dear husband, would that I remain in the city with your child. He should grow up to be civilized here. Surely you do not want him to become an animal roaming around in the New World?"

When that did not change Turnbull's mind, she had pleaded, "Please, my darling. You know I would do anything for you. Have as many romps with me as you like before you go. Just grace me with permission to raise my child with others of our stature here in proper society."

Turnbull ignored her outburst and filled his travel bags with his clothes from the armoire. Turning back to her on the stairway landing, he said, "I shall be gone tonight, enjoying my evening in the company of a friendly woman or two. When dawn breaks, you had best be packed and waiting for me by the door. Or I shall burn this house to the ground, leaving you alone and penniless. We leave London tomorrow for the port and shall wait there until the child is born before we sail. I shall not hear another word of it."

Finally Jane had screeched loudly, "You are a cruel beast to force on me an ocean sailing. My health is poorly and you know I would not survive. I must stay here. How would you raise a child without me? Come and have your way with me, then begone, leaving me and mine forever."

Turnbull grabbed her furiously. It took all of his willpower not to strike her. Instead, he took out his anger in a rough romp with her. For her part, his pregnant wife refused to quiet herself. She resorted to another tantrum.

He started down the stairs and added, "One more thing. When we arrive in Georgia, you shall be an obedient wife and not complain when I demand that you perform your wifely duties. Or the child shall learn quickly how to get on in the world without a mother to care for him and I shall take him once a year to visit your grave."

Turnbull smirked, proud of himself. Why should he treat that scandalous woman any better than those heathen Acadian prisoners? She betrayed him. It would serve her right if he left her and went to the New World alone. Why should he be loyal to her? The child was not his son. But he needed an heir and, despite all the romps he had taken with Jane, had failed to produce one.

As he walked out of the house and felt the brisk rain on his face, Turnbull laughed aloud. "I shall get my vengeance," he whispered. "I shall turn the boy against her. I shall bring him with me to the prison and she shall be all alone in that wilderness. That should be her reward for crossing me."

The next morning when Turnbull arrived, bleary-eyed and still hungover from a night of drinking and romping at Madame Taylor's brothel, he stepped over the threshold. A letter had been dropped on the floor. He carried it into his office and sat down to read it. He was surprised to see Jane's writing. The note was short, but certainly not sweet.

"Husband,

"I have taken my leave of you and moved in with the gentleman who truly loves me and our future child, his true father Dunley. He says if you try to take the child when he is born, he shall kill you. If you try to take me back, I shall kill you meself.

"Go to the Georgia Colony. You belong with the criminals and the animals roaming those uncivilized woods there."

"Without regret, Jane.

"PS. You never knew how to properly plant your seed in me."

Nathan Turnbull stood up and screamed as loud as he can. The pox on her. The pox on Dunley. The pox on anyone who could hear him. He shouted loudly as he rummaged through his desk, tossing out papers, files and records from years of work which had never been appreciated.

At last he found what he was looking for – his handgun. He stuffed Jane's letter into his mouth and pushed the cold steel piece inside his jaws. Then he pulled the trigger. The paper absorbed a bit of the blood and guts.

*

Months passed at the Gate in an uneventful manner. Pinckney kept to his word and fed Gabriel and Marc well. Then one evening, the routine changed. Pinckney called out to Gabriel through the food chute. "Stand back while I unlock the door."

Gabriel was unsure of what was happening, but he obliged without question. Pinckney entered with two overstuffed travel bags and dropped them the floor. The old guard handed Gabriel a document and said quietly, "Today's list."

Gabriel shook his head and refused to take it. "I cannot look at any more death warrants. Tell me if this is my hanging day. If so, I must pray harder than usual."

"Methinks you should find this one of interest," the old man insisted.

Gabriel picked up the list and glanced at it. His eyes lit up and he grabbed Pinckney, hugging him nearly to death. "Pinckney, you are a gem. This says I am to be released today. And Marc. How did this happen? Are those our travel papers?"

Pinckney nodded. "Least the Warden can do for youse. He used to ship the Frenchies off to for seven years to farms after four or five years here at the Gate. Made a few coins on the deal. It was Turnbull what kept youse here. Guess the Warden figured ye nearly done your time here in conditions a lot worse than them fields. Ye gots it coming."

He handed one of the travel bags to Gabriel, who found it filled with clothes, shoes, and a bag of dried meat, cheese, bread and apples. Gabriel hugged the old man, who seemed near tears himself. Gabriel choked as he said, "I had begun to doubt I would ever leave here alive."

"Warden said he is pleased as puffed pantaloons to get rid of youse. Didn't want any of them prisoner changes the two Kings do when they tire of sending out them armies to kill each other." Pinckney chewed on his old cud as he talked, mangling his words.

Gabriel was confused. "Why would England want to change us for English prisoners?"

Pinckney shrugged. "Word is, just a matter of time before there be another peace treaty. Gotta empty the jails for the next lot in the next war."

At that point, Gabriel did not need to know anymore. He was getting his freedom. More importantly, he would be able to search for Evangeline! Gabriel only hoped he was not too late to find her and that she was still alive. The thought made him at once gleeful and restless to start the journey.

Pinckney interrupted Gabriel's daydream by handing him a small pouch of coins. "Change yer rags into them new clothes so's I can get youse out. Both of youse."

Then he hobbled over to Marc's cell, unlocked it and tossed him the other bag and a bag of coins. Marc was overjoyed. "You have given me my life back. I can do nothing except give my eternal gratitude."

Pinckney said, "Just go find your special ladies. And think kindly of me even if I was your jailer." He reached into his pocket and pulled out the gold wedding ring Gabriel had entrusted years before. Gabriel had not forgotten it, but how could he have asked for its return when Pinckney had already given him many times the value of the little piece of jewelry?

Gabriel grabbed the old man and hugged him so hard Pinckney nearly lost his balance. "You shall always have a place in my heart."

With his English reserve, Pinckney patted Gabriel quickly on the back and disengaged from the embrace.

Upon their release from the prison, Gabriel and Marc practically ran through the iron gates and were immediately caught up in the daily market. Vendors barked the benefits of their wares from their stalls as locals sniffed vegetables, pulled on the beaks of ducks and chickens and mulled over this fabric or that bunch of poseys. The market buzzed with activity. The best part to Gabriel was that he was an invisible part of the chaos. No one knew him and no one cared. But he was free and could now find his love.

As the two Acadians walked the crowds, a hapless young ruffian approached. He was dirty and looked as if he had not had a meal in a week.

"Spare a tuppence, mister?"

Gabriel's heart went out to the young man, and he opened the sack of coins Pinckney had given him. Before he knew it, the boy grabbed most of the coins in the sack and disappeared in the crowd. Gabriel could not be certain but it looked as if he had slipped under the cloth on the table of a nearby merchant. He ran to the stall and pulled up the cloth but the young thief had vanished. He and Marc ran through the rows of vendors but never saw the boy again.

Marc consoles his friend. "The wages of kindness, my friend. We were fortunate to never experience that back home."

Gabriel ruefully agrees. "We cannot waste time trying to find him. We must buy our passage, though I may not have the funds now."

Marc generously said, "Take anything you need from my share. You must get to France. With Lord Le Blanc's royal status, they will no doubt offer the King's resources to help you find Evangeline."

Gabriel shook his head. "I would have gone there, but for one of the last things Turnbull said to me. Remember, he said Evangeline survived and was sent to Bostontown for the slave markets."

"And you believed him? He lied to us at every turn."

"I cannot take the chance that he was not telling the truth. If it is true, I do not want her to spend one more day living that life. I would never forgive myself."

Marc warned, "But the war is still going on. The British in the Colonies shall surely imprison you again, or worse, if they catch you."

Gabriel nodded, "I must take the risk. I must find a way."

They walked ahead but found themselves lost in a seedy area near the port. Facing them on both sides of the streets were shabby hotels, pubs and brothels. They walked into the nearest pub, a very noisy one. When they walked in, the shouts and hollers stopped. Gabriel walked up to the proprietor at the bar. "Where might the harbor master be?"

The men in the pub burst into laughter, deriding and taunting them.

"Listen to them Frenchies."

"Don't them French speak the King's English?"

"Where did them heathens come from?"

"Ye ain't welcomed here. Get ye gone," scoffed the proprietor.

Gabriel ignored their ridicule as he and Marc took their leave. They walked down the filthy, winding cobblestone streets for hours. Marc said what both men were thinking, "It feels like we have been walking in circles. Did we not see that pub only a while ago?"

Gabriel agreed, "We have walked uphill and downhill and around the hill but we must be getting close. Oh wait – I believe I see a mast."

Marc followed the direction he pointed. "Where? Where?" Then he exclaimed victoriously when he saw it, "Halleluiah! We have found it."

They rushed down the street, trying to find an opening between the shops and pubs built nearly on top of one another. At last they spied a narrow alleyway and ran through it to arrive at the docks.

The port was a hectic scene, even as late as it was. In the dark, torches set in fixtures on top of the wharf's pilings shot out smoky light for the workmen to see where to load cargo onto the ships. Gabriel and Marc looked up and down the pier for the ships ready to set sail.

They found two tall ships whose decks were filled with sailors working in a frenzy. Running to the port officer's station, Gabriel breathlessly asked, "Where are those two transports going?"

The man pointed to the closer one, "English one there is headed to Santo Domingo. Captain usually goes to Louisiana, but with the war on, British ships cannot even get close to the port. He decided to offload his cargo in the Caribbean."

Marc nodded. "I shall board that one and hope I can find a ship to take me to New Orleans."

"And the other ship?" queried Gabriel. When the officer told him, "Bostontown, Gabriel grinned and clasped Marc by the shoulder. "This is where we part company, my friend. I shall book passage and find my Evangeline."

Marc hugged him and said, "We shall forever be brothers."

Gabriel nodded, "We shall reunite in New Orleans, no matter what."

Each man was determined to find and marry the woman of his dreams. But considering the inherent risks in their destinations, whether they would achieve success was unknown.

CHAPTER 71
Pompadour

Palace of Versailles

The huge marble tub was filled with scented water and rose petals which, at the moment, Louis XV was splashing onto the thick hand-woven rugs. He amused himself by tossing water at his servants who continued to refresh the scent by pouring more vials of heated oil into his bath. The aroma permeated throughout the massive bed chamber and into the antechamber and hallways.

To the left of the tub sat his newly-appointed foreign minister Étienne-Francois, Duke de Choiseul. To the King's right, his First Mistress Marquise de Pompadour lounged on her favorite couch. The King refused to hold any meeting, official or not, unless she attended. With the great power she wielded at Court and her sought-after salons, she had an uncanny ability to elicit information that would otherwise be hidden from her royal lover.

Étienne-Francois intended to ask His Majesty about the spies the King had located in many foreign capitals who worked at odds against the monarch's public policies. The Duke was not aware of the King's political mastery that kept foreign leaders guessing as to Louis XV's true intentions, so conflicted were his announced strategies with his secret agendas.

But in the midst of the war with England, the King's focus was on raising new sources of revenues to fill his quickly-diminishing coffers. To do so, he withheld from the minister his intentions to levy more taxes on landowners in his island territories. He wanted the minister to come up with the idea on his own, which would elicit approval from his entire cabinet who rubber-stamped whatever any minister proposed, no matter the title. Besides, what did the other ministers know of the King's foreign lands? Each minister reasoned it was better to agree with each other and retain a position on the cabinet than to disagree and risk His Majesty's wrath.

The King played in his tub as servants hopped among him and his guests, refilling champagne glasses and serving food on solid gold plates. He waved his hand, "Scribe?" The young man stood at attention, trembling as he responded, "Yes, Your Majesty." He had arranged a row of quills and pots of ink next to a stack of parchment. The King could be verbose, and the scribe did not want to risk missing a word. Everyone knew that the former scribe was cast out of the Palace for running out of ink and now he was an outcast who begged Cook for scraps outside the kitchen every day.

The King spoke and the scribe recorded his words to the letter. "Last year we were 'Bien-Aimé' beloved by all. This year, they grumble about our love life. Do they not realize we must spend substantial sums on our adorable Pompadour?" He was mesmerized by her voluptuous breasts spilling out of her satin corset as she leaned forward and blew him a kiss.

"Heaven knows, we must keep her in the style to which she is accustomed, for she is the only one who dares tell us the truth. There continues to be much treachery and betrayal at Court. Alas, we are prevented from removing these dissenters because our ancestors granted too many letters patent catapulting mere commoners to the nobility."

Choiseul was unsure of his footing with the King, appointed a few months earlier. Louis said, "We are woefully under-funded on our islands. We wish to hear your solution to the problem at hand."

Pompadour smiled. She knew the issue troubled Louis and she had suggested the solution. But both wanted to know how his new minister would tackle the situation. Choiseul blurted, "Surely taxes could be raised. But why burden land owners who have been your loyal subjects for years?"

The King coughed, indicating his displeasure, but the minister was unaware of the signal. He added, "To increase funds for the Treasury, you must increase the sales of sugar from the plantations, since they generate heavy taxes." The King rolled his eyes at the comment, so obvious to anyone who knew anything about money. But he let Choiseul speak to either redeem himself with brilliance or hang himself with stupidity. The minister added, "The plantations needs more workers to tend more fields."

Pompadour spoke up, more to amuse herself than out of a great interest in his discourse. "And how do you propose that be done, Minister?"

Choiseul realized, too late, it was a trap. He slowly sipped his glass of bubbly to allow more time to formulate his thoughts, then he quietly replied, "Offer His Majesty's subjects free passage to the Caribbean in exchange for seven years of plantation labor with ownership of a small plot of land thereafter. This rids your kingdom of detractors unhappy with their lot and allows them to become landowners, which they could never do in France."

Pompadour set her goblet on the server's tray and clapped vigorously, "I approve His Majesty's new foreign minister and his answer."

King Louis snapped his fingers and the servants rushed around in a frenzy with more food and drink. He was pleased he would have more taxes next year. "You have our permission to institute the program at once."

Choiseul stood and bowed gratefully. "I am at His Majesty's service."

Pompadour whispered loudly to the King, "You may go."

The King repeated it, "You may go."

The minister backed out in a bow until he had exited. Louis clapped with glee. "We shall have much money. What can we buy our Marquise?"

Madame shook her curly wig, "I am utterly content with His Majesty's love. A diamond bracelet does compare with his brilliant company."

Louis understood her desire immediately. "Diamonds it is, my love."

They grinned and toasted before the King rose out of the tub in all his glory. He refused to be wrapped in a towel and ordered, "You are dismissed. We shall have a private meeting with our little Pompadour."

He pulled his black satin cape from the bedpost, whipped it over his shoulders and put the hood on his head, then grabbed Madame. When he tossed her onto the bed, her shrieks of delight and his shouts of passion could be heard in the antechamber through the double doors to which the servants' ears were glued.

*

Evangeline counted the days until the month had passed and once again, she found herself in Madame de Pompadour's receiving room. She sipped the obligatory champagne, willing herself to be calm though she was impatient for Madame to relay the status of her fiancé Gabriel.

"Well, Evangeline, you are looking quite well today."

"Thank you, Madame. I am grateful for the opportunity to see you again. May I compliment you on your stunning gown and jeweled hair?"

"Thank you, dear. I have news. My dear Duke of Nivernais sent a spy, Monsieur de Launay, to Westminster Gatehouse. Bribery is quite common there, but when he tried to offer the guards a payment, the Warden stepped in. He took the money, and then threatened de Launay with pain of death if he should ever return to England. However, the spy managed to stay in the country undetected for a time thereafter. But his message is quite old."

Evangeline was crestfallen. "So that means…?"

Madame nodded and motioned to her servant to refill her champagne glass. When he had done so, she drank half the liquid.

"That means, my dear, that he was unable to see your fiancé or any other prisoner. What is more, he failed in his reconnaissance mission to learn about the prison and its weaknesses. We do not know how to arrange a break to remove the Acadians even if it were approved. We know nothing."

"I see," Evangeline said in a small voice. "Thank you for trying. It is much more than anyone has done for me."

"Are you still serious about your dream to buy back the Acadian exiles from the slave farms in Bostontown? If so, I am willing to fund your entire trip. It is the least I can do for our poor countrymen who have been displaced for their loyalty to His Majesty. What is more, I believe I have the right man for the job. He has my complete confidence and is already in Bostontown."

"Madame, you would have my eternal gratitude. Gabriel inspired me to when he formed the militia in Grand Pré. I cannot fight to help our fellow Acadians, but my plan can work. I know it."

"You must not be recognized as an Acadian yourself. If you are, of course, the entire scheme fails."

"Of course, Madame. I have not completely thought of all the details."

"Shall we both consider what would be most likely to succeed? I shall contact you with I have some ideas."

"Thank you, Madame, thank you from the bottom of my heart."

"I only wish I could have succeeded with details about your fiancé. But fear not, I do have a surprise for you. Guillaume?"

From a hidden room, Evangeline's uncle, the Count de Beaufort, entered. He carried a half-full champagne goblet and glared at the servant until the cowering man refilled it with the bubbly nectar.

Madame took the lead, "Guillaume, meet Eugenie's daughter, Evangeline. This is your uncle Count Guillaume de Beaufort, child."

Evangeline threw away convention and ran up to her uncle, hugging him tightly. He was struck by her emotion and wrapped his arms around her. They parted and sat on opposite sides of a small marble table.

Guillaume spoke first. "You look so much like Eugenie. In fact, you remind me of her at your age. It is uncanny, I must say."

"Tell me about her. I never knew her."

Madame interrupted, "You can both withdraw from here and get to know each other better. My purpose here is done."

The Count bowed and kissed the hand that Pompadour held out awaiting his sign of respect. He waited until Evangeline curtsied, then escorted her out of the rooms to the main hallway away from any prying eyes, or so she thought.

Little did Evangeline know that in frames, paintings, wall molding, and doors were hidden tiny peepholes. Anyone with access to the tunnel system at Versailles could use the holes at any time to spy on others at Court. That was only one element that made life at Versailles so intriguing.

Guillaume's voice turned icy cold. "If you think to take the fortune that I waited my entire life for, you are sadly mistaken, Lady or not."

"But Uncle, I don't want...."

He pulled two small velvet bags from his jacket and thrust them into her hands. "Take these. One is filled with the only jewels your mother left at the château before she married. She must have taken or sold all the rest. And for her sake, I am giving you a purse of gold coins. That is all you shall ever get from me. I strongly recommend you remove yourself from this place. Your mother hated it. It would have killed her but for René marrying her and taking her away. That should have saved her life, yet, we know what happened next. She should never have borne a child. You caused her death."

"You cannot mean that, Uncle."

He shook his head. "Never contact me again. Do not talk to me if you see me at Court. Do not visit my château if you are in Provence again. And advise those bothersome Rocheforts not to contact me on your behalf."

"But we are family. You are my uncle. I am your niece. You are all I have left of my mother."

"You are nothing to me. My twin sister is gone because of you. I lost a part of myself when she died. I never wish to see you again."

He turned and, instead of returning to the residences inside the Palace, he exited via the main doors. He roughly pushed aside the Royal Guards at the entries and flew down the steps to the gravel driveway.

Evangeline choked back tears as she watched him climb into his ornate carriage. A moment later, the driver rode off at break-neck speed. She knew she would never see her uncle again. All she could wonder was what she could have done differently to earn his love and respect.

With that thought, Evangeline burst into tears. She was slightly comforted that no one was there to see her. The last thing she wanted was to be the subject of gossip at Versailles. Unbeknownst to Evangeline, a large eye peering through a hole in the decorative wall trim behind her blinked away tears several times.

Behind the hole in the wall, the King, wearing his black satin hooded cape, turned from the peephole and marched down the dank stone corridor lit only by his torch. His footsteps echoed throughout the tunnel as he splashed into puddles of water caused by seepage from above.

Evangeline returned to her rooms in low spirits. King Louis had continued to refuse audiences with anyone and prohibited open dinners and banquets in the spacious Palace dining halls. The members of Court became cross having to eat with their families in their rooms. Since the Arnauds had departed, Evangeline was content to stay in her set of small rooms, which provided more space than she had ever enjoyed in Grand Pré.

That evening, she sipped the soup that Lianne had set out on the dining table in her rooms. But she had no appetite for the delicious crusty bread and fresh creamy butter. She curled up on the bed and cried herself to sleep.

*

The following week, Evangeline awoke to find an invitation from La Pompadour that had been slipped under her door sometime during the night. She rang the bell and Lianne dressed her in her finest green satin dress. Then the servant piled Evangeline's hair on top of her head in the latest fashion. Evangeline preferred not to powder or rouge her face but to let her youthful appearance speak for itself.

She opened the sack of jewelry that Guillaume had given her and was amazed at the dazzling display of necklaces, bracelets and rings. She chose an exquisite emerald choker, thanked Lianne and packed the remaining jewels into her black satin bag before setting off for Madame de Pompadour's rooms in the Palace.

This time, when she arrived at Madame's suite, the dwarfs escorted her directly into the inner chamber. Madame stood up and kissed Evangeline on both cheeks, repeating, "Poor child. You poor, poor, dear. Whatever got into the Count? It must have been a terrible blow, was it not?"

Evangeline was taken aback, thinking her conversation was private. But she chided herself that she should have known nothing stays a secret very long in Versailles. She responded, "He explained his feelings. I believe he is still in grief over the death of my mother. At least it seemed that way."

They both took their seats as Madame waved off the thought. "He is simply a greedy bastard who wants the entire inheritance. Half of it is rightly yours, but for the title. We shall engage a smart lawyer."

Madame waved to the waiters who served a beautiful luncheon in gold plates to her and Evangeline. Eating heartily, Evangeline decided to take charge of her destiny. "Thank you for your concern, Madame, but the matter is ended. I do not want the family money or lands or even the château. Uncle Guillaume deserves that. He gave me my mother's jewelry which means more to me than a piece of ground ever could."

Madame was impressed with her and raised a new issue. "We have some rather urgent business to take care of at present. My connection in England was able to obtain more recent information about your fiancé."

Evangeline drew in her breath sharply. "Gabriel? Have you news?"

Madame nodded. "Our spy arrived last night with the news that Gabriel was released from prison early. He saved the life of an important guard or some such incident."

"That sounds like Gabriel. Putting another's life ahead of his own."

"Quite," said la Pompadour. "But the news is even more interesting than that. After his release, he booked passage back to the New World."

"He left England? Where did he go? Oh, Madame, I must know."

The old dame cleared her throat and replied, "I am getting to that. He told the guard he wanted to find you. And he reported that a Captain Trimble –"

Evangeline interrupted without thinking, "Captain Turnbull?"

Madame continued with a curt nod, "That he said you had survived his musket balls and had been exiled to Bostontown to be sold in the slave markets. We have confirmed that our Acadian countrymen have, indeed, been sold to harvest their fields and work in their manor houses."

"But could Gabriel enter that city without being arrested?"

"De Launay hired an agent in that very city. He learned the port is filled with merchant ships and sailors from throughout the world. If Gabriel bribed the captain of the transport that carried him across the seas, he might be able to obtain a crew uniform and walk off the ship under the noses of the port officials."

"Oh, say it is true. Tell me he was able to slip past the enemy."

"Alas, my child, that is the last information we were able to obtain. Does he speak English, per chance?" Madame was more than curious. She obviously had a reason for the question.

"Very well, as a matter of fact. He speaks better than I do, though I pride myself that my accent is difficult to detect when I speak the language."

"Speak to me in English. I shall be the judge of it."

Evangeline seamlessly converted her speech and mannerisms to that of an English titled lady. "Madame," she began, "It has been my honor to converse with you today. The subject matter was most profound and the information you imparted most valuable. I shall act on it prudently."

Madame clapped and chuckled with delight. "Yes, yes, there you have it. Not every French woman can speak English without an accent. But you have mastered the language beautifully. If your fiancé did so, he most likely succeeded in his plan and so shall you."

"Let us hope and pray that he did," Evangeline replied. "And now I must go to him. I must find him. If he is in Bostontown searching for me, I must travel to him. It is possible we could meet in a matter of months!"

Madame de Pompadour stood as if she were ending the audience. Evangeline jumped up in response, but Madame merely went over to her writing table and brought back a leather case filled with papers and money.

"You shall be in need of travel papers and your ship's passage. I have also arranged the agent named Hampton to work for you. He and his servants can be completely trusted. In addition to making all the arrangements, he shall be at your side as your guard and also serves as a political minister, of sorts." Madame pulled a stack of official-looking documents covered in stamps and seals and ribbons from the case. "Your identity for this scheme is a widowed British Countess from the English countryside. You are relocating to the Massachusetts Bay Colony to buy a small plantation and start your life anew. Your husband was recently drowned in a boating accident, so you do not wish to live in Bostontown.

Too close to the sea. Your loss is fresh and you want nothing to remind you of the seas."

Evangeline added, "So, having no husband to hire and supervise field workers, I am obliged to buy slaves. Those of the Acadian kind. In the midst of these activities, I shall meet Acadians who might know of Gabriel's whereabouts. If he is hiding, he may have reached out to them to find me."

Madame opened the case to show her stacks of English bills and coins. "Courtesy of an English nobleman whose carriage had an unfortunate accident. The spoke of a wheel broke along the same route de Launay took to return to France. Shocking, such a theft, is it not?"

Evangeline replied, "Your kindness leaves me without words."

Madame drew her to her voluptuous breast as if caressing a child. "I shall miss you, my dear. But I ask you for one favor before you depart."

"Anything you ask, if I am able, I shall do it at once."

"Lie on this chaise longue and let me sketch you. I am somewhat of an amateur artist and like to draw my friends. Like you, my dear."

Evangeline happily complied. Within an hour, Madame had completed two sketches in charcoal of Evangeline lying on the velvet chair with a mysterious smile on her face. Madame rolled up one drawing and melted a stick of red wax with a candle over the edge of the canvas. She pressed her gold signet ring into the hot wax, firmly sealing it in place. She handed it to Evangeline, saying, "Remember this as a souvenir of our conversations."

Evangeline replied softly, "I shall treasure it and my time with you."

Madame asked, "Do you mean you shall never return, not even to present yourself to King Louis, our gracious Holy Majesty?"

Evangeline jumped back. "Oh, of course I have a great desire to return and have an audience with His Majesty. If it could be arranged, that is."

"I believe he truly wants to meet you. But now, you shall leave, find your fiancé and return together as husband and wife. If that happy day arrives, I shall host a grand banquet in your honor." She kissed Evangeline squarely on each cheek. Evangeline asked, "How can I ever repay you?"

"Return to us, my dear, so I can play with your children in my garden."

"I shall, I promise," Evangeline responded.

As Evangeline walked out of the room through the open doors held by the two dwarfs, she looked back wistfully. She watched Madame give orders to her servants to set up a tea service for her next guests.

Evangeline was all but forgotten as Marquise de Pompadour continued her busy day filled with appointments. For Madame had many admirers and hangers-on, but only a limited number of hours in the day.

CHAPTER 72

Pox

*France * Philadelphia*

In his chamber, Delacroix was absorbed in reviewing documents. Suddenly, he felt an urge to scratch his arm. He raised his lacy blouse to reveal large red blotches all over his skin. Some of the blemishes had formed sores. He pressed one and it released a pus that spilled over his arm. He wiped it with his handkerchief, now bloody from his constant coughing. His eyes grew as big as saucers.

He asked himself, "Is this the pox? That is impossible. Preposterous to have the commoners' disease. I have not lain with anyone lower than the Baroness Faubert. But I must find out before I do anything else. I am a busy man. Surely the Court Physician can rid me of these spots."

He started to send a message to Evangeline, but changed his mind. Instead, he scurried back into the Hall of Mirrors and pressed a hidden button on the large gilted frame. A door opened and closed again as soon as he disappeared into the hidden hallway.

Running through the dank stone corridor lit every few feet by a torch, he looked up and down until he saw a small sign saying "First Physician." He pulled a lever and the wall opened up. He entered a dark room lined with shelves lined with jars full of organs pickling in colored liquids, then closed the wall. He jumped onto a long table stained with blood, which did not bother Delacroix in the least. Everyone had to let blood to be healed.

In the adjoining room, a physician in a blood-stained waistcoat sliced the heart out of a cadaver and placed it into a jar filled with colored water. He was nearly finished with cutting out the liver when he heard a shout from the back room.

"Doctor Potier? Are you here? I need you."

The harried physician rushed in, wiping his bloody hands on his coat. "Delacroix? What brings you here?"

Without saying a word, the Notaire raised his shirt sleeve. The red sores were a dead give-away. "Do whatever you must but rid me of these – horrid things -- and quickly. Tell me I shall not die from this."

"Are you a physician now as well as a Notaire?" The Doctor put on his spectacles and tied a cloth over his mouth and nose. He carefully inspected Delacroix's arm with a magnified lens.

The doctor shook his head. "Have you had fever or aches?"

Delacroix feared the worst but hoped for the best and nodded, "Both."

"Any oral deposits in your chamber pot?"

"Once this morning and a second time a little while ago. What does that mean? Please tell me this is an insect bite."

"It is the pox. Of that I am certain. You may have waited too late, but you shall get my best leeches in any case." He grabbed a jar filled with green leaves teeming with life. Black worm-like creatures moved in and out of the greenery. Using a small pinching tool, he laid a leech on each of the red sores. "You are to remain here in quarantine indefinitely."

Delacroix jumped up and winced. The sudden jerk of his arm caused the leeches to dig into his skin more deeply. Blood and pus oozed and dripped from the red blotches. "I must see the King. I have important information for him."

"And infect His Royal Majesty? Are you mad? I trust you touched no one since your sores appeared?"

Delacroix shook his head. He thought of Evangeline. Did he kiss her hand? Or touch her lovely skin? He could not recall. "I met with Lady Evangeline, daughter of the late Lady Eugenie de Beaufort and the King's Notaire René Le Blanc de Verdure. But I made no contact with her."

Potier grunted, "Lady Evangeline? I do not know her. She must be new to Court."

The Notaire stared nervously at the leeches. "She arrived some time ago, but I have not seen her of late. Is this the cure?"

Potier shrugged. "About half the time. For the other half, the remedy is a prayer for a swift end."

He wiped his bloody hands and led Delacroix down a narrow hallway into an enclosed room with a dozen cots in it. Arm restraints were on each cot where a person's arms and legs would rest. Potier pulled a long cord outside the room.

Delacroix shook his head. "I prefer my own rooms. You can trust me to stay within them and not see anyone else."

Two burly guards appeared at the end of the hallway, blocking any attempt by Delacroix to leave the room. They stayed far enough away so Delacroix could not touch them or even breathe on them. The Notaire entered the room meekly. He allowed Doctor Potier to lock his hands and feet in the locks and wept. "Please give me some parchment so I may write a note to the King."

Potier ignored him and closed the door, locking it from the hallway. "What an idea. How could he think I would allow His Royal Majesty to touch a document that had been written by a poxed hand?"

Potier motioned to the two guards to approach. When they had walked half the distance from the doorway to him, he held up his hand. "Find the Lady Evangeline. She must be quarantined."

The two thugs stomped their way out into another corridor. When they had disappeared from view, Potier returned to the cadaver in his office and started rooting around for other organs to cut out.

Unfortunately, Delacroix passed away during the night from the pox. Doctor Potier ordered that the body and everything Delacroix had touched be burned in a pit that was dug in the far corner of the Versailles property. The physician promptly dismissed the idea of contacting Evangeline. He figured she would live or she would die, but it was not up to him to find her.

*

Evangeline took a last walk through her rooms. The armoire was emptied, and all that remained was a stack of boxes and travel bags for her departure. She rang the servant's bell. Within moments, the maid Lianne appeared and curtsied. "Yes, my Lady?"

"Please have my bags taken to the side entry. A carriage is waiting."

"I shall be sorry to see you go, my Lady. When might you return?"

Evangeline turned to speak and suddenly felt so nauseous she ran into her room. She grasped hold of a chamber pot on the table and threw up in it. Lianne was concerned, but Evangeline waved her away. "I ate some shellfish at luncheon today that must have disagreed with me. I am fine. I have no immediate plans but should I return I shall ask for you to assist me."

Lianne grinned and curtsied, then disappeared. She soon arrived with wo valets to carry the boxes, bags and cartons and escort Evangeline to the exit. Walking along the corridor, Evangeline felt nauseous again. She sat down for a few moments, and the feeling passed but was replaced by such severe head pain that it seemed her skull was splitting in two.

She walked out to the porte cochere and the driver of her carriage pulled up in front of her. The footman assisted her into the carriage and the coachman took the bags from the valet and stowed them. Once Evangeline was inside the coach, she closed the curtains to eliminate the light. Her head felt slightly better, but she felt flushed and ached to her bones.

The driver sped away, flanked by Royal Horsemen, promptly hitting every pothole, rock and stone in the road. If Evangeline had not felt so ill, she would have been proud that her family still ranked the honor of the

Royal Horseman providing security for her journey. She pulled the ivory fan from her purse and fanned her face until she felt cooler.

Without warning, another wave of nausea hit her. She dumped the contents of her satin purse on the floor and vomited the rest of Madame's luncheon into the custom bag that Adèle had lovingly sewn for her.

Evangeline felt better for a while, but after a few hours in the carriage, Evangeline directed the driver to stop at the first inn on the road to Le Havre. She immediately went to sleep in the private room, paying for rooms and food for everyone traveling with her.

Each day, Evangeline insisted on stopping at an inn after only half a day's drive, so she would not feel so queasy. Rather than sleeping in the carriage, despite its luxurious design, she preferred a bed that did not bounce and jiggle at every turn. Because she desired the additional comfort, the length of her trip was extended by two additional weeks before they reached Le Havre.

From the port road, the carriage moved up the hill and finally arrived at Highpoint. By the time Claire Broussard had settled Evangeline into her rooms, Evangeline had a burning fever and constantly complained of nausea and severe headaches. She had not noticed that her skin was covered with red splotchy marks.

Claire called the same doctor who had treated Evangeline after her fall in the harbor. He recognized the red patches on her skin instantly and quarantined her to one end of the house, forbidding Claire or the servants from opening the door. The physician was certain the disease could be carried in the air, so he closed all the windows and stuffed linens in the opening between the door and the threshold.

The cook staff left meals for Evangeline at her doorway and knocked, then rushed off, afraid to breath any air seeping through the linens under the door. Evangeline was forced to leave her bed and carry her meals inside her room. Her lack of strength and the exhaustion of that simple act caused her fever to spike and her headache to throb harder. Worse, each time she climbed out of bed, she vomited in the chamber pot.

She tried to sleep but when a sliver of light poured in between the drapes and the window edge, her head hurt even more. She felt aches and soreness through every part of her body. It felt like her insides were coming out with the stomach pain and the matter she threw up in her chamber pot.

As time went by, Evangeline drifted in and out of consciousness. The doctor came every few days, always with his nose and mouth covered by a tie-on cloth to protect him from catching the disease in the air currents. He conducted the leeching procedure, leaving the pulsating insects to do their work and remove the liquid from the pustules on her arms and legs.

When Evangeline woke, she was usually delirious and did not understand that the doctor was forcing her to eat and drink to keep up her strength. When she was unconscious, the doctor performed additional leeching.

One day Evangeline slowly opened her eyes. She did not know where she was, nor how long she had been there. Gradually, she remembered that she was at Highpoint in Le Havre, and that she was going to take a ship Bostontown.

She looked over at her arm, filled with red marks that were fading. Looking closer, she realized they were red circles around bite marks. She felt somewhat relieved because she finally realized the soreness had been caused by leeches that the doctor had applied when she was too ill to notice the procedure.

She went into a deep sleep, and was still sleeping when the physician stopped in the next day. She woke to find him standing over her with a bottle of leeches. She tried to speak but her throat was so parched. She called out, "Water." He handed her a glass filled with the liquid which she hastily drank. "No more leeches, Doctor," she was able to say.

He stared at her quizzically. "The leeches sucked out the pox which has helped you recover in large part. But the poisonous disease still flows through your veins. Do you wish to succumb to it again?"

Evangeline grimaced. "The pox? I had the pox? Wherever did I catch the pox? I have not been anywhere in this country but for carriages, châteaus and this inn?"

"Perhaps you met someone who had it? Someone touched your arm? Kissed your cheek?"

She shook her head, though she could not remember much. "What happened?"

The physician answered matter-of-factly, "You have been very ill. You have struggled in and out of consciousness these last months. I was concerned that the sickness would do you in. Fortunately, you were strong enough to overcome the illness. At least for now. But I must warn you, you still have the disease and it could exhibit itself three times as worse. Especially if you do not allow me to leech you again."

She shook her head. "No leeches."

He shrugged and put the jar away in his black bag. Then he poured an elixir into a giant spoon and bade her to drink it. "This will help your strength." She took a small sip, but it was bitter and she turned her head. He insisted, "Drink it all, my Lady. Else it shall be of no effect." She complied but grimaced as she swallowed the vile liquid. He closed his black bag and exited the room.

She caught him as he crossed the threshold. "Shall I see you again?"

286 | M. M. Le BLANC

He shook his head. "I think it should be unnecessary. I have done all I can do here. I pray for your health. Good day." He closed the door and walked down the hallway.

She absentmindedly said, "Thank you, doctor." Then she cried out, "Hello? Claire? Are you there?" She heard a knock at the door. "Yes, do come in," said Evangeline.

The door opened a crack but Claire was nowhere to be seen. A timid housemaid stood in the hallway and asked, "Need something, miss?" She held her hand over her nose as if she would be safe from the disease if she did not enter the room and did not breathe the air directly.

Evangeline nodded. "I am famished. Could I please have some food? And water. I am quite thirsty but want no wine. Only water. Thank you."

The maid curtsied, shut the door and disappeared.

A short while later, Evangeline heard a faint knocking on the door. By the time she opened the door, no one was there. Likewise the hallway was empty. At her feet were a tray of food and a pitcher of water. She carried the tray to the little table in the room and noticed a folded card on the tray. She opened it quickly.

"Evangeline,

"I am glad you are at long last feeling better. Please understand the doctor advised us to stay away lest we catch the disease. We – Michel and I -- look forward to visiting in person when he gives his blessing.

"He said you refused the leeching. You should not have done that. The disease is fickle and could return at any moment.

"Let us know if you need anything, anything at all. We pray for your full recovery.

"Your friend, Claire Mercier Broussard."

Evangeline put the note aside and penned her response to Madame de Pompadour.

Unbeknownst to Evangeline, when the doctor left, he met with Claire and Michel to warn them. "Without another leeching, I fear the disease will return with a vengeance. It is best to make final arrangements for the Lady. Does she have any family nearby?"

Claire and Michel looked at each other. "I shall write my sister whom you met last time you were here. They were close in Grand Pré."

The doctor nodded. "Stress the urgency. She should come within the week if they wish to say their goodbyes."

Michel asked, "Perhaps we could convince her to allow the leeching?"

The doctor shook his head. "It would give some relief, but there is no cure for the pox. The best thing I can say is that when the end comes, it is quick. She can feel well one day but cough the next and die in the night."

Claire felt so helpless. "What can I do?"

The doctor said, "Set out bowls of fresh water several times a day with clean linens for her to cool her body. But burn anything she touches."

Claire wiped her eyes, swollen with tears. "I understand. We shall continue to pray for her. Shall you sup with us when you return next week?"

The doctor sighed and shook his head sadly, "My work is done here. If I were in your stead, I should call the undertaker for the rest of the job."

*

In Versailles, in his palatial room, King Louis XV felt ill. It was not a physical sickness but rather a queasy feeling in his heart. He should have done this years ago, his Pompadour had said. But, be that as it may, he would make things right at this time. Propped up by massive pillows in his oversized bed, he clapped his hands, commanding, "We wish to write."

His diminutive, bespectacled secretary sat attentively in a corner at a writing desk with paper, quills and ink pots. "At your leisure, Majesty." The secretary lit a candle under the royal red wax pot to warm the wax then dipped a quill in the ink which promptly broke. He had to select another.

"Dearest Evangeline," the King stared at the secretary who wrote quickly then looked up and nodded. "We must reveal some important family secrets. My dear little angel -- that is what your name means, you know. Little angel. We must share with you some information about your mother. And your uncle of late."

The secretary's quill broke and he grabbed another, dipped it in the ink and looked up. The King glared, "Faster. Or you shall be cleaning stables."

"Yes, Your Majesty," he responded, as another quill broke.

"Our Pompadour has told us you heading to Bostontown and that she has an agent there, so we send our letter and our prayers to you there."

*

On the other side of the ocean from France, in the Pennsylvania Colony, the haggard old woman bent over a man shivering in the small bed. She tried to lessen his fever and comfort him with cloths dipped in a fresh bowl of cool water. "Sir, can you hear me? Sir?"

The man tossed and turned, and the cloths fell off his forehead onto the linens of the small bed.

She tried once more. "Sir, I beg you, wake up! Can you hear me? You must rid yourself of this illness."

René slowly opened his eyes. He felt groggy, but where was that cloth? He needed it to shield his eyes from the blinding light. "What? Where am I? Who are you? I am sorry, but do I know you?"

"I am Madame Cozzen. Call me Margaret. What is your name? Remember anything? Know where you came from?" When the man rubbed his head trying to remember but said nothing, the woman patted his hand and crept out of the room.

In the adjoining room, she turned to her husband. "From his accent when he done talked to me, I know he is French. Probably one of them Acadians who done escaped the ships. He hid better than the others, I must say. How long have soldiers combed these woods looking for runaways?"

Her husband Frederick whittled a piece of wood that was taking the shape of a pipe, even as he smoked his tobacco in one, blowing smoke into the fireplace. "Three or four years? Forget him. You know what you have to do."

Margaret said, "Please, not this time, husband. The last prisoners we turned over were shot by them soldiers in the barn. This one is different."

"What makes you think that?"

"How he talks. He almost sounds royal if I didn't know no better."

"They is war prisoners. The army wants them. 'Sides, we need the money they pay for 'em. What they do with 'em is none of our concern."

Margaret pleaded, "Do not take him in his pitiful state. Leastways, let me fix him up. Make him feel a bit better."

Frederick harrumphed loudly. "You want to waste your time healing him before they kill him, that is up to you. But when he can walk, you tell me. I shall ride him over to that there English fort and get some coins in trade. The likes of him is worth a new plough."

She shrugged. "If you insist."

"You know I insist, woman. Now hush and let me whittle in peace."

Margaret filled a cracked bowl with soup from a pot on the hearth and walked to the door of the little room. Opening it, she saw René toss and turn in his sleep, mumbling. She was determined to listen. She sat by his bed. If she could learn who he was, she could prove her intuition right. And if he was an important man, then he might be worth even more alive than dead.

She whispered to René again. "Sir, you must eat. You have been ill for days and have not taken much food or drink. Try this and get your strength back." The woman held up the bowl with a spoon.

René pushed himself up on the bed to eat. She fed him a spoonful. The broth was tasty, filled with potatoes, carrots and onions. She was proud of her vegetable garden that grew like wildfire after she planted the seeds bought with money she secretly took from Frederick's purse. He had refused to give her money for "extravagances" as he called the seeds. But when the winter freeze killed the other corps, he blessed her for buying the dratted seeds that meant they would not go hungry.

After a few spoonfuls, René looked at the spoon. "May I?" he asked simply. Margaret nodded. He began to feed himself, slowly at first, then faster until he had finished the entire bowl. She handed him a piece of crusty bread and some old cheese. He ate it quickly as well. "Thank you. It was delicious. I am sorry. So tired." Before René spoke again, he fell asleep.

She left the room proud of herself for making progress. She decided to take her meals with the stranger and wheedle more details out of him. Anything she learned she planned to keep to herself. Perhaps he could buy his freedom. He might even pay more than the English military, though he had no coins on him when she found him delirious behind the barn.

Over the coming weeks, Margaret tended her garden, cooked the vegetables, wrung a chicken's neck once a week to add some chunks of chicken to a soup, and tended to René's illness.

One day, out of the blue, René asked her, "How did I end up here?"

She replied, "Do you remember your home? Start at the beginning."

He squeezed his eyes together, then opened them with as if he had seen a vision. "I was forced from my home in Grand Pré onto a ship. It sank, but I survived and washed ashore on Îsle Royale. A kind family nursed me back to health and helped me return to Grand Pré to look for my daughter and my fiancée. But they had been exiled, too, so I headed for Quebec City to book passage to Louisiana. I remember walking for weeks. Months, maybe, I don't know. I was in a forest. It was snowing. I heard thunderous hooves behind me. I dove under some bushes and stayed there for a long time. The next thing I remember is I woke up here."

Margaret marveled at the tale, saying "That is some story. What did you do at your home?"

"I was -- I am -- Royal Consul to King Louis XV in Nova Scotia."

The woman could hardly contain her glee. He was rich. He had to be rich. He was chosen by the King. And the King was rich. Which meant she and her husband would be rich.

"If you are thinking that I should pay you –"

"Oh no, sir, I weren't thinking that at all. Me husband and me, we just want to help you get well. No reward or nothing like that."

"Despite your protests, I promise when I arrive to Louisiana, I shall send you a reward. A very sizeable one."

"Well, then, we shan't turn down a sizeable sum. Harvest weren't no good last year. We could do with some extra coins here and there."

"You shall not want for anything if you nurse me back to health and help me get out of British territory. Where are we, anyway?"

"Just outside Philadelphia. You could get a ship at the port."

René asked, "Are French citizen welcomed here?"

She laughed. "No sir, absolutely not. If the army knew you was here, they would grab you and string you up in our barn here and now."

René clutched his throat. "But I have done nothing wrong."

"Well, now, the army gots their own way of thinking about things and that is what they think, rightly or not."

He reached for her hand. "I beg of you. Do not turn me over to the English. Protect me and help me get to a boat. Do that, and I promise you shall have all the funds you need. Please?"

She nodded reluctantly. "My husband wants to get you to the fort soon as you can walk. Just don't walk is all I am saying. If he sees you, pretend to be too sick to move. I'm thinking of a way to get you out of here. And I'm thinking Mister Cozzen will forgive me when I do. But I want a red petticoat for meself when you send that money. I hear them French ladies all wear red petticoats 'neath their dresses. Makes them feel pretty. I ain't felt pretty in a long while."

He nodded. "Agreed. We can keep this our private secret."

She grinned. "That is what we shall do, long as you gots the coin."

René assured her, "Oh, I have the coin."

CHAPTER 73
Journey

British Colonies * New Orleans

"**D**rat!" Gabriel stepped in a fresh pile of nightsoil dumped from the third floor down into the street. He scraped his shoe but was certain the stink would follow him wherever he went that day. He spied a horse trough down the road and dipped his boot in it. That should be better, he thought.

Unbeknownst to Gabriel, a shopkeeper named George Tallenbook watched him from his stool behind a counter. It was too early for customers but Tallenbook liked getting to his shop hours before the streets of Boston filled with people. It was quiet then. And he liked quiet. Unlike his home. He had just left his house after complaining about the breakfast his stingy wife had given him, a crusty bread without butter. "You are too fat, Mr. Tallenbook. No more butter or jam for you," she screeched. No amount of cajoling, pleading, or even kissing the little woman could change her mind. So he resigned himself to go hungry until she brought his lunch pail.

Tallenbook sold leather goods, which he crafted himself from hides that the local tanner sold him. He offered straps, belts, bags, satchels, pouches, wallets and money bags. While waiting for customers, Tallenbook had become a watcher of people. He had become quite good at divining their occupation from the looks, their demeanor and their clothes.

As Gabriel stared in the window at the array of Tallenbook's leather products, the shopkeeper thought something seemed odd about him. Gabriel was dressed in a mariner's uniform, which was common enough. He could be a worker on any of the numerous ships in the Bostontown harbor. But a real sailor would not be concerned about horse droppings or nightsoil on his boots. He would simply ignore the stink and go about his day. Tallenbook waved Gabriel in, so he entered the store. That was Gabriel's first mistake.

"Good morn, sir," Tallenbook was nothing if not polite. He was always ready to sell his wares to anyone.

"And a good day it is, sir." Gabriel spoke flawless English.

Tallenbook was instantly suspicious but wanted to keep the man in his store. "What can I show you today? A leather wallet? A money pouch?"

Gabriel shook his head and perused the stock on the shelves behind Tallenbook. The shopkeeper kept none of his items on counters or tables due to the thieves. Young boys would run in and grab an item then escape and sell it on the street for half the shop price. Tallenbook had lost a goodly stack of newly-dyed belts and he was not about to do so again.

Gabriel nodded at an item behind Tallenbook. "How much for that?"

George turned around and picked up the leather piece. "You want this?"

Gabriel nodded. "Indeed. What is the cost?"

Tallenbook sized up Gabriel before he spoke. As a sailor, he most likely had half a year's salary, if he had been at sea that long. At least a minimum of three months, so he could afford to ask a good price. "Ten pounds."

Gabriel was taken aback. "Ten pounds? Thank you, sir, but I do not need a leather-bound journal after all." He turned to leave.

Tallenbook knew he had to negotiate to make the sale. "Wait, sir. Seeing as you are His Majesty's sailor, I could let it go for seven pounds."

Something in his tone alerted Gabriel that Tallenbook was suspicious. He wanted to run as fast as he could but restrained himself. "I can pay two."

"Five."

"Three," Gabriel countered, holding out the coins. Tallenbook greedily grabbed the money and slapped the journal in Gabriel's hands.

But he could not resist, "Come now, sir, you cannot work on a ship. Your hands are too elegant, like the hands of a nobleman."

Gabriel withdrew his hands and laughed. "Appearances can be deceiving, 'tis true, but I have been on a ship for the last three months. See that one in the harbor there? Ask Captain Jones if you do not believe me."

Tallenbook looked at the ship Gabriel pointed to and held up his hands. "My mistake, sir. Enjoy your purchase."

Gabriel nodded and said coolly, "Good day, sir."

Tallenbook thought the man's tone sounded almost angry. He was certain the man was hiding something. He locked his shop and headed to the harbor to ask the Captain about the stranger. But George changed his mind and stealthily followed Gabriel. Something was not right about him. Tallenbook wondered if he was fugitive with a bounty on his head.

When Gabriel exited the shop, he walked up the street as quickly as polite society would allow. He wanted to blend in, not call attention to himself. He turned onto a side street and disappeared from view. Turning into a narrow alley, Gabriel arrived at the small boarding house where he had rented a room the day before.

Tallenbook trailed Gabriel until he entered the building. Then George turned back, heading to the harbor. He made it a point to watch for strangers in this part of town and inform the authorities of people who did not belong there. And he was convinced that the stranger was one of those fish out of water. He passed a constable who tipped his hat and gave him an idea.

Gabriel climbed the stairs to his second-floor room and locked the door behind him. Feeling secure in the small lodgings he had rented, Gabriel laid all of his purchases on the small table. The leather journal sat next to a set of quills and a small ink pot. He lit a small candle, took a seat and began to write, slowly reading aloud as he did.

"My dearest darling Evangeline,

"I feel I am getting closer to finding you each day. After my miraculous release from Westminster Gatehouse, I had planned to make my way to Louisiana. But something Captain Turnbull had told me kept gnawing at me. I did not know if it were true but he said you were sent to Bostontown where all Acadians are put on the auction block to work on the plantations. I knew you had defied him in the water and I hoped against hope that you had been rescued by Kitok, and if not, then by the English who would take you to Bostontown.

"I knew I had to see for myself. Now that I am here, I shall endeavor to discover where you are. Perhaps by learning when you arrived, I shall be able to find you and whisk you away from here to the safety of my arms and the love of my heart.

"Though I am unable to post this letter, it brings me comfort knowing that you and I shall be reunited in the very near term.

"I send all of my love, your Gabriel."

Gabriel had been taking his supper in his room each night since he arrived. He did not want to jeopardize his plan with a misspoken word in English or a mannerism that was not distinctly British. But tonight he decided to join the other boarders in the dining room. When he was halfway down the stairs, he saw Tallenbook and a constable talking in low tones with the landlord. Though he did not understand, he saw the landlord point upstairs in the direction of his room.

Creeping back upstairs to his room, he hurriedly stuffed his satchel with his extra uniform, his letter to Evangeline and the purchases he had made in town. Opening the window, he jumped from the second floor to the ground, then began to run down the alley in back of the building.

He imagined, fairly accurately, that the proprietor of the boarding house had led the constable and the shopkeeper up the stairs. After knocking loudly on his door, the landlord would have unlocked the door and seen the open window. With that, the constable would have blown his whistle and run outside to the back of the building to chase and capture Gabriel.

Gabriel ran into the forest to evade capture and finally stopped to catch his breath. He thought he heard a whistle coming from town, but it could have been the wind. He had to keep going. He could not allow himself to come this close to Evangeline only to be arrested or shipped off again.

Hours later, Gabriel slowed his gait to avoid stumbling over fallen trees and getting caught in underbrush. He heard the cries of foxes and the sounds of scurrying nocturnal animals. Searching for shelter for the night, he spied twinkling lights ahead. He ran closer and saw a row of shacks lit by candles.

Gabriel thought he dreamt hearing voices singing in French. But edging closer to the hovels, he recognized Acadians who had been in his militia. Captain Turnbull did not know them, so they were not sent to the Gate. One of the men saw Gabriel's English sailor uniform and warned, "Englishman. Get to your houses and bolt the door." The Acadians scattered and the man held up a piece of wood menacingly, growling, "Who are you and why are you watching us? We are protected by the owner. Show yourself."

Gabriel came out of the shadows with his hands held high. He spoke in French, "Philippe Melancon? It is Gabriel. Gabriel Mius d'Entremont."

The man dropped the wood and rushed to Gabriel, hugging him like a long-lost brother. "Gabriel. We thought you had been sent to London."

Gabriel nodded and said, "I was. It is a long story. I want to share it with everyone, but I need your help."

Philippe slapped Gabriel on the back. "You are still my leader. All you need do is ask. Come. Are you hungry?"

"Starved," Gabriel admitted. Philippe fixed Gabriel a hearty meal which he devoured. Then, they walked into the clearing and Philippe called the other Acadians to join them. Their reunion was poignant and powerful. Gabriel imparted his story and made his plea asking for news of Evangeline. Though no one had any news, they exchanged stories of their exile until dawn. The Acadians repaired to their huts, knowing they would only have time to fix a cold breakfast before their work day began.

*

René felt a cramp in his leg. But he was too crammed into the wooden cargo box to be able to knead out the pain.

Margaret peered into the box. "Remember my red petticoat. And the money. Youse better be good fer it."

He nodded and held his fist tightly at his sides, "I shall remember."

She harrumphed and said, "Me husband will kill me when he learns what I done, but I want that petticoat. This here's me brother Raymond what works on ships and builds them boxes for them captains."

René squatted into the cramped box, but shook his head, "We must find another way. It is too small to stay here for many weeks."

The carpenter scratched his head, "Cap'n Swillingham hired me to build some store bins for his hold. I can build them to fit a man that won't shut off his breathing. And he can keep vittles and a jug of rum in it with him."

Margaret looked at René. "Well? What'll it be? The box or the fort?"

René turned to the carpenter and reluctantly said, "Just do not nail it shut. They might forget about me and leave me stuck when I get into port."

The carpenter shrugged, "I can put fasteners to hold one end down and lift up the other. As for the rest, that's 'tween you and the cap'n. What I hear, ye can even eat well on his ship if ye gots the coin."

Margaret shouted, "If he gots the coin? Course he gots the coin, brother. Would I be here talking to the likes of youse if he don't gots the coin?"

René echoed her words, "I have the coin."

*

The French navy had blockaded the New Orleans port to all ships originating in England. In London, Marc de la Tour Landry had booked passage on a British merchant ship heading for Santo Domingo. He figured to find a New Orleans-bound ship on the island. But the London ship was recalled for use by the English navy before it left the harbor, leaving Marc stranded after Gabriel had left for Bostontown.

Marc used his passage money to pay an English fisherman to haul him across the English Channel and drop him off on the French coast. The fisherman brought him close enough to Le Havre that he could walk several days to the harbor but not so close that the fishing boat would be impounded by the French. Once he arrived in Le Havre, Marc was lucky enough to board a French merchant ship that set sail directly for New Orleans.

All Marc could think about was that his fiancée Jeanne had pledged to meet him in the Louisiana port city, though he had no way of knowing if she had been able to keep her promise. If he had known her painful experience in Cornhandle's slave auction and her resulting servitude, he would have felt the pain nearly as strongly as she had. He prayed he would find her there.

*

The month before the first transports had arrived in Grand Pré, Lieutenant-Colonel Winslow had arrested their parish priest, Père Rivière, sent him to Bostontown and seized his rectory as his base of operations. The Acadians were caught by surprise, especially Evangeline and Gabriel who were to be married by the priest shortly after the reading of the Edict.

Word had spread like wildfire throughout Bostontown of Rivière's status as a priest and that he had been sold like an animal on the auction block. A successful fisherman, Edward Stampley, heard the news and was incensed. He had taught his family to respect all religions, unlike the prejudiced

Bostonians. Stampley convinced other fishermen to form a network and help Acadians escape the plantations by hiding them on their boats and sailing to other locations, which they could do without suspicion.

Edward and his sons sold their catch to the wealthy mistresses of large plantations and learned that Rivière was on one of their patron's estates. One day, Edward kept the plantation owner's wife busy with making selections from an unusually large selection of fish. Meanwhile, two of his sons found the priest in the barn. "Quickly, come with us, Père," they said.

"But who are you? How do you know my name?" asked the priest.

"We are friends ready to remove you from here."

The priest was not convinced, "Where shall I go?"

"We have found a tolerant Colony where you may say your Masses and build a church," the eldest son said.

"God bless you, my sons," Rivière said as his eyes swelled with tears. "My prayers have been answered without even knowing your name."

"Best we keep that to ourselves," they said as they whisked him out of the barn and into the wagon. In between barrels filled with fish, Rivière climbed into a stinky barrel recently emptied of dried cod. When the wagon left, no one was the wiser. After hiding Rivière in his cellar that night, Stampley whisked him away at dawn in his fishing boat, keeping him below deck in the hold behind barrels of the family's catch. They sailed out of Bostontown harbor heading south for the Colony of Mary Land.

The next morning, the overseer knew Rivière had escaped when he did not show up for the master's morning prayers, but no one understood how he could have escaped. Thus, Stampley's underground network stayed intact.

Stampley sailed his boat into the harbor of Annapolis in Mary Land less than a week after he departed. As Rivière disembarked, Stampley informed him, "A local fishmonger awaits you on the wharf. He and his family are Catholic and have longed for a priest. He has arranged housing for you and has purchased an old shed you can turn into a church."

Rivière turned to him. "You have my blessings and eternal gratitude."

Stampley reiterated his beliefs to the priest, saying, "No one, especially a holy man, should have to endure what you did. I hope you enjoy life here."

Père Rivière and his parishioners constructed the church where he preached and served for a year before he caught the dreaded pox and was buried in the cemetery of the church he helped build.

The escape operation had taken only a few months of careful planning and was implemented other times before Evangeline arrived and rescued the remaining Acadians.

It would be years before his Acadian parishioners from Grand Pré learned his fate.

CHAPTER 74
Countess

Bostontown

The mysterious English Countess Eleanor of Devon arrived on the passenger ship from Liverpool. Descending the gangplank to the harbor teeming with activity, the woman wore an expensive black fur cloak and a black hat with a long black veil covering her face. She ignored the chaos around her, as if she floated through the lines of frenzied laborers. From all accounts she was English, though the veil covered her face so no one could actually remember seeing what she looked like.

The ship's crew wondered why she had not stayed longer each afternoon when she had taken a brief walk on deck for some fresh air. The cook's assistants had reported they had left a tray for each meal by her door, and that by the next meal the empty tray had been placed neatly on the floor.

On the wharf, she waltzed around the cartmen pushing their wagons at breakneck speed to get their goods to market. She strode up to a private carriage that had refused passengers all morning. The driver, Francis, sat up in the box and nodded but said nothing. He had been paid in advance to take orders from the Countess for as long as she wished.

Hampton, a tall, sinewy man in a black cloak jumped to attention when she walked up. He bowed and assisted her into the carriage. He had been hired on her behalf by the shadowy figure whom he had assisted in a plot to oust the Bostontown Mayor. The scheme had worked and the official placed in the office was more amenable to the desires of his contact's employers. The shadowy figure had been very grateful with additional compensation and the promise of more work. This job came about through the shadow's acquaintance with the French spy, Monsieur de Launay, who knew Marquise de Pompadour, which completed the circle that brought Hampton to carry out Evangeline's strategy to free the Acadian slaves.

The Countess nodded, inviting him into the carriage. He climbed in and shut the door then took the seat opposite her. The carriage lurched before driving off in a snow flurry. He tipped his cocked hat, saying, "Hampton, at your service, Lady Eleanor. Our mutual friend Madame de Pompadour has sent the first month's payment for myself and your driver. He is my brother, Stephen. Rest assured, should you desire additional staff, I shall fill the need in short order with well-trained personnel."

Evangeline nodded in the style of the nobility, polite but without emotion, as she replied, "A small staff is my preference. My imperatives are loyalty and discretion. I am told you offer both in following an employer's directives."

"My Lady, you have only to issue your demands. I shall carry them out quickly, silently and without alerting the many eyes and ears that lurk around every corner in Bostontown. The colonial officials pay dearly for information that can add to their wealth, crush an opponent or increase their power. Because we are so far removed from London, the power structure can change at will. Trust no one. Reveal your true plans to no one. Have a plausible explanation for everything you do, and assure that your plan does not appear to cross any of the political lines which are altered as quickly as the winds blow the beach sand near the port."

"You are aware that my mission may encroach on established beliefs, and perhaps even, shall we say, disagree with city ordinances."

"My Lady, greasing palms in this city generates long memory lapses where the law is concerned. I can make arrangements for that so long as I know in advance."

"You shall be informed when the time comes. Now let us talk about what I shall need you to do with this carriage. I trust you know a discreet carpenter?"

"I can procure any craftsmen that you need."

Evangeline lifted her veil and showed him a drawing that she had sketched of changes she wanted to make to the coach, the seats and the underbody. After reviewing the document, Hampton responded, "Very good, my Lady. It shall be done forthwith."

Evangeline's mentor, Madame de Pompadour, had certainly advised her correctly, Evangeline thought. No one would guess she was a French Catholic Acadian in the midst of the papist-haters. Bostonians continued to pass laws restricting Catholics from practicing their religion, earning wages, traveling after dark, and much more. In fact, the only stares she got were from curious citizens who had never seen nobility before.

Hampton asked, "Where do you wish to go first, my Lady?"

"The City Surveyor, please."

Hampton reported her directives to Stephen and away they went. Walking into the land office, Evangeline introduced herself. "Eleanor, Countess of Devon to see Mister Panderwick, if you please."

The surveyor's young son who worked in the office as an apprentice bowed and led Evangeline to his father's office. "Yes, my lady Countess, right away, my lady. This way, my lady."

"Papa, the Countess is here," stammered the boy. Embarrassed, he ran and hid under a nearby table.

The surveyor ran from around his desk and bowed deeply to her. "What an honor, Lady Eleanor. I did not expect you till next week. These ships. Who can keep to a schedule? The winds must have been favorable. Would you like some tea? What can I do for you today?"

Evangeline cut off his babbling with a slight wave of her hand. She was amused that he was starstruck at the thought of English nobility in his office. She remained gracious. She needed him to work fast on her behalf. "Kind sir, as you were advised, I wish to buy a large plantation outside Bostontown. Have you knowledge of any such properties for sale?"

Panderwick was flustered. A Countess was asking him for his advice. Of course, all property buyers went to his office first, but he was too flustered to realize she was doing what was required by the procedure for buying land in the territory.

"Lady Eleanor, I have all the maps and plats ready for your perusal. Follow me, please. I think you shall find at least one of the estates quite to your liking."

He led her to a dusty room with a large flat wooden table covered with rolled-up parchment. He blew on the table, dispersing the dust everywhere. Fortunately, Evangeline's veil protected her nose from the dust storm swirling around the room.

Over the course of the afternoon, the surveyor had explained the pros and cons of each piece of property. Evangeline scrutinized each map, appearing to favor one over the other but actually seeking the property closest to the boundary of a neighboring Colony.

Finally, she made her decision. Pointing to one map, she said, "This one is acceptable."

Panderwick was surprised, but hid his thoughts, saying "Very good, my Lady. Excellent choice." Her choice was one of the smaller properties, far away from Bostontown and near the uncivilized British Colony of Connecticut. The price was smaller, too, which meant Panderwick's commission would be less than he expected. He had counted on selling a much larger estate to a wealthy Countess.

Without quibbling over the price, Evangeline paid with a stack of English bills, and added several other bills for his fees and the taxes.

Panderwick sent his son to the taxing officer with the deed. Within minutes, the boy had returned with the document stamped and decorated with a large red wax seal.

Panderwick bowed again and handed the deed and map to her, "My Lady, we are honored that you are now a landowner in the Colony of Massachusetts Bay."

Underneath her veil, Evangeline smiled. The city fathers had no idea what was about to befall their structure of selling and working Acadians on their lands. Their idea of politics was child's play compared to the political intrigue, trickery and vicious schemes she had learned in the salons of Madame de Pompadour.

The Countess was assisted into the carriage by one of the two coachmen who rode on the back. She was safely delivered to the largest hotel in the city. Once again, Hampton handled all the details with the hotel manager. While Evangeline waited in the carriage, he arranged for a clerk to carry her travel bags and open the windows. The winter air would freshen the room after the cigar-smoking brother of the Mayor who was the former occupant of the suite. Hampton even managed to procure a vase of fresh flowers for her rooms. When all was ready, Hampton escorted Evangeline to her suite.

The rooms were quiet, just as she liked it. A server brought up the light supper Hampton had ordered. She dined on English fare and drank wine as she studied the map of her property. When she had the scheme in mind, she crawled into the oversized bed, but had only a fitful sleep. More than once, she woke during the night wondering where Gabriel was, whether he had been captured and sold into slavery, if any of her friends were in service on the plantations, and how she would implement her plan.

In the morning, after a quick morning meal, she descended the staircase. Due to her veiled face, she was able to watch the reaction of those in the hotel lobby who could not determine her true identity.

Stephen and Hampton waited with the carriage outside the hotel until Evangeline arrived. As Hampton helped her into the carriage, she gave the orders for the day. "Were you able to determine the leading trader in the city?"

He nodded as he took his seat opposite her, "Yes, My Lady. Jonas Cornhandle is expecting you today at your leisure."

She replied, "At present is the best time. Let us get on with it."

The coachman hopped back onto the carriage and Stephen trotted the horses through town. Evangeline had lifted her veil inside the carriage and viewed the stores and street vendors through sheer curtains although passers-by could not see in. She took note of everything she saw. The shops, how women dressed, what men said as they conversed with each other on the street, the height of the buildings, the quality of the other carriages, and other details of life in Bostontown. She even noticed the type of shoes people wore as they traipsed through the snowy, muddy streets.

Before long, had traveled the length of the main street and were headed toward the harbor. The carriage stopped in front of a modest-looking building, small in size compared to the multi-story structures in town. They had been purposefully built with shop space on the main floor and several floors above for owners' residences. As she had expected, the little office had a view of the seaport. No doubt the auctioneer fixed his gaze on every ship coming into the port. After all, that was his business.

The coachman rapped on the door and she opened the latch. "Wait here," she told Hampton. "I shan't be long." When Evangeline knocked on the door with the brass fixture, the proprietor, Jonas Cornhandle, bowed deeply. With his paunch belly, bending was difficult for his breathing, but he made a good go of it.

"Lady Eleanor! I am honored you grace me with your presence in my humble establishment," he crowed. He had already sized up her wealth simply by the expensive gown she wore set off by her dazzling jewelry. Rings on each of her hands, bracelets and a diamond choker, were all in full view of the greedy slave trader. The only thing running through Cornhandle's mind was how to get his hands on as much of her funds as he could, and how quickly he could do so.

The news had spread like wildfire throughout the city of the arrival of the Countess of Devon. First, Panderwick had told his friends at his favorite pub, and they told their wives, who repeated it to the shopkeepers in the morning. Cornhandle thought it dubious that there remained in town one person who did not know about the Countess and her purchase of the old Skinley plantation. It was one of the oldest plantations in the Colony, far from Bostontown, rumored to be haunted by the souls of the slaves old Skinley had mistreated.

But it mattered not to Cornhandle what property she bought. He knew he would be able to procure her entire cadre of labor and felt giddy at the opportunity to make a small fortune off the woman. Not having had the pleasure of attending one of his auctions, she was unaware of the prices. That meant she would need his counsel, which Cornhandle would be only too happy to give. Naturally, his advice would suggest three times the slaves that she would need to work the fields and in the manor house, though they were only half the size of other plantations in the Colony.

"Tea, My Lady?" Cornhandle's voice was lined with a false sweetness that Evangeline instantly recognized.

"But of course," she replied politely. She dared not touch her lips to the cup he presented to her, but she nodded and placed it carefully on the table. "Shall we do business, Mister Cornhandle?"

Her abrupt nature took Jonas by surprise. He recovered quickly, however, imagining the pile of gold coins that would flow from her bankers to his. "What services may I provide for you today?"

"Let us not play games. I appreciate a man who is forthright. You and I both know why I am here. Can you help me?"

"Of course, of course. You are at the right place. Cornhandle is always at your service to do your bidding. Shall I see a map of your lands?"

He played into her hands as she had expected. She had figured that Panderwick would not be able to keep a secret as tantalizing as the purchase of an entire plantation sight unseen. That meant that practically everyone in town knew about her and her new plantation. That gave her instant legitimacy that she would need when she initiated her plan.

Evangeline unfurled the rolled-up map on the table where they sat. Cornhandle leaned in to the map, turning his spectacles this way and that until he understood the size and boundaries of her newly-purchased lands.

"Yes, my Lady. I do believe I have just what you need. Your lands need laborers, do you not?"

"You know that they do. Do you have any to be procured?"

"Unfortunately, we have not had a ship in quite some time. You know, most of them came from Nova Scotia. Difficult business, this English expansionism. The French were transported here, many of them, and they were quickly auctioned off at farms and fields throughout the Colony. Then a second wave of shipments came last year, followed by a third which just ended."

"So why did you agree to see me? I have no time to waste. Clearly, I have misjudged you."

"Now wait just a minute, if you please, Madam. I can help you. In fact, I believe I am the only one who can."

"And how is that," she asked.

"I can procure shipments from Africa or other places if that suits you?"

Evangeline stood, and as she did, Cornhandle saw his dreams of her coins float out of his pockets. She said flatly, "That is not my interest. I thought my coachman was clear. I am only interested in the Acadians. They have a reputation of being excellent workers, obedient and polite. Any other nationality would be too difficult and time-consuming to train. I must have workers very quickly as the spring planting season is approaching."

"Hold on a minute," he barked, realizing instantly the faux pas he committed by talking to her like any other woman in Boston. That would not do. He would have to lower his price, he feared, due to his rudeness. But he could not let the goose with the golden egg leave his shop. Her lands were too far away. She might seek workers in the Connecticut Colony which was close to her plantation. He knew for certain that she would leave

Bostontown and she would take her fortune with her. He could not afford to let that happen.

"I beg your pardon, Lady Eleanor. What I meant to say is that I am the one who transacted all of the Acadian sales in this entire Colony. I had a commission with the Governor, so no one knows this population of slave labor better than I."

She played the game and slowly took her seat again. "You have my interest. Go on," she fed his ego and knew that he would take the bait.

"There is a distinct possibility that some of the plantation owners, and mistresses actually, are not happy with their workers. They might be persuaded to sell them, if the price were right. Would you be willing to engage me as your agent to search out these possible acquisitions?"

She smiled beneath her veil. Those words were music to her ears. It had to be Cornhandle's idea when things unraveled as they would in the coming weeks and months. Finding Gabriel would be more difficult as she could not let on who she was actually looking for. But this would be advantageous to her in that she could actually free some of the Acadians as she searched for her love.

She stood and handed Cornhandle a small purse. He opened it and his eyes nearly jumped out of his head. It was filled with gold coins. She held out her hand and he returned the purse to her. She took out a handful of coins and placed it in his hands.

"Consider this an advance against your fee for services."

Cornhandle bowed. The payment today was far more than he had expected for the first delivery, but he did not divulge his glee.

Evangeline waited to see if the merchant protested the fee was too high or returned some of the coins. When he did not, she was reassured that she had whetted Cornhandle's appetite with her intentional overpayment. Hampton had done his homework and had obtained the prices paid for Acadians over the last year. Many an overseer spilled valuable information over a leg of mutton and a tank of ale. Hampton's research cost surprisingly little to yield such valuable information.

Evangeline was now convinced Cornhandle would do whatever she asked. She understood greedy people. Her uncle Guillaume was one. They were self-centered and concentrated their focus on increasing their wealth. That was an easy thing for Evangeline to do, thanks to the foresight of Pompadour.

"I should like the names of the landowners and the names of the slaves they have, from whence they came, ages, male or female, and the like. I am sure you have kept those records, have you not?"

Cornhandle prided himself in keeping records. He wrote everything in his journal. His philosophy was to keep as much information as possible in every transaction. He never could tell when a bit of information could be used to close a business deal, or blackmail an unwilling partner. Information was never more powerful than it was in Bostontown.

"Leave it to me, My Lady, and I shall have all of the information for you in short order."

"I leave a week hence to inspect my lands. I should require the list before my departure. Contact my man Hampton. He shall bring it to me. Then I shall make my choices."

"Very good, my Lady. Very, very, good," he cackled with delight.

As she walked to the door, she wanted his assurances once more, asking, "Before I embark on this venture with you, can you assure me with no hesitation that I shall be able to acquire any of the names on the list?"

"Most assuredly. I have no doubt I can procure what you wish," Cornhandle squealed.

"Very well. I shall look forward to receiving your information in a fortnight." She took her leave, knowing full well that Cornhandle was watching her every move until her carriage drove away.

Once Evangeline left, Prudence waddled into the room from behind the curtain. "Well, how much did she give you? Fork it over."

Anticipating his wife's nagging demand, Cornhandle had hidden all but two of the coins in his jacket pocket. He gave her one. She bit into it. It was real. She kissed it and dropped it into her ample bosom.

"Methinks I need a fancy new cloak. Like the one in Merrick's window. And some new boots."

Cornhandle rolled his eyes, "Yes, dear. They would look lovely on you. You heard the Lady. I have much work to do and precious little time to complete it. Shoo, unless you want me to lose this commission."

She tiptoed and leaned over to her husband, kissed him chastely on the cheek and sashayed out of the office, closing the door behind her.

CHAPTER 75
Overseers

C ornhandle asked, "Tea, Lady Eleanor? Even with the embargo and the protests against taxation without representation, I do have the real thing," he crowed. His wife was proud of their status in the community and often boasted to the neighbors, "We have real tea." He could not bear to tell her that city fathers held him in esteem not for his charm but rather because he kept their confidential vices secret.

Evangeline accepted the tea cup and noted it was an expensive import from Limoges, France trimmed in gold. At least the trader had good taste, though how he could stomach selling her Acadian friends was beyond her. She could not take a sip with the bitterness in her mouth about the man.

"Shall we conclude the business we spoke of last week?" Evangeline had to speak slowly to keep her disgust from spilling into her speech.

"But of course," he gleefully responded, handing her a long page with a list of plantations and the Acadian slaves sold to each owner.

She carefully perused the list, often raising her eyebrows at the names. Many were members of families she knew in Grand Pré named Broussard, de la Tour Landry, Cormier, Bellivau, Hébert, Bourgeois, Lambert, Gaudet, Melançon, and others.

"Yes, I think this should do. What is the price?" asked Evangeline without so much as a flinch. She intended to free everyone if she had to pay a pretty penny to do so. It was poetic justice, she thought. The English locked up her fiancé on false charges. Now they would pay for the return of her Acadian compatriots at their cost, as their plantations would lose productivity and with the loss of product, the taxes the Governor demanded.

"Well, my dear Lady Eleanor, that is a difficult question to answer. For my part, I would gladly sell you all of them. But of late, the city has just passed an ordinance making the sales of slaves illegal. Of course, anyone who is a slave now shall remain so. However, I am, as of last month, out of business, so to speak."

"Is that so? Does that mean that you cannot conclude this transaction? Perhaps I should seek out another merchant suited to the task?"

"No, no, no, no, no, my Lady. No need. Of course I can make the transaction. I only meant that the plantation owners may not be as willing to sell, since that reduces the number of laborers for their own fields."

"You understand that is not my concern, and I am prepared to pay now?"

"Yes, Lady Eleanor, that is perfectly clear. Shall I be allowed to make a suggestion?"

Evangeline motioned that he should proceed. He looked at the list and pointed to the first plantation. "For example, this is Mister Poundgate's farm. He sold off a small part of his land recently to his brother. Seems logical he would be willing to sell some of his stock."

Evangeline stifled a grimace at the word "stock" and was outraged at the thought of them treating the Acadians as badly as animals. Or perhaps worse. But she nodded, "That sounds reasonable. What about the others? This is a long list."

"Indeed it is. Shall we continue and let me recall what I know about their operations. That shall give us an idea of how many laborers you might end up with. Of course, this is completely up to the owners."

"Get on with it, Mister Cornhandle, shall we?" She was losing patience with his dilly-dallying, though she realized he was trying to calculate the commission he could charge her. To Evangeline, the money was inconsequential. What she cared about was paying the owners for the Acadians – she could not bring herself to think of buying them -- and arranging their safe transport out of the British Colonies into the French territory of Louisiana.

She knew that ocean travel was far too dangerous, due to the ongoing war. No one underestimated the might of the British naval forces, which were formidable. She imagined any English warships that came across French merchant ships would impound and seize French Acadians discovered on board, if not torture or murder them. She shuddered at the thought. No, she realized she would have to arrange an overland journey for the Acadians until they reached safety in the Louisiana territory. From there, they could travel down the Mississippi River to the port of New Orleans.

Cornhandle noticed her sudden shiver and, ever concerned for her health until she paid him, he politely asked, "Is it too chilly for my Lady? Please sit closer to the fire." He stoked the logs in the large hearth until the flames shot up and crackled throughout the room.

Though the cold had not been the cause of her tremor, she appreciated the fire that warmed her hands as she leaned closer to it. Likewise, her heart warmed to the possibility that Cornhandle could be quite useful, for a price.

Evangeline blurted out her thoughts, which, though uncharacteristic of her, sounded perfectly acceptable. "Mister Cornhandle, I wonder if you might procure travel papers for my new laborers. My plantation will be in need of supplies and, being located so far away from Bostontown shops and merchants, I may need to send some of them to a nearby Colony from time to time."

Cornhandle scrutinized her. What was she saying? He could not read her solemn face as she sat so primly in the chair. "Of course, my Lady. But may I suggest that you hire an overseer who would do the actual buying?" When her countenance remained unchanged, he added, "What I mean to say is, of course you could send the workers but can they be trusted with large sums? What if they ran away? Or tried to escape?"

She brushed his remarks off, "Nonsense. I shall only pay for the ones who seem honest and industrious to me. Have you a list of those? Surely you noticed those characteristics when you put them on the auction block?"

He silently patted himself on the back. Of course he took copious notes of their behavior, attitude and demeanor. He always charged more for the ones who were appropriate in all situations. "I have a good understanding of the qualities you seek in the ones I sold. But it seems that their value has increased tremendously now that they cannot be replaced. Are you prepared to pay the price for such workers?"

Evangeline was tiring of his game and his concerns about money. "If it is reasonable, of course. But mark my words, should I learn that others are buying similar workers for lower prices, the Governor of the Colony shall hear about you."

At that threat, Cornhandle paled. She could not have said anything that would have frightened him more. He could not afford for Governor Shirley to learn about the resales. His agreement with the Governor had been far-reaching and required payment to Shirley for subsequent sales of the same Acadians to different buyers. Drat! He would have to share his commission. No, he would nip this in the bud.

"No need for that, I assure you. My price shall merely be a portion on top of the price that you negotiate. Should we say ten percent? You should pay the buyer directly, and then pay my commission to me. Since you are a landowner now, I have great hopes that we shall enjoy a long-lasting business relationship. I stand ready to provide other services to you."

"Like travel papers?"

"Exactly," he grinned.

"And the limits of your discretion? I would not want my business being splattered about town like local gossip. Had you heard of my arrival in town before my man Hampton contacted you?"

He did not know how to answer, but decided to use the truth to his advantage. At least this once. He pretended to latch and lock his lips, then throw away the imaginary key. "Consider my lips sealed. Unlike the local tax clerk and land office surveyor. They are the ones who spread the word about you. That is not how I do business, my Lady."

"When may I conduct the inspections of the workers?"

Cornhandle took her bejeweled fingers in his chubby little hand and kissed them. "As you wish, day or night."

"Very well. Hampton shall make the arrangements."

When the Countess was locked in her carriage and it drove away, Cornhandle's wife confronted him. "Why did you only ask for ten percent? You could have gotten more, you oaf!"

He tried to calm her down. "Missus Cornhandle, have I not kept you in the style to which you have become accustomed? Do I not buy you everything you wish and then some?"

She sheepishly admitted. "You do."

"Then leave me to my business and go spend some more of my money." He handed her another coin along with the lint in his pocket.

She kissed his cheek and bounced out of the door, happy as a lark and eager to buy as much as she could with the funds.

*

As Evangeline's carriage rolled back to her hotel, Gabriel silently hid under the floorboards of Philippe's shack all day. At sundown, the Acadians on Samuel Uttinger's plantation returned to their shanties. In the main house, he saw from under the shack that the lamps were lit. He heard the clinking of glasses and the laughs of the owner and his family as they enjoyed the food that several Acadian women had worked all day to cook.

Philippe stomped on the floor of his shack, which was the sign for Gabriel to come out of hiding. He began to crawl out into the clearing in front of the huts. Just then, Northam, the plantation overseer, galloped past the hovels and stopped in front of Philippe's shed. Clearly drunk, Northam nearly fell off his horse as he dismounted. Gabriel rolled himself back under the shack as far back as he could so that he could not be seen in the dark.

Northam pulled out a large bell and proceeded to hit it with a stick. At the signal, all the Acadians stepped out of their houses and formed a line in the clearing. Northam rode up and down the line, checking them and counting the number. When he had finished, he pulled his horse up to Philippe's hut, expecting him to follow.

The overseer stomped up the steps and yanked open the door, then pushed inside. When Philippe entered, Northam began to berate him in unintelligible language that Gabriel could not decipher. What he did hear, however, was a growl from an unknown animal whose sleep under the floorboards he had disturbed.

Gabriel did not turn to face the animal, fearing fangs and claws. Instead, he scooted forward to the front of the hut. But rather than stop, the growling continued to get louder. Gabriel peeked out into the clearing. Northam's horse was still there, but he was still shouting at Philippe in his hut.

Gabriel chose to take the risk of being seen by Northam rather than to be clawed, so he slipped out into the clearing. The horse was startled and it bucked and whinnied loudly. Gabriel rushed into the next house, taking an Acadian woman by surprise.

"Gabriel! I am packed and ready to go."

He shushed her. "The overseer is out there. Where can I hide?"

She pulled up the blanket on her little cot and when he clambered in, she tossed the blanket on him.

The growling animal, an angry fox, picked that moment to rush out of its hiding place and attack the horse. It neighed loudly and kicked the fox until the little animal whimpered and limped into the woods.

Hearing the noise, Northam ran out of Philippe's shack, fell down the stairs and cursed everyone. "The pox on all of youse worthless scumps. Ne'er-do-wells. Youse should be living in them woods. These houses is too good for youse." He tried to mount his horse several times before he got one foot in the stirrup. The horse bolted with Northam hanging on for dear life.

Philippe came out of his shack and looked underneath the raised floorboards. "Gabriel, are you there? Overseer is gone." When Gabriel was not there, Philippe ran into the clearing and called him again, "Gabriel!" This time, Gabriel ran out of the house and said, "We should go now, before the overseer returns."

The woman knocked on the doors of the other huts. Soon, the clearing was filled with Acadians, each carrying a small bag, ready to go. Philippe reminded them, "Remember, until we get to the border, we must not stay too close together. Sometimes the military are on patrol. If they find us, we shall be arrested."

Gabriel thought of another concern. "But we have no travel papers. You said your life is in jeopardy if you leave the plantation property without them. And you have never been given any. What are the consequences?"

Philippe answered, "Most owners leave it up to their overseers. Northam warned us he has authority to punish any runaway as he sees fit. He threatened beatings and promised to hang one of us as a message to the others."

Gabriel responded, "This may your best chance to escape."

Philippe agreed, "This is our only chance. We had not the courage before you came. We all agreed our life was worth the risk."

Gabriel nodded slowly and said, "Remember, move in small groups and head for the woods." In short order, all the Acadians had crossed the clearing and run through the fields into the woods beyond the plantation. Gabriel stayed a careful distance away from them. Should he be recognized, and there might be a good chance the shopkeeper could identify him, he could cause severe punishment to the Acadians he was helping escape.

At dawn, when Northam rode into the cleaning and clanged the bell, the doors to the shacks stayed closed. He hit the bell again, harder this time. Still nothing. He jumped off his horse and beat on Philippe's door. It bounced open to reveal the empty hut. Northam ran from one hut to the other, furiously cursing them for being abandoned.

He jumped back onto his steed infuriated. "Scrump runaways. Youse heathens will get what is finally coming to youse. Master Samuel!" he shouted as he galloped away. "The louses done run away. Every last one."

*

While Gabriel and the Acadians from the Uttinger plantation trekked toward the adjacent Connecticut Colony, Evangeline suffered in silence as Cornhandle prattled on about the luxury of her carriage. As they bounced along the road, Evangeline sat on one side with Hampton and a chatty Cornhandle on the other. Every time the carriage hit a pothole, Cornhandle bounced and fell onto Hampton, pushing him into the side of the carriage. By the time they had righted themselves, the wheels hit another hole in the road and they had to re-adjust themselves again.

Cornhandle prattled on. "Lady Eleanor, indeed, you have exquisite taste. Such soft velvet cushions make it a pleasure to ride for hours. And the lovely lace curtains. My missus would relish a gander at them handiworks."

She was having none of it. They had agreed to his fee which she would not change, no matter how much he flattered her or her exquisite taste. "Tell me about Mister Uttinger. What is he like? Why did he select those particular Acadians to serve him?"

Cornhandle loved to spout forth information. Usually he charged a nominal fee for his knowledge. But in this instance, he knew he was guaranteed a small fortune to transact the resales, so he happily imparted everything Evangeline asked.

"He is kind unless his orders are not obeyed. Then he directs his overseer to make an example out of the one who refused to follow orders. No matter if it was a mistake, or forgetfulness, or illness. No excuses. Ever."

"He sounds very much a tyrant," she said.

"I saw some of his servants when I returned to deliver two additional kitchen workers. They seemed happy enough."

"Did you see any signs of abuse? Bruises from beatings, for example?

He shook his head vehemently. "Never." He was quick to add, "But that does not mean that punishment never occurred. It happens on every estate. The owners believe that discipline cleanses the soul. That they must instill fear in the servants. If they ever planned an escape, they could easily overrun the family members in the house. And no plantation owner can ever allow that. Hence, the ironclad policy with no exceptions."

"I see." But she still did not understand how a wealthy plantation owner could do so. She glanced out of the window, taking in Cornhandle's words. She was angry at herself that she had not been able to get there sooner to help the Acadians. She was committed to help them escape, not only from the Uttinger plantation but from every place they had been sold.

Hours later, when Evangeline's carriage finally arrived at the manor house, it was past mid-day. Cornhandle assisted her to descend the stairs and escorted her to the front entry.

"Mister Uttinger is generally in his salon in the afternoon."

The merchant rapped the brass knocker on the door. No answer. He knocked louder this time. When he heard nothing, he made an excuse. "He may be in another part of the house. It is very large."

Cornhandle tried a third time without success. Looking around, they saw no one. It looked to Evangeline as though the plantation had been abandoned. They saw no house workers through the open windows in the salon. The fields in the back of the expansive home were empty of workers. The barn doors were open but were void of horses and people.

Cornhandle pulled the knocker again, but received no answer. In a panic about the money he could lose if the Countess were upset with him, or if there were a delay, he made a suggestion. "Shall we walk to the back of the house?"

Evangeline demurred. "I prefer to wait in the carriage."

Cornhandle rushed around the building, peering in windows along the side of the house and jumping on the back porch. The door was open. He peered in, but he saw no one. He rushed to the outbuilding and poked his head through the archway into the kitchen. A cook stood at the fireplace stirring a pot of soup that smelled delicious. But that was not Cornhandle's mission. "Where is Mister Uttinger? We are to see him today."

The cook shook her head, "No Master here. He and overseer Northam took all the friends and neighbors hunting runaways.

"Runaways? The slaves ran away?"

312 | M. M. Le BLANC

"They sent a fast rider to the Governor asking for the military to be sent out. Master is a powerful man in these parts. I saw soldiers marching past here two days ago."

"Can you tell me where I might find them?"

"They went out a far piece past Master's lands. Sent a carriage for me to bring supper last night. Don't know if I could find it again. When I was serving, I saw one of our field hands tied to a tree. He was beaten so hard his back was just a mush of blood. Northam told Master he gave up the ringleader. Said it was an Acadian criminal named Gabriel."

"Did they catch all of them, or just the one?"

"Just the one I know of. Said they will hunt them all down like dogs, since they know the name of the man they called an agitator. Don't know what that means, but it don't sound good. Don't sound good at all."

"Well, they shall get the punishment they were warned of. But was there an Acadian cook here?" Cornhandle asked.

"Them up and left, too. Lived in the shacks over that way." She pointed down the road to the clearing where the hovels sat on either side of the dirt path. "I was Mistress Sarah's personal cook. When them Frenchies did not show the other morning, she done got me out of bed to cook for the whole lot. Everybody wanted something different. I just fixed a couple of dishes and said they could eat it or go hungry."

"I see."

Cook proudly announced the results of her ultimatum. "They all ate it. Done cleaned every pot and bowl. Nothing left."

"Where is Madame Uttinger now?"

"In her bed, I expect. Nobody here to dress her or fix her hair or set her jewels on her neckbone. Nothing for her to do but stay in bed, I suppose."

"May I see her?"

"No, sir. She would tan my hide even though I've been here for years. Nobody can see Mistress. Not even the Master can see her lessen she leave a white scarf hanging on the door. No scarf been on that door for years."

Cornhandle pressed a small coin in her hand and she bit into it then stuck it in her apron. She went back to stirring and spicing up her soup as if he were not there. He took his time walking back to the carriage, feeling dejected and furious at the same time. But mostly he feared the wrath of the Countess when he reported the news. She might end her operation with him and engage a different merchant for her transactions.

Evangeline waited patiently, realizing that nothing was going to happen today. When Cornhandle grunted his way into the carriage, he recounted the cook's tale. When he got to the part about Gabriel's involvement in riling up the workers, she gasped aloud.

Cornhandle was instantly suspicious. Why would that bother an English Countess who knew no one here. "Does that name mean something to you?

She recovered quickly and acted insulted. "I am wondering how the owner would be so lax with his security that a perfect stranger could meet the Acadians and hatch a plot for them to escape. Do tell, how in the world could that happen?"

He relaxed, understanding she was worried whether her workers would leave as these had. "For one thing, my Lady, they have no travel papers. If they are caught, as the straggler whom they beat the truth out of, they will not get far. Not with English troops tracking them."

She shook her head and said a silent prayer for Gabriel. How could she have just missed him? If she had not waited a week for Cornhandle, would she have been able to help him escape? She had so many questions, but now she could only suggest, "Shall we move on to the next estate on the list?"

Cornhandle asked gently, "Are you hungry? I could ask the cook to prepare a supper."

"I should prefer to move on. Hampton packed a basket if you want something to eat. Under the seat just there."

Cornhandle was always hungry. He looked in the basket at the variety of eats available for the taking. He grabbed some bread, cheese, ham and strawberry preserves. And a bottle of wine. A veritable feast. Evangeline tapped on the ceiling of the carriage and they began moving down the road. She opened one of the curtains to watch the countryside as Cornhandle noisily stuffed his face. She wanted to keep a lookout for Gabriel. She had to find him before anyone else did.

*

When Stephen pulled Evangeline's carriage into the entry courtyard of the estate owned by Edgar Chiddlewick, Cornhandle verified that the owner was at home. He graciously invited both Cornhandle and his mysterious guest with the hat veil over her face to join him in the parlor.

Cornhandle gave a glowing introduction of Evangeline as Countess Eleanor of Devon. Proud of his house servants, Edgar showed them off as they served tea and refreshments.

Evangeline was concerned that the two Acadian girls waiting on them would give away her identity. However, as it turns out, they were not from Grand Pré. She asked one of the girls where she had come from, but the owner interrupted her.

"They do not speak English. They are all traitors to His Majesty and were shipped here as punishment. Isn't that about it, Cornhandle?

Jonas agreed, responding as he stuffed his face with little cakes and meat pies. "Mmm...umm...mmm." Swallowing a mouthful, he reminded the owner of their prior transactions. "Madame, er, that is, Lady Eleanor, would like to acquire those servants for which you have no more use. We understand you, like Mister Uttinger, have sold off some of your properties. I just thought we could take them off your hands."

"It is true they can eat one out of house and home. They claim they need the extra food because they are working sunup to sundown. Nonsense. I work up a powerful hunger just riding my horse out to the edge of my property and back, yet I ask for no extra food. So, in answer to your proposal, I would be willing to sell some of them. For the right price."

Cornhandle nodded and turned to Evangeline, sitting silently, watching from under her veil every move that Chiddlewick made. Cornhandle opened the process. "You recall that I made you a very good price on the kitchen girls and the house servants."

The owner nodded, "But I paid nearly twice what Uttinger did for the field hands. So ye got the better end of the bargain. Ye shall not cheat me again. I want thrice what I paid."

Cornhandle exploded. "Thrice? Thrice, you say? That is robbery just as the highwaymen in the countryside."

Chiddlewick stood and raised his fists. "Ye shall not take me for a fool. If ye wants me stock, ye shall pay for them. And a pretty penny at that."

Cornhandle realized his temper could cause him to lose the sale, so he calmed himself. "Mister Chiddlewick, sir, my apologies. Of course, the price is up to you and the Countess. Whatever you and she agree to, of course, is none of my business."

Chiddlewick rolled his eyes, knowing full well that the merchant was making a fee off the sale, though he would never know exactly how much.

Evangeline sat silently through the tirade and cooling-off period. When both men had taken their seats, she spoke. "Mister Chiddlewick, I understand you set great store by your workers. And I am in need of some. What say you to double the price you paid? I can take them off your hands within the week."

Chiddlewick looked at Cornhandle, who agreed with Evangeline. "It is a fair price, and we all know it."

The plantation owner nodded and told Cornhandle, since he was not going to do business with a woman, "Prepare the papers and make the arrangements to pick them up within a week. They shall be ready."

She stood and turned to the owner, "I must inspect them before I make any payment."

Chiddlewick was stunned. "Now? You want to see them now? They are in the fields."

"Now. If you want my price. And I insist that no beatings or punishment be meted out between today and the day I pick them up. Are we agreed?"

Chiddlewick sputtered, "If I tell my overseer that, they will run wild."

Evangeline disagreed softly but firmly. "I shall tell them they are being relocated to my properties. You shall not have any problems with them. In fact, you may actually get greater output between now and then."

Cornhandle argued in support of her idea. "She is right. They shall see her and think it shall be an easy job for them. They shall want to do whatever you demand during this interim period."

Chiddlewick nodded. Cornhandle shook the owner's hand and quickly ushered Evangeline out of the house. He did not want the cheating Chiddlewick to change his mind. He had a deal! And he was already counting his commission.

In the barn, Chiddlewick's groom assisted him to mount his horse. The horse galloped into the fields where the groom gave the instructions to the overseer. Within no time at all, the overseer had marched the Acadians from the fields to the side of the house. He lined them up for inspection.

Evangeline stepped down. As the two men flanked her, she said in no uncertain terms, "I shall inspect them alone."

Cornhandle was worried about her safety. "But they are dangerous."

She brushed him away with her hand. "They respect women. I can feel it. Have no worries about me."

She left the men at the carriage and strode over to the line of Acadians. She walked up to each one, and inspected shoulders or backs or teeth while she whispered in French, "Have no fear. I am here to help you and take you away in one week. Do not reveal my identity if you recognize me."

She saw several friends of Gabriel's in the crowd. As she whispered to them, she asked, "I heard Gabriel organized the escape at the Uttinger place. He is being hunted. Keep your eyes out to help him and the runaways." They nodded in understanding. She asked them in English, "Open your mouth so I can inspect." They did so as part of the charade while the two men looked on from afar.

After the inspection, Evangeline returned to the carriage and nodded curtly to Chiddlewick. "All is in order. We shall return within a week."

The owner assured them, "They shall be ready."

Evangeline was exhausted by the process and asked Cornhandle, "Is there a nearby inn where we might bed for the night?"

He replied, "Of course, only an hour from here. It is close to the next plantation should you desire to go in the morning?"

"Yes," she agreed. "Give the directions to Hampton and he shall take care of it."

That night, Evangeline slept soundly in her private room in the inn. She paid extra for individual rooms for her entire party. She could not allow the innkeeper to put a bundling board in the big beds and rent the empty spaces to strangers seeking a night's rest. She needed the space to be alone and think. How could she convince Cornhandle to provide travel papers for all the slaves, not just a handful who would be buying supplies for her?

Early the next morning, Evangeline was woken by a squawking chicken. She peered out of the narrow window and saw the innkeeper's wife chasing after the bird until she grabbed it, wrung its neck and put it on a spit. For the next hour, the wife's two young sons rotated until the hen was cooked. The owner's daughter served Evangeline a hearty breakfast of the roasted chicken with bread, cheese, jams, jellies and tea. Soon the Countess and Cornhandle were ensconced in her carriage discussing the next landowner and what Acadians on the list he might be willing to sell.

So intent in her discussion was Evangeline that she did not see the two dozen bedraggled Acadians picking berries for food from bushes near the road. At the sound of the wagon wheels, the men and women dove into the brush and hid until the carriage had passed.

Gabriel watched the coach drive by just as a gust of wind fluttered the curtains open. He could have sworn he saw a silhouette of Evangeline's face. To be sure, the woman's hair was styled a bit differently and she was slightly older than the last time they had seen each other in Grand Pré.

The image was forever emblazoned in his memory of Evangeline braving the freezing waters of the Grand Pré harbor to see him before his ship sailed away. He remembered how his heart had stopped when Turnbull had fired his musket at her, turning the waters red. All he could do was pray that she survived and offer his life to see her, hold her, kiss her, once more.

Gabriel was so convinced the woman he saw was Evangeline that he thought for an instant about running up to the carriage or standing in the road to stop it from moving ahead. But he knew such an act would expose the Acadians he had helped rescue from Uttinger's plantation. He was willing to risk his own life, but not theirs. So he watched helplessly as the carriage rolled by. Soon it was nothing but a mirage swallowed by the dust bowl blowing in the road.

In his heart, Gabriel felt that Evangeline was still alive and had already reached the safety of the French Louisiana Territory. He was determined to let nothing stop him from reaching that destination. If he could bring the escaped Acadians with him, it would make their trek so much the sweeter.

CHAPTER 76
Papers

Bostontown

Jonas Cornhandle was a busy man. But nothing seemed more important to him than the demands of Countess Eleanor of Devon. He had no inkling of her real identity, but if he had, would it have made any different to him? He was a merchant inside and out, offering services and charging a pretty penny for them. If the Countess had wanted a herd of elephants and dancing fire-eaters, no doubt he would have discovered a way to fulfill her desire.

Today, Cornhandle found himself wrestling with a new experience – a moral dilemma. Never before had he concerned himself with judging a request as "right" or "wrong." Nothing was morally repugnant or ethically required. He simply did as he was bid, and paid to do.

He struggled with the latest request the Countess made for travel papers for all the Acadians she was buying. But she had agreements with the owners of ten plantations thus far. Why did she need papers for all those slaves? They were bound to a plantation and did not need to travel anywhere. Should he prepare the documents or report her to the authorities?

Getting the authentic papers was easy enough. He has greased the palm of a clerk in the Governor's office. The man had provided Cornhandle with stamped documents for the family of several criminals whom they were able to whisk out of the Colony before the trial. He had no problem with criminals. But property that he had sold? Could he be arrested for aiding and abetting someone to steal property? Thieves were punished for less in London. He had heard about hungry boys losing their right hands for stealing bread. And any man who stole the horse of a noble was hanged on the spot pursuant to the new simplified justice of King George II.

Cornhandle thought he had heard the Countess confirm the papers were only for the Acadians to travel to the nearest storehouses to buy supplies for her estate. Because they would cross into the adjacent Colony, official travel papers were required at the border.

He wondered what would happen to him if he reported the Countess' request? She had immense wealth, that was obvious. Could she turn the tables on him and have him taken in by the constable, or worse, by the English military? He did not want to find out.

At the same time, he did not want to lose such a large commission. He hemmed and hawed before he finally decided what he would do. He prepared the travel documents that the Countess needed for all the adults, but not for the children. He would simply tell her that papers were not needed for any Acadian under the age of fifteen. Hopefully, she would not know that the law required a separate set of papers for each person, not each adult. If she attempted to bring children across the colonial borders, she would reap the punishment she sowed. But he would be able to make his fee and still sleep at night.

Evangeline walked into his office before Cornhandle realized it. He held out his hand, expecting her to fill it with gold coins she had in her purse. However, she insisted on reading each document before she paid him. He was nervous the entire time.

"You have listed their names in English. Very good. That should not draw attention," she said.

Cornhandle warned, "Unless they forget and begin to speak French. If so, they could be arrested even with the proper documents."

"I see you are missing papers for the two young girls at the Winborne estate and the boy at Chiddlewick's. You listed his name as Peter Pine Gaudet. Is that what he goes by – Pine?"

Cornhandle lied with a smile. "I believe the youngster's name is Pierre, but I do not know where Pine comes from."

"Are you certain you shall not need the child's name on a separate paper? He is listed on the page with Bertrand Gaudet. Is that his father?"

"This is my business. I have made no mistake. Children cross the border on the same travel paper as an adult. The man is his uncle, I believe. You know those large Acadian families. Who can tell who is related to who?"

By the time she had finished, Cornhandle's eyes were as large as the pile of gold laying in front of him. He bowed and escorted her to the door, when the bell tinkled as she walked out.

"Good day to you. I trust you shall think of Cornhandle if you need anything else for your plantation."

"Good day, sir." Evangeline exited and disappeared into her carriage. Hampton cast a glowering look at Cornhandle. The man seemed very untrustworthy to him.

The week flew by and at dawn, Evangeline stepped into her carriage. Hampton had arranged a line of drivers with large wagons and carts to follow and pick up the Acadians when Evangeline paid the owners. She had laid out the plan, which he would then implement.

"Hampton, collect all of the Acadians once I have paid for them and deliver them to the manor house on my estate. We shall help them cross in small groups, making certain each is led by a man who speaks English. Otherwise they will call attention to themselves."

Hampton did not know Evangeline's true identity and thought she was actually an English noblewoman pursuing a higher moral cause in freeing the Acadians. There was nothing wrong with buying property and letting it go, but the Massachusetts Bay Colony officials were skittish about the subject, especially since their wealthy friends were landowners forbidden to buy more laborers for their farms.

As a sympathizer to the Acadian plight, Hampton had pledged his loyalty to her. "Shall we try to help those on the plantations escape the same day we collect the ones you were able to free?"

"We must wait at least a week, perhaps a month, before doing so. Otherwise, we risk a landowner's claim that we are the ones perpetrating the deed. By now, the Acadians will have heard of the escape by the man named Gabriel." She stopped suddenly to catch her breath and hold back the tears at the mention of her fiancé. Then she continued, "That means the owners will be more cautious, even wary, of strangers."

"Do you think they shall suspect us?"

"They shall be looking for every explanation, and we cannot take any risks. But once we do free all the Acadians from one farm, we must proceed to the next one the following night, and another the night thereafter, until they are all freed. We shall not be able to wait weeks in between. There is the strong possibility the military will be called in and our plan will be for naught. We must help each and every one of them to escape into the Louisiana territory."

Hampton assured her, "All is ready. We shall succeed."

Evangeline completed the transaction at the Uttinger farm, then at the Chiddlewick plantation. When her carriage pulled up to the Dillingbird estate, the owner and his wife accepted the payment with glee and directed their overseer to load the selected Acadians into the waiting wagons.

The Dillingbirds insisted she stay for tea, though their purpose was to showcase the supposed talent of their daughter. She played off-key music on the harpsichord as Evangeline listened politely. Her parents encouraged the girl to attempt every song she knew. Finally, a rap at the front door gave Evangeline a much-needed reprieve.

Hampton appeared with an urgent message for Lady Eleanor. He whispered to her, "The Acadians in the wagon said they heard Bostontown troops plan to move into the area by nightfall."

Hearing that, Evangeline thanked the host and hostess and their well-meaning, but poorly-trained, daughter. They left immediately with all the Acadians and disappeared around the bend in the road.

As they traveled on the road, Hampton asked Evangeline, "Should we postpone the rescue for another night?"

She responded thoughtfully, "We may not have another opportunity. Let us hope the Dillingbirds are so tired after listening to their daughter all day that they are sound asleep. We should be able to whisk them away in short order, if they are ready."

"The Acadians promised me those who remain are prepared. They only await my signal."

"Make certain they escape quickly and quietly. Tell them not to burden themselves with their possessions. I shall procure what they need. And make certain the young boy Peter Pine stays with his uncle."

Hampton slipped out of the carriage and disappeared into the woods. Evangeline stayed in the carriage but blew out the candles inside so she would not be detected. In the dark, she heard the noises in the forest of animals moving, trees blowing in the wind, branches scratching against the carriage top and finally, whispered voices.

She observed Hampton lead the male adult Acadians into the false bottom built in her carriage for that purpose. They piled in until there was no additional room. Then he assisted the women and Pine Gaudet into the carriage. He lifted up the seat cushions which hid large compartments where the rest of the Acadians stowed away. Before Pine climbed into the hiding place, Evangeline hugged him. "I know your mother and sister very well. Once we get to Louisiana, I shall help you find them."

"Thank you, Countess," said Pine.

Evangeline could not tell any of the Acadians her actual name, although she recognized many from Grand Pré. Seeing neighbors who did not recognize her broke her heart but strengthened her resolve to carry through with her mission. She knew she was doing the right thing. Besides, she reasoned that Mr. Dillingbird had been paid more than the total he had expended in the first place for all of the Acadians. He had not lost anything and the Acadians had gained their lives back.

Evangeline asked, "Is everything ready to rescue the Dillingbird Acadians? We are nearly a day's journey from the Chiddlewick estate, so the news of their loss should not travel so quickly."

Hampton was more cautious. "I do not like it, my Lady. Even with the distance, they are still neighbors. No doubt they know each other. It seems the Dillingbirds would be the first to get the news of the escape tomorrow.

"Yet, each day we delay brings more pain and suffering to the Acadians. The risk is a small price to pay.

Hampton nodded halfheartedly and bowed. "Then we must pray that you are not discovered before then, my Lady."

*

After the Chiddlewick and Dillingbird purchases, Evangeline was frustrated with the extraordinary amount of time Cornhandle spent in contacting the other landowners as to their interest in selling their property. Evangeline waited impatiently as Cornhandle corresponded back and forth with the owners to schedule appointments then travel for hours to meet and negotiate the deals.

At each meeting, the landowner agreed to transfer his Acadian servants to Evangeline. The only question was the price. Sometimes Cornhandle negotiated half the number of Acadians on the estate, and sometimes it was for only a handful. Subsequently, after some time had passed, Hampton carried the remaining Acadians away. Due to the distance between estates and the rare visits among owners of neighboring lands, Evangeline's scheme was not detected.

There remained only one plantation whose owner had refused to sell Evangeline any of his Acadian workers. On a large plantation on the western side of the Colony, not far from Evangeline's estate, Elliott Poundgate lived with his sister Martha.

Elliott was a wiry, wizened old fellow with a shiny bald head and pock marks all over his face. He had never married, not because he had never asked, but because none of his proposals were ever accepted. He focused instead on working his fields into some of the most profitable in the region. He had built his wealth steadily and had invested his profits in acquiring nearby properties until his estate was the largest in the Colony.

His sister Martha was a short, stubby woman with long hairs that grew out of a huge brown mole on her chin. A homely woman, she had never married, not because she turned down any suitors, but because she never had any to begin with. Her entire life revolved around her brother, which was the way she wanted it. An excellent cook, she refused to have kitchen help even after Elliott bought many Acadian house servants from Cornhandle. Martha insisted on running the household without any interference from the heathens.

Cornhandle had attempted several times to strike a deal with Poundgate, to no avail. Evangeline was not satisfied with his attempts. She called Hampton to the main house and issued a directive, "I do not trust

Cornhandle to handle this business any longer. He has failed to make an arrangement for the Poundgate Acadians. I must meet with the landowner myself. Please make the arrangements."

"Of course, my Lady. When do we leave?"

"On the morrow at dawn."

Because the property was in the same general vicinity within the Colony, the trip was not but a half-day's journey. She arrived at the property and Hampton struck the wooden knocker. A wizened old man appeared whom Hampton took for a servant.

"Good man, I have urgent business for Mister Poundgate."

"Yer talking to him in the flesh. What is this urgency?"

"Begging your pardon, sir, Countess Eleanor of Devon would like--"

Poundgate interrupted abruptly, "Who? I have nothing to do with a countess. What is this? Go away, young man."

Poundgate slammed the door in his face. Hampton was taken aback but rapped on the door with the knocker again. The owner again opened the door. This time Hampton stuck his foot in the doorway so Poundgate could not slam it shut. "Please, Mister Poundgate, if you have no immediate business, what would it hurt to hear what my Lady Eleanor has to say?"

The old man stroked his long gray beard for a moment and nodded. He crept into his main room, leaving the door wide open. Hampton escorted Evangeline into the house. It looked like it had not been dusted since it was built. Hampton brushed off the dirt from a chair with his handkerchief for Evangeline. He stood by her side.

Poundgate swigged a bottle of beer. "So? What is yer talking point with me?" he asked gruffly.

"Sir," Evangeline began, "I am here to help you and offer to buy some of your -- workers."

"Eh, what's that? Why do yer think I needs to be helped? Me fields make me more money than can be spent. Why should I sell my slaves?"

His sister entered the room quietly and whispered in his ear. He nodded. "She tells me it's time for me sleep. Let me think on yer words. Come back in the morrow." He walked out, leaning on his sister's arm. Turning back at the archway leading to the hall, he turned back and said, "Me sister invites you to sup then, too."

Evangeline was surprised but gratified, "It would be a great pleasure. We shall return tomorrow, sir." She and Hampton returned to the carriage. On the road back to her house, she spoke her thoughts.

"That went better than expected. At least he shall consider it. But perhaps his sister makes the decisions. Her gaze lingered on you for a bit, I noticed. I am certain you can put that to good use."

"As I am in your service, anything you ask that is within my power shall be done. And that is something within my power."

The next evening, Evangeline and Hampton dined with Elliott and Martha Poundgate. The table groaned under the weight of platters filled with meats, fruits, cakes, breads and cheeses. Hampton smiled at Martha every time she glanced his way. While Martha said nothing, she took note of the value Evangeline placed on the workers.

Elliott told her, "I ain't selling at any price, but eat up." Martha whispered her thoughts into his ear. Immediately, Elliott asked, "What be yer price?" Clearly, he valued Martha's opinion, for he changed his tune whenever she spoke to him.

Evangeline quoted a price, "Three times what you paid." She had substantial funds and did not want to risk losing these last Acadians.

That evening, after supper, Martha took Elliott off to bed but turned and said, "Wait here. I shall return."

Evangeline and Hampton sat patiently in the dining room and were not disappointed. Martha returned and said simply, "We accept. Pay now and take yer pick of half in the barn. Boy counts as a man, not half-price."

Evangeline knew about the boy and wanted to make certain he came with her tonight. She nodded, "I understand and agree."

Hampton asked, "Should I meet with your overseer?"

She held out her hand. "Fired him. Ain't got one now." Evangeline counted out more gold pieces than she had paid any other farmer. The money was immaterial to Evangeline. She was proudest of the transaction with the Poundgates because it completed her mission to rescue all Acadians working on farms and plantations in the Massachusetts Bay Colony. And in less than one year!

Even Hampton, quite used to bringing to fruition the impossible, recognized her efforts as heroic accomplishments considering the vast territory that had been covered, the number of landowners who had to be convinced to sell, the delicate price negotiations, the inspection, and finally the payment and collection.

Evangeline was amazed that the owners had not connected her with the Acadian escapes on so many plantations and farms. But as Hampton had told her, "My Lady, you are of the highest English class, only second to the Royal Family. No one would suspect you at all, because you have the means to pay for what you want. You have no reason on earth to steal."

With her fist full of gold coins, Martha nodded her thanks and left them with her parting words, "As my brother said, choose the ones you want in the barn."

Hampton escorted Evangeline out and they went into the barn, where Hampton loaded the agreed-upon number of Acadians into a large enclosed

324 | M. M. Le BLANC

wagon. Evangeline advised those left in the barn to expect a signal late at night within the next month. She also cautioned them not to discuss it amongst themselves nor to anyone else, for fear that the scheme would be discovered and foiled.

Once the Acadians were securely seated in the wagon, the driver flicked his whip and trailed Evangeline's carriage a short distance behind.

As Evangeline and Hampton rode in the carriage on their way to her estate, she told him, "I shall have Stephen drive me to Connecticut in order to deposit the first group of Acadians across the border. Once that has been done safely and we know that the routine does not arouse suspicion, I shall return to the manor. Then we shall repeat the procedure until they are all safe. I trust you shall make the arrangements to pick up the remaining Acadians from Poundgate's farm. I shall participate in that operation, which will be my final act to remove all of the Acadians from this Colony."

Hampton dutifully replied, "My Lady, it would do no good to dissuade from this dangerous mission. You are well aware of the danger of being caught and arrested. However, anything could happen when an angry landowner finds the culprit who took his property. That said, I know your mind is fixed. Therefore, I shall have all the arrangements made when you return from the border transfer."

"And please book passage for me on the ship leaving for New Orleans after we finish our work." Her intuition told her to leave at that very moment and seek Gabriel. But she knew she could not betray her moral duty and her commitment to rescue the remaining Acadians and take them across the border. She was in the position to do so without arousing suspicion.

She prayed Gabriel was on the overland trail to the Louisiana Territory. She understood it would take him through the Connecticut Colony into the northern part of Louisiana, where he could travel down the Mississippi River to the French port city of New Orleans.

PART VIII

Paradise Found
1760 – 1763

Carpe diem.

- Horace

CHAPTER 77
Trails

Virginia Colony

To the naked eye, Evangeline appeared to be a single woman traveling alone with her driver and two burly coachmen who held on to leather straps, sometimes for dear life, in the rumble seat on the back of the coach. She had marveled at Hampton's ingenious idea to build seat boxes under the cushions inside the carriage in addition to her schematic of adding a false floor beneath the floorboards. She watched Hampton hide the first group of Acadians escapees in the two compartments.

But as she sat in her carriage that rolled along the muddy road out of her estate and approached the Connecticut Colony border, her heart beat faster. She was not at all certain her plan would work and allow all of the Acadians to escape the Massachusetts Bay Colony. For that reason, she was only willing to risk using two sets of travel papers that Cornhandle had procured for her. She had paid him handsomely but had no doubt that he employed nefarious means, like bribes or threats, to obtain the documents stamped with official colonial seals.

She could lose the money she invested, but she was not willing to risk the lives of all the innocents in her care if the travel papers were discovered to be fakes or poor forgeries. The carriage stopped and she heard voices outside. It would not be long now. She pulled the curtain back slightly to observe the border check process.

A small shack sat at a crossroads, with an open gate that had rusted. Three young men in mismatched military uniforms held up their muskets as a show of strength, or perhaps to strengthen their resolve.

One of the guards, a mere boy of thirteen, held his hand out to the driver for the travel papers. He glanced momentarily at the two huge Acadian men,

Jacques Gaubert and Robert Primeau, then checked the travel papers for them and Stephen, the driver. Then the young guard knocked on the window of the carriage and Evangeline drew open the curtain.

"Begging yer pardon, Miss, but I need yer papers."

"Of course," Evangeline said and placed them through the window with her gloved hand.

The boy hardly glanced at the documents, sealed with royal red wax, ribbons and the appropriate number of signatures. She was grateful that Madame de Pompadour's relationship with her spies in England had made bribing British officials for the official documents a painless procedure.

Evangeline had very much hoped for an audience with the King, who had apparently adored both of her parents. But since it could have been months, or longer, until the King decided to hold audiences again, she was thankful for his First Mistress' counsel and assistance in setting up her new identity in the Colonies.

The guard abruptly returned the document to her. She noticed he had looked at it upside-down. So the guards, at least this one, could not even read! The revelation immediately set her mind, and her heart, at ease. Cornhandle's travel papers appeared impeccable, but even if they had not been, it was clear the young soldiers at the border crossing were more interested in gossip than in doing their job.

The young man tipped his cocked hat and waved the driver through the gate, which appeared to be open day and night. Evangeline watched through the window as the driver turned down a road with a sign reading, "General Store and Inn." She was pleased that Hampton had employed a man on the ground there to research the terrain, the border checkpoint and the closest store. Perhaps she would find not only supplies for the Acadians, but also lodging for herself. The journey from her plantation was only five hours long, but Evangeline felt fatigued to her bones.

She was not naïve enough to think that Massachusetts Bay would not have spies living here. That would be the best way to keep track of people going from one Colony to the other, and to report back to the powerful Governor, William Shirley. But she realized she would not need the pretext of buying supplies for her estates in her future trips to deposit the Acadians in the adjoining Colony.

The driver stopped directly in front of a wooden building that offered supplies, rum and lodging. Before she exited the carriage, she warned the Acadians who had piled into the seat boxes and the hidden compartment of the carriage.

In a loud whisper, she said, "Stay hidden. We shall be able to obtain foodstuffs for your journey before we deposit you in the woods ahead. Then we shall return for the next group."

She climbed the steps of the small building with two Acadian men walking behind her, as she had pre-arranged. She introduced herself to the English couple standing behind the counter.

"Good day. I am Countess Eleanor of Devon, the new owner of the plantation that abuts the Colony line."

She curtsied and he bowed before responding in unison, "Good day, my Lady."

"We should like to procure food and supplies to stock my manor house. My workers could also use winter clothes, woolen sweaters in particular. My men here shall bring everything to my carriage."

The man and woman gave each other a knowing look. The shopkeeper directed the Acadian men to the food area with sacks of flour and rice, jugs of beer and rum, bottles of wine, and jars with jams, jellies, preserved fruits, pickled vegetables and other edibles.

His wife pulled Evangeline aside and showed her linens, blankets, woolen sweaters, hats and gloves. As Evangeline selected nearly everything she inspected, the woman whispered, "We are sympathizers. We know what you are trying to do and applaud your mission."

Evangeline was stunned. How did she know? She only had two men. She had not slipped in her pronunciation of English. What gave her away? But she pretended not to understand. "My mission, Madame, is equipping my house and workers so we can commence working my fields."

The woman persisted. "Have no fear. We are far away from the nearest military station. The Connecticut officials may know what we are doing but they leave us be. My husband and I moved from Bostontown expressly to help runaway slaves. We have never agreed with the policy."

Evangeline looked at her intently but said nothing. On the other side of the store, the Acadians took one load out to the carriage and returned for more. At that point, the shopkeeper joined the two women. His wife told him, "I was right. She is assisting runaways. Imagine that! An English Countess is one of us," the woman said proudly.

Evangeline started to warn the Acadian men to leave, but the woman put her hand on Evangeline's arm. "Do not be alarmed. Let us help you."

Before he could speak, Evangeline opened her coin purse and handed them a gold piece. Their eyes bugged wide. They had never actually seen one before. But the man actually tried to hand it back to her. "It is our honor to assist you. No need for payment."

Evangeline insistently said, "Use it for your mission. It will allow you to buy more food and blankets, and give more aid."

The wife nodded to her husband, who replied, "Thank you, my Lady. Our store is a welcome light for Acadians and others in their situation. While they do not enter through the front door, we often discover them rooting through the trash in the back of the shop. That is when we can offer some supper and a warm, dry spot for the night."

"We keep our barn filled with animals but have a hidden cellar under the horse stalls. We can accept as many as twenty at a time."

Evangeline queried, "Do you see many Acadians?"

Mrs. Normand said ruefully, "We do not encounter them very often. When we do, more often than not, they are half-dead from the cold. Or badly wounded from a musket ball or two."

Her husband agreed. "We recently housed a group of Acadians who had escaped from one of the plantations several days' walk from here."

At that, Evangeline's eyes lit up. Perhaps she had seen her love. "Do you have the names of anyone in that group? Their leader, perhaps?"

The storekeeper's wife shook her head. "It has been several weeks. I may have heard the name Gabe."

"Could it have been Gabriel?"

She shook her head. "Perhaps. I really don't remember. They were a large group, but one man was definitely their leader. He spoke perfect English. Wore a sailor's uniform."

Evangeline looked toward heaven and said a silent prayer of thanks. That meant he survived the farmer search parties, soldier hunts and dog trackers that had no doubt been sent after him and the Acadians he had helped to safety.

It was nearly sundown, and Mrs. Normand said, "Please join us for supper. And our daughters shall prepare a room for you in the lodge."

Evangeline was grateful, "That would be most kind. Thank you."

They enjoyed a quiet supper while the Normand daughters delivered a food pail to the driver and a large supper tray to the two Acadian men. Evangeline had directed them to sit in the carriage. That way, they were able to open the seat boxes and one of the false floorboards and hand food to the Acadians hiding below.

During the meal, the three discussed the procedure that would extricate the Acadians from the carriage without attracting attention.

Normand explained their process, "When we see signs that runaways are nearby, we leave a tray of food in the back of the building. No one has dared enter the store, but we reach out to them when they take the food. We offer them shelter and safety in our cellar. The trap door is hidden beneath the counter in the store. No one has ever suspected it is there. From there, we load the Acadians into a hidden box inside our supply wagon, and drive them with our supplies to the next town. A family there feeds and shelters them for the night, then transports them to the next town, and so on."

Evangeline was intrigued, "In effect, you have arranged an underground network to protect the runaways. Where do most of them go?"

Mrs. Normand responded quickly, "They all want to go to France, but realize it is impossible with the ongoing war. The English blockade captures any ships heading for France. So most head for the Louisiana territory."

Her husband interrupted the conversation as night had fallen and all was quiet. "It is time." He directed the undertaking resulting in all of the Acadians pouring out of Evangeline's carriage into the Normands' cellar.

Before Evangeline left, she left the group of Acadians with some gold pieces and a request, "When you arrive in New Orleans, please find Gabriel Mius d'Entremont and tell him I will be there soon." The Acadians assured her they would deliver the message if they found him there.

At that moment, Gabriel was well on his way to Louisiana. He and the Acadians he had rescue from Uttinger's plantation were traveling down the Mississippi River. They had paid a trapper planning to sell his furs in the port city of New Orleans to take them with him. Gabriel believed his fiancée Evangeline had already arrived and that he would find her there.

*

Martha Poundgate served tea and homemade shortcake to her brother Elliott's guests, fellow plantation owners Chiddlewick and Dillingbird. Then she sat quietly behind the men who raised serious issues.

Dillingbird began the conversation, "I sold half my Acadians to that Countess of Devon. Made a pretty penny if I do say so myself. But a fortnight later the rest of 'em went missing."

Mr. Chiddlewick stood up and stomped around the room indignantly, "Mine, too. I only sold a handful. Needed the rest to work my fields this season. But I took the missus on a trip. Stayed in the best hotel in Bostontown. She insisted on spending some of the coin in every shop there. When we got back, nary a one was in their huts."

Elliott Poundgate connected the stories and asked, "Do we think this Countess had something to do with this?"

Dillingbird folded his arms and leaned back in his chair. "Mighty curious that one woman is suddenly interested in buying all of them, and neither of us wants to sell everything we own. So did she just take 'em?"

Martha whispered in her brother's ear. Elliott leaned forward and told his two friends. "Methinks we can make a plan. We still have some Acadians here. What if she is planning to take the ones I refused to sell?"

The three landowners plotted and schemed, tossed out ideas and changed their minds. Martha sat back and sipped her tea, listening to the arguments. She knew all it would take was a whisper into her brother's ear and the problem would be solved. But she enjoyed watching the three old men fuss and fight.

*

Back in her manor house, Evangeline and Hampton finalized the details of the rescue of the Acadians from the Poundgate estate. This was the only one in which she decided to participate, over Hampton's warnings of danger. She gave him a sack of gold coins as a sign of her gratitude, knowing that she would not see him again. Hampton was traveling in the wagon with the Acadians driven by his cousin, Jasper. After the mission was completed, Stephen would drive Evangeline to the dock in Bostontown and see her off.

Due to the naval blockade, she would travel in her identity as an English Countess to the Georgia Colony, where she would complete her journey overland to Louisiana. With the plans arranged and the ticket purchased, she sensed the bittersweet ending to their working relationship.

"You and your brother Stephen have been invaluable in helping me complete this mission."

Hampton nodded his thanks and simply said, "It is time."

Jasper drove the wagon out of her main estate road and within a few hours had arrived near the Poundgate house. Stephen drove the carriage at a slower pace and arrived an hour later, parking the carriage by the road but out of eyesight of the Poundgate main house.

Hampton crept up to the carriage and assisted Evangeline out. She had dressed in the clothes of a shopkeeper's wife, courtesy of Mrs. Normand. She did not even look the same, with her hair pulled back into a stringent bun and an apron over her blouse and skirt. She wore black stockings and flat black boots, for which she was thankful as she traipsed across the muddy farmland towards the barn.

As a precaution, Evangeline had tied the bag of her remaining gold coins inside her petticoat. With the passage already paid for, she needed nothing until she reached Georgia, where she had already prepaid a guide to take her overland. She felt the money she had was sufficient. That was her first mistake.

Rather than risk a lantern being seen by the Poundgates, Evangeline and Hampton relied on the moonlight above to show them the way. It was slow going through the thick underbrush, bushes and vegetation until they reached a clearing. Their goal was to enter the barn without being seen by anyone in the manor house.

They finally reached their destination. Hampton opened the barn door wide enough to slip in and held it open for Evangeline. She hesitated and turned to gaze at the Poundgate main house. She saw a wagon and a carriage sitting on the side of the house, which were not there when she had visited before. However, she did not give it a second thought and crept into the barn. That was her second mistake.

Inside, Hampton woke the Acadians lying in the hay in the barn. He pointed upstairs to the loft. Evangeline climbed the narrow ladder up to the loft and quietly woke the other Acadians up there, and waited for them to descend to the barn floor. Hampton led the Acadians out of the barn into the dark and Evangeline followed.

Hampton had loaded so many other Acadian groups that his directions had been honed to perfection. Not a minute was wasted. Once the workers were in the boxes, he closed them and pulled over boxes of supplies to cover the latches.

Evangeline rushed to her carriage and Jasper pulled the horses out slowly. The wagon followed until they came to the crossroads. Evangeline suddenly remembered something. She tapped on the carriage and Jasper stopped. Not waiting for assistance, she jumped out of the carriage and ran to the wagon, fearing to call out. Hampton had, fortunately, looked back and had seen her running so he stopped the wagon.

"Where is the young boy?" Evangeline asked.

Hampton shook his head. "Surely we have him with us."

She repeated, "Simon. Where is Simon? He was in the hayloft. But I do not remember watching him climb down and join you."

Hampton was mystified. "My Lady, we are losing precious time. Once day breaks, we stand a greater chance of getting caught."

Evangeline was fearful. "I fear he is still in the barn. We must make sure. It would not do to leave a helpless child in the care of the Poundgate family. It would not do at all. I shudder to think what would happen."

Hampton nodded and jumped down. "We should not drive the wagon back. I shall run back and check the loft."

As he started running, Evangeline joined him. They reached the barn and ran inside.

*

Outside the manor house, Elliott Poundgate and his neighbors Chiddlewick and Dillingbird were taking long strides toward the barn. They each held a musket and bags of powder and musket balls.

"That hussy comes near me, she'll get a hide full of musket balls. Nobody steals my slaves, for sure no woman," Poundgate announced.

Chiddlewick agreed, "If it is that Countess, I shall give her thirty lashes myself."

"You shall have nothing to lash if I have my way with a rope and a tree," Dillingbird adamantly declared.

"Hanging's too good for the likes of her. Killing her slow and easy. That there's the way," said Martha Poundgate who, unbeknownst to the men, had caught up with them, running with her short little legs as fast as they could go. She was a sight to see, her musket nearly as tall as she, taking three steps for every one of her brother's. The three men looked aghast at her. She was dead serious, but they nodded to her in agreement as their little band continued toward the barn.

*

Hampton climbed up the barn stairs and found Simon still sleeping. He roused the boy and half-carried him down the stairs where Evangeline was waiting. "Be very quiet. A wagon waits for you down at the end of the path. If we get separated, run to the end of the road and tell the driver Jasper that I told him to take all of you to freedom."

Simon was half-asleep but he knew enough to be afraid. "You must leave, Madame. Master Poundgate will shoot you. That is what he said. If anyone comes to get me, he will shoot."

"Do not concern yourself with that. Move quickly now."

Hampton nodded, and Evangeline opened the barn door wide enough for the three of them to exit the door. That was her third mistake.

As they exited, the three men and Martha were fast-approaching the door. Elliott was the first to see Evangeline. He yelled out, "There she is. Fire away. Fill her hide full of musket balls!"

He fired, aiming for Evangeline. He was so flustered the gun shot straight up in the air. Hampton pushed Evangeline back in the barn, but Simon ran for his life down the road. Dillingbird and Chiddlewick both aimed at the moving target and fired. Simon fell to the ground, dead.

The two men did not even check the boy to see if he was still alive. Martha ignored him as well. Instead, they proceeded to stuff their muskets and ready them to shoot. They fired at the barn door, which Hampton had barred from the inside. He and Evangeline had run away from the door, seeking another way out of the barn, but they had closed off their only entrance. One horse remained in the barn, which whinnied sensing fear.

Hampton found an axe and started chopping a hole in the side of the barn opposite the door. "Start a fire. That way, if they break down the door, the horse will kick down his stall and run out, scattering the group that is out there."

Evangeline piled small sticks, hay, leaves, and other small matter she found on the barn floor. Then she began to rub two of the sticks together. After the sticks emitted smoke for a moment, they burst into flame. The horse began to stomp and whinny louder. She rubbed the horse's mane, trying to keep him calm.

Hampton called out to her, "Strengthen the fire now, my Lady."

She obliged and soon there was a roaring fire in the middle of the barn. Hampton had chopped a small hole with the axe and was enlarging it to make it large enough for at least one at a time. The horse was stomping and neighing loudly as the acrid smoke hit its nostrils.

Hampton and Evangeline were still crouching out of the line of fire as Dillingbird, Chiddlewick and the Poundgate siblings were still shooting at the barn door.

Poundgate yelled out, "Come out and face yer punishment. Slave thief justice is the same as for a horse thief."

Finally, Hampton broke through and he called out, "My Lady. Go quickly."

When Evangeline had managed to get through the hole in the wall, she waited for Hampton. He told her, "Do not wait. Go back to the carriage and tell them not to go to the docks. You must go back to the Connecticut Colony."

"But what will you do?" she wailed?

"Worry not. I shall be fine. I assure you. I shall hold them off if they break through the door to give you time to escape. Please, go, before it is too late."

Just then, the horse bolted and ran to the hole in the wall. Rearing back and kicking it in, the horse neighed when it could not get through. "Hampton, please chop enough so the horse can exit." She grabbed a saddle and reins and calmed the horse so she could place both on the animal.

"My Lady, you must leave but that horse is not safe. He is too afraid to take on a rider," he protested even as he struck the axe at the wall with all his might and broke several more boards. Evangeline whispered to the horse to calm it and allow her to mount it.

"Hampton, are you sure you can still take the Acadians to the underground network?"

"Yes, I promise I shall finish your mission. But I worry for you. The horse is skittish. It is too dangerous to ride."

"I have ridden since I was a small child. I shall be fine. Be well, and thank you." She quickly jumped onto the horse, led it out of the hole and rode around the side of the barn since the underbrush was too thick to ride through. She knew she would have to take a chance but this was her only way out.

Evangeline bent low and whispered into the horse's ear, "Take me to safety, boy. Take me away."

She kicked the horse, which took off. She started galloping down the road. But Martha Poundgate had been watching the side of the barn anticipating she might try to escape. She had her musket loaded. She aimed and fired. Bang!

Down went the horse after a direct hit to its leg. Fortunately, Evangeline was not trapped but was still on top of the animal. She climbed off and ran through the underbrush and into the woods. Martha screamed, "Come back here you strumpet! Rapscallion! Thief!"

Evangeline wore flat-footed boots and easily moved faster through serpentine vines and thick foliage than could Martha Poundgate. The poor woman traipsed slowly through the underbrush in her fashionable heels on which she had spent a substantial sum of her brother's fortune.

Elliott shouted out, "You heathen. I should have known youse weren't no countess. Youse is a heathen Frenchie."

The members of the Poundgate party gave their position away by their voices and their lantern lights, which sparkled like jewels in the night. After an hour, they were still chasing her. Evangeline heard the voices getting closer. How could that be? Had she just traveled in a circle? Their lantern lights had grown larger. She looked around. Should she climb a tree? She looked but there were no low-lying branches to help her hoist herself above. Besides, she would be an easy target if they looked up. That was not a good idea. Instead, she pushed forward, staying low in the underbrush.

Because Evangeline had lived with the Mi'Kmaqs and had learned their ways of living off the land or in a forest, she was confident in her ability to travel silently. She crept slowly through the brush, careful not to step on twigs or leaves that would reveal her position. Gradually, the lantern lights in the distance became smaller and smaller until they disappeared. By then, Evangeline was able to avoid the thick underbrush and run swiftly through the trees.

After a while, Evangeline found herself deep in the woods. Sitting for a moment on a fallen log, she felt a stinging on her arm. She looked down and saw she was bleeding. One of the musket balls had grazed her arm. She looked around at the plants and saw one that she recognized would make the "red river paste" that White Bird had taught her. She pulled the leaves and tore them apart to reveal a white paste. She spit in the white stuff and mixed it together, then lathered the concoction on her arm. Relief came immediately. She did not dare to sit for more than a moment as she kept her ears peeled for any sounds of the hunters chasing her.

She knew the Poundgates had carriages and could call for military reinforcements. How would she be able to stay ahead of them on foot if they brought hounds and horses? She knew the only way she would survive was to outsmart them.

*

Evangeline had decided not to venture into a town or village on her trek, as she presumed the influence and wealth of the Poundgates extended beyond the Massachusetts Bay Colony. She was not willing to risk buying food or clothes even with the money she had. Instead, she drew on the skills she had acquired from both the Acadians and Mi'Kmaqs she had known.

From Kitok, Evangeline had learned how to make traps for small animals and cook them with a minimal of visible smoke. He had also taught her how to use every part of the animal, including bones which made delicious soups. She silently thanked him when she caught a small rabbit and enjoyed a hearty stew that night and the next morning, which sustained her strength the entire day.

Christine had taught her to identify which plants were safe to eat and which were poisonous. Cutting a branch to make a digging stick, Evangeline discovered wild mushrooms, edible roots, leafy plants and small pools of water. Even when she caught no animals, she was able to nourish herself during her journey.

The difficulty Evangeline faced was not finding food but choosing a safe sleeping location. She did not wander too deep in forests and woods, though she was able to use them as cover. Instead, she selected thick foliage and bushes with underbrush that hid her from passersby on the nearby paths and roads, but did not expose her to wild animals roaming at night. During the day, she lit fires to cook the animals she had caught, then protected herself by covering herself with leaves and branches to stay hidden at night.

Weeks later, Evangeline found herself still walking overland trying to reach the Mississippi River. The rough terrain and harsh conditions did not deter her from her destination of New Orleans. But she knew not where the boundary was between the English Colonies and the French territory of Louisiana. After two months of crossing forested land and open fields, she reached mountainous territory. Realizing the temperatures would drop, even though it was spring weather at the base, she knew she would need warmer clothing. She noticed a small town in the valley below the woods where she had spent the night.

From her vantage point in the forest above the town, she observed the goings-on along the single main street. She saw no British militia or fort, so she decided to take the risk of a possible capture to buy the necessary food and supplies. There would be little food in the mountains except large animals which she was not trained to hunt, so she planned to spend some of her coins on foodstuffs before taking on the mountain.

Because she had lived in the mountains with the Mi'Kmaqs, she was not intimidated by natural ranges. She had learned to respect the beauty as well as the power of the majestic peaks rather than to fight them. The best way she knew to do that was to prepare herself with food, supplies, hunting equipment and tools.

Leaving the safety of the woods, she walked past the small, faded sign reading, "Virginia Colony" and entered what she saw was a small village. It offered little more than a dirt path between lean-tos, shacks and small buildings on either side of the street. She headed for the largest structure which had crates of goods stacked outside and a small sign reading,

"Supplies." Walking into the crowded building, she stepped up to the counter.

The proprietor greeted her skeptically. "Eh, missy, ain't seen you around here. New to town?"

"Good day, sir. I need to cross the mountains. Can you help me?"

He eyed her carefully, scrutinizing her disheveled appearance. He was doubtful she had the means to pay for even a cup of coffee, and, if that were the case, he did not want to waste his time. "Ye gots some coins to pay fer things yer need?"

She held up one of her gold coins. His eyes sparkled as much as his gold tooth when he grinned broadly. Grabbing the coin, he crowed, "Ye come to the right place. The right place, fer sure. What's yer order today, missy?"

"I shall need heavy clothing, weapons and equipment. And food stores as well."

"Fine, just fine. I got plenty left from my annual shipment of mountain gear. Had a big group of travelers here a month or two ago who bought some of it."

Evangeline was startled. "A month ago? Do you know who they were? Did they say where they were from?"

He stepped back when she peppered him with questions. "Whoa, missy. They was Frenchies headed to the port of New Orleans, is all they said. Didn't have much money but they got what they could pay fer and they got going."

"I am trying to catch up to them. Did you happen to hear any names?"

"Nary a one. But they met up with a guide. A native from one of them tribes. Spoke French too, he did," the clerk mumbled. He ambled over to shelves and cupboards and grabbed a travel bag, blankets, bearskins, wool sweaters, heavy gloves, a cloak, a wool cap, a pair of leather boots and other warm clothes that would serve Evangeline well in the higher altitudes.

Evangeline tried to elicit more information again. "Can you remember a name for the guide? Or the tribe?"

He shook his head. "Need hunting tools?" Without waiting for her response, he set out large and small axes, hunting knives, animal skinning tools, and a couple of muskets.

Evangeline shook her head. "No guns. I'll be fine without them."

He shrugged. "Suit yerself. Giving ye what I'd take for meself. Just make sure ye stay away from them bears. Got plenty up there. As fer food, how long ye gonna be up there?"

"How long do most people stay?"

He laughed. "Most people don't go up at all. Them mountains is not friendly. But trappers, they go for the winter. Get some bearskins and sell 'em for a sizeable profit. But ye ain't hunting bears, is ye?"

"I just need to get over the pass. How long will it take?"

"Month or two. I'll get ye the vittles and stuffs ye need." A thought occurred to him that he had overlooked. "Say, missy, where be yer man? Ye don't plan on going up there alone? Lots of folks get lost. Too many mountain trails leading to nowhere."

For the first time, she felt fearful. He had raised an issue she had never thought of before. She did not know the way and it could be very dangerous.

"Do you know a reliable guide for hire?"

He pointed to the stables at the end of the dusty main street. "Ask for William. Tell him George sent you. Ain't seen one in town fer some time but if anyone knows, he does. Where's yer cart? I'll load it up fer ye."

She shook her head. "No cart."

"Ye ain't got no cart? How do ye expect to get over them mountains on them trails up there? Ye need a cart."

"Where can I buy one?"

He pointed at the stables. "Same place. If he got one, he'll give ye a good price. But usually, he ain't got none."

She nodded and walked out of the store. George watched as she rushed down the street to the stables. "Is William here?"

"Who's asking?"

"George sent me. I am looking for a guide. And I will need some sort of small cart or wagon to take into the mountains. He thought you might have one."

He shook his head. "We get some Indian guides this way but nary a one in town now. Them is expert trackers and can find you a cave in a snowstorm. As for wagons, sold the last of 'em three months ago. Ain't got no new parts to build any new ones."

She was not ready to give up. "Perhaps you have an old one that could be repaired? Or one that is too small for most people? I just need something to get me over that mountain, even if it breaks down on the other side. And a horse, of course."

He stroked his beard and his eyes lit up. "Ye want a mule, not a horse. And that ain't no problem. Take yer pick. But a wagon? Ain't got none, except a buyer left an old one in back when he bought a new one. Never needed it so's I never took a gander at it. But if ye wants it, I can make ye a good price."

He took Evangeline out to inspect it. As she told him all of the things on the wagon that needed repairs, he was amazed at her knowledge of his craft. But he drove a hard bargain. She badgered him for a better price and he relented in the end, selling it for half of what he had originally asked. At that price, both parties were satisfied. He hooked the wagon up to the horse she bought and away she went.

She drove back to the store and George loaded all her supplies. As she drove off, he shook his head. "Women. They all gots to be fools. Whoever heard of a female crossing them mountains by her lonesome?"

*

Three weeks later, Evangeline found herself in a dire predicament. Her wagon wheel had broken, and of course, she had not thought to buy another. The skies had turned an ominous gray, foretelling a storm. She had to find shelter to ride out the weather.

She walked farther up the path looking for a cave in the rocks. It took her an hour's walk uphill, but she finally found one. She had made a small fire and lit some heavy branches to make torches. She knew they would only last a few hours, but she had to make certain the cave was empty. She entered slowly, cautiously, looking for tracks, droppings, any sign that animals had made this their home, or were still living there. No critters anywhere to be seen, and no signs that any had ever been there. She knew she was in luck. She stuck the torch in an opening in the wall hoping it would still be burning when she returned with her supplies.

For hours, she trekked her supplies uphill into the cave, then rushed back down for another load. She took everything from the wagon, then thought that she might need wood for a fire, especially if she had to hole up during a storm. She took the axe and started with the seat. Chopping it into manageable pieces that would burn well, she loaded it into one of the bags George had sold her and lugged it uphill. It was nearly dark, so she stopped for the night and built a fire at the entrance of the cave. She had to prevent any unwanted creatures from wandering in while she was sleeping.

She woke, freezing, and feeling like she had slept for days though it had only been a matter of hours. She sat up, relishing the warmth of the blankets and the bearskin. All that remained of the blazing fire was a pile of glowing embers dancing in the cave due to the winds whistling at the entrance. She wrapped herself in a blanket and the bearskin and lit another fire using the wagon wood.

Within minutes, she had built a fiery barrier at the entry of the cavern, with the bright glow illuminating the cave. She gazed into the flames and thought she saw an image of Gabriel with outstretched arms, pleading for her to join him in Louisiana. But her fatigue got the best of her and she curled up under the warm bearskin. Soon she fell asleep and dreamed of meeting Gabriel in New Orleans.

CHAPTER 78
Overland

Louisiana Territory

Climbing a steep hill, Kitok led two pack mules loaded with provisions, blankets and muskets he had bought from the Virginia Colony store owned by a man named George. He had also bought the mules from the local stables owner named William. Both men had made a pretty penny off his charges, the Jules Martel family of fifteen Acadian runaways.

At a turn in the mountain path, Kitok waited for the family as they slowly made their way towards him. He both admonished and encouraged them. "We rest at the next plateau. Keep going. Push harder. We must reach shelter before dark."

Hours later, it was nearly dusk before the group finally arrived on the flats on the mountain. Kitok had cleaned out a cave as their shelter for the night and Jules helped his family members settle in. They warmed themselves in front of the roaring fire where Kitok had cooked a feast of squirrels, cornbread and potatoes.

During the dinner, Jules asked Kitok, "Why do you work as a guide in this territory so far from your home?"

Kitok brushed a tear from his eye, and turned his gaze directly to the Acadian. "I was away from our Mi'Kmaq winter home in the mountains helping a very important Acadian escape the English military. She was the daughter of the French Consul. During my absence, English soldiers acted on a rumor that our family sheltered Acadians. We had helped many who escaped the Exile. Some stayed a while before leaving for Île Royale and New France, but many were still living with my family. The English commander sent a hunting party into the mountains and massacred my entire family and all of our Acadian friends. Not even a child was left alive."

Jules and his wife and thirteen children were awestruck. They could not imagine losing their family members to natural deaths. But to have everyone killed must have been devastating.

Jules spoke for his family, "Words cannot express our sorrow for you."

Kitok nodded, "My mission now is helping fugitive Acadians reach the Louisiana Territory. Like you. I am only one man, but the English will kill them – will kill you -- if I fail. I must not."

They finished their meal in silence, reflecting on the seriousness of Kitok's undertaking, especially in their case. The Martel family settled for the night under blankets and skins, each one thanking God that Kitok was helping them.

Kitok was not sleepy, so he squatted by the fire, feeding it more branches and twigs. When the flames rose and crackled in the otherwise dark cave, he stood and walked to the archway carved in the rock.

Raising his eyes to the sky, he looked at the stars and spoke in a soft whisper, "I shall avenge your death, my family, Sitting Fox, Running Bear, my brothers, all of you. I shall not rest until I deliver every Acadian from the reach of English troops."

*

Even as Kitok was helping the Martel family climb up through the pass, Evangeline was miles ahead in the same mountain range. She had not eaten in two days because she was unable to trap any animals. She had climbed too high in the mountains to find many plants that could provide nourishment. And the temperatures dropped so low at night that she feared moving forward with the uncertainty of shelter.

Evangeline had settled into a small cave carved into the rocks and had gathered every piece of wood, every branch and every twig she could find. She had tried to close off the entry with the largest branches to keep out the freezing wind and cold. She had run out of the food she had bought. With her cart long ago used for firewood, she could only travel on foot. The higher she went, the more biting the winds and the stronger the snow flurries. She knew she had a choice – stay where she was and risk a slow death by starvation, or trek forward and risk death by freezing at night or by a large animal attack at any time. Neither choice was acceptable.

She had no way of knowing that Kitok and the Acadian family he was guiding were at that very moment less than an hour's journey from her. All she could think of was keeping warm, staying alive and fighting to survive another day to her trek to meet Gabriel.

She felt a rush of cold air. She shivered, then turned around. She felt her bare neck, where the hairs were standing up. "Gabriel, is that you?" She looked around, but no one was there. She made a fire, and saw an image of Gabriel in the smoke. But when she reached out to it, the image disappeared.

When the wood died down to only burning embers, Evangeline curled up under her blankets and fell asleep.

*

Kitok had roused the Martel family and fed them a quick breakfast of corn cakes. He had already packed up their possessions on his pack of mules and they set out to reach the mountain peak.

Halfway there, the family members sat on large rocks along a ridge to catch their breath. Kitok surveyed the plateau seeking shelter and food. He spied a faint trail of smoke spilling from a cave at the far end of the ridge, which meant someone was in the cave. Eager to learn who was there, but wary that the English may have sent their hunting parties this far south of Massachusetts Bay Colony, Kitok furtively approached the cave. Without making a sound, he peered through the branches blocking the front entry and saw a figure move slightly, then collapse.

Evangeline saw a figure through the branches at the opening of the cave. She feared it might be an English soldier, but she was desperate for water and tried to get the attention of the stranger. Her mouth was so parched from lack of water that she mouthed the words but no sounds came out. She tried to push herself up to move closer to the entry, but she was in such a weakened state that she simply dropped back to the ground.

Kitok slashed at the branches with his knife until he made an opening large enough to push through them into the cave. He rushed up to the person lying on the ground near the dying fire. To his shock, he recognized Evangeline. He held up her head and poured water from his bota into her mouth. She was so weak, half the liquid spurted out all over her and Kitok.

She looked at him gratefully and whispered, "Kitok? Oh, thank heaven, my prayers are answered."

Kitok offered her more water. This time she drank several long sips greedily. He helped her to sit up, making certain she was otherwise alright. "I shall return with provisions and an Acadian family that I am guiding. We shall travel together now."

Evangeline nodded. Kitok sprinted back out through the branches. When he returned, he used his axe to chop down the obstruction at the cave's entry. The Martel family entered with wood, water and food. Jules' wife Nan stayed at Evangeline's side and served her food and water until she was strong enough to walk.

That evening, Evangeline felt well enough to sit by the cracking fire and share in a feast of venison that Kitok had caught. Laughing and sharing stories, she looked around the cave at the Acadians who felt hopeful about their future for the first time in years.

The next day, Kitok led the group to the peak, where they crammed together in a small cave through a snowstorm. When it cleared, they crossed the plateau and started down the other side. They found the downhill trek went much faster than their uphill hike.

As the days passed, Nan continued cared for Evangeline, and her health began to improve dramatically.

On one occasion, Kitok guided them to a mountain stream. The sky was clear and the sun was shining, and soon all the members of the Martel family were at the water's edge, drinking the cold water and filling their animal skin pouches for the days ahead.

Evangeline eschewed the water, instead heading for an outcropping overlooking the rock bed in the stream. Suddenly her foot slipped. She would have fallen onto the rocks had Kitok not been behind her. He supported her and was able to right her precarious stance so that she found her footing and reached the top of the ledge.

They stood and stared at the beautiful expanse of earth, sky and water. Evangeline broke the silence, saying, "Gabriel would love it here."

Kitok nodded. Neither saw a snake slither across the ledge and head toward Evangeline. Just then, the snake rattled. Kitok saw the viper and whispered, "Do not move. Your life depends on it."

Evangeline heard the rattle and whimpered, jerking involuntarily out of fear. The snake lunged and attacked. Its fangs broke through her layers of skirts and petticoats and sank deep into her leg.

Kitok sprang into action. He hacked the snake in half with his machete and pulled the head off Evangeline's leg. She turned white and began to breathe in gasps. He pulled up her skirts and ripped her petticoat to form a tourniquet that he tied above the fang marks. He then cut holes in her leg with his knife and sucked out the venom before he spit it out. He repeated the process time and again, watching Evangeline's face lose its color.

When Kitok had finished sucking out the poison, Evangeline was unconscious. He tried to breathe life into her from his mouth to hers, then listened to see if she was breathing on her own. After three attempts, he heard a faint heartbeat and slight, but regular, intakes and exhales of air.

She opened her eyes, "Tell Gabriel how much I wanted to be his wife. Tell him...." She shook her head, so filled with emotions was she. "...I love him," she finished.

He washed her bloody wound with water from his bota. Then he cleansed the poison from the fang marks on her leg. "Fear not, dear friend. You shall tell him yourself." He wrapped the wound in leaves that he pulled from a pouch tied to his waist, silently thanking White Bird for teaching him and the other braves how to prepare and use remedies from forest and mountain plants. Evangeline gasped for air, until he placed his hand on hers to calm her. Kitok spoke in a soothing voice, "You shall heal. Rest now. Sleep." She listened to him and closed her eyes. Soon she was fast asleep.

CHAPTER 79
Masks

New Orleans, Louisiana Territory

After Evangeline recovered from the snake bite, she and the Martel family trudged down the mountain until they reached the bottom, where a valley stretched before them as far as the eye could see. Kitok led them to an abandoned hunter's cabin where they rested for a week, but he would not let them stay longer. He had to keep them moving, so they trudged across the plain until each was about to reach the point of exhaustion. The next day, Kitok led them to an earthen embankment. When they climbed to the top, they saw a raging waterway below.

"We have reached the lower part of the Mississippi River. We follow the River and it leads to the port of New Orleans."

The Martel family and Evangeline shouted for joy, and praised Kitok for pushing them to continue. They knew they still had a way to go to their destination, but they knew they were getting closer every day. Everyone felt a renewed spirit and made great progress trekking on top of the levee. Their only view was the muddy water below and trees on the other side of the bank, but they continued to walk forward.

One day, a young Martel boy cried out, "I see it. I see the town." He and his siblings dashed ahead to the edge of the levee before the adults joined them. They were in awe of the hustle and bustle of the port and the grand riverfront city.

Jules Martel exclaimed, "How can we ever repay you, Kitok? You have given my family the opportunity to have a new life, safe from the English."

Kitok brushed them off, "Your freedom is my reward."

Still, Martel placed a pouch of coins in Kitok's hands. "I insist. Please do not insult me by refusing." Kitok understood the significance of the gift and he humbly accepted it. The Martels gathered their children and departed down the levee road towards the city below.

Evangeline waited until they had left before turning to Kitok. "Will you not stay? Gabriel would want to see you."

Kitok shook his head, "I have done what I promised him. I brought you safely here. It is your destiny to find him. I know you shall."

They stood without speaking until she commented, "We shall not meet again, shall we?"

He shook his head and replied, "You are already but a dream to me."

True to Evangeline's prediction, that was the last time they ever saw each other. Kitok helped hundreds more Acadians fugitives flee the British Colonies on the overland trail to Louisiana. But a month before the treaty was signed ending the Seven Years War between England and France in 1763, Kitok was caught by British troops and executed as a spy.

*

From the port of New Orleans, Gabriel walked to the Square in front of the Cathedral. Entering the open expanse, he was surrounded by carpenters and workers buzzing around him as they made preparations for a grand celebration. Gabriel hailed a builder working on a large bandstand and dance floor. "Sir, can you tell me what festivities are to be celebrated here?"

The worker grinned, showing his missing front teeth. "They say France turned us over to Spain, so the Spanish King rules us now. All me family cares about is the grand fireworks to be lit up." He returned to his work and banged his hammer, nailing the legs of the platform for the band. Gabriel nodded his thanks and walked past a central stage decorated with French and Spanish flags. A painter stood back to admire his work. His freshly-painted sign read, *"MASKED BALL FRIDAY NIGHT HONORING SPANISH ACQUISITION OF LUISIANA. FIREWORKS FOR ALL."*

Gabriel continued walking and entered the St. Louis Cathedral, which had been named for the French King Louis IX. He lit a candle near the altar, raised his eyes heavenward and whispered his prayer aloud. "Dear Lord, I can feel that Evangeline is near. Please lead me to her."

*

At dawn, Christine dashed from her Acadian Tearoom to the open-air market near the Mississippi River. On her arm, she carried a large wicker hamper and arrived as vendors were setting up their carts and stalls.

She always went early, a woman on a mission searching for the best ingredients for the day's menu. Pondering the dishes she planned to serve, she picked fresh peppers, okra, tomatoes and corn from farmers' carts. She promenaded by the boats at the wharf and pored over the fishermen's chests displaying fresh fish, shrimp and crabs. She easily could have filled her basket just with the seafood but she decided to buy only shrimp for her gumbo. Then she stopped by her favorite bakery and selected freshly-baked bread and cakes that she would serve in the Tearoom.

Once she had filled her hamper with everything she needed, Christine turned and made her way back through the now-crowded market. She spent a few hours each morning looking at new offerings to make certain she did not miss any unique items for her patrons. Then, she scurried down a side street away from the River where the fresh flower sellers always set out their bouquets. She had made it a practice to decorate each table in the Tearoom with a small glass vase filled with a single rose. She selected an armful of beautiful red roses and, with that, Christine had finished her shopping.

She walked into the Square, looking straight ahead as she hurried toward her restaurant. Gabriel exited the Cathedral just as she walked past. He called out, "Christine de Castille? Can that be you?"

She stopped in mid-stride, turned and recognized him immediately. She rushed to hug him with all her might. "Gabriel? How is it possible? You were sent to Westminster Gatehouse. We thought you were...." Christine stopped short of saying what was on her mind, but Gabriel understood.

He offered his arm to her and she wrapped her arm in his. "That is a tale that shall take some time."

She said, "I know just the place," as she led him toward the Tearoom.

*

In the hold of the ship, René tried to open the lid of the box he was in, but it was stuck. In actuality, boxes were stacked-high above the box, as Swillingham had demanded. The crew sweated as they lugged the boxes up to the deck. Pine Gaudet, a deck hand, stopped to take a breather. He was jostled by a heavyset crew member at the edge of the boat and nearly fell overboard but was nimble enough to grab the ropes and swing back onto the deck. The other crew members applauded him and patted him on the back. He was one of them. He loved his job, but he missed seeing his sister. He planned to surprise her later today, not having written in advance.

The goods that Swillingham bought in the Colonies would be snatched up at record prices by merchants and wealthy French families alike, despite the war. When it came to women getting the things they wanted, they were not going to let a little war stop them from having frilly things, hats with feathers, and bolts of satins and silks that their seamstresses could turn into head-turning gowns for the many balls and parties held in the city.

When the Captain climbed down into the hold, it was empty but for the storage boxes that his favorite carpenter, Raymond Cozzen, had built. Swillingham opened the hatch of the box where René was. He handed him a jug of grog and a huge chunk of cheese. René took a swig and downed the cheese. He had eaten the last of his foodstuffs the day before, but it had taken the crew extra time to empty out all the additional cargo they carried.

When René stepped out of the box, he coughed and was hoarse. His throat was sore and red and he was coming down with a fever. "Thank you, Captain. I shall send payment to you once I obtain the King's coin for my services to the Acadians."

Swillingham remarked, "I'm easy to find. The port master knows me. I took on some Acadians as sailors. Good lads they are, too. I remember an Acadian lady sailed here several years ago from Santo Domingo."

René's ears perked up. "Do you remember her name?"

Swillingham shook his beard and the food particles sprayed all over. "From time to time I drop in to see her. She owns a Tearoom, a a meeting place of sorts. Caters to Acadians. You might know some that congregate there."

"I shall. Thank you again, Captain." René waved to him as he disembarked. At the bottom of the wharf, he remembered to ask, "Where did you say that meeting room was?"

Swillingham said, "Rue Conti or thereabouts. Can't miss it. The owner lady has flaming red hair. Everybody knows the place."

René could not believe his ears. A lady with red hair? An Acadian who was exiled? Could it be possible? He hoped against hope that the woman Swillingham described was his Christine. He ran as fast as he could off the wharf and through the port area to the main street.

He stopped in a shop near the Square in front of the Cathedral and asked the clerk, "Could you tell me how to get to rue Conti?" The man happily pointed out the street which was not far away.

When René turned the corner onto the street, he saw the welcoming sign, "Acadian Tearoom." His heart was beating madly as he pushed the door open and the bell tinkled, letting the owner know a patron had entered.

*

Jeanne stepped out onto the deck of the ship that arrived from Bostontown and looked down at the bustling port. She pinched herself. She really was in New Orleans! She hoped she would soon find Marc and become his wife, as he promised to meet her here. Carrying the travel bag Cornhandle had given her, she approached the sailor verifying the passengers who disembarked. He did not even look up at her. "Name?"

She was flustered but responded, "Jeanne Lambert."

He scratched off her name on his paper and called out, "Next!"

But Jeanne could not be brushed off so quickly and asked, "Sir?"

He ignored her, motioning to the man behind her. She tapped his shoulder. "Sir?" Finally, the sailor looked up, feeling harried. "What do you want? You are no longer on my passenger list. Descend the gangplank."

"I simply want to know where a young woman can find lodging here."

He shrugged his shoulders, "Do I look like I own a hotel? But I did hear something about a convent near the big cathedral."

She asked, "What cathedral?"

He pointed to the tall church steeple not far from the wharf, then impatiently pointed to the next person in line, "Sir? Your name?"

"Thank you," Jeanne called out as she ran down the plank to the wharf, dodging carts, workers and hawkers selling food and useful items to new colonists and visitors at the port. It did not take Jeanne long to reach the St. Louis Cathedral and speak to Father Poirson. He gave precise directions to the Ursuline nunnery. Jeanne rang the bell, and nearly fainted when the gate was opened by none other than her friend from Grand Pré, Béatrice Gaudet.

"Béatrice! Or do I call you Sister?"

Béatrice exclaimed at the same time, "Jeanne! How happy I am to see you alive and well." The two women hugged, but even before they separated, Béatrice asked, "Please tell me my mother arrived with you."

Jeanne lowered her eyes, "I am so sorry, dear. So very sorry."

Béatrice nodded as her eyes flooded with tears. "I prayed so hard we would meet here. My poor mother. Pine will be devastated."

"I did not know Pine was here. How wonderful for you. Where is he?"

Béatrice said, "He hired on a merchant ship for a Captain Swillingham. We see each other every year or two. It was Evangeline who rescued him and my uncle Bertrand, too, who works at the docks now."

At hearing her friend's name, Jeanne shrieked, "Evangeline?" Nothing could not have shocked her more. "Evangeline is alive? Is she here?"

Béatrice laughed softly. "Shall we talk over a cup of tea? If you aren't too tired, I know the perfect place. Do you remember Christine de Castille?

Jeanne gasped, "Is she here, too?"

Béatrice invited Jeanne to step inside the convent. "I must ask permission to take you to the Acadian Tearoom." Béatrice slipped away and did not hear Jeanne's question, "What is the Acadian Tearoom?"

*

In the Tearoom, Christine was in the midst of preparing lunch for her patrons and did not look up when the bell on the door sounded. René stood there, gazing at her beautiful smile, her ravishing red hair, her flour-covered hands kneading dough for beignets. He walked slowly up to her.

Without looking up, she asked, "What would you like today?"

He knelt as he spoke, "Your heart, Christine. Marry me. Today. Let us go to the church this instant. I cannot live one more minute without you."

Christine stared at him in shock, dropping the dough she was preparing, and rushed into his arms, sobbing. He whispered to her, "If you need more time, of course I can wait. I shall wait for you forever."

She pulled apart from him and said, "More time? I need no more time. These are tears of joy. I have waited so long to be your wife. Yes, oh yes!"

They embraced sweetly at first, then passionately. Christine introduced him to the patrons, "Meet Lord René Le Blanc de Verdure, Royal Consul to His Majesty. We are getting married today! I must close now. I hope you understand." The customers applauded loudly and piled out.

René called to the patrons, "Who shall loan me a wedding band?"

One customer pulled her band off her hand. "Do not let Christine out of your sight. She is a true gem. She helps anyone who needs it."

Christine closed the Tearoom for the rest of the day and she and René were wed in the Cathedral by Father Poirson. After René kissed his new bride, he took her shopping. First, they walked to the private bank on rue Royale. The bank manager accepted his title as Royal Consul to King Louis XV and advanced a substantial sum. The banker also arranged to send a sizeable sum to a Mrs. Frederick (Margaret) Cozzen in Philadelphia.

Then René bought Christine an emerald wedding ring to replace the borrowed band. At his request, Christine selected a red petticoat for Margaret and he bought a pipe for Frederick that the shopkeepers dispatched by courier to Captain Swillingham's ship. René hoped the gifts would show Margaret how much he appreciated the freedom she had given him.

The newlyweds returned to the empty Tearoom and made their way upstairs into Christine's quarters. There, they consummated their love with a passion that had burned for years and would endure for many more.

When Christine opened the Tearoom the next day, Gabriel was waiting. Gabriel and René embraced and exchanged stories of how they fled the Exile. Then they studied Christine's lists of missing and deceased Acadians, searching for Evangeline's name.

Gabriel asked, "Where is Evangeline? Have you any news of her? I had the strangest sensation that I saw her in a fine carriage near a plantation outside Bostontown. Could it be possible she is living in a British Colony?"

Christine said, "I thought it odd that no one had seen Evangeline despite hundreds of Acadians arriving here daily. Then some Acadians sold in Bostontown said she was disguised as an English Countess and helped them escape. Since then, no one has seen her. She has simply disappeared."

Christine and René smiled encouragingly. René said, "Have faith. She will be here." He dipped a quill in the ink pot and added "Alive. In New Orleans" to his name on the "Missing" list. He wrote on the death list the names of the men on his ship who had died and said a silent prayer for each.

Gabriel sat opposite René and scratched his name off the "Missing" list, wrote the names on the death list of those who had died in Westminster Gatehouse prison, and noted by Marc's name, "En route to New Orleans." Gabriel had trusted his instincts to save his life, but he also knew Evangeline was resourceful. He insisted, "I did see her! I knew it. We promised to meet each other here. If she is not already in the city, I know in my heart she will arrive before long."

Christine nodded. "Nothing would please me more than to see the two of you finally married. In fact, I have her beautiful wedding dress. I could not leave it in Grand Pré, so I took it with me and have kept it all this time. I pray she shall wear it at your wedding."

Gabriel nodded slowly, "I should go. Perhaps she is outside the city and needs my help."

"You don't intend to leave when the biggest event in the city shall occur tomorrow night? You must attend the masked ball. Everyone shall be there."

He shook his head. "I should keep looking for her."

Christine urged, "You cannot do so at night. Especially not at the celebration. It will be difficult to move around as the city has planned to have music and dancing in the streets. They will be filled with masked dancers and costumed revelers."

Gabriel relented a bit, "Perhaps I shall attend after all."

"It is an opportunity to meet Acadians who survived and live here."

He replied thoughtfully, "They may have news of Evangeline. You have convinced me. I shall meet you and the Consul there. Thank you."

Christine added, "Could you can return this afternoon? I want you to meet another Acadian you know. Shall we say four o'clock?"

Gabriel nodded and left the Tearoom. Christine returned to serving her patrons, as René made the rounds among the tables. Everyone from Grand Pré reminisced with their Consul. The Acadians from other areas knew René by reputation and clamored to meet him. Christine rushed to the door when she saw Jeanne and Béatrice walk in.

After a tearful reunion, Christine expressed her condolences to Béatrice on the loss of her mother and shared tea and beignets over their news.

Jeanne held her breath as she reviewed the lists of dead Acadians. She saw her parents' names, but not Marc's. She said a silent prayer. Then she read the note about Marc and screamed, "Marc is on his way! He is alive!"

Béatrice congratulated her, then dipped a quill in ink and sadly added "Anne Gaudet, Bostontown (d 1756)" to the list of the deceased.

Christine asked, "I was about to send you a message, Béatrice. Could you return about four to meet a special visitor?"

Béatrice agreed, then she and Jeanne left the Tearoom for the convent. Mother Superior installed Jeanne in a cell where she promptly fell asleep.

When Béatrice returned to the Tearoom, Gabriel was waiting to meet the unknown Acadian. Béatrice hugged him, which startled him. He did not recognize the young woman. She exclaimed, "Gabriel, how do you not recognize me? Béatrice Gaudet from Grand Pré."

Gabriel laughed, "How could I? When I saw you last, you were but a child. Look at you now. Quite the young lady."

She nodded and said solemnly, "Many of us had to grow up quickly or perish. No child should have to endure what we did."

Christine ushered them to a table and they shared their stories and talked of their friends whom they lost. They left at dusk and Gabriel offered, "May I escort you home?"

Béatrice smiled. He looked as handsome as ever. Perhaps even moreso with a new ruggedness he had about him. "It is not far. This way."

At the Ursuline gate, he was surprised, "I had no idea you were a nun."

Béatrice laughed, "I'm not. At least, not yet. Would you join me tomorrow for luncheon? A picnic in the park? I should like to speak with you about something important."

He laughed, "A possible nun and an exiled militia leader. You have ignited my curiosity. I shall be here at noon tomorrow." Sister Catherine made her way to the locked gate and let Béatrice enter before closing it again. Gabriel watched them until they disappeared in the convent.

*

After leaving Kitok, an exhausted Evangeline had slept in a tree trunk that had fallen and had been gouged out by the elements. The next morning, she ate some roots and plants before she trudged down the levee road to a ridge overlooking a park. Needing a respite, Evangeline wrapped her cloak around her and sat on a large rock. Looking down, she noticed a couple enjoying a picnic. Seeing their happiness brought memories flooding back of happier times when Gabriel took her on such outings.

Watching the man and young woman, she vividly pictured herself with the man she loved. So vividly that she thought the man she observed was Gabriel. Were her eyes playing tricks on her? Could it be possible that the man in the park was the man she was in love with? She considered it in her confusion. Yes, it was possible. After all, he had led a group of Acadians overland to Louisiana. And he had promised to meet her in New Orleans.

It took a moment for Evangeline to realize she was not dreaming. She was watching Gabriel laughing and talking with a woman in the park. Overjoyed, she nearly called out his name until she saw Gabriel kiss the woman's hand. Her fiancé was polite and she considered it a respectful gesture. But she stifled a scream when the young woman kissed his cheek, a personal liberty that a mere friend would not take. A ray of sunlight shone on the ring the woman wore. A wedding ring? Had the love of her life married another? Did he believe she died when Captain Turnbull shot her?

Dejected and utterly defeated, Evangeline fought back tears. She did not want to believe he had betrayed her. Finally, she let go and cried so hard her body ached, trying to release the love she had felt for him for years. The fire in her heart had never waned. Now, she was in the same city as he was at the same time. Why had he not waited for her? As the questions raced through her mind, she decided she would leave New Orleans and return to France. She would ask Madame de Pompadour and, perhaps even His Majesty, to convince her uncle to accept her as family. But she needed lodging till then.

Evangeline took one last look at the couple enjoying their picnic lunch, who were unaware that she was on the ridge. She trekked down the road into the city and headed for the Cathedral with the tall spire she had seen.

Gabriel and Béatrice chatted, ignoring strolling passers-by. She was so animated that he admitted, "You remind me of Evangeline so. When she was your age, she was very much like you."

They laughed, reminiscing about their life in Grand Pré and how they first met. Béatrice reminded him, "You bought all of my posies for Evangeline's birthday. Remember?"

"Of course. And I paid you extra to keep my identity a secret."

Their eyes met and they sat there for a long moment. He broke their gaze by looking at the gold band on her hand. She merely smiled and asked, "You are going to the masked ball tonight, are you not? I hear it shall be wondrous. Imagine all those ladies in their finery meeting their gentlemen and swirling the night away."

He replied, "I do not feel at all like dancing. I have not yet found Evangeline."

She asked, "Please join me, join us, in the Square. Most of the Acadians in town are going. The Governor promises music, dancing and even fireworks. Mother Superior has given me permission to attend the events this evening and later tonight. It might be the last time I am able to dance."

"Have you made your decision about joining the convent?"

"I shall after tonight. That is why it is a momentous occasion for me."

"But the ring," he queried, "Why do you wear it?"

"The Mother Superior in France gave it to those of us who traveled from Paris to the Order here. It gave me extra security, especially after the Exile, and I asked Mother to keep it until I make my final decision."

Gabriel nodded in understanding. "It must have been so much more difficult for the women in the Exile. At least the men could try to escape and, if not, had only to work in the fields."

Béatrice tried to close the subject gently. "We did what we had to do, and many of us survived in that way. So, shall you escort me to the event?"

Gabriel smiled, "I am grateful for the invitation from you and Christine. The Exile has bonded all of us in a complicated but valuable way for the rest of our lives. We should be with each other as often as we can. Moreover, I cannot explain my feeling that something momentous shall happen tonight. So it is settled." Gabriel kissed her hand as they packed up and walked off.

*

"Thank you, Father," Evangeline told the priest in the rectory of the Cathedral who had given her directions to the place she sought. She slipped the hood over her head and held her black cloak tightly about her. She reached under the cloak to her pouch of gold coins. It had been her security and had enabled her to help many Acadians escape. She wondered how the Acadians who had not been as fortunate were able to start their lives anew.

Turning the corner and walking several blocks in the biting winter winds, Evangeline finally reached her destination. She gazed at the austere building of stucco-covered brick, with an arched entry door and its second-floor dormers, through which a winding staircase could be seen. The entire building was surrounded by a black iron fence, which made the structure appear forbidding, yet a small sign reading, "Ursuline Order" seemed to welcome her.

Ringing the bell at the gate, Evangeline shivered, not only because of the cold but because she knew she had no future in New Orleans. When Sister Catherine walked up to the gate, Evangeline asked, "May I speak with your Mother Superior? Father Poirson at the Cathedral sent me."

The nun replied, "Who is calling on her?"

"Lady Evangeline Le Blanc de Verdure, of Nova Scotia and France."

"This way, my Lady." She opened the gate for Evangeline, then locked it behind her and led Evangeline into the building. On the landing, the wind blew the hood off her hair. For a slight moment, she turned to look back at the gate. A man who looked like Gabriel was walking up. But Evangeline knew he would have no reason to be at a nunnery. Sister Catherine led Evangeline upstairs to Mother Superior's office and introduced her.

Then Sister Catherine returned to the gate and met Gabriel, who greeted her, "Good evening. I am to escort Béatrice Gaudet to the celebration."

Béatrice bounded out from the back kitchen, wearing a dark cloak. "Thank you, Sister. You must taste the new dish that Sister Therese is cooking. Delicious."

The nun reminded her, "Tonight is an exception to your curfew, so do not be late. Mother shall refuse you any other requests if you do."

"I was granted permission to stay until the fireworks are over. After all, how many times does Louisiana change governments?"

Béatrice asked Christine and René, "Shall you join us for fireworks?"

Christine shook her head. "We are enjoying our honeymoon at last."

René echoed her sentiments, "Thank you, but enjoy the celebration."

Gabriel and Béatrice put on their masks and meandered over to the Square. Crowds had already gathered for the occasion. Béatrice waved to her friends, and Gabriel followed her to meet up with them.

Evangeline, her hood covering her head, rushed past Gabriel and Béatrice. Seeing them together again, she wiped a tear from her eyes as she passed them by and headed away from the Square.

Christine heard the bell ring in the Tearoom below. She looked below from the window but did not recognize the woman in the cape. Rushing downstairs, she was shocked. Evangeline fell into her arms, sobbing.

"Mother Superior told me you were here. May I stay here tonight?"

"Of course, my dearest Evangeline. For as long as you like."

Christine led her up the stairs where René was waiting. Evangeline rushed into his arms. "Papa. Papa, I missed you so."

René embraced his daughter tightly and said, "My prayer was granted. You are safe. You are here. And now you have a step-mother."

Evangeline turned to Christine and hugged her. "I am so pleased. You both deserve each other. Both so wonderful. Both so loving."

Christine said, "Gabriel was here earlier updating the Acadian lists. Have you seen him?"

"I did but he has chosen another. I have seen him twice with another woman. A young, pretty woman who looks familiar but I cannot name her."

Christine shook her head, "No, dear. Since he arrived, he has only spoken of you. He has scoured every street and lodging searching for you."

"Gabriel is not married? But who is the woman he was with?"

"If my dearest husband agrees, we shall escort you to the Square. You shall see Gabriel is with a group of Acadians from Grand Pré."

René smiled and kissed Christine. "I would not have it any other way, darling wife."

Evangeline looked at her tattered clothes. "But what shall I wear?"

Christine said, "It is a masked ball. And you shall be the belle. I have an idea. Come with me." She led Evangeline into the bedroom as René waited.

*

On the stage in the Square opposite the Cathedral, a small orchestra of musicians played the final notes of a song. Couples danced a lively jig. displaying elaborate costumes and unusual masks. They were as spectacular as Venetian art, made in intricate designs. Many featured feathers, jewels, wigs and flowers. One was even designed to recreate the fountains of Versailles Palace.

When the music stopped, the crowd moved back from the stage, giving way to two small delegations of officials who walked through the costumed revelers. Flag-bearers proudly carried the French and Spanish flags ahead of each small group of men. The head of the French delegation, the French Governor Charles Phillippe Aubry, spoke first.

"Fellow citizens of Louisiana and friends in the City of New Orleans, we are at an important crossroads. Spain, France and England signed the

Treaty of Fontainebleau which transferred the territory of Louisiana from France to Spain. We are grateful to the Spanish monarch for not only providing transports for our Acadians to New Orleans, but also for providing them with free land, tools, cattle and starter seeds for their fields." He continued, "And now, I hereby turn over the city of New Orleans and the territory of Louisiana to Spain and its first Governor, Antonio de Ulloa."

The reaction from the crowd was mixed. While loud applause was heard, intermittent cries of, "Spanish interlopers!" and "Go back to Spain," could be heard above the din as the mustachioed Spaniard accepted the keys to the City and a large proclamation.

"It is my honor to accept on behalf of His Majesty Carlos of Spain. I look forward to ruling Louisiana kindly. Let the fireworks begin."

The Governor motioned for the fireworks to start. The sights and sounds of the bright lights bursting into many colors in the sky subdued the dissent. Unbeknownst to the revelers, armed Spanish soldiers in masks and costumes had been moving throughout the crowd, arresting the protesters.

Dozens of wine stewards poured wine from large oak barrels and distributed glasses of wine to the cheering throng. Following the sounds of the music, masked couples made their way into the section of the Square that had been roped-off for dancing. An orchestra played a lively tune where couples danced in a line and then with their partners.

When the music ended, the couples applauded the musicians and then milled about the Square as they awaited the next dance or speculated on the identity of other masked people. The excitement was so great that perfect strangers danced with each other to celebrate the occasion.

The musicians started playing again and vendors walked throughout the crowd hawking cheap masks and dark capes. Gabriel tried to make his way from the stage to the other side of the Square. However, a lady in a dark blue cape trapped him into dancing with her. He was too polite to refuse, but when the music ended, he bowed and walked off to meet the Acadians.

Christine and René arrived with Evangeline. Christine instructed her, "Stand here, away from the crowd. Gabriel must walk this way to get home. He shall not miss seeing you. We must return to the Tearoom to prepare food for tomorrow and host a wedding reception for two Acadians from Cobequid who found each other at my shop. Good night, my dear." Christine and René each embraced Evangeline before they left.

Finally, Gabriel started again to make his way through a sea of costumed dancers in the Square to the other side which was the direction of his lodgings. As he did so, he was stunned by the sight of a young woman in spectacular white finery resembling a wedding dress. She wore a white lace and feather mask that hid her eyes but allowed him to drink in the vision of her beautiful face.

Gabriel was enchanted at the sight of her, yet he felt guilty. He was undeniably committed to his love, yet the woman he saw somehow reminded him of Evangeline. He had to meet the mysterious woman. Gabriel bowed to her, "Mademoiselle, would you honor me with a dance?

Evangeline nodded without a word and followed him into the crowd of dancers. The musicians played a waltz, and Gabriel held Evangeline firmly yet respectfully as he expertly whirled her through the crowd. "May I have your name, Mademoiselle?"

Evangeline shook her head as if she were shy. She did not want to give herself away. She wanted him to recognize her on his own.

Gabriel tried again, "I am new to the city. Have I met you before? You seem familiar, yet I am at a disadvantage. I cannot recognize you under your delightful mask."

Evangeline shook her head. Gabriel continued, "Dancing with you takes me back to the last time I danced. It was with a young woman that I...." He stopped in mid-sentence. Did Evangeline image it or did Gabriel wipe a tear from his eye underneath his mask?

Evangeline wanted to prolong her secret and hear Gabriel express his feelings about her. But a young masked woman glided by on the arm of a tall masked dancer. Evangeline thought it could be Béatrice, though she seemed much more poised and restrained than the girl she knew back in Grand Pré. The young woman waved to Gabriel, "Hello, my friend."

The masked man released his hold on Béatrice, bowed and cut in on Gabriel, asking Evangeline, "May I, Mademoiselle?" By custom, Gabriel bowed and relinquished Evangeline to the man before she could say a word. She turned to see the woman and Gabriel dance in the opposite direction.

Béatrice was amused. "You seem to be enjoying yourself."

Gabriel turned to look at Evangeline, who quickly disappeared into the crowd. "Being with that young woman brought back so many memories of dancing with Evangeline. Remember her birthday? And the Church dance?"

"Those were happy times, but seem so long ago. When I watched you and Evangeline then, I knew you were both deeply in love with each other."

Gabriel thought he saw the woman in white on the opposite side of the dance floor. She looked ethereal, and for a moment he was convinced it was Evangeline. He turned to Béatrice, "Please excuse me for one moment. I shall return."

Gabriel made his way through the revelers to the other end of the Square but the woman was gone. Dejected, he walked the dance floor looking at every woman to see if he could find the mysterious beauty again, but she had vanished.

He returned and offered his arm to Béatrice, then walked with her to the convent gate and stayed until Sister Catherine unlocked it.

Béatrice imagined she knew what he was thinking and tried to make him feel better. "She looked so much like Evangeline, I almost called out her name. You shall find her, Gabriel. And you shall marry and have many children and grow old together. I feel it. And I pray every day that you do."

She started to leave as Sister Catherine locked the iron gate. But Béatrice remembered something and turned to Gabriel. She reached around her neck, pulling off Evangeline's chain and locket. Handing it to Gabriel through the bars of the iron fence, she said, "My mother found this on the Grand Pré beach."

He looked at it ruefully, "I must believe I shall find her. I promised her." He walked away from the convent and heard music and laughter in the Square. Foregoing the celebration, he slipped into the Cathedral.

Despite the revelry in the Square, the church was quiet and peaceful. Gabriel knelt on the prie-dieu and bowed his head, praying fervently, "Please, Lord, please send my Evangeline to me. I have done what You have asked. If this is Your will, please answer my prayer."

He rose and walked toward the big oak doors. To his amazement, entering the Cathedral was the mysterious figure in white. She stood unmoving at the door, the feather mask still covering her eyes. At first, he believed she was an apparition. But then he knew. He knew before she took off her mask. He ran toward her and shouted her name, "Evangeline!" He had nearly reached her when Evangeline tore off her mask.

She stood trembling as tears streamed down her cheeks. She whispered as if she spoke it aloud, it would not be true, "Gabriel, my love!"

He rushed up to her and embraced her tenderly. She hugged him tightly and their passionate embrace ended years of longing, searching, waiting.

He finally released her and looked into her eyes, "You are my love. You have been my only love. I have finally found you and I promise you, I shall never let you go."

She cried through her tears, "You are the answer to my prayers. We shall never part as long as we shall live."

Gabriel placed the chain with the locket around her neck. She opened it and looked at his portrait and hers and smiled up at him. Gabriel took both of her hands and kissed them tenderly, then he embraced her again with passion.

CHAPTER 80
Bells

France * Louisiana

King Louis XV called his couriers into his chamber. He was seated at a small dining table and had his scribes prepare rolled parchment orders for the men. "Travel to the four corners of France and call all nobles to Versailles within the month. This war must stop. It has gone on nearly seven long years. We shall devise a solution to end the madness."

Within a few weeks, posh carriages and ornate coaches began to arrive at the Palace. Hordes of assistants, aides, dressers, coachmen, hair stylists, tailors and the like followed their nobles in ordinary wagons. Versailles became a hive of activity as the nobility descended upon the Palace.

When all the noble families were represented and the various branches of the King's royal relatives were present, Louis' first announcement at Court was to appoint his chief negotiator.

"We name Mazarini, Duke of Nivernais, as our chief negotiator to the London peace talks. They have been arranged for five weeks hence. Until then, none of you shall dance, or hunt, or gorge yourself with food and wine, or play cards, or flirt, or even sleep. You were called to do your duty to your King. Provide specific points to put into a peace proposal to present to George of England. Once that is determined, then we shall allow you a respite and hold a spectacular banquet with fireworks to celebrate our plan."

The nobility and the royals in the King's presence knew better than to do anything except clap loudly and continuously until the King took his leave. When he had gone, Nivernais called the heads of the families to an enormous round table in one wing of the Palace. Once they were seated, Nivernais presented a long list of grievances that France had with England.

Over the next two weeks, the nobles worked, discussed, argued, shouted over each other and tried to work out compromises. So that they did not leave, the Duke had ordered a never-ending supply of food and wine. A plethora of servants scurried to and fro refilling plates and goblets for all in the midst of the negotiations. If the King's representatives from all parts of the kingdom could agree on a reasonable plan to end the war, then Louis reasoned he would be able to convince King George to accept it.

Finally, the peace plan was presented to the King. "Your Majesty, we believe this is the proposal that England will accept."

The King perused the plan before responding. "Why should we have to give up all our interests in the north of the New World? Quebec is very important to our expansion there."

Nivernais disagreed. "Majesty, we have Louisiana in the south, with rich lands surrounding an important waterway. We can afford to give up Quebec, but we must have big bait to hook the big fish that is England."

The King relented. "You have our blessing to represent us at the talks." The Duke bowed and backed out of the room with his personal secretary, Alexandre Robert d'Hilaire de la Rochette.

Nivernais and de la Rochette, joined by several French noblemen and a delegation of the Royal Guard, left Le Havre and arrived in England on New Year's Eve 1762. The weather cooperated with their plan to arrive several weeks in advance of the meeting with the George's negotiators.

The Duke sent Rochette to speak with the Acadian exiles. He traveled to the town of Liverpool and inspected the poor houses and work houses in which hundreds of exiles had been dumped seven years earlier. "Our King has promised to resettle you anywhere in his realm if you leave once we have a peace treaty signed," said Rochette.

The self-proclaimed Acadian leader, Luc Hébert, responded. "We shall be more than pleased to be relocated anywhere that His Royal Majesty desires." The Acadians proceeded to cheer and clap with such an outpouring of joy that the British guards at the houses were scandalized.

*

Mother Superior waved Béatrice into her office. "Come in, come in, child. It is time to talk about your intentions with our Order."

"Yes, Mother," Béatrice said dutifully.

"You know we are an order of poverty. On entering, we give all of our possessions to the poor."

Béatrice hid her hand in her pocket. The ring on her finger suddenly felt as if it were burning her flesh. She could not give it up. That little piece of gold, simple as it was, had carried her from Paris to Louisiana. It gave her the security she wanted to feel for the rest of her life. "Everything?"

"We cut our hair. We give all of our clothes to the poor. Except shoes. With the war against England, leather is difficult to procure for shoes."

"Mother, may I have some water, please?"

The old nun answered, "Of course, child."

As the nun turned away, Béatrice hid the ring in her shoe. She took the cup gratefully and sipped it slowly to give her time to think. What was she going to do?

Mother Superior dismissed her, saying, "Pray about your decision, child and we shall talk again soon."

Béatrice nodded, and walked into the dining hall. She struck up a conversation about her life in Grand Pré with Lucette, who had already taken her final vows. As Sister Madeleine, she had urged Béatrice to join her in the Order. Fleur had also taken her vows and received the name Sister Cecile.

Béatrice began, "You have never seen such beautiful trees as those in Acadia. The name comes from a region of Ancient Greece where the trees were so beautiful, people wept."

Sister Madeleine remarked, "I have seen similar trees here, not far from the river, when I take walks along the bank."

"Oh, Sister, take me with you, please. I would so enjoy the view," Béatrice pleaded.

"We shall see. Mother Superior decides who may leave the building once you are a novitiate, you know."

Béatrice nodded. "I suppose it is fortunate I have not taken any vows. Excuse me. I must talk to Mother Superior." She left her friends and walked back to Mother Superior's office and knocked.

"Enter, my child," Mother Superior said through the open door.

Béatrice rushed in and laid her head on Mother's knees. "I am ready." She pulled the ring out of her shoe. "I have been untruthful. I have had this valuable ring. It has meant more to me than anything, except my family. I return it to you and ask forgiveness."

Mother Superior smiled, "Child, do not fret over material things. But if this ring is of such importance, you shall receive this very one again when you take your vows."

Béatrice looked up at the nun and smiled. "I am so grateful to be home."

Mother Superior smiled and said, "We shall make preparations for your ceremony."

A week later, Béatrice knelt at the altar of the small convent chapel. The nuns in the Order sat in the pews and offered their silent support. Each had undergone the same ritual in the past. For some, that had been a matter of only a few months, like Lucette and Fleur, or a few years like Sister Laure. For others, it was a lifetime ago, like Mother Superior.

Mother Superior raised the scissors to Béatrice's long locks. Béatrice saw the scissors and cried out, "No, wait, Mother. Please, wait."

The nun whispered to her, "I, too was unsure for my first vows. It gets easier through the years for the second and the final vows. Would you like to return to your cell and pray about your decision?"

Béatrice changed her mind and embraced her vocation. "No, thank you, Mother. I am ready now." But she still winced when Mother Superior cut off the first lock of curls.

The nuns walked together from the convent to the St. Louis Cathedral. They walked in the side entrance and took their seats behind the iron grill on the side of the altar. They watched the guests enter the nave of the Cathedral, softly lit by candlelight that glowed throughout the church.

The Acadians who knew Béatrice took the first five rows of pews. Next, French families whose daughters were taught by Béatrice at the Ursuline Convent school filled the long wooden pews. They were here to honor their daughters' favorite teacher. And last, townspeople and friends attended to honor their friend.

When the investiture ceremony began, Béatrice Gaudet took her vows into the Ursuline Order. Dressed in a simple white floor-length gown, she lay face-down on a white cloth covering the stone floor. While Father Poirson and priests from surrounding towns walked around her, swinging urns with burning incense and chanting prayers, she lay perfectly still. Her only thoughts were of the immense joy she felt at taking her vows.

Mother Superior assisted Béatrice to stand and slipped black robes over her long white gown, then placed and adjusted a long black veil over Béatrice's short hair. Father Poirson anointed her with holy water as he softly prayed in Latin and finished with a loud, "Amen."

Mother Superior pronounced, "Béatrice Gaudet, your request has been granted. You have been given special approval to advance your vocation and take your first vows as your final ones. Now you are now a full member of our Ursuline Order. Forever shall you be named Sister Agnes. May God bless you and keep you always."

At that moment, the ceremony was rudely interrupted when the heavy doors opened and a young man in a sailor uniform called out, "Béatrice!" It was Pine. Béatrice saw him and looked at Mother Superior pleading with her eyes for permission to go to him. The nun understood and nodded. Béatrice ran down the aisle and hugged her brother, to the delight of the people in the audience.

As the church bells pealed loudly outside, the friends of Sister Agnes inside clapped as she walked arm-in-arm with her brother back to the front, then walked back down the main aisle of the church, exiting the front doors. She gave a wide smile on her way out to the Acadians who applauded her for her selfless commitment to a life of service.

*

On February 10, 1763, church bells all over Paris clanged and echoed throughout the city, as if a thousand weddings and baptisms and other happy occasions had simultaneously occurred. In fact, the prayers of King Louis XV were answered when England's King George signed the treaty ending the war which had dragged on for seven years between the two countries.

Since the accord was signed in the city, and not at Versailles Palace, the agreement would forever be known as the Treaty of Paris.

King Louis had previously signed a secret treaty with Spain that ceded it the Louisiana territory if the Acadians were relocated at Spain's expense there. He returned to Versailles free of the heavy financial burden of the Acadians and a happy man to return home to his Pompadour.

The King retired to his chamber and called for his old, feeble Notaire Jean Lajeunesse, who had replaced Jean-Luc Delacroix after his untimely death. Lajeunesse carted the heavy document in. The Notaire bowed and handed it to the King, saying, "This ends the war and is the first step to restoring the Treasury."

Louis changed the subject abruptly, waving his hands at the old man. "We know that. But what news of our cousin Lord René Le Blanc and the daughter, Evangeline?"

Lajeunesse reported sadly, "No news, Majesty. We continue to pay our spies and informants, but we have heard nothing yet."

"Be sure that I am the first to know what you know in this regard."

Lajeunesse walked backwards in a deep bow, "Of course, Majesty."

*

The bell on the entry door of the Acadian Tearoom continually rang with joy as friends entered the room to celebrate a newly-married couple. The groom was none other than Gabriel's best friend, Marc de la Tour Landry. His bride was his long-time love, Jeanne Lambert.

René and Christine toasted the bride and groom.

She said, "To your happiness for years, Marc and Jeanne."

René added, "May you have a long and beautiful life together."

The crowd shouted, "Hear, hear!" They enjoyed Christine's delicious marriage cake and downed French champagne until there was no more. Each guest imparted their good wishes to the couple before departing.

Gabriel gave Marc a bear hug. "I knew this day would come for you, my friend. But how did you get here after we parted in London?"

Marc said, "Love has no bounds. The English ship was conscripted so a fisherman took me to Le Havre and a French merchant ship sailed here. We got caught in a bad storm, but I never wavered in the belief that my Jeanne was waiting for me. I made a promise, as did you. And look at us now."

Evangeline hugged Jeanne. "Never was a bride lovelier, Jeanne."

Jeanne smiled, "Now it is your turn. We shall see you at your wedding."

*

The bells of the St. Louis Cathedral pealed joyously. A luxurious carriage decorated with white tulle and roses pulled up to the front of the Cathedral. Marc de la Tour Landry climbed out from the carriage and extended his arm to help the bride step out. "I wish your father were here."

She nodded brushing aside a tear. "He is feeling better. The doctor says he shall be out of the hospital in no time."

Marc encouraged her, "This is your day. Your greatest moment of joy. The day you have waited for. He is here in spirit and all of your friends are waiting to share in your happiness. Are you ready?"

She nodded, stepping out of the carriage in the wedding dress and veil that had been lovingly made by Adèle Arnaud in Grand Pré. The bride clutched a gold locket around her neck. Christine fussed over the bride's veil, making certain it covered her face as they climbed the steps and entered the Cathedral. In the vestibule, Christine adjusted the train.

Inside the church, wedding guests dressed in their finery filled all the rows of wooden pews. The Acadians who attended the reception for Marc and Jeanne were there, as were regulars at the Acadian Tearoom.

Father Poirson waited at the altar for the bride and groom. Gabriel walked up the main aisle, took his place next to him, and waited anxiously for his bride to walk down the aisle.

Christine slipped into the front pew and turned back toward the entrance of the Cathedral, awaiting the bride's arrival. Jeanne sat next to Christine and smiled as she rubbed her wedding band.

A sole trumpeter standing near the altar played the bridal march and all heads turned back to the entry of the cathedral. The veiled bride, holding a single red rose, walked down the aisle on Marc's arm. The bride floated by in the beautiful white confection that had traveled halfway across the world with Christine. Women wept into their handkerchiefs as Marc and the bride passed them on their way to the altar. In front of the priest, Marc placed the bride's hand into Gabriel's and whispered, "May you both be happy forever."

Then Marc stepped to the side of Gabriel to serve as his best man. They would not start without him. He had the ring. He looked out at the audience of Acadians and other friends. Jeanne blew him a kiss from the front row. Marc blushed, nodded and then turned to Gabriel.

Gabriel and the bride stood before the priest and she lifted her veil. Her back was to the audience and anyone who did not know the bride would still not know until later in the ceremony.

Father Poirson turned to Gabriel and asked, "Do you, Gabriel Mius d'Entremont, take this woman as your lawful wedded wife, to have and to hold until death do you part?"

Gabriel gazed lovingly at his bride, his life-long love. "Yes, Father. Oh, yes, I certainly do."

Gentle laughs emanated from the audience at his response. When Evangeline raised her veil and turned to him, everyone saw the looks of love that the pair exchanged. They broke tradition as they stood and clapped loudly. Gabriel lifted Evangeline's chin and gently kissed her.

The priest held up his hands to the wedding guests and stopped Gabriel. "Not yet, Gabriel. I still have one more question." He turned to Evangeline.

"Do you, Evangeline Marie de Beaufort Le Blanc de Verdure take this man to be your lawful wedded husband, to have and to hold until death do you part?"

She nodded, "I do. I certainly do."

The priest said hurriedly, "The ring, Gabriel. Where is the ring?"

Marc pulled from his coat pocket the simple gold band that Gabriel had entrusted to Pinckney. He looked at it, then at the bride and groom and over at his wife Jeanne, and marveled. It seemed like a lifetime had passed, but he knew all of their lives were just beginning. Marc handed the ring to Gabriel, who placed it on Evangeline's finger.

Gabriel then turned to Father Poirson and said, "Sorry, Father, but I have waited long enough." Gabriel took Evangeline in his arms and kissed her once, twice, thrice, to the delight of the crowd.

As he did so, the priest cried out, "I now pronounce you husband and wife. You may kiss the bride. Again."

Gabriel looked at the guests then back at Evangeline, grinned at her and kissed her again. The audience broke out in cheers and applause.

Standing behind the iron grill on the side of the altar, the Ursuline nuns sang joyously as the newlyweds strode down the aisle. Sister Agnes, in her black nun's habit, stood on the front row with the other nuns and Mother Superior. Béatrice wiped a tear from her eye then smiled and rubbed the gold wedding ring on her finger. Mother Superior clasped her hands over Béatrice's and they nodded to each other with gratitude.

The bells clanged and pealed loudly as Evangeline and Gabriel ran out of the Cathedral. The newlyweds stepped into their carriage and the driver gently nudged the horses forward through a stream of rose petals thrown at them by a cheering throng of Acadian friends and well-wishing guests.

The crowd followed behind as the carriage made its way to the Acadian Tearoom for the grand wedding feast hosted by Christine. She outdid herself with the food using the recipes she obtained from the Ursulines. She had made delicious gumbo, etouffée and courtbullion. She had cooked tantalizing soups and stews featuring duck, fish, chicken and shrimp. But nothing outdid her multi-layer wedding cake decorated with fruits, nuts and roses.

While enjoying the feast, the guests partook of champagne and wine which flowed freely. The Acadians reveled for three hours before the bride and groom took their leave, to another shower of rose petals. As the carriage drove away, the wedding guests thanked Christine and left in small groups for their own homes.

The newlyweds' carriage ride was short, however, and the driver pulled up in front of the large brick hospital not far from the Tearoom. Gabriel lifted Evangeline out of the carriage and escorted her inside. She looked at him questioningly. "Is Papa worse? Why are we here?"

Gabriel smiled and hugged her. "He is still recovering and asked to see us after the wedding. He gave no special reason, so let us share our joy with him." Evangeline nodded as they passed the nurse and walked down the hall to René's room.

*

Christine was about to lock the door of the Tearoom when a messenger in a Spanish military uniform walked in. He bowed as he spoke.

"Good evening, Madame. Please excuse the disruption in your evening. I am Diego Lopez, aide to Governor de Ulloa. The Governor understands this Tearoom attracts many Acadians. Are you the owner?"

Christine nodded. "I am. How can I help His Excellency?"

"It is of the utmost urgency that I speak to one of the Acadians. Hopefully you will know how to reach her. Evangeline de Beaufort LeBlanc de Verdure."

"Actually, she was just married and her name is Mius d'Entremont now. But I shall be pleased to pass along the message. What is it?"

He held up an envelope addressed to Evangeline with a variety of addresses crossed-out in different types of inks, and covered with numerous stamps and seals. "I am ordered to deliver it only into her hands. It must be quite important. The King's seal." He pointed to the red seal with the King's signet imprint on the back.

"I understand," Christine said. "With all the seals and writings, it appears to have been in transit for some time. From whence did it arrive?"

Diego shrugged and said, "Governor Ulloa found it stuck in the back of an old desk drawer when he moved into his quarters. It could have been there for years, since the last Governor was there."

Christine nodded, "I am on my way to meet Evangeline now. Should you like to follow?"

He bowed again, "Allow me to escort you in the Governor's carriage."

Christine blew out the remaining candles, locked the Tearoom and climbed into the carriage. As soon as Diego entered the coach, he tapped on the ceiling. Hearing the signal, the driver cracked the whip and the carriage hurried down the street.

*

A nurse wiped the forehead of the patient, a man who looked much older than he was. René coughed quietly as he lay in his hospital bed. Evangeline rushed in the door and ran to her father. Gabriel entered behind her as the nurse discreetly exited, closing the door behind the couple.

Evangeline sat beside René, kissed his forehead and held his hand. Gabriel put his hand on Evangeline's shoulder in a show of support.

"Papa," Evangeline asked, "How do you feel?

He spoke in a weak voice, "I am stronger now, with you at my side. I had a coughing spell and I asked Gabriel and Christine not to tell you. I wanted nothing to cloud your glorious day. The physician says I am doing better. But the most important thing is that you have found your true love."

"Shame on you, but I am so gratified that you are doing better."

Christine entered the room quietly and walked to the opposite side of the bed and sat down next to him. He looked up to her and smiled, then coughed several times. He stopped, then had a coughing fit. Christine hovered over him, and spoon-fed him medicine encouragingly.

René swallowed the medication and gazed tenderly at Christine, saying, "I found my love, too. And we have news."

Christine put her hand on her belly and grinned widely, "We did not want to interfere with your special event. I am with child."

René laughed, "Now I can die in peace."

Evangeline shushed him, "Papa, you shall do no such thing."

René motioned for Evangeline to move closer to him. She did and he whispered, "I have waited for the right moment, but there was never a good time to tell you, not even the day I was separated from you and Christine."

Evangeline sat back, unsure of his meaning, "Tell me what, Papa?"

He spoke quietly, "I am not your father. I was never certain of who he was until your mother told me on her deathbed."

He began to cough again. Evangeline looked to Christine, pleading with her eyes for Christine to heal him. But René stopped as quickly as he started and continued, "You must believe me when I say I could not have loved you more than if you were my own child."

Evangeline kissed René's cheek. "I know that, Papa. I do. And no daughter could love you more than I. But who is my father if not you?"

Just then, the Spanish courier burst the door open, without realizing he interrupted René's important conversation with his daughter.

"Pardon me, but I have most urgent correspondence for Mademoiselle Evangeline Le Blanc de Verdure. Would she be here?" He looked at Evangeline questioningly.

Evangeline stood and corrected him, "I am married now. It is Madame Mius d'Entremont," as she gazed lovingly at Gabriel.

"A thousand pardons, Madame. A letter from His Majesty King Louis XV for you." He bowed to everyone, "My apologies for the intrusion. The Governor sends his deepest regards and well wishes to you, Monsieur le Consul Le Blanc de Verdure."

René nodded, "Please send my gratitude to His Excellency." Diego nodded and dashed out.

Evangeline took a seat, looked up at Gabriel who nodded his support, and then broke the King's red seal on the letter. Opening it, she scrutinized it and, with a look of both shock and joy, handed it to Gabriel.

She pointed out a particular part of the letter. He read it and turned to her in surprise.

René asked, "What did the King say?"

Christine exclaimed, "Do not keep us in suspense."

Evangeline nodded for Gabriel to read it aloud. He began, "By these presents do we hereby acknowledge that you are our legitimate daughter by our love, Eugenie de Beaufort...."

Gabriel looked at René, fearing his scorn. Instead, René sighed with relief. "His Majesty did seem relieved at our wedding, even though he had arranged our betrothal himself."

Evangeline was incredulous. "King Louis XV is my real father?"

René nodded, then coughed again several times. Christine attentively handed him a goblet of water but he declined. "I am fine. And pleased that Evangeline knows the truth now. But there is more, is there not?"

Gabriel returned to the letter, "We regret to inform you of the untimely demise of Count Guillaume de Beaufort. A scoundrel accused him of cheating at cards and the Count challenged him to a duel. However, the man pulled the trigger at nine paces instead of ten. He was later hanged for stealing the Count's horses, but it was too late for your uncle. Thus, we have titled the entire de Beaufort château, lands and all properties in the estate in your name, which you claim by presenting yourself in person."

Gabriel looked up to see Evangeline still in shock, "We look forward to a private meeting, and we shall hold your rooms for you awaiting your return to our Palace of Versailles, my little angel, Evangeline."

As René and Christine clasped hands, Gabriel kissed Evangeline tenderly, gazing at her with devotion. "Should you like to move to your new properties in France, my love?"

Evangeline looked at her husband, then at René and Christine, before turning back to Gabriel. The newlyweds gazed into each other's eyes. Instantly, Evangeline knew her answer.

She said in a strong, clear voice, "I think not. I am finally home."

ABOUT THE AUTHOR

M. M. Le Blanc, JD, MBA, SRS, LSS, is a multi-award-winning author of sixteen books of fiction and non-fiction and of numerous award-winning screenplays. Her trilogy *Evangeline: Paradise Stolen,* Volumes I, II and II of the series *Evangeline: The True Story of the Cajuns* has won six book awards and was selected as an Official Gift Selection for the VIP filmmakers at the Sundance International Film Festival. She has also authored dozens of articles and columns published in law, real estate, business and entertainment industry journals in the USA, Europe and Asia.

Le Blanc is also an experienced international entertainment, real estate and film financing attorney and a veteran Hollywood film and television studio executive previously at film and television studios including Fox, Disney/ABC, Universal/Canal+ and Metro-Goldwyn-Mayer Studios/United Artists, among others. Le Blanc has worked on over one hundred fifty film and television productions, both as an executive and as an award-winning writer/producer. Her film, "Cajun Renaissance Man" was an Official Film Selection at international film festivals including in Cannes, Montreal, New York, New Orleans, Chicago and many others, and garnered the "Audience Favorite Film" Award.

Her academic and educational administrative experience includes positions as Founding Academic Dean, Department Chair and Professor of Law, Business and Finance at universities, film schools, law schools and graduate business schools in the United States and Europe.

Le Blanc is a frequent speaker at historical and genealogical societies and conferences as well as at film festivals, pitchfests, film and television markets and entertainment industry conferences throughout the world, from Cannes to China. Le Blanc was selected one of the "Top Ten Working Women in America," was awarded an international Writing Fellowship from the Fondation d'Art Paris-New York and is a member of the Academy of Television Arts and Sciences.

CONTACT THE AUTHOR or PUBLISHER
Email: bizentinepress@gmail.com
www.bizentinepress.com